The School Mistress of Emerson Pass:
"Sometimes we all need to step away from our lives and sink into a safe, happy place where family and love are the main ingredients for surviving. You'll find that and more in The School Mistress of Emerson Pass. I delighted in every turn of the story and when away from it found myself eager to return to Emerson Pass. I can't wait for the next book." - *Kay Bratt, Bestselling author of Wish Me Home and True to Me.*
"I frequently found myself getting lost in the characters and forgetting that I was reading a book." - *Camille Di Maio, Bestselling author of The Memory of Us.*
"Highly recommended." - *Christine Nolfi, Award winning author of The Sweet Lake Series.*
"I loved this book!" - *Karen McQuestion, Bestselling author of Hello Love and Good Man, Dalton.*

Traded: Brody and Kara:
"I loved the sweetness of Tess Thompson's writing - the camaraderie and long-lasting friendships make you want to move to Cliffside and become one of the gang! Rated Hallmark for romance!" - *Stephanie Little BookPage*

"This story was well written. You felt what the characters were going through. It's one of those "I got to know what happens next" books. So intriguing you won't want to put it down." - *Lena Loves Books*

"This story has so much going on, but it intertwines within itself. You get second chance, lost loves, and new love. I could not put this book down! I am excited to start this series and have love for this little Bayside town that I am now fond off!" - *Crystal's Book World*

"This is a small town romance story at its best and I look forward to the next book in the series." - *Gillek2, Vine Voice*

"This is one of those books that make you love to be a reader and fan of the author." -*Pamela Lunder, Vine Voice*

Blue Midnight:
"This is a beautiful book with an unexpected twist that takes the story from romance to mystery and back again. I've already started the 2nd book in the series!" - *Mama O*

"This beautiful book captured my attention and never let it go. I did not want it to end and so very much look forward to reading the next book." - *Pris Shartle*

"I enjoyed this new book cover to cover. I read it on my long flight home from Ireland and it helped the time fly by, I wish it had been longer so my whole flight could have been lost to this lovely novel about second chances and finding the truth. Written with wisdom and humor this novel shares the raw emotions a new divorce can leave behind." - *J. Sorenson*

"Tess Thompson is definitely one of my auto-buy authors! I love her writing style. Her characters are so real to life that you just can't put the book down once you start! Blue Midnight makes you believe in second chances. It makes you believe that everyone deserves an HEA. I loved the twists and turns in this book, the mystery and suspense, the family dynamics and the restoration of trust and security." - *Angela MacIntyre*

"Tess writes books with real characters in them, characters with flaws and baggage and gives them a second chance. (Real people, some remind me of myself and my girlfriends.) Then she cleverly and thoroughly develops those characters and makes you feel deeply for them. Characters are complex and multi-faceted, and the plot seems to unfold naturally, and never feels contrived." - *K. Lescinsky*

Caramel and Magnolias:

"Nobody writes characters like Tess Thompson. It's like she looks into our lives and creates her characters based on our best friends, our lovers, and our neighbors. Caramel and Magnolias, and the authors debut novel Riversong, have some of the best characters I've ever had a chance to fall in love with. I don't like leaving spoilers in reviews so just trust me, Nicholas Sparks has nothing on Tess Thompson, her writing flows so smoothly you can't help but to want to read on!" - *T. M. Frazier*

"I love Tess Thompson's books because I love good writing. Her prose is clean and tight, which are increasingly rare qualities, and manages to evoke a full range of emotions with both subtlety and power. Her fiction goes well beyond art imitating life. Thompson's characters are alive and fully-realized, the action is believable, and the story unfolds with the right balance of tension and exuberance. CARAMEL AND MAGNOLIAS is a pleasure to read." - *Tsuruoka*

"The author has an incredible way of painting an image with her words. Her storytelling is beautiful, and leaves you wanting more! I love that the story is about friendship (2 best friends) and love. The characters are richly drawn and I found myself rooting for them from the very beginning. I think you will, too!" - *Fogvision*

"I got swept off my feet, my heartstrings were pulled, I held my breath, and tightened my muscles in suspense. Tess paints stunning scenery with her words and draws you in to the lives of her characters."- *T. Bean*

Duet For Three Hands:

"Tears trickled down the side of my face when I reached the end of this road. Not because the story left me feeling sad or disappointed, no. Rather, because I already missed them. My friends. Though it isn't goodbye, but see you later. And so I will sit impatiently waiting, with desperate eagerness to hear where life has taken you, what burdens have you downtrodden, and what triumphs warm your heart. And in the meantime, I will go out and live, keeping your lessons and friendship and love close, the light to guide me through any darkness. And to the author I say thank you. My heart, my soul -all of me - needed these words, these friends, this love. I am forever changed by the beauty of your talent." - *Lisa M.Gott*

"I am a great fan of Tess Thompson's books and this new one definitely shows her branching out with an engaging enjoyable historical drama/love story. She is a true pro in the way she weaves her storyline, develops true to life characters that you love! The background and setting is so picturesque and visible just from her words. Each book shows her expanding, growing and excelling in her art. Yet another one not to miss. Buy it you won't be disappointed. The ONLY disappointment is when it ends!!!" - *Sparky's Last*

"There are some definite villains in this book. Ohhhh, how I loved to hate them. But I have to give Thompson credit because they never came off as caricatures or one dimensional. They all felt authentic to me and (sadly) I could easily picture them. I loved to love some and loved to hate others." - *The Baking Bookworm*

"I stayed up the entire night reading Duet For Three Hands and unbeknownst to myself, I fell asleep in the middle of reading the book. I literally woke up the next morning with Tyler the Kindle beside me (thankfully, still safe and intact) with no ounce of battery left. I shouldn't have worried about deadlines because, guess what? Duet For Three Hands was the epitome of unputdownable." - *The Bookish Owl*

Miller's Secret

"From the very first page, I was captivated by this wonderful tale. The cast of characters amazing - very fleshed out and multi-dimensional. The descriptions were perfect - just enough to make you feel like you were transported back to the 20's and 40's.... This book was the perfect escape, filled with so many twists and turns I was on the edge of my seat for the entire read." - *Hilary Grossman*

"The sad story of a freezing-cold orphan looking out the window at his rich benefactors on Christmas Eve started me off with Horatio-Alger expectations for this book. But I quickly got pulled into a completely different world--the complex five-character braid that the plot weaves. The three men and two women characters are so alive I felt I could walk up and start talking to any one of them, and I'd love to have lunch with Henry. Then the plot quickly turned sinister enough to keep me turning the pages.

Class is set against class, poor and rich struggle for happiness and security, yet it is love all but one of them are hungry for. ......Where does love come from? What do you do about it? The story kept me going, and gave me hope. For a little bonus, there are Thompson's delightful observations, like: "You'd never know we could make something this good out of the milk from an animal who eats hats." A really good read!" - *Kay in Seattle*

"She paints vivid word pictures such that I could smell the ocean

and hear the doves. Then there are the stories within a story that twist and turn until they all come together in the end. I really had a hard time putting it down. Five stars aren't enough!"
- M.R. Williams

ALSO BY TESS THOMPSON

CLIFFSIDE BAY

Traded: Brody and Kara

Deleted: Jackson and Maggie

Jaded: Zane and Honor

Marred: Kyle and Violet

Tainted: Lance and Mary

Cliffside Bay Christmas, The Season of Cats and Babies (Cliffside Bay Novella to be read after Tainted)

Missed: Rafael and Lisa

Cliffside Bay Christmas Wedding (Cliffside Bay Novella to be read after Missed)

Healed: Stone and Pepper

Chateau Wedding (Cliffside Bay Novella to be read after Healed)

Scarred: Trey and Autumn

Jilted: Nico and Sophie

Kissed (Cliffside Bay Novella to be read after Jilted)

Departed: David and Sara

Cliffside Bay Bundle , Books 1,2,3

BLUE MOUNTAIN SERIES

Blue Mountain Bundle, Books 1,2,3

Blue Midnight

Blue Moon

Blue Ink

Blue String

EMERSON PASS

The School Mistress of Emerson Pass

The Sugar Queen of Emerson Pass

RIVER VALLEY

Riversong

Riverbend

Riverstar

Riversnow

Riverstorm

Tommy's Wish

River Valley Bundle, Books 1-4

LEGLEY BAY

Caramel and Magnolias

Tea and Primroses

STANDALONES

The Santa Trial

Duet for Three Hands

Miller's Secret

DEPARTED: DAVID AND SARA

CLIFFSIDE BAY SERIES, BOOK 10

TESS THOMPSON

DEDICATION

This one is for the Tessers.
They know why.

A NOTE TO READERS

Dear Readers,

Thank you for being on this journey with me. If you've gotten to the tenth book in the series, I'm assuming you're a true fan. I can't tell you how much it means to me that readers have responded so favorably to this series. I always write straight from my heart, and that's a vulnerable place most of the time. That said, I figure if I make my characters be vulnerable, I should be, too. I've spent the last two years writing these books. I have to say that again for emphasis. Two years of my life! It kind of boggles my mind to think of how many hours I've spent at this desk telling the stories of the Dogs and Wolves. No matter how you look at it, that's a lot of #ButtInSeat. From the first to the last, these characters have given me nothing but joy. I hope reading them has been as much fun as writing them.

When I first started writing the tenth book of the Cliffside Bay saga, I thought it would be the last of the series. I was sad to say goodbye to the Dogs, Wags, Wolves, and Bobcats. However, as my dad says, the party can't go on forever. Plus, when one door closes, another opens, right? In this case, it is a spinoff series called Emerson Pass. Do you remember the little town where Stone and Pepper were snowed in and later, Lisa and Rafael married?

I fell in love with that little town and decided Emerson Pass, Colorado, would be the setting for a new ten-book series. Since then, I've written the first two in the series and plotted out the others. I've played with series convention in that five of the books will be set between 1910 and 1920, and five will be contemporary, featuring the descendants of the historical characters. One of the contemporaries will feature Trey's sister, Jamie Wattson, and her one-night stand, Darby the Dickens expert from book 9 of Cliffside Bay. As often happens in romance novels, they unexpectedly meet again in Emerson Pass. Without giving too much away, sparks fly in more ways than one.

The School Mistress of Emerson Pass (historical book 1) and The Sugar Queen (contemporary book 1) are now available from the retailer of your choice. Simply click on the title to purchase.

But I'm getting ahead of myself. For now, we're still in Cliffside Bay with David and Sara. We know from the previous book that Sara can't stand David. What we don't know is how he feels about her. Keep reading to find out!

All this to say, I'm playing with the idea of a Part III Cliffside Bay. This would be with five new couples, while keeping up with our original ten. This time, it would feature five best girlfriends. Just to tease you, I give a little hint about who might be featured in various places in this book. Tell me, though. Would you be interested in continuing this saga? Let me know. Drop me a note at tess@tthompsonwrites.com.

Don't miss any of my news! Visit my website at https://tesswrites.com/ to sign up for my newsletter.

Sending you a hug and the wish for a cozy spot in which to fall into the pages of my humble offering.

Much love,

Tess

S ara
In Sara Ness's experience, the phone never rang before seven a.m. unless it was bad news. When her mobile shrieked her awake that morning from a deep sleep, she bolted upright and prepared herself for the worst. Someone was dead. Or in the hospital. Maybe jail?

"Hello." She wiped her tired eyes.

"Sara Ness?"

"Yes, this is she."

"This is Stephen Lodge. I'm your grandfather's attorney."

"My grandfather?" She sat up and by habit looked at the baby monitor. Harper was asleep on her back with her arms thrown over her head.

"Lincoln Ness, yes," Lodge said.

"Why would you be calling about him?" Lincoln Ness was her father's father. She'd never even met him. Hadn't thought of him in years and had no idea he was still alive. She searched her memory for a trace of him. An old photograph she'd found tucked into the pages of her father's Bible after her parents' deaths came to mind. He'd been tall and angular with high cheekbones and eyes shaped like her father's. Except they weren't kind like his.

Sharp, cruel eyes had stared back at her, reminding her of a rattlesnake she'd seen coiled outside the gates of her parents' estate in Colorado when she was a little girl. As if its bite could be poisonous, she'd dumped the photo in the trash. At twenty years old, she'd had no interest in knowing the man who had caused her father so much pain.

"He and my father had a fight before I was born," she said now to Mr. Lodge. "This was thirty years ago. They never spoke again." The dispute had been about differing opinions on her father's future. He'd wanted to marry Sara's mother, for one thing. Secondly, he hadn't wanted to take over at the helm of Lincoln's conglomerate. He wanted to start and run his own business. Lincoln Ness, from all accounts, had been a manipulative, greedy man. When he didn't get his way, he'd disowned his only son and cut him off financially. This was no small thing, as Lincoln Ness was worth a fortune. The joke was on him. Sara's father, Matthew Ness, borrowed money and started his own venture. Ness Brewing Company had made him wealthy beyond his wildest dreams. He'd told Sara once that being ousted from the family was one of the best things that had ever happened to him. "Marrying your mother was the other," he'd said.

"I'm sorry to disturb you so early, but I have bad news," Lodge said, bringing her back to the present. "Your grandfather died last night."

"Was he ill?" she asked.

"No, he turned ninety last week. He died peacefully in his sleep. I'm calling about his will."

"Did he even know I existed?" She hadn't thought so.

"Yes, he was aware of you. He's left you the bulk of his fortune."

"What? Why would he do such a thing?

"He was an eccentric man, to say the least." Lodge cleared his throat. "There are some contingencies."

"Contingencies?" She threw back the covers and slipped out of bed. The rug caressed her bare feet as she padded over to a window and opened the shades. Another beautiful day in Cliffside Bay. Positioned at the top of the southern slope, her newly built home faced the Pacific. "Like I said, he was eccentric," Lodge said. "There are no other heirs, as your father was his only child."

No other family. This was not new information, yet it ushered in the familiar sadness. Dead parents. A murdered husband. All that was left of them were her and Harper.

"The fortune is quite significant," he said.

"I don't need money." After her parents' death, she'd sold the company. She didn't like to think about it much, because it wasn't money she'd earned herself. According to *Forbes*, she was one of the wealthiest women in the country. Sara's gaze followed the stone paths that meandered through the massive lawns and kidney-shaped pool. Leaves from the clump of trees they'd left when they cleared the land fluttered in the breeze. Fall was only weeks away, but summer weather remained.

"I'm aware of that," Lodge said. "Still, turning away a billion dollars isn't something one does, despite how much they already have. Wouldn't you agree?"

"True." Her interest heightened. She could start her own foundation, as Bill and Melinda Gates had done. There was so much good she could do with that kind of money. "What are his terms?"

"You're to inherit it all. However, you have to be married," Lodge said.

"Did you say married?" She must have heard him incorrectly. "Why would that matter?"

"People have all kinds of reasons for things, Miss Ness."

"Did he know my husband was murdered?" she asked. "I was married. Does that count?"

"He was aware of your difficulties, yes." He paused. "The

will is very specific. You have to marry within thirty days after his death, or the money goes to his dog."

"His dog?" Not only had her grandfather been cruel, he was obviously not in his right mind.

"Between you and me, he was…how shall I say it? A bit of a misogynist. He was under the assumption that women couldn't handle money without a man. In addition, he thought your daughter should have a father."

"That's insane."

"I'd have to agree. Still, it's the way he had me draw it up. There's nothing to be done."

"I can't possibly get married within thirty days. I don't even have a boyfriend." Unless peanut butter cups counted as a companion.

"Furthermore, you have to be married for a year before you're granted the money."

"Does it have to be a real marriage?"

"Real? What do you mean by real?" Lodge's voice lowered, obviously embarrassed. "Do you mean sex?"

"Yes, sex. A love match. A real relationship. Or will there be a test like they do during immigration hearings?" She bit back a laugh.

"Miss Ness, the answer is yes. This is very similar to an immigration-type case. Your grandfather hired a private detective who will follow you around and interview friends and family for the first six weeks after the marriage. After that, he will interview you to determine how close you really are. If he believes the marriage is real, he'll communicate that to me. I'll have it notarized, and at the end of the year, the money will be yours.

She sighed and turned away from the window. "This is absurd. I'm not going to be married any time soon. I don't want some psycho my grandfather hired following me or harassing my friends."

"The choice is yours, Miss Ness. I'm only the messenger."

"What happens if the dog inherits this money?"

"Per the will, the dog was left to your grandfather's companion, Moxie King. She was your grandfather's caregiver for the last few years of his life. She had a great deal of influence on him. I'm fairly certain she convinced him to set up his will this way. Basically, she'll inherit the money." He went quiet for a moment. "I've been Lincoln's attorney for the better part of thirty years. Before he became involved with the young woman, he'd always named you as his heir. He felt strongly that his money be left to his only living relative. The young woman— Moxie...can you think of a more appropriate name for a conniving young woman?"

She had to admit. Moxie seemed just right.

"Anyway, this Moxie was more than his caregiver. If you know what I mean?"

"I do, yes." Sara was familiar with how this worked. For that matter, her husband had used her in the same way. He'd wanted her for her money.

"I believe all this was her idea," Lodge said. "If I'm correct, she understood your situation and decided to take advantage of it."

"My situation?"

"I'm referring to your husband's murder and that you're raising a child on your own, which were detailed in the press."

The headline from the paper flashed before her eyes. *Husband of Ness Breweries Heiress Murdered by Girlfriend's Husband.*

Everything one needed to know about her personal life in nine words.

She perched on the edge of her easy chair and ran a finger along the blue-and-tan stripes. Her talented interior designer, Trey Wattson, had chosen a soothing Nantucket blue for the walls, but at the moment it was not calming her. "Are you saying she understands it would be impossible for me to remarry this quickly after such a tragedy?"

"Precisely."

"This Moxie must be smarter than her name suggests."

"I'm afraid so."

"Is there any chance she might do good with the money?" Sara asked.

"Unlikely."

The baby monitor crackled. She looked over to see that Harper was now sitting up and calling, "Mama."

"My little girl is up," she said. "Can I think about all this and call you later?"

"Yes, I'm around all day. I hope you'll at least consider complying with the request of the will. There's perhaps a friend you could think of?"

"I'm not sure, Mr. Lodge, but I promise to give you an answer of some kind sooner rather than later."

She hung up the phone and grabbed her robe from the end of the bed. Harper needed her. She'd have to put the rest of this out of her mind for the next few minutes.

By the time Sara entered the nursery, Harper was standing with her fat fingers wrapped around the bars of her crib. "Mama. Out."

Sara reached into the crib and pulled her daughter up and into her arms. "Good morning. Are you ready for your breakfast?" She kissed her smooth cheek. "Let's get you changed first."

She put the baby on the changing table and unzipped her onesie. The diaper was full but hadn't leaked. A good beginning to the day. She efficiently wiped and powdered and fastened her adorable bottom into a fresh diaper. "Are you hungry?"

"Nana." Harper grinned, showing her eight teeth. She'd just turned one and was learning new words at a rapid rate.

"Yes, you may have a banana," Sara said. "And some oatmeal."

Harper wriggled and pointed toward the kitchen. Sara settled her on her hip and wandered down the hallway toward the kitchen. The hardwood floor was cool under her feet. Harper babbled and kicked her legs while holding on to a clump of Sara's hair.

Sunlight flooded the white-and-gray kitchen. Large windows looked out to the patio. She tucked the baby into her high chair and secured her in with the strap, then slid the tray into place. Her nanny, Zoey, didn't show up until around nine. Sara liked to do the morning routine with Harper herself. After Zoey arrived, Sara took her morning swim in the pool, showered, dressed, and closed herself in her office to work on managing her various charities. She was a member of several boards, consisting of about twenty hours of work a week. After her husband died, she'd taken on more duties to keep her mind occupied. Between that and caring for Harper, the days flew by. The nights were lonely, though, and when the dark thoughts possessed her.

Zoey took off for the day around five so that Sara and Harper could have their dinner together. Harper went down around seven thirty. The rest of the evening dragged until it was time for bed. If she went to bed before ten, she lay awake for hours. Instead, she watched television and drank wine. There were too many nights she talked herself into chocolate. If it weren't for her morning swims, the fifty pounds she'd lost after college were sure to return.

She cut up banana for Harper and put steel-cut oats and water into a pan on the stove. Harper stuffed one of the half slices into her mouth and let out a happy note of appreciation. Sara made herself an espresso from the machine and stood against the sink to drink it and watch her child enjoy breakfast. Motherhood had knocked her for a loop. The amount of love she felt for this baby was unlike anything she'd ever known. After losing her parents during her first year of college, she'd been essentially without family. Now that she was a mother, she understood how much her parents had loved her. She'd known it growing up, of course. Matthew and Sheri Ness had been loving and attentive parents. They were at every piano recital, school science project contest, and school play. Her father had recorded everything. She couldn't have asked for a more idyllic childhood in the wealthy suburb of Denver. Private school and clothes and a car when she turned sixteen might have made her rotten to the core except for her parents' decency and insistence that they give back in any way they could in the form of philanthropy.

What she hadn't known until Harper, though, was the intensity of that love. She knew, now that she was a mother, that the last thought her parents had before they died was of her. This made her miss them in a whole new way.

She smiled back at Harper, who was offering her some of the banana. "No, thank you, doll. I have my coffee." Her eyes stung with the promise of tears. What she would give for her parents to be here to see this beautiful baby.

The oatmeal was done by then. She poured a small amount into one of Harper's plastic bowls and added milk. Harper liked to feed herself these days, so Sara set the bowl and one of her small plastic-coated spoons on the tray. Most of the oatmeal would end up in places other than her mouth, but it didn't matter. Learning to be independent was important at this stage of development.

Sara, a bit of a nervous mother, had the growing stages memorized. Harper had hit them all with no troubles. Thank God. Sara wasn't sure she could have coped if her precious child had struggled. Keeping herself together was a daily chore of will. Harper was her source of joy in a life that would otherwise be bleak.

As she ate her oatmeal, doused with a few tablespoons of slivered almonds, she contemplated the strange phone call. Money contingent on a marriage? Who did that kind of thing in this day and age? As much as she wanted the money for her foundation and to keep it away from this Moxie woman, marrying for the sole purpose of complying with the will was impossible. Who would she ask? Some stranger on the street? The fact that they would have to physically reside in her home was the deal breaker. No amount of money was worth risking the safety or well-being of her child.

By the time she'd finished her breakfast, she'd decided. There was no way she could make a fake marriage work. Not even for her foundation. Harper had to be the top priority in her life. Disrupting her home life was not something Sara could do and live with herself.

Zoey came in through the patio door. "Morning," she said.

"Morning. How was your date last night?"

"Awful. I remembered why I don't do online dating," Zoey said.

Zoey was twenty-five and adorable. How she couldn't have luck with men was anyone's guess. Whatever the reason, it informed Sara that her decision to be celibate and alone for the rest of her life was the right decision.

Zoey closed her intense green eyes and shook her head as if she couldn't quite believe what she was going to say. "He smelled like he'd never heard of deodorant and then left me with the check." She scurried over to Harper and planted a kiss on her head. "Hello, cutie. Are you ready for story time at the library?"

Zoey wore jean overalls and a T-shirt etched with tiny yellow daisies, making her look no older than a teenager. The freckles scattered over her fair skin added to the sense of youthfulness.

Harper clapped her sticky hands together. "Zozo."

"What're you up to today?" Zoey asked Sara as she yanked a paper towel from the roll.

"I'm going to take my swim, then meet Autumn in town for lunch. In the afternoon, there's a conference call for one of my charities. The ladies love to hear themselves talk, so it'll probably take most of the afternoon."

"I don't know how you stand it." Zoey ran the towel under water. "I'm starting to dislike other humans more every day." She walked back to the high chair. "Except for ones named Harper." She smiled at the baby as she leaned over to give her another kiss on the head. "You're the perfect human."

Harper reached for Zoey's dark braid. Zoey darted away in the nick of time. With efficient swipes, she cleaned Harper's face and hands, then lifted the tray away before it was necessary to redo the same action.

"All right, let's have a kiss before I go swim." Sara undid the belt around Harper's waist and lifted her into the air. "You have a fun morning at story time." She kissed Harper's cheek and snuggled her for a moment before setting her on the floor. "I'll be back by three if you want to take off a few hours this afternoon. There's only so many beach days left, so you should take advantage of them. I have that thing this evening, so I'll need you to come back around six."

"I remembered. And that *thing* is going to be great for you," Zoey said.

Sara let out a sigh. "I really doubt it, but Autumn made me promise I'd go."

"Isn't that what best friends are for?" Zoey asked. "To nag you into doing stuff that's good for you?"

"Whether it's good or not is yet to be discovered." A flyer for a six-week grief support group had caught Autumn's eye. Ever since then, Autumn had been on Sara to attend.

"When I lost my mom, it really helped," Zoey said.

"Maybe I should've gone to one when I lost my parents, and I'd have been healthy enough to choose a better husband."

"But then you wouldn't have this angel," Zoey said as she lifted Harper off the floor. "Have a good swim, okay? And lunch. You deserve a little fun."

Deserve might be strong word. There were so many ways she'd messed up her life. All she cared about now was making sure her daughter had the kind of childhood she'd had.

2

————————————

David

David Perry held his hand under the cold-water tap. He'd burned his finger making French toast. The darn metal handles on the pans had gotten him again. What kind of designer thought those were a good idea? For that matter, why had he thought making a hot breakfast was wise? It was the monotony. The same breakfast of bran cereal with raisins was gnawing at him as much as the kids.

Since his wife's death, putting together meals challenged him more than it should. After all, how hard was it to put food on the table? His mother had always done it exceptionally well. Lisa, his twin, could whip up something edible with her eyes closed. Even his wife, who'd been supplying illegal drugs to half of Iowa, still made it home in time to put a decent meal on the table. The men in the family, however, were challenged. Since David's father had moved in with them after his divorce, they'd survived on frozen pizzas and takeout from the grocery store deli.

He took his hand away from the water and put some ice in a plastic bag to hold against the burn. Nothing serious, but the skin had blistered.

His daughter, Laine, was at the table buckled into her booster chair. At two and a half, she'd graduated from her high chair. Thank God for small favors. That thing had made the compact kitchen even more crowded. Laine had grown a lot during their time in Cliffside Bay, less baby and more little girl than when they arrived over a year ago. Or was it a year and a half? Those first months had been a blur.

Blond and fair with big sapphire eyes, she resembled his twin. When he compared baby pictures, it was hard to tell them apart. Laine reminded him of Lisa, too. A little timid, with the same kind heart. Except that Laine hardly spoke. For the past nine months, she hadn't uttered a word. Dr. Waller had said she was capable of speaking but that she didn't want to for whatever reason. David knew why. Her mother's death and their subsequent move to California had damaged her. Not surprising, really. More surprising was how well-adjusted Oliver was, especially since he remembered his mother. Laine seemed to have no recollection. Other than her subconscious, he supposed.

Both of his children stared at the stack of angry, mostly burned French toast.

"Can we have cereal instead?" Oliver asked. He'd just turned five. Too short for the chair but refusing the indignity of a booster, his chin was level with the tabletop. If he'd wanted to, he could rest his chin on the surface. He had slightly darker blond hair than his sister and blue eyes as round as nickels. Everyone said he looked like David had at that age.

"Yes, I suppose you can," David said. "Sorry about the French toast."

"You tried your best." Oliver's expression brightened. "That's what's important." He hopped out of his chair and lugged the carton of milk David had left on the counter over to the table.

David smiled as he fetched the cereal from the pantry. He loved it when Oliver parroted phrases back to him. Perhaps he wasn't a complete failure as a father. He poured them each a bowl of cereal while Oliver took two spoons from the drawer.

"Here you go, Lainey," Oliver said to Laine as he set a spoon at her place.

Laine smiled at her brother but didn't say anything.

David's father entered the kitchen, humming under his breath. Dad lit up, as he always did, at the sight of the children. "How are my amazing grandchildren today?"

"We're fine and dandy." Oliver lifted his chin and smiled up at his grandfather. His little son adored his "Papa" and had started mimicking some of his sayings. "Except Daddy burned his finger and said a bad word."

"You all right?" Dad asked. "Let me see."

"Nothing serious." David held out his hand.

"Keep the ice on it," Dad said.

David winced as he placed the bag of ice on his burn. "I got it under cold water right away."

Dad patted his shoulder and went over to kiss his grandchildren on the tops of their heads.

"Papa, do you want cereal?" Oliver asked.

"Let me think about that for a moment while I have my coffee," Dad said.

David turned to get a better look at his father. Freshly showered, shaved, and dressed in jeans and a polo shirt, he looked relaxed and well-rested. "Good night's sleep?"

Dad's gaze darted to the window before he answered. "Sure was."

"I don't know how you can sleep on that couch every night," David said. "I wish you'd take my room."

"The couch is fine for me," Dad said.

"If you'd take Lisa up on her offer to buy you a house, you wouldn't have to live here with us," David said.

"When you take her up on that same offer, I will too." Dad poured himself a cup of coffee from the fresh pot.

"You know I can't," David said. "It's not right for me to live off the charity of my sister."

"I feel the same way," Dad said.

"It's different for you," David said. "You're her father. You sacrificed for her."

"I won't be like your mother," Dad said.

David leaned his backside against the sink and lifted the bag of ice from his burn to see if it had helped at all. "To be fair, Mom's husband's footing the bill now."

"Are we sure about that? Or is Lisa slipping her money?" Dad asked.

Lisa had convinced their mother to take a year in France, on her dime, after their parents had announced they were getting divorced. Unlike Dad, who was too proud to take money from his famous, rich daughter, Lois Perry had agreed. She was now living with her new husband in Paris. Her husband who was the same age as her children.

"Anyway, I like being here to help you out with the kids." Dad opened the refrigerator and pulled out the creamer. "I'll find a place eventually."

"Were you out this morning?" His father hadn't been on the couch when David woke that morning.

"Yep. Sure was. Took a walk." Dad turned his back on him as he poured cream into his coffee. Was he avoiding eye contact? His answer had been quick, as though he made it up beforehand.

"Where to?" David asked, casually, as if he were simply interested in his father's walking routine.

"You know, around." Dad gestured toward David's hand. "How did you burn your finger?"

"On the handle of the frying pan." He motioned toward the sink. "My sad attempt to make a hot breakfast. Somehow I managed to burn the bread and undercook it at the same time."

"I'll eat them." Dad took a clean plate from the dishwasher. Yet another task David hadn't gotten to yet. "Anything's edible doused with syrup."

"Eat at your own risk," David said.

"I'm extra hungry this morning," Dad said as he took the chair next to Oliver. He stuck a fork into the top two pieces of the charred, limp toast and set them on a plate. "My mother taught us never to waste food."

"Even if it tastes yucky?" Oliver asked.

"My mother was a better cook than your dad." His father winked at David. "No offense."

"None taken," David said. "I remember Grammie's cooking and have to agree. She made the best fried chicken."

Dad squirted syrup over his stack. "What I wouldn't do for a few pieces of that. And her mashed potatoes slathered with gravy."

"Maybe we could order that from a restaurant," Oliver said. "I don't see gravy happening here."

David laughed. "You have a good point there, Ollie."

"Or Aunt Lisa could make it for us," Dad said. "She has the family recipe."

"Let's ask her," Oliver said. "I want mashed potatoes."

Laine, who had been steadily eating her cereal one flake at a time, raised her head, then patted her tummy.

"You want mashed potatoes?" David asked his daughter.

Laine's mouth lifted in a brief, benign smile, as if the answer were obvious, then returned to her methodical examination of each bran flake.

Dad cut his French toast into smaller pieces and began to eat. "See there? I was right. Tastes like maple syrup."

David poured himself another cup of coffee and sat in the last available chair at the table. "What's our plan for today? I need to go into the office. We have an emergency meeting." Last night, Trey had called. His sister's inn, which they'd remodeled from a large house built over a hundred years ago in Emerson Pass, had burned down in a forest fire. She'd been open for only a few days when the fire raged out of control, taking out her inn, some houses, an ice rink, and the high school. Trey wanted to talk about what they could do for Jamie and anyone else in Emerson Pass who needed to rebuild.

"The weather's supposed to be great again today," Dad said. "I was thinking the kids and I could have a beach day. Dominic and Rosa want to join us. And Ria." He added the last part as if it were an afterthought.

"Yay," Oliver said.

Laine clapped her hands together.

"That sounds terrific," David said.

"It's supposed to be nice for at least the next week," Dad said. "Make hay while the sun shines."

Oliver giggled. "Papa, you're funny."

"I'm here all week, kid," Dad said.

What was it with his father that had him so happy lately? Living here agreed with him. Tanned and fit, he looked about ten years younger than he had a year ago.

"Thanks, Dad. I'm going to get a shower and head into work. Can you guys help Papa with the dishes?"

They both nodded.

"That's my troupers," David said. "I'll see you tonight for dinner. Maybe I'll pick up some takeout from the deli?"

"Don't worry about that," Dad said. "Ria and Rosa are making tamales. They're sending some up for our dinner."

"God bless them," David said.

If raising children took a village, he had the best one in the world.

"Before you go," Dad said, rising from the table, "I saw this and thought it might be a good idea for you." He handed him a piece of paper folded into a square.

David shook it open. It was a flyer for a grief support group over at the church.

"I think you should go," Dad said.

"I don't need a group." David pressed his thumb into his cheekbone. What was his dad thinking? Support groups were not for Perry men. They licked their wounds in private, talking to no one. Keeping it all inside so that no one pitied them. Hadn't his father done that for most of his life?

"I disagree," Dad said.

"Why would this help me? Talking about stuff? Hearing other people's sad stories? I'll feel worse."

"You'll find people who understand what you're going through. Where you've been and where you need to go."

"Dad, how would you know anything about this?"

"I attend a divorce support group." Dad walked over to the window. With his gaze out toward the street, he shrugged his shoulders in conjunction with placing his hands in the pockets of his khaki pants. "Talking with others has helped me move forward."

This information stung him in that place between surprise and hurt. How come he felt the need to go outside the family? He and Lisa should be all Dad needed. "If you wanted someone to talk to, I'm here."

Dad turned slowly to look at him. "Talking to my son about my failed marriage is what the experts would call unhealthy boundaries. I need to talk to people who aren't family. Others who are going through the same heartbreak that I've experienced."

"That's fine for you, I guess. But it's not something I need."

"Let me put it to you this way, son. I don't ask you for much. Never have. I'm asking you to do this. For me."

"Why?"

"Because it hurts me to see you this way."

David took a long hard look at his father. "Fine. If it means that much to you, I'll go to one meeting. But if it's worthless, I won't go again."

"You've always been as stubborn as a mule."

"I get it from my mother," David said. "But you know that."

Dad gave him a weak smile. "Yes, son, I surely do."

3

Sara

A breeze fluttered the fabric of the umbrella where Sara sat with Autumn on the patio of Dog's Brewery. Temperatures hovered in the low eighties. Overhead, the bright sun shone down from a cloudless sky. The patio was full this afternoon. Diners chatted and laughed. Half a dozen children played on the grass, shouting and running while their mothers enjoyed lunch. School started soon. They were having their fun while they could.

"Are you going to the support group tonight?" Autumn leaned forward slightly with her forearms pressed against the tabletop.

Sara tapped fake sweetener into her iced tea. "I told you I'd go, so I will. However, I don't want to, and I'll be very grumpy the whole time and later with you."

"I think it will be good for you." Pure green eyes stared back at her. Autumn Hickman, now Wattson, could peer right into Sara's soul. They'd been friends for twelve years, and in all that time, she'd never been able to keep anything from her.

"Why?" Sara asked as her elbow knocked over the sweetener container.

"Because you have anger issues, and it's time for you to move on. Start dating."

Sara narrowed her eyes. Autumn was all cinnamon and cream, with her light red hair and dewy skin. Since her marriage to Trey, she glowed with happiness. "Dating? I don't think so." If Autumn only knew about her grandfather's will. The thought of a date or two was small compared to finding someone to marry her in less than a month.

She yearned to share this strange request with Autumn. But it was too absurd to even go there. Still, there was this small, niggling thought that perhaps she should do it. She could hire an actor to play the part in exchange for cash. If she did, it was imperative that she keep the secret between them. Even Autumn couldn't know. For one thing, her best friend was a terrible liar. Even if she didn't accidentally spill the truth with her transparent expressions, a detective could easily trick her into talking. Plus, she'd never keep a secret like that from Trey. If Trey knew, all the Wolves would know. Then the truth was sure to come out, blowing her chances to start the foundation.

Not that any of that mattered. She wasn't going to do it. She'd already decided. The foundation idea was too big, anyway. Harper was the priority for now. Disrupting both their lives to have a stranger live with them and pretend to be happy newlyweds was the worst idea she'd had since marrying Harper's father. Autumn's thin brows came together as she peered at her. "What's going on with you? Are you keeping something from me?"

Sara sipped her tea to avoid answering the question. "Not a thing."

"Fine. But I'm serious about the support group." Autumn stacked the spilled sweetener packets neatly into their ceramic container.

"I don't want to share my feelings with strangers. Anyway, I have you."

"But I don't totally get it. Not like people who are also grieving a spouse."

"I'm not grieving a spouse. I hate his guts and hope he's burning in hell right now."

Autumn's mouth turned downward into a sad frown. "Do you see what I mean? Anger is running your life. If you remain like this, you'll never be open to meeting someone."

"There's no one in this town who's still single, so I'm not sure it matters if I'm open or not."

"What about David Perry? The more I get to know him, the more I think he'd be perfect for you."

"Are you kidding me? He is *not* my type. Not at all."

"But why? You said he was so kind to you the other night."

"I don't dislike him. Not after I puked all over his shoes and he still took me home." Sara flushed, remembering that night. One reckless night out after months of being a shut-in single mother. That was all it took. One stupid, drunken night where she'd succumbed to a gargantuan amount of self-pity and had too many martinis. As the mother of an infant, she rarely drank more than a glass or two of wine, which had made her consumption even more potent. David had happened to be out that same night. Being a gentleman, if not a giant bore, he'd offered to take her home. They'd only just crossed the parking lot of Dog's Brewery when the eruption had spewed from her like a wanton fire hydrant. "I'm not sure I can ever face him again after what happened."

"It's not that bad," Autumn said.

"I'm not sure about that." Puking on her archenemy's shoes wasn't the worst thing that had ever happened to her. Not even close. Still, she'd rather not have added ruining David Perry's loafers to her list of humiliations.

"It's been weeks. I'm sure he's already forgotten about it."

"I really doubt that," Sara said. "Even if I did like him that way, which I don't, he would never be attracted to me. Even without the puking incident."

"Why would you say that?" Autumn asked.

"Guys like him don't like girls like me unless they're interested in my money."

"That was your husband, not all men." Autumn gazed back at her with a glint of determination in her eyes. "You will go to that support meeting. Do you understand?"

"If it means so much to you, I'll go. One time, but if it's excruciating, I won't be returning."

Zane Shaw, owner of Dog's Brewery, arrived with their salads. "Hello, ladies. I saw you two out here and thought I'd better bring these myself." He set identical Cobb salads in front of each of them. Blond and tanned with shoulders as wide as the surfboard he was often on, he could be on a poster advertising Cliffside Bay. "It's great to see you both."

"You too," Autumn said. "How's it coming with The Oar? Any news on when the guys can start rebuilding?"

Zane and his sister, Sophie, who was engaged to Nico, one of the partners of Wolf Enterprises, owned what had been a family bar and grill for generations. The Oar had burned to the ground a few months back, and Wolf Enterprises had been hired for the rebuild.

"Should be any day now," Zane said. "Permits and insurance have slowed us down."

"Do they have any leads on who started the fire?" Sara asked.

"None that they've made public, other than the witness who claimed to see a woman dressed in black running out the side door of the kitchen," Zane said. "And that they'd decided it wasn't connected to the fire at your mom's apartment building in Stoweaway."

Autumn's mother had moved to Cliffside Bay after the fire demolished the complex where she'd rented an apartment. With the connection to her sons and daughter, the authorities had at first theorized that the fires were set by the same person.

"The whole thing's so awful," Sara said. "I'm sorry you guys have had to deal with this."

"Ironically, losing The Oar made it possible for her and Nico to get together, so it's all worked out in the end," Zane said. "After I got out of their way. I had no idea I'd be such an over-protective big brother. But now that I have Sophie back in my life, I can't deal with the thought of anything happening to her."

"You're a good brother," Autumn said. "As are my two knuckleheaded brothers."

Stone and Kyle loved their wives and families with a passion that made Sara actually hurt with jealousy. She hadn't had the good fortune to pick a man like them. An image of her husband flashed before her. Dark eyes and his full mouth had been so irresistible. If only she'd seen through his good looks to the man beneath the surface. Instead, she'd been so damn grateful. A fat girl with the guy who looked like a movie star.

"I'll let you two enjoy your lunch," Zane said. "I just wanted to say hello."

"Give Honor my love," Autumn said.

"Will do."

After he left, they turned their attention to the salads. Sara moved a slice of avocado to the side of her plate. She would have only a few bites of the fattening avocado and blue cheese. Just enough to be satiated.

Autumn scooted the blue cheese from her salad onto a napkin.

"Do you feel all right?" Sara asked. "You love blue cheese."

Autumn grinned and tossed her hair behind her shoulders. "I can't have soft cheeses. For at least another seven or eight months."

"Oh my God."

"Yep. I'm pregnant."

A happy thrill went through her. Autumn had wanted a husband and a family for years. "I'm so happy for you." Sara reached across to squeeze Autumn's arm. "How far along?"

"Eight weeks. I know it's too early to tell people, but I was too excited not to tell my best friend."

"Trey must be so pleased."

"He is. He's already planning the nursery."

"What color?" Sara asked.

"Yellow and soft greens. He claims those are fine for either gender."

"Were you trying?" Sara asked.

"Not trying exactly, but not taking precautions either."

"Harper will be a year older. Not exactly the same age, but close enough."

"Just like we always wanted," Autumn said.

They chatted for a while about when the baby would be born. Either late April or early May, depending on exactly when the baby had been conceived.

"I'm worried about going back to work," Autumn said. "I'd like to stay home with the baby, but we need the money."

Was this another sign? They'd always talked about Autumn helping her to run a foundation if she were ever to start one. Sara could give her a big salary, and Autumn could work at home. Or, if she had a building, she could hire other women with young children and offer a day care at the facility. She could make it a mission to hire women. Yet another reason to find a husband. Could she do it? Would she? What was a year of her life, really? It's not as if she had the inclination or wherewithal to find actual love. So what if she had to hire an actor to play the part? Maybe she'd ask Lisa or Pepper if they had any out-of-work actor friends who needed money. But no, that wouldn't work, because then they'd know she had to hire someone to be her husband. How pathetic was that? She had to hire a man to be in her life. If she thought about it too hard, that's what she'd done the first time. Only she hadn't known he was playing the part of devoted husband.

Autumn smiled and reached across the table to squeeze her arm. "Now, don't worry about me. Trey and I will figure something out."

"Yes, of course you will. Things like that always work out.

Worst case, you'll let me gift you a nanny for the first couple years."

Autumn glared at her. "You know that's not a possibility. We've talked about this too many times."

Sara sighed. "I wish you'd just let me help."

"Even if Trey would agree to it, which he won't because he's too proud, there's no way I'm taking your money. This is my life, and I have to make it work just like all the other moms in the world. You're my best friend, not the bank."

"You've done so much for me, though," Sara said. "I'd like to pay you back somehow."

"Your friendship is all I want. That's all I've ever wanted. You and me, always."

"Yes, you and me." *You loved me when I was fat*, she thought. And when her husband and his mistress had been murdered and the proverbial floor dropped out from under her, Autumn had been there. "Come to Cliffside Bay and build a house that over-looks the sea," she'd said. "Let the salt air heal you and let me take care of you." So she had. And because of that, her life had been bearable.

4

D avid

David sat at the conference table with his business partners in the office space of Wolf Enterprises. The building itself was on a back street of town and had once been the old schoolhouse. They'd bought it from the city, and David's design had brought it into this century. The ground floor was essentially one big room where they met with potential clients and also spent time together brainstorming. Upstairs was another open space where they each had a desk. Of the five, David spent the most time there, working at his drafting table by the large windows that let in light no matter the time of year.

Rafael Soto ran the business but worked primarily from his home office or on the road. He accompanied Lisa when she traveled to movie sets or did publicity in Los Angeles or New York. Fortunately, Rafael could do his work from anywhere, as he primarily managed their finances and secured new work.

Stone Hickman, their general contractor, was in and out, depending on if he needed to be on the work site to manage the subcontractors and their crews. Now that they were profitable and steadily busy, Stone spent less time doing physical work and more time supervising. David had noticed he'd seemed restless since he'd returned home from working on Jamie's inn. The giant man needed physical work or he started building projects on his own property. His wife, Pepper, had begged him not to put up another project for fear they'd take out all the natural foliage in the area. He'd already built a garden shed, pool house, and workroom. His latest project was a tree house in one of the oaks. For future children, he'd said, when David had dropped by to see him perched on a thick branch hammering the platform together.

Nico, the landscape architect, did his design work on the computer here at the office, but he was often out buying plants and supervising his crew. He preferred to be outside and paced like a caged panther on days it was too rainy or windy to plant.

Trey spent a fair amount of time in the office. However, as their interior designer, he traveled to shops and antique stores for product. Of the partners, he spent the most time with clients, which sometimes exhausted him. There was no accounting for taste, he sometimes said, then shuddered. David understood this zealotry when it came to design work. Each home design represented his aesthetic. Architecting houses was his small contribution in his mission to make the world more beautiful. However, often the client wanted what they wanted. Like the heart.

This left David alone most days to do his drafting work in the quiet. He preferred this. He turned on classical music and entered the zone. Hours would go by before he looked up from his work.

"Yeah, so the whole inn is demolished," Trey said. "Jamie's devastated. She'd only been open a few days."

"What can we do?" Rafael asked. His dark eyebrows came together in a frown. "This is such a tough break for her. She worked so hard to save the money."

"Insurance will cover the damage." Stone folded his large hands together on the tabletop. "But given how long it's taking to get the insurance check for The Oar, it could be a while."

"She's thinking about coming home to Cliffside Bay and just

calling it quits," Trey said. "I've never heard her like this. Our dad's voice is echoing through her head, telling her she's a loser and to give up. Honestly, I can't say I blame her. What's she supposed to do now? Spend another year scraping together money while she waits for insurance checks and building permits? There's no way she can recover from this."

"Once the insurance money comes in, she can build a new inn," David said. "If she wants, I can replicate what we did with the remodel."

He'd managed to take an old, crumbling mansion and turn it into a beautiful inn. Trey's interiors had added the extra layer of detail and charm. Stone's team had left no detail unattended. They'd been proud of the work and happy for Jamie. Now, like so much in life, all had been lost in an instant.

"What will she live on between now and then?" Trey asked. "Everything she had was sunk into that place. She's up to her eyeballs in debt, and now she has a business that won't turn a profit for at least a year. I mean, if we could even rebuild it in that amount of time. I hate to say it, but I think she's right. She should bag the idea and use the insurance money to pay off her bills."

"What's she supposed to do here?" Stone asked. "Go back to waitressing after tasting the thrill of running her own business?"

"We can do all the work pro bono again," Rafael said.

"She already told me no," Trey said. "She feels guilty for all the work we did for free the first time around."

"She shouldn't," Nico said. "That's what family's for. We're not letting your little sister hang out to dry. Not after how hard she worked to open the place."

"The Wolves are family," Stone said. "Which means she's as much our little sister as yours."

"Thanks, you guys. Seriously." Trey cupped his hands under his chin. "I'll pass it on to her, but I think she's too defeated. I'm not in a position to help her out, either. We're about to have a lot of expenses. Autumn's pregnant."

The other men exploded into congratulations. "Way to go." Stone, sitting next to Trey, thumped him on the shoulder.

"I'm thrilled, of course, but also nervous about money. Autumn wants to stay home with the baby. I'm not sure how we'll survive on one income, let alone take care of my sister."

"These things have a way of working themselves out," Stone said. "One way or another."

"True," Rafael said. "Plus, you've got us."

"Selfishly, I'm glad to hear that you guys are having a baby," Stone said. "Maybe it'll rub off on Pepper. She keeps putting me off on the whole baby thing. For some reason, she thinks it'll change our lives."

David laughed. "It will, man, but in good ways. Pepper will be an awesome mother."

"It's that Kyle has so many. She's getting a bad impression," Stone said. "I can't believe he talked Violet into another one."

"Wait, what?" Nico asked. "Number five?"

"Yeah, number five," Trey said. "They announced it at family dinner last week. They're due a few months before Autumn."

"Kyle's a brave man," Rafael said.

"Brave or foolish, I'm not sure which," Stone said. "Violet said he just wouldn't let it go. He insists there's one more soul out there waiting to be their child."

"That's the sweetest thing I've ever heard," Nico said.

"If misguided. Five kids?" David shuddered. "Two are kicking my ass and I have a village behind me."

"Nico, you know what this means for us, though?" Rafael asked. "Sophie and Lisa will be full-court press on starting a family."

Nico groaned. "Sophie already is. I guess she's probably right. If I don't get started now, I'll be a hundred years old before they graduate from college."

"You're the same age as the rest of us," Stone said. "Thirty-five is still a respectable age to become a father."

"But to your point, we better get going," Rafael said. "Lisa and I have been enjoying it just being us, but time stops for no man."

"Sophie agreed to wait until after we get The Oar reopened. I was going to wait until tonight over beers to tell you this, but now seems as good a time as any. Sophie finally got the insurance check. We can get started next week on construction."

"Fantastic," David said. He'd designed the new bar and grill to Sophie's specifications. She wanted California bar meets Paris café. "The designs and building permits have all been approved by the city."

"It'll be great to have our second office back," Stone said. "I was thinking we were going to have to install a keg in here."

Once a week, the Wolves had met at The Oar to discuss a little business but mostly to shoot the breeze and bond. David wasn't much for conversation, but he enjoyed their time together more than he thought possible. There were moments over the past year that those couple hours a week were what had saved him from a complete depression.

For the next thirty minutes, they discussed the project plan for The Oar, then moved on to Jamie's inn. David couldn't help but feel spooked about the fires. They still had no leads on the arsonist who had taken down The Oar. The forest fire in Colorado had nothing to do with the torching of The Oar, yet it unsettled him. Since moving to California, he was so much more aware of how fire danger threatened the western part of America. Every summer, fires took out entire communities. In addition, he hoped the arsonist wasn't about to target another local business. Or, God forbid, the Victorian.

"Last on the agenda," Rafael said. "I have more good news for us. I'm happy to report that through Jamie's connections, two of the people who lost homes in Emerson Pass have asked us to lead their projects. Apparently, our reputation for good work has circled through the community."

"The weird part," Stone said, "is that one of the houses lost in the fire was The Lake House, where Pepper and I were snowed in." He grinned. "And where I charmed the pants off her."

"Quite literally," Rafael said.

"The Lake House was bought by someone else after we used it for the wedding." Stone's eyes twinkled as he paused dramatically. "And you won't believe who it is."

"It's somebody famous," Nico said. "I can tell from your face."

"Not another Hollywood star, I hope," Trey said. "No offense to your wives, but that YouTube star Pepper sent us about finished me off."

"No, thank God," Stone said. "Our new client is Patrick Wilder's widow. Her name's Crystal Whalen."

"The tech guy?" Trey asked. "Wasn't he like one of the richest men in the world?"

"That's right," Rafael said. "He was right up there with all the big guys. That's what happens when you invent technology every person in the free world uses on their phones."

"I don't," Stone said. "I like to keep it old-school."

"Mostly because you don't know how to use your phone," Nico said.

"What else do I need it for other than to send sexy messages to my wife?" Stone asked.

Rafael rolled his eyes. "Can we stay focused here?"

"Yeah, sorry," Stone said. "After Patrick Wilder's death, his widow, Crystal, moved to Emerson Pass because she visited her grandparents there in the summers. She wants to rebuild as soon as possible."

"David, this is a great opportunity for you," Rafael said. "She has deep pockets, obviously, and wants to get started now. She said she'll worry about the insurance check later." He glanced at his watch. "In fact, she wants us to video conference with her. She's waiting for our call."

Rafael turned on his laptop, which was connected to a large-screen television on the wall. A few seconds later, a slender woman with high cheekbones and dark blond hair that fell over her shoulders showed up on the screen. Even on a video call, David could see how beautiful she was. The rich guys always got the best women. That left nothing for a guy like him.

"Hi, Crystal. It's Rafael and the other Wolves."

"Hello, everyone. Thanks so much for making time to talk today."

"Our pleasure," Rafael said.

They went around the table quickly to introduce themselves.

"I've heard nothing but wonderful things about Wolf Enterprises," Crystal said. "And when I learned that Stone and Pepper had been snowed in at my house before it was my house, it felt right to hire you guys to build a new one."

"Do you want to rebuild it as it was?" David asked.

"Not necessarily," Crystal said. "I loved The Lake House, but having the chance to design a new one exactly how I want is rather intoxicating." She looked away from the center of the camera, as if embarrassed. Her hair hid her face for a moment before she smoothed it back and returned her gaze to the camera. "I'm trying to find the silver lining in all this."

"Let's schedule a phone call with just the two of us," David said. "We can talk more about your tastes. In the meantime, send me photographs of homes you admire." He gave her his work email. "I'll look forward to your project."

"There's one other thing I wanted to ask you about," she said. "Actually two. Trey, I'm acquainted with your sister and what's happened with her inn. I feel terrible about it." She hesitated. Again, the curtain of hair covered her face as she looked downward. When she lifted her chin, she tucked one side of her hair behind her ear. "This is going to sound strange but I'd like to set up an anonymous fund for her to live on during the construction. In addition, I'd like to give her the money to start the rebuilding process right away, including your fees. I have the inside track on the city officers who grant building permits, so I can move things along as needed. Legally, of course."

David glanced over at Trey. He was staring at the image on the screen as if Crystal had been speaking another language. She was in a way, David thought. The language of money. To those without it, the concept of the kind of money Crystal Whalen had was inconceivable.

"I don't know what to say," Trey said finally. "It's so generous of you. I have to ask, why?"

"She's a young woman trying to do something very hard," Crystal said. "I was her not very long ago. I'm trained as a chef, and when I met my husband, I was working in a restaurant, barely making enough to afford my overpriced Seattle rent. I could've used a little help. When I heard about her newly opened inn and how devastated she was, I wanted to help. Have you ever had a visceral reaction to the news of someone's plight? Like it's happening to you? That's what I felt when I heard about Jamie. Then I thought, I can actually do something to help here. What's the use of money if you can't do good with it?"

"This will save her life," Trey said. "Opening an inn has been her dream since she was a kid. She called me this morning about giving up and just coming home. It's been a month and all she's gotten from the insurance company is the runaround."

"I understand perfectly," Crystal said. "But please, will you keep my secret? I don't want her to feel strange around me. Or indebted to me."

"Our lips are sealed," Stone said.

"Also, the other client Jamie sent you?" Crystal asked. "Has he been in contact yet?"

"Are you referring to Garth Welte?" Rafael asked. "If so, yes, we've exchanged emails and are set to talk tomorrow."

"He's my neighbor," Crystal said. "And good friend. If it's between working on my house or his, please focus on him. I have an apartment close to my kitchen shop and am perfectly happy living here for as long as I have to."

"We'll put together a project plan for both these and let you know," Stone said. "The trouble will be finding subcontractors, given how many local resources will have to focus on building you folks a new high school."

"And the weather here," Crystal said. "There's no way to build in the winter months because of snow."

"I remember your winter only too well," Stone said.

Crystal laughed. "Right, I suppose you do."

"But being snowed in with Pepper is how I got her to fall in love with me," Stone said. "Which makes me darn fond of the place."

"Mr. Lake told me more than one couple fell in love in that house," Crystal said. "Can you put a little magic into the new one?"

"We'll do our best," Rafael said.

They said goodbyes and hung up.

"Wow," Trey said. "I'm blown away."

"Me too," Nico said. "But I'll tell you what—since moving here, I'm amazed by the kindness and generosity of so many people. I mean, look what Judi did for Sophie and me."

"You're just a lucky bastard," David said. "It's because you're so pretty."

"Takes one to know one," Nico said.

"It's a fact that beautiful people have it easier," Stone said. "Which explains why I have to work so much harder than the rest of you jerks."

5

Sara

Sara saw David Perry the moment she descended the narrow, creaky stairway into the church basement. He stood just outside the kitchen, staring into a paper cup of the terrible coffee. She cursed silently. What were the odds that he'd come to the exact same grief support group on the exact same evening? Pretty good, actually. This was Cliffside Bay. There were only a few thousand residents. This group was open to anyone. He'd probably seen the same stupid flyer Autumn had.

Her gaze darted to his feet. Yes, there they were. The shoes. Or, rather, the exact replica of the shoes she'd vomited all over— the very same ones she'd ordered and had sent to his home with a hasty apology note.

Dressed in khaki pants and a button-down striped shirt, he looked as tidy, self-contained, and proper as always. His sandy-brown hair, long on the top and short on the sides, fell over his forehead. She knew from the months they'd conspired on her house design that his eyes were the color of the sea on a sunny day. Intelligent eyes that took in every detail of whatever he was examining at the moment. She didn't like the way he'd often looked at her as if he saw flaws in her design and would fix her if he could. Many times, she'd wanted to cover her face and hide under baggy clothing. He'd made her feel exposed.

Which was why she didn't like him.

He looked up from his cup and straight at her. He waved and headed toward her. It was too late to pretend she'd somehow made it into the basement in error on her way to somewhere else. She lifted the corners of her mouth into a fake smile.

"Hey, Sara. You trying this out too, huh?" David asked in his slow, Midwestern intonation. The guy rarely spoke, but when he did, it took him twice as long as everyone else. She supposed they had more time for chitchat in Iowa. He ran an index finger over his bottom lip. A habitual movement she'd noticed during their meetings. One he did while he was thinking.

And there was the problem of his mouth. Lips on the thin side but somehow totally sexy. Far too many times she'd wondered what his mouth would feel like against hers. Another reason she didn't like him.

"Autumn saw the flyer," Sara said, "and basically forced me to come."

"My dad did too. Lisa, my sister, has been on me to do this for months now." His voice wavered, then tapered off. He cleared his throat.

The scent of the stale coffee from his cup made her nervous stomach queasy. Perhaps sensing this, he stepped over to the nearby trash can and tossed the cup into it before returning to stand next to her.

"I'm not sure I'll stay the whole time," she said. "Zoey had to give up her night off to stay with Harper." Maybe she should make a run for it before the meeting began? It would be less rude to leave now.

"I didn't want to come, either," David said. "I don't know what good it'll do anyway."

She looked up at him, surprised at the soft quality of his voice. "I mean, what's the point, right? No amount of talking will make what happened better."

A muscle in David's cheek twitched, as if a gnat had flown too close to his face. "That's exactly what I said to my dad."

"And what are we supposed to do? Share our most personal feelings with the entire group?"

"I believe that's the idea, yes." He smiled, rather grimly, then spoke through clenched teeth. "Should we make a run for it?"

"How'd you know that's what I was thinking?"

"Because I was thinking the same thing."

She looked over at the older woman positioning chairs into a circle. Clearly the leader of the group. She'd already seen them. Leaving now would be completely immature and rude. "I don't think we can without bringing attention to ourselves."

"Bad manners to go before it even starts," he said. "Right?"

She almost laughed when he shot her a conspiratorial glance. "Yes, bad manners and chicken. Here's the plan," she said under her breath. "One hour and we never have to come here again."

"Good plan," he said.

A few seconds of awkward silence passed.

She gestured toward his loafers. "I'm glad they fit."

"They do, yes. Thanks again for sending them. Totally unnecessary."

"I'm so embarrassed about that night," Sara said. "I was in a bad place."

"We've all been there." He paused, dipping his chin as if contemplating what to say next. "I should tell you about my wife's funeral sometime. In case you were curious, too much whiskey before getting up to speak about your backstabbing wife is not a good idea."

She groaned softly. "Yes, I'm sure it's not." An image of her husband's funeral flashed across her mind. His mother had sobbed during the entire service. Sara, numb, could only stare into the face of her infant, praying it would soon be over and she could take her baby far, far away. Autumn had been next to her, their shoulders touching. She'd thought later that the warmth of the baby in her lap and Autumn's presence had made the entire ordeal bearable. "I wondered if I could even attend my husband's funeral. I remember thinking, what's the protocol for widows of spouses who died in the arms of their mistress?"

"But then you thought about your baby," David said. "You knew you had to go because he was your child's father."

She met his eyes. *So blue,* she thought. *Empathetic and sincere.* No one in the world could understand quite as he did. Perhaps this group was a good idea after all.

"That's what I kept telling myself, anyway," David said.

In all the times they'd met about her house design, he hadn't said one thing about his personal life. She'd had the feeling he hadn't thought her worthy of conversation. She'd guessed he thought she was just a spoiled rich girl with no purpose in life. Maybe she'd misinterpreted his reticence. Could he be shy instead of aloof?

Before she could say anything else, Zane Shaw walked in and headed toward them with a friendly wave of one perfect hand. What was Zane doing here? Didn't he have the perfect life with his perfect blonde wife and two perfect children and a thriving brewery? What did he have to grieve over? Then she remembered he'd lost his father a few years back. Hugh Shaw had been a hero in Cliffside Bay. They'd renamed the main street of town Hugh Shaw Avenue.

"Hey, Sara," Zane said. "David. You guys ever done something like this before?"

"No," David said. "And we were just discussing how we really wish we hadn't."

Zane chuckled. "Yeah, me too. But my wife's making me, so I'm screwed."

The thought hadn't occurred to Sara that she would actually know people here. This made the whole evening worse. How could she share her innermost thoughts with people she actually knew? Like everything, she had no control. Life was a series of lessons in how little power she had over anything, including her dead husband and his dead girlfriend.

She should have gone with her instinct and told Autumn no. A night without her baby should have been spent with friends for dinner, not with strangers in this room that smelled of mildew and bad coffee. She could be home right now stuffing her face with chocolate and watching a Netflix movie.

She wanted to run. But no. Something in her life had to change. The chocolate consumption was starting to show in her waistline.

Anyway, she had an ally of sorts in David. That was something.

"Looks like we're starting," Zane said. He gestured toward the tall woman now sitting in one of the chairs.

"Too late now," David muttered under his breath.

"One hour and we're free," she answered back in the same tone.

She lowered herself into one of the rickety chairs nearest the door and waited for the torture to begin.

There were five of them, plus the leader. Besides Sara, David, and Zane, there was an older woman she didn't recognize wearing the most fabulous black boots. In addition, a man with closely cropped silver hair stood in the corner, looking as if he, too, wanted to bolt for the door.

"Come sit." The woman gestured for the rest to take chairs. Once everyone was in the circle, she introduced herself. "I'm Ria. Thank you all for coming. I'd like to begin our first session by introducing ourselves and saying why we're here." Ria, thin with dark skin and big brown eyes, wore a soft knit wrap dress and red cowgirl boots. Sara guessed her to be in her late fifties.

"I'll start," Ria said. "I lost my son twelve years ago to gang violence. After he passed, I nearly died from grief. A group like this one saved my life. I used to run groups in my old neighborhood in Oakland. I'm not a licensed therapist—just a person who lost her entire life when I lost my son. Talking with others who've lost children or loved ones is the only thing that's helped me cope. The world is divided between those of us who've lost the person they loved most and the ones who haven't. We, as those who've lost, will gather together to grieve and provide support to one another." She turned toward the woman with the great boots. "Would you like to tell us why you're here?" Ria asked.

She nodded as she set her designer handbag under her chair. For a second, Sara thought she might change her mind. Her small features clenched in obvious pain before she composed herself and began. "My name's Judi Coventry. I've never really gotten over my husband's death. It's been several years since I lost him." She spoke with a Southern accent, and her hands moved about restlessly as if she wished she'd kept hold of her purse. "He was the love of my life, and after he passed, I retreated inside myself. And into my house. There were weeks at a time I didn't leave. I don't know if you know this, but you can have almost everything delivered these days. I've mostly endured in silence, like a good Southern woman does. My mama always said to fix your hair and put on your lipstick even when you're hurting. I've been in California for many decades, so I figured it was time I started embracing a few of the more progressive ways and talk about my feelings. I won't, however, under any circumstances, be eating kale."

The tension in the room eased as everyone laughed.

"What was the tipping point that made you decide to be here tonight?" Ria asked when they'd quieted.

"There are two young people who essentially brought me back to life." She turned toward Zane. "I'm speaking of your younger sister and her fiancé, Nico."

Zane smiled. "I figured as much."

Sophie and Nico. Yet another Cliffside Bay couple that had fallen in love. All this love in this saltwater town was like salt in her wounds.

Judi turned back to Ria. "They reminded me that I'm still here, and despite my abhorrence of kale or anything else good for me, seem to be poised for at least another decade of life."

"I'm glad you've come," Ria said. "I hope you'll find comfort among those who understand."

Ria nodded toward Zane. "Would you like to go next?"

"I'm Zane Shaw. In case you don't know me from my dad's bar." His voice broke.

Sara's mouth dropped open when his eyes filled with tears.

"I'm sorry," Zane said.

"In here, we don't apologize for our grief," Ria said. "Go ahead. Tell us why you're with us tonight."

"The short answer is because my wife made me," Zane said.

David and Judi chuckled.

"The longer answer is that my dad died a few years ago. He'd been lost to me before then, due to dementia. At the time, I was super focused on keeping the business he devoted his life to up and running, not to mention paying for the memory care facility. When the bar and grill he built with his blood, sweat, and tears burned to the ground, I fell apart. It was like losing him all over again. My wife thinks I didn't grieve him properly, and now it's caught up with me. So I'm here to talk about my feelings or whatever it is we do here."

Ria smiled kindly. "Thank you, Zane." She turned her gaze toward David.

"My turn?" David asked, with a slight hitch in his voice.

"If you're ready," Ria said.

"Sure, yeah. I mean, I'm not really ready, and I don't have a clue how to talk about my feelings. But I'm here because my twin sister and my dad encouraged me to come. When I say encouraged, I mean they're totally sick of my crap."

"What do you mean by crap?" Ria asked.

"I guess just a disinterest in living," David said. "Other than my children needing me, I'm not sure I'd get out of bed most days."

Sara's chest ached. She knew exactly what he meant.

"Will you share with us who you lost?" Ria asked.

"My wife." David shifted in his chair, crossing one leg, then the other. "She was murdered." His chest rose and fell as he took in a ragged breath. "I had no idea at the time, but she was delivering drugs via our minivan with my children in the back seat. The people she worked for killed her when the Feds figured out what she was doing. They didn't want her to talk. Which is ironic because from the time I met her, she never shut up." His mouth twisted into a bitter smile. "I'm angry. All the time."

Me too.

"I'd like to be less so," David said. "Although anger fuels me. Gets me out of bed. So I wonder if it's a good idea or not."

"Talking about how we feel will help," Ria said. "Even though I can see you're not quite sure that's true."

David shifted in his chair. "Yeah, I'm on the fence."

"There's nothing wrong with how you're feeling," Ria said.

"Thanks," David said.

Ria turned to Sara. "And you, dear?"

"I'm Sara. My husband was murdered by the husband of his girlfriend." She paused as a manic giggle erupted from her chest. Horrified, she clutched the gold cross that hung in the hollow of her neck. "I'm sorry. It's not funny. It just sounds like a soap opera when I say it out loud. But it's the truth. My husband was having an affair with a friend of ours. Her husband, who was upended by drugs and jealousy, killed them." Everyone stared at her with sympathetic eyes. Her vision blurred from the tears that had come from nowhere. Good God, was she crying in front of these people?

Sara watched the floor, wishing for one of those famous California earthquakes to split the room apart. Anything would be better than all the pity that seemed to radiate from every member of the group. She swiped at her cheeks. "I'm angry, too. I can't seem to get past it, and I want to, for my daughter's sake. I'm like this bitter old lady." As her grandfather had been. She continued to clutch her necklace. "Maybe I came because I thought it might make me feel less alone."

"You're not alone," Ria said. "We're here."

Sara waited for her to say more, but what else could she say, really? "Thanks," Sara mumbled. "For the opportunity." Opportunity? That was the wrong word. This wasn't a job interview.

"Bobby, would you like to share next?" Ria asked.

Bobby from the bar? Sara squinted to get a better look. It *was* him. She was acquainted with Bobby from the brewery. He worked for Zane and Sophie as a bartender. She hadn't recognized him at first because he'd cut his long hair. Much better, in her opinion, than the ponytail. Fit and muscular, he had a definite aging surfer vibe.

"I'm Bobby. Thanks for having me." He had a voice like an aged bottle of whiskey. "I lost my sweetheart a few summers ago to cancer. We'd been together since we were twenty years old. We had a good forty-five years together and then she was gone. The nights are long now." He stroked the gray stubble on his chin. "I saw the notice about this group when I was leaving work the other night, and I thought I might give it a try. I'm new to town. Still getting my feet under me. I know it's time to start living again. I started with cutting my hair a few days ago. This is going to sound loony, but I hadn't cut it since my wife died."

"And why is that?" Ria asked.

"Her fingers had touched it." He cracked a knuckle on his right hand as he shook his head ruefully. "I was right. It does sound crazy."

"Not to us," Judi said.

"Definitely not," Sara found herself saying. "I can totally see how you would feel that way. It's a symbol."

The two younger men in the circle shifted, making their chairs squeak.

Bobby smiled as he wiped the corners of his wet eyes. "Why is it kindness from others always makes me cry?"

"Because it makes us feel understood," Ria said. "And seen."

"My wife would've hated my long hair," Bobby said. "When I first met her, I wore it long. Boy, was I proud of my hair. I thought it made me look like a rock star. I was a surfer back then. She made me cut all of it off and get a job."

"Smart lady," Judi said.

"She was that. And tough. She fought so hard." His voice broke. He ducked his head and covered his mouth with one hand before speaking. "She knew I'd be lost without her. She just kept fighting to stay alive. I had to let her know, there at the end, that it was all right to let go. I couldn't watch her suffer any longer."

"You loved her very much," Ria said.

"From the moment I met her," Bobby said. "She wasn't so sure about me."

"You're lucky to have had that," David said. "I was unhappy in my marriage. Now that she's gone, and I know what she did, I hate her. All I am is angry."

"Me too." Sara hadn't planned to speak. The words had simply erupted from her. "I hate my husband too. I'm exhausted from hating him."

David slowly turned his gaze to her, almost as if he moved through quicksand. His head dipped in a quick nod. "Yes, exactly. I had no idea anger could make me this tired."

"The difference for me is that I wasn't unhappy in my marriage." Sara's voice thickened. She continued, even though it felt as if a golf ball were lodged in her throat. "I was blissfully ignorant that Brent was having sex with my friend the entire time I was pregnant."

Judi gasped. "You poor dear."

Ria's placid expression didn't change, other than a slight softening in her eyes. Zane scratched the back of his neck and kept his gaze on his lap.

David, however, didn't move. She could feel him staring at her. When she lifted her gaze to him, their eyes locked. *He's in pain like me*, she thought. How could she not have seen that before now? It wasn't superiority but grief that kept him from engaging with others.

Sara placed the fingers of her right hand around the spot where her wedding ring had once been. For months after she took it off, the indentation remained. Now it was only skin. Other than the baby girl who had just taken her first steps last month, all traces of her husband were gone. The baby she'd wanted so badly. The baby who had changed everything. "He never wanted a child. When I got pregnant, he wanted me to get rid of her." She took in a deep breath before continuing. "He called her an 'it.' Get rid of 'it.' But I refused. I had the power in the relationship because I was the one with money."

"And it was your body, your child," Ria said.

"I would never have even considered...that...even though I knew from the first moment I told him I was pregnant that our marriage was doomed." She'd practically danced down their spiral staircase in their Colorado home waving the pregnancy stick around like one of those sparkly things on July Fourth. "The first thing out of his mouth, and I quote, 'But what about Vail next week?'"

"What did that mean, honey?" Ria asked.

"Vail was code for partying with our friends," Sara said. "The jet-setting kind of friends."

"I know just the type," Judi said. "They live for the next party instead of figuring out the purpose for their wealth. The good they could do with all that money."

"Yes. He'd rather have had Vail than a child. Or me." He'd stopped touching her and refused to participate in anything baby-related. "I went to the birthing classes by myself. Those were some of the evenings he brought her into my bed." Her throat constricted as the pain racked her body. She held her breath, willing herself not to break down into big ugly sobs.

"He acted like a child instead of stepping up like a man should," Zane said.

"And slept with your friend," David said. "Like a rebellious teenager who didn't get his way."

"Yes," Sara whispered as tears spilled from her eyes. "Exactly that."

"Sweetheart, of course that hurt like a son of a bitch," Bobby said. "No one breathing would feel any other way."

"Doesn't leave much to mourn," Zane said. "A man like that doesn't deserve your grief."

"I wonder how a woman does that?" Sara asked. "What kind of woman can sleep with another woman's husband in his wife's bedroom?"

"One without empathy," Judi said. "Otherwise known as a sociopath."

A bitter laugh rose up from Sara's belly. "I hate myself for mourning either of them, but once in a while a memory pops into my brain of a good time we had together. You know, before their affair. I'd thought she was a real friend. I had no idea he was cheating on me. I feel like such an idiot."

"It's easy to see, now that you know how the story ended," David said, leaning forward slightly. "But at the time you didn't know. You loved him."

"I did," Sara said. "I thought he loved me. Even when I was fat, he loved me. Only it turns out it was just the money and the lifestyle he wanted."

Why hadn't she married a man like Zane or David? A man who knew what a privilege it was to be a father instead of a narcissistic child?

"I'd be unapologetically angry." Judi's eyes snapped like lightning bugs on a black night. "Trying to squelch all that rage will give you wrinkles, darling. Just let it all out. We can take it."

Sara let out a laugh and sob all at once, then hiccuped. Embarrassed, she clutched her cross again and looked around at the faces staring back at her. "And then there's all the chocolate I've been eating."

"Eating to feel better?" Ria asked.

"Yes. I know I shouldn't, but I'm so lonely at night. Since I'll probably never have sex again, maybe it doesn't matter if I gain back the fifty pounds."

"You'll have sex again," Zane said, sounding amused.

"I don't think I can ever trust a man enough to do that," Sara said. "I mean, seriously. How could I?"

"Because most men are good," Judi said. "Not like that rat bastard of a husband of yours."

"I'm sorry," Sara said. Why had she talked this much? Why had she admitted to her love affair with chocolate? "I seem to have monopolized this entire session."

Ria shook her head. "I have a rule. No apologizing for our feelings. In here, we can be angry, sad, or anything else."

"Thank you. I promise not to do this at every meeting." Sara wiped under her eyes and sniffed.

"That sounded like an apology," David said softly.

Sara looked over at him. "I've been apologizing for my presence my whole life. The subtleties are lost on me."

"Darlin', we need to change that up right now," Judi said. "You're too pretty and smart to apologize for your presence. Ever. Whoever made you feel that way, and I'm assuming it was way before your adolescent husband, deserves a special place in hell."

"Agreed," Bobby said.

"Yes, ma'am," Zane said.

David, once again, gave her an almost imperceptible nod.

And once again, that simple gesture said it all. He understood.

6

David
All the way home from the meeting, David fumed. How could Sara's husband have done such a thing? Having an affair during his wife's pregnancy was despicable. Despite their troubles, he would rather have jumped off a building than abandon Marigold or their children. Some might say that was part of his problem. He'd been too loyal to his wife.

From the time they were fourteen years old, she'd clung to him and never let go. He'd wanted out but never quite managed to do so. When he was at college and met Liz, he'd been determined to break it off with Marigold. He and Liz had become close friends after being partnered on a project in their architecture program. He'd never said anything about his romantic feelings toward her. His plan was to be free first, then make his move. He'd gone home that Christmas break sure he would be able to let her down gently. As good as his resolve had been, he'd wavered under the pressure of his mother and Marigold. They were already planning the wedding. Marigold had bought a dress and secured the grange for the reception. He'd felt it was too late to back out. He couldn't let anyone down. Doing the right thing was more important than his own selfish desires.

He came from it naturally. Hadn't his father demonstrated that same behavior all his life?

I got the children out of it, he reminded himself as he trudged up the stairs to the second-floor apartment of the Victorian. He let himself in using his key. The lamps on either side of the couch were dimmed. His father's pillow and blanket were stacked on the couch. Toys had been tidily scooped into the bin he kept in the corner. All signs that Lisa was here.

His sister had offered to make him dinner. Given the scent of butter and garlic coming from the kitchen, she'd made good on said promise. His stomach growled in response. Thank God for small favors. He glanced at his watch. It was after eight, so the children would be tucked into bed. Lisa had probably brought an expensive bottle of wine from her cellar. They'd be able to have a good chat without interruption.

He took off his shoes and left them by the door. Before he went to the kitchen, he veered off to the bedroom to check on Laine and Oliver. They were both asleep in their toddler beds. The night-lights lit the room well enough that he could see clearly without fear of tripping over a toy. He crept over to Laine's bed and knelt next to her. He brushed back a lock of her shoulder-length blond hair and kissed her cheek. Next, he went to Oliver and did the same. How was it that his baby boy would start kindergarten in a few weeks? As slow and painful as the last few years had been, watching him grow from a baby to a boy had never ceased to amaze him.

He left the door open a few inches and crossed through the living room to the kitchen. Lisa greeted him with her stunning smile. "Hey there. How was it?" She pointed to a glass of wine on the table. "That's for you. Dinner's almost ready. Have a seat and tell me everything."

He drank from his glass before answering. "It was better than I thought it would be. Nice group of folks. You know how it is here. I recognized most of them."

Lisa dumped a pile of steaming noodles into a strainer she'd placed in the sink. "Not surprising."

"I should've expected it, I guess." He hadn't. He'd been too busy worrying and dreading actually attending to think about who might be there.

"Who was it?" Lisa asked.

"Zane Shaw. Bobby from the bar. Judi Coventry. Ria was the group leader, which did surprise me. I had no idea she did that kind of thing." Ria lived downstairs in the apartment across from Mama Soto. She and Dad sometimes played bridge with Mama Soto and Uncle Dominic. In true Cliffside Bay style, Rafael's mother had married his uncle. "And Sara Ness." His stomach fluttered as he said her name. That was strange. Yes, he'd always thought she was gorgeous, but she'd been a client. Even if he'd wanted to pursue a woman, she wouldn't have been the right choice. She was way too classy for him. And rich. Plus, she didn't like him. He didn't know why exactly.

"Sara? I'm glad to hear that she was there," Lisa said. "The poor woman has had a terrible time. Autumn worries about her."

"They're best friends from college, right?" he asked.

"That's right." Lisa mixed the fettuccine into a saucepan on the stove. "You don't like her much, do you?"

"Why would you say that?"

"I don't know. Something in your tone just now."

"No, not at all. I liked her fine. She has phenomenal taste. I enjoyed designing her house more than I can say. It's the opposite. She doesn't like me for some reason. I don't know what I did, but she gets this sour look on her face every time she sees me."

"Even after you took her home from the brewery?"

He grimaced. "She felt really bad about that. Did I tell you she sent me a new pair of shoes?"

"That was sweet." Lisa placed a steaming bowl of fettuccine Alfredo in front of him.

"This smells amazing." He smiled up at her. "You're my favorite sister."

"I'm your only sister, but thank you." She poured herself half a glass of wine and sat across from him.

"Aren't you eating?"

"I ate a salad and chicken earlier. I report to set next week and don't want to look like a whale." She rested one cheek in her hand and gazed at him with her sapphire eyes.

"You do not look like a whale." He wrapped noodles around his fork. Despite the fact that she was paid millions of dollars a movie, his sister still thought of herself as the chubby teen she'd once been. He thought briefly about Sara. The same demons plagued her as did his sister. The world was a harsh, judgmental place. Especially for women.

"Did you talk during the meeting?" Lisa asked.

"Quite a bit. More than I'd planned. Ria pretty much forced us to."

"Did it feel good?"

He twirled more pasta onto his fork. Had it felt good? Different and exposing, but comforting at the same time. "You know, it did. I especially related to Sara. Like me, she's angry. After what her husband did and what my wife did, we have every right to be. The rest of the group are mourning these wonderful people who they had loving relationships with. Not like my situation. Or Sara's."

"Maybe you two can get together after next session and talk?" Lisa sipped from her wine as her brow wrinkled. "You might give each other a lot of comfort and understanding."

"Except she doesn't like me. Oh, and she's rich. I'm still struggling to make ends meet every month." His house in Iowa still hadn't sold, which meant he had to pay a mortgage for a home he didn't live in. Marigold, despite her lucrative drug-running business, had run up twenty thousand dollars in credit card bills before she was killed.

Business had been steady, but splitting the profits among the five of them wasn't making any of them rich. Rafael and Stone were married to wealthy women, one being his sister. They didn't need the paycheck the way he, Trey, and Nico did.

Still studying him, Lisa touched her fingers briefly to her mouth. "Are you sure you don't want some help? I could pay off those debts tomorrow."

"We've discussed this." He gave her the look that told her to drop it.

"Fine. I won't bring it up again."

"Liar."

She got up from the table to grab the bottle of wine. "Regardless, you could still reach out to Sara. I'm sure you could both use a friend."

"If you have ideas that we're going to hit it off and fall in love, it's never going to happen. Other than tragic marriages, we have nothing in common."

"You're so stubborn sometimes."

"I'm not."

"You are. Anyway, if not her, then maybe someone else? You need to get back into the dating pool."

"Are you insane? I'd rather cut off my arm than get back into a relationship."

"You don't mean that," Lisa said.

"I do. I'll never let myself be that vulnerable again. My only priority is my kids. I've got to focus on them and work. All I need is a relationship to screw me up just when I'm starting to function like a human being again."

She rested her forearms on the table. "Just because you had a bad marriage the first time around doesn't mean it will happen again. Look at Rafael, for example. He's my prince after so many frogs."

"I have two little kids. What woman wants to take that on?"

"They're the loveliest children in the world," Lisa said.

"You're biased."

"Maybe, but I'm still right." She stretched her arms overhead and yawned. "Speaking of Rafael, I should probably get home. I've got an early day tomorrow."

"What? Already?" He'd been hoping for more time with her. This is how it was now. She was a famous movie star. No time for her loser brother.

"Don't look like that," Lisa said. "I have a call with a producer tomorrow morning and I haven't finished reading the script."

"Thank you for tonight," David said. "I don't know what I'd do without you and Dad."

"It's my pleasure. I love spending time with them." She got up and tucked the chair under the table. "I'll give you a buzz tomorrow to check in on you guys."

He stood and held out his arms. They embraced. "Hang in there," she said. "I'm proud of you for going tonight."

"Thanks, sis. I better walk you down to your car." She'd parked in the lot behind the building. This was Cliffside Bay and probably safe, but he wasn't taking any chances with his sister.

They walked down the stairs together, being careful to be keep quiet. It was before nine, so not officially quiet hours, but half the building was occupied by people over fifty-five and known to go to bed early.

They had almost reached the first floor when they saw their father. They both froze. Dad stood in front of Ria's apartment, clearly waiting for her to answer the door. A split second later, the door opened, and Ria pulled Dad into an embrace. They kissed. Like a movie kiss. David gripped Lisa's forearm.

"Dad?" Lisa voice squeaked like a scared child.

Their father and Ria jumped apart. Her hand flew to cover her mouth, as if to hide the evidence of the kiss. Dad took Ria's other hand in his. "Hello, kids."

"Dad?" Lisa asked again.

He smiled at them sheepishly, as if he'd just been caught in the cookie jar. "I didn't mean for you to find out this way. Ria and I are seeing each other."

Ria nodded. "Hi there."

How had he not seen them together before now? Had they been purposely sneaking around?

"How long?" David asked.

"A few months now," Dad said. "We wanted to see where it was going before we said anything."

"I'm surprised," Lisa said as a gentle smile crossed her face. "But pleased for you both."

Knowing her as he did, David detected the cracks between the words. This had jolted her. *Why is it we always expect the ones we love to remain exactly as they were?*

"Thank you, Lisa," Dad said. "We should all have dinner when you get back. Out at the brewery. What do you say?"

"Sure," David said. "Sounds like fun."

"Great. You two have a good night," Dad said. "I'll be staying here tonight, David, so don't wait up." Then he led Ria into her apartment and shut the door.

David and Lisa walked the rest of the way down the stairs to the first floor and out the front before saying anything. The evening had cooled, and a breeze brought the scent of the ocean. A faint sound of waves crashing to shore could be heard in the quiet.

"Oh my God," Lisa whispered. "I had no idea."

"Me either. And I live upstairs."

They strolled across the wraparound porch to the back where her car was parked. David waited for her to unlock the car, then opened her door for her. Once inside, she rolled down the window.

He rested his forearms on the frame. "This is nothing to worry over," he said.

"I hope not. Dad's been hurt, you know. He doesn't need it to happen again."

"Ria's good people," David said. "She's lost a lot in her life, too. I don't think she's the kind to toy with Dad's heart."

"I certainly hope not," Lisa said. "We just discovered who he really is without Mom pushing him around. He's seemed so light and free."

"Maybe Ria has something to do with that?"

"Maybe." She turned on her car. "Anyway, we'll just have to wait and see how it goes, won't we?"

"Drive home safe, sis. See you later."

He moved aside and watched as her car pulled out of the driveway and onto the street that ran parallel to Hugh Shaw Avenue. A cricket chirped as he crossed back around the building and through the front door.

His father and Ria? He should have known from observing their interactions over the last few months. As he trudged back up the flights of stairs, his shoulders sagged. Good for Dad. If anyone deserved some love in his life, it was him. Still, another pairing of his friends and family highlighted how alone he was. Everyone had someone but him.

One more peek into the children's bedroom assured him they were fine. Since Dad wasn't returning, he could watch television from the couch. He lounged on the couch with his feet on the coffee table and cycled through channels. When he was married, he'd wished for control of the remote. Marigold had been in charge of it, as she had of most things. The thought of his complacency made him cringe. What a sap he'd been. It had been easier to comply and avoid conflict. In hindsight, he could see how that had worn away at his sense of self. He'd become a robot, checked out and emotionless. Would fighting back have made things better or worse? Who knew? At this point, it didn't matter.

His thoughts drifted to Sara Ness. Her story tonight had moved him. Although she was way too pretty. Every time he was near her, he couldn't think of one thing to say. It was as if he'd suddenly transformed back to his thirteen-year-old self— pimples, braces, and feet way too large for his scrawny frame. She smelled damn good, too. Very distracting.

She didn't like him. He knew it to be true, although it

perplexed him. The night he'd taken her home she'd mumbled something about his arrogance. Which couldn't be further from the truth. He was a broken man, humbled and beaten up by life. His quietness stemmed from his awkwardness and shyness, not arrogance.

He had the sudden urge to call her. Not that he would. What a loser he must seem to her. An architect with no house. Living in this small two-bedroom with his little kids and his father. Barely hanging on to his sanity. Worrying about money day and night. No wonder she didn't like him.

A River Runs Through It was playing on one of the movie channels. He settled further into the couch cushion and watched a shot of Brad Pitt's character fly-fishing in the clear waters of a river in Montana. Was he like Brad Pitt's character? Doomed to failure and mistakes and fated to die early, alone and afraid?

No, a voice whispered to him. *That's not how your story ends. You have to fight harder to reclaim your life.*

Tomorrow, he thought. *Tomorrow is another day. Another shot at redemption.*

7

S ara

Around eight the next day, Sara stood near the bench that overlooked the long stretch of beach. For the first time in months, the temperatures were chilly enough that she'd dressed in leggings and a sweatshirt over a tank for a brisk walk along the path that ran parallel to the sand. The air was still and the water calm. Morning fog had already lifted, leaving blue sky and sea for as far as she could see. She stretched her arms overhead as she took in the particular shades of blue this morning offered. How many variations were there? She suspected as many as there were days in the year.

Harper, in the jogging stroller, babbled and kicked her legs. She loved the sea air as much as her mother. All summer, they'd made it down for a walk at least five mornings a week. Unlike the old saying about salt in a wound, the briny air soothed Sara's soul. She felt free here, unburdened, as if all that had come before could no longer hurt.

Surfers in wet suits dotted the water, hanging out where the waves crested, waiting for a swell worthy of their efforts. But this hour would not bring the breakers that beckoned the thrill-seeking board riders. Today was for bobbing and floating in the gentle ripples.

She knelt to tie a shoestring that had come loose. A surfer, clad in a wet suit that hung from his waist, ascended the path from the sand to the grassy bank. She straightened to see that it was David, bare-chested. What was it lately? Everywhere she turned, there he was. She'd much rather have avoided him or anyone from the support group. Her embarrassment about the night before lingered like a sunburn after a great afternoon at the beach. Exposing herself as she'd done felt good at the time, but she regretted it afterward. If only they made sunscreen for baring of the soul.

For hours last night she'd tossed and turned, replaying every stupid thing she'd said. What they all must think of her. She'd acted unhinged, like a woman on the verge of a breakdown. Perhaps she was.

He lifted a hand in greeting. She did the same. *Just walk on by. No need to stop and make small talk.*

"Good morning," he said as he approached.

"Hey. Morning swim?" She'd never seen him shirtless before. His chest and arms were lean and muscular. Damp chest hair had flattened against his skin. For a split second, she imagined her fingers trailing down his chest to his navel. A swift shudder of desire coursed through her.

What was she doing? Thinking about David Perry that way? No, no. Not a good idea.

"Morning surf." David's damp hair curled over his forehead and ears. She'd never seen him unkempt before. Sadly, it made him even more attractive. "I already put my board in the back of my truck and realized I'd forgotten a sweatshirt down on the sand." He lifted a red lifeguard sweatshirt to show her.

Had he been a lifeguard? He seemed the type, actually. She could easily imagine him all bronzed and muscular sitting on the lifeguard perch. Every girl in town in love with him.

"Aren't you cold?" she asked. As in, *put your shirt on so I can think straight.*

"Not yet. Attempting to actually get up on the surfboard is hard work."

"Do you surf alone?" That seemed dangerous.

"No, Nico and Trey were with me. They've been teaching this Iowa boy how to ride the waves. Like I said, I'm terrible."

"Good for you." She played with her ponytail and wished she could think of something to say that didn't make her sound awkward and silly.

"Last night was pretty good, right?" David asked. "The meeting, that is. Better than I expected."

"I wanted to die of embarrassment afterward." She'd blurted that out. Clearly she couldn't trust her own mouth.

"Why?" He tilted his head and peered at her with more intensity than she cared for.

"All that stuff I said. It was almost as bad as the night I wrecked your shoes."

He smiled, and the creases near his eyes crinkled in a disconcertingly sexy way. "You were fantastic last night. I walked away thinking how strong you are. There's so much to admire about you."

"There is?" She studied him. Was he making fun of her?

His blue eyes stared right back at her. "Isn't it strange we never really got to know each other when we worked together? Considering what we have in common."

"Oh, well, you know, I was your client. We kept it professional, which was appropriate. Or, you did at least. I mean, you set that tone." *Stop talking.* God, what was it about this guy that made her act like a complete fool?

"You don't like me, so there's that." He raised his head to the sky and squinted into the sunlight. "I never knew why until the night I took you home. You told me I was arrogant. Do you remember that?"

A wave of heat shot through her. "No, I do not remember. I'm so sorry."

He clutched the sweatshirt to his chest. "I feel the need, for some reason, to set you straight on that. I'm not arrogant. I'm broken and afraid and really, really tired." His features twisted in obvious pain before they rearranged into his usual stoicism.

She stared at him. What could she say to that? "I'm sorry. I know what that's like. I'm living the exact same way."

"I apologize that my awkward silences seemed like arrogance." David looked at his feet. "It doesn't bode well for my client relations," he said with a sarcastic lilt in his tone.

"No, you were very professional."

"I lack warmth. I've heard that before from other client feedback. Back in Iowa, anyway. I was with the same woman from the time I was a teenager. I'm never sure how to act around women. I get tongue-tied and act aloof, when really I'm just nervous. Especially around beautiful women. Being anywhere near you makes me feel like I'm thirteen years old in front of the prettiest girl in town."

Another wave of heat went through her, only this time it was because she was pleased. "What? No way."

"Yes way. You're lovely and smart and accomplished, and it makes me feel inadequate." He lifted his gaze briefly to look at her. "I just wanted to tell you that. I'm not sure why."

"Well, if we're being all honest and vulnerable, I'll confess that you made me feel like a spoiled rich girl with nothing to show for myself other than money. Then there's you—talented and hardworking, plus raising two kids by yourself. I felt unworthy, which translated into dislike. That was about me, not you."

His mouth lifted into a slow, sleepy smile as his eyes softened. "I guess we both made assumptions that were incorrect."

"I guess so."

"I'm around, you know, if you ever just want to talk or hang out and not talk. I have a lot of friends and my sister, but no one understands the kind of betrayal I've had to maneuver through. You do, though, don't you?" He asked this last part almost under his breath.

"I do. I wish neither of us knew what this particular hell feels like."

He shifted his body slightly toward the shore and squinted as he gazed out to sea. "Do you ever think back and wonder where the point of no return was? Like the decision that could've changed the trajectory of your life?"

"All the time."

"It's not good, though. Those thoughts make things worse."

"Yes. Because we can't go back."

"We can only go forward," David said. "Isn't that what everyone keeps telling us? But I feel stuck."

"Yeah, I know. I get it."

"Did you look back at things, later, after you knew the truth, and think, 'How could I not have seen it?'"

She had an urge to rest her cheek against his chest and wrap her arms around his waist. "Of everything that comes with betrayal, that might be the worst part. All night long, scenes play over and over in my head. The pieces coming together like a puzzle you never wanted to put together."

"It's like that for me too," David said. "I also play the 'if I'd only done this or that, none of it would've happened' game."

"I can trace that sucker back to a thousand wrong decisions." Starting with the first time she'd noticed Brent sitting outside the commons area at college. He'd sat in the sun near a fountain, and the way the light sparkled in his curls had undone her. When he lifted his face and caught her eye, for once she didn't run. She'd stared right back at him. That was the moment of vulnerability that started the whole thing.

"There was another woman I was interested in during college." David closed his eyes, as if the memory pained him. "I wanted to break it off with Marigold, but I couldn't go through with it. I think about that decision a lot. Like what would've happened if I'd had the courage to do what I wanted?"

"Or, if I'd had more self-confidence, would I have seen through him?"

"Was Judi right?" David asked. "Was there something in your past that made you feel unworthy of love?"

She took a second to form her answer. "My parents were wonderful. I had every privilege and opportunity. But I was a fat kid. The one in class everyone made fun of and bullied."

"It's hard to imagine," David said.

"Food was my only comfort." Her throat constricted and ached. Even if she wanted to, she wouldn't be able to go on.

"My sister struggled with weight when she was a kid, too," he said. "Look at you both now. So you got the last laugh."

A dragonfly landed on the back of the bench, drawing her gaze.

"I always thought if I lost the weight all my problems would be solved," Sara said. "That's not how it works."

"Can I say something that's completely inappropriate and without any sense of boundaries?" David asked.

"I guess so." She laughed nervously. "I mean, go ahead."

"You're special. Any man would be lucky to have you. Be picky next time around. Only the best man wins."

There wouldn't be another man. She knew it in her bones. No one would be allowed in to hurt her ever again.

"I'm not interested in going another round." She smiled at him, hoping to convey her appreciation for his kind words. "But thanks just the same."

"Like I said, let me know if you ever need anything. You have my number."

"Thank you. I'm sorry we got off to a rocky start."

"No worries. We'll just put that behind us." He gestured toward the cars in the lot. "I should go. See you next week at the meeting."

She nodded and watched him walk over the grass in the

direction of his car. How could a man look that good wearing half a wet suit? *Oh well, he's not for you,* she told herself. A friend, maybe, but it would stop there. All she needed was to mess up her life by wanting a man. Even a good one like David.

8

———————

David

David arrived at the meeting a few minutes early with the idea that he would talk with Ria about the situation with his father. He didn't want her to feel awkward. Even though he felt awkward.

She was at the coffee machine scooping fresh coffee into a filter. "Hello, David."

"Hi, Ria." He pulled at the sleeves of his shirt. "I thought I'd come early and check in. I mean, is this weird if I'm in your support group?"

"I'm sorry if you're feeling that way. If it means anything, everything we say here is confidential. I'd hope you'd feel like you can share freely."

"Yeah, that's the thing. A lot of my stress right now is my living situation. My dad's the best, don't get me wrong. But with him and the kids in the apartment, I feel like I can't breathe."

"I understand. Please, feel free to share about that or anything else." She made a zipper motion over her mouth. "Everything stays with me."

"Thanks, I appreciate it."

"I know you're on the fence about whether this will help you or not," Ria said. "I think it will. Also, maybe you'll make new friends. People who understand what you're going through."

He didn't have time to answer, because Sara Ness walked in, followed by Zane. The pulse at his neck quickened at the sight of her. Her curvy body in that clingy dress was enough to distract him for the rest of the night. He waited to see where she sat, but she went over to the coffeepot. He took a seat next to Zane. They shook hands. "How you been?" Zane asked.

"Good. Thanks," David said. "How's business?"

"Booming. But we're at the end of tourist season, so who knows what'll happen next month. Feast or famine in the restaurant business."

"We're worried about the winter as well," David said. "Work dries up as soon as that rain starts to fall."

"Hopefully we'll have The Oar project under way by then," Zane said. "If the insurance crap ever gets figured out."

"We'll be ready. In fact, did Sophie show you the plans I drew up?" David asked.

"Yeah, man. Quality. She's in love with the ways you incorporated the French cafés that inspired her. Truthfully, it's hers now. I want her to have whatever she wants."

The others had joined them. Bobby and Judi sat next to each other on the other side of the circle. Sara, who'd been lingering by the coffee, took the only seat left. Right next to him. Her sweet scent drove him to distraction.

"Thanks for coming tonight," Ria said. She looked around at the circle of attendees and landed on David. "Would you like to go first? How has your week been?"

He shifted in his chair. Why had she called on him first? Was she like a cat who always went to the person who despised cats over everyone else in the room?

"I've been all right," he said.

"What does all right mean to you?" Ria asked.

"What I mean is, not great. I'm struggling financially and living in an apartment with two little kids, and my dad is making me insane." He scratched the back of his neck. "I kind of feel like I'm at the breaking point. The house I own in Iowa is still on the market. I can't seem to off-load that place to save my life. Quite literally, actually. If I could sell it, I might have a chance to find a house here. Even if it was just a damn rental. None of this has anything to do with grief. I mean, the fact that I'm broke."

"You feel it's your wife's fault, though?" Ria asked. "She left you with an extremely difficult situation."

"She did, yeah." David dropped his head into his hands. "And then I just loop back to Angry Bird land."

Sara laughed. He looked up to see her clamp her hand over her mouth. "Sorry. That struck me as funny."

He smiled, despite feeling miserable. She could light up any man's heart with her beautiful smile. Even his, which was, let's face it, basically dead.

"How about you, Sara?" Ria asked. "What's your week been like?"

"Fine, I guess. About the same. I mean, I'm not really sure what I'm supposed to talk about," Sara said. "I already told you guys about what happened. What else is there to say?"

"How much chocolate did you have since we last saw you?" Judi flashed as mischievous grin. "That's a place to start."

Sara tossed her hair behind one shoulder and chuckled. "I've had less this week than last."

"Progress then," Judi said.

"What do you think made the difference between this week and last?" Ria asked.

Sarah glanced down at her lap. "I almost hate to admit this because I came kicking and screaming to this meeting last week, but I think it's all of you. After I left here, I felt less alone." She looked over at David. "David, sharing your story really helped me."

"That's the reason we're all here. To feel less alone and hopefully understood," Ria said. "Would anyone else like to share?"

Zane raised his hand. "I have something." He shifted in his chair before starting. "I had a dream a few nights ago. In it, my dad was sitting in the easy chair in the bedroom. I asked him what he was doing here. He answered. 'I'm always here, even when you can't see me. It's okay to move onward, son. I'm doing just fine.' Then I woke up and he wasn't there. Obviously."

"How did you feel when you woke?" Ria asked.

"Like I'd actually been talking to him," Zane said. "For a second, I felt warm and happy. Then the reality that he is truly gone hit me like it was brand-new information. I'd have given anything for a few more seconds. I had to get out of bed and go downstairs. I sat in the dark…" He trailed off. "Well, you know what I did. You've all been there."

"That awful empty feeling," Bobby said. "When you'd sell your soul just to see them one more time."

Zane nodded. "Yeah, that."

"I've had my husband call out to me a few times while I was asleep," Judi said. "I sat straight up in bed and fully expected him to be standing there. For a few seconds, even after I woke, I could feel him."

"I hope it happens again." Zane played with his wedding ring. "My wife thought maybe coming to this group made the dream possible."

"Why does she think so?" Ria asked.

"I'm actively grieving now, instead of pushing it aside," Zane said. "Which allows room for me to dream about him."

"Makes sense to me," Bobby said. "As men, it's hard for us to talk about our feelings. We do a great job keeping ourselves occupied, hoping that'll keep the pain away. It doesn't work."

"No, it doesn't," Zane said. "The grief's there anyway."

"How was your week, Bobby?" Ria asked.

"I donated boxes of my wife's clothes to a shelter," Bobby said. "I'd had them packed up for months but couldn't bring myself to do it. It felt like progress." He winced and covered his eyes with his hand for a moment. "No, that's a lie. Not progress but a betrayal."

"Does moving on feel like cheating?" Judi asked. "Or like you're being disloyal somehow?"

"Right, yes," Bobby said. "Even though I know she would want me to keep living. She would want me to meet someone new and have another happy marriage. However, the thought seems completely impossible."

"I understand," Judi said. "Only too well."

"The same's true for me," David said. "But not in the same way. I can't imagine being stupid enough to give my heart to a woman. Not after what happened with my wife."

"Trusting someone again would be difficult for you?" Ria asked.

"Yes. That's what I've found in general." David hesitated for a second, trying to find the right words. "It's like I can't stop looking at people and wondering what they're hiding. I'm suspicious of everyone."

"After what happened, it's totally understandable," Sara said. "I'm the same way. I look at these two." She gestured toward Judi and Bobby. "And I'm actually jealous. Isn't that awful? I'm envious that you have these wonderful people to mourn. Spouses you loved with all your heart and who loved you that same way." She smoothed a hand over her shiny hair as her gaze turned toward the basement windows. "I wonder what it is about me that I can't have that? Am I fundamentally flawed? Unlovable? Too stupid to have seen the truth about the man I loved?"

"Not stupid." David's fingers twitched in his lap. "What happened isn't your fault." He wanted to touch her and soothe her with a hug or wrap his arm around her shoulders. *It's just that you relate so much to her*, he told himself. *That's all this is.*

"I feel like it is," Sara said. "And then there's my little daughter. She's stuck with me for a mother and the legacy of her father being murdered by his girlfriend's husband. How is she supposed to feel about men?"

"There will be others," Zane said. "Friends who can be surrogate uncles, for example."

"It's not the same," Sara said.

"This is probably out of line," Zane said. "But you two are wrong about remarrying. You'll find someone, eventually, who will be worth it to open up to and trust. It seems impossible right now, but take it from me, it's not."

"You're both young and sinfully gorgeous," Judi said. "I'm going to have to agree with Zane on this one."

He felt Sara tense beside him. "Right now that idea seems about a million-to-one chance of ever happening," she said.

"Agree," David said. "Not to mention I'm so beat by the end of the day, the last thing I want is to go on a date."

Sara laughed. "Right?"

"Y'all are making me sad." Judi's expression was one of sympathy but also made him feel as though he was disappointing their room mother. "But I can understand how the effort it takes to date seems completely overwhelming."

"What about you, Judi?" Sara asked. "You've been widowed for years. Aren't you ever curious to see who's out there?"

"At my age, darlin', there's not enough gas in the old tank to even think about having sex with a man," Judi said. "No one would want to touch this old skin anyway."

"Not true," Bobby said. "You're extremely attractive."

"Oh, shush now," Judi said. "You're old and clearly in need of some glasses."

Bobby chuckled. "I'm old, but I know a pretty lady when I see one."

David, amused, hid a smile behind his hand. For two people who had just sworn they were uninterested in dating, they seemed surprisingly flirtatious.

"I'd like to introduce a challenge for next week," Ria said. "I want each of you to do something you used to do before you lost your loved one. An activity you shared with your spouse that's been too painful to do without them. Or one you did before you were married that you perhaps gave up because of your spouse's wishes."

"Like what?" David asked. He could barely remember anything from his life before Marigold. He'd floated through time, each day like the next. Sunday dinners with his parents. Marigold's constant nagging about what he was or wasn't doing. All the things she wanted: a vacation in the tropics, a better car, new curtains for the living room. There was always more, more, more. This unquenchable thirst for a life he could never have provided her. Not on an architect's salary. She'd known who and what he was when they married, but somehow she'd expected to wake up one day married to a millionaire.

Ria's gaze swept over each of them. "What's the first thing that comes to mind?"

David knew the answer to that question without a doubt. He'd liked to draw. Back in high school, he'd spent hours on drawings.

"For me," Zane said, "it's probably going on long drives and listening to music. In the summers, my dad and I used to do that on the one afternoon he took off from the bar. On Monday afternoons, he'd close up for the day and we'd pack a lunch and some fishing gear and just drive up or down the coast. We never talked much. Just listened to the music and watched the sights." He sucked in his bottom lip for a second before continuing. "Those were some of the best hours of my life."

"Did you stop doing them because it was too painful?" Judi asked.

Zane pinched the bridge of his nose, as if he were trying to remember. "I don't know, honestly. After I finished college and stayed in LA, I guess it just naturally happened. When I moved back to take care of him after his diagnosis of dementia, I was too busy with the bar and figuring out what to do about him. Taking a drive was not on the list of priorities."

"What about now?" Ria asked. "Could you do that with your wife and children? Start a new tradition?"

"They'd like that," Zane said. "I could teach Jubie how to fish."

Jubie was Zane's adopted daughter. David wasn't sure, but he thought she was around eight. She could sing like an angel. In church last week, her voice had brought him to tears.

"It's a way to honor your father," Ria said. "And keep him close to your heart. You can tell Jubie stories of what it was like when you were a boy."

Zane's eyes glistened. He didn't say anything further, but nodded his head in agreement.

"What about the rest of you?" Ria asked.

"I loved going to dinner with my husband," Judi said. "Nice places where they knew how to make a proper martini and had caviar on the menu. Don't say it, I know it's terrifically pretentious. But I'm a Southern woman. I like my dresses and pearls and nice dinners."

"Do you not go out now?" Ria asked.

"Only if Nico and Sophie drag me out to Dog's Brewery, which is tasty. Don't get me wrong, I love a good burger." She gestured toward Zane, then Bobby. "Both these men make a mean martini."

"But you're talking about a date-night type of place," Sara said.

"Yes, exactly," Judi said. "Where I can wear high heels and a fancy cocktail dress. But what's the point if it's without him?"

"Are you saying you wouldn't enjoy an elegant night out if you were alone?" Ria asked.

Judi crossed one slender leg over the other. She wore silky butter-hued slacks that looked like a long skirt paired with a sleeveless white blouse. David didn't know anything about clothes, but he had a feeling the ensemble cost more than his rent. "I like my own company fine, but yes, I guess that's what

I'm saying. Eating alone seems pathetic. I might as well stay home and make my own martini."

"I could take you," Bobby said. "Think of it as a night out with a new friend. Not the same as dinner with your husband, but to Ria's point, we're doing ourselves harm by not participating in life the way we used to."

"Making new friendships is important," Ria said. "Especially with those in the same situation."

"Fine," Judi said. "I'd like that."

Bobby smiled over at her. "It will be my pleasure. I know a great place up in Stoweaway."

What a sweet guy, David thought. Gentle and thoughtful. Judi could do worse.

"Bobby, what about you?" Ria asked. "What's something you no longer do?"

"I haven't surfed since I lost my wife, which is weird," Bobby said. "When she was alive, there were many times I didn't go out because I knew how much it worried her. A brother had drowned in a lake when she was a child. She wouldn't go past her shins in the ocean. Since she's been gone, I haven't touched my board. Which is ridiculous, because she's no longer here to worry about me."

"To surf would be a betrayal, perhaps?" Ria asked.

"Yes, yes, I suppose that's it," Bobby said.

"I surf most mornings," Zane said. "You want to meet me tomorrow?"

Bobby's face lit up. "You don't mind surfing with an old guy?"

"As you said to Judi, it would be my pleasure," Zane said. "Six?"

"I'll be there," Bobby said.

"And you, Sara?" Ria asked.

David turned to look at Sara, curious to see what she'd say.

She winced slightly and scooted forward in her chair. "This is embarrassing, but I guess you guys know all my secrets by now anyway. I majored in creative writing in college. My dream was to be a novelist."

"What happened?" Ria asked.

"After I married, it seemed stupid," Sara said.

"Why?" David asked.

"He read a few of my stories and said they were awful," Sara said. "He was probably right, by the way. But regardless, it sucked all my self-confidence away, and I decided to focus my energies on my charity work. Writing was such a selfish, self-centered thing anyway. Especially if I have no talent."

"Did your teachers say that you had no talent?" David asked.

She turned to meet his gaze. "No. The opposite."

"There you go then," David said.

"Maybe devote an hour a day to it," Judi said. "And see what you come up with."

"Write for therapy reasons, if nothing else," Bobby said. "Catharsis about what happened to you might really help."

"Yes, you're right," Sara said softly. "It's just that I feel foolish."

"What's foolish about doing something you love?" Judi asked.

"I don't know. Poor little rich girl and all that," Sara said.

"We're all born into circumstances," Zane said. "Ones we didn't pick or control. You don't have to be ashamed that you were born into wealth just as I don't have to apologize for being the son of a bar owner. It's what you do with what you have that matters. Seems to me you've done a lot for other people through your philanthropic work. You can give yourself this gift."

"I agree," David said. "Tell him to screw off. He had no right to destroy your confidence. Use your anger as fuel. Write the memoir or novel or whatever it is just to spite him."

Sara laughed. "It's nice to be around someone as angry as myself."

David grinned. "True statement."

"What about you?" Sara asked. "You haven't told us yours."

"Mine is similar to you," he said. "When I was a kid, I loved to draw and paint. I took a few classes in college for fun." He paused, wondering how much to include. "During college I was engaged to Marigold, but she'd stayed home in the town we grew up in, so I was free to do as I pleased. I never told her about the art classes. That probably sounds weird, but that's the way it was with us. I felt ashamed to tell her who I really was. Like your experience, Sara, she would've mocked me or told me I had no talent. All as a way to control me."

"It sounds like you have an assignment, then," Ria said. "You need to draw or paint before we see you next."

"I'll write if you draw," Sara said as she held out her hand. "Deal?"

He shook her hand, so warm and soft in his. "Deal."

9

S ara
　　After the meeting, Sara sat in her kitchen with a glass of wine. She hadn't thought about her writing for years. Were they right? Would writing about her experiences help? She went to a drawer and pulled out a small notebook. Usually she used it to jot down a grocery list or whatever. She sat back at the island and opened it to a blank page.

I can't remember much from the night my husband was murdered.

She chewed on the end of the pen. What was she supposed to write? Would putting it on paper make it better or worse?

Sara looked up from her pad and dropped the pen into the crease of the notebook. She remembered a female cop had made her sit on the couch. They hadn't wanted her upstairs. Matilda, the nanny, had brought Harper to her. As they'd gone through the standard proceedings of a murder-suicide, she'd nursed her infant.

She'd thought about that later. How strange that she was giving her baby sustenance while they put her husband in a body bag.

Another memory came to her. One of the cops said to

another, "Classic tale. Husband takes out his wife and lover and then turns the gun on himself."

She wrote in her notebook.

A classic tale. Is that true? What does that mean?

The story was all over the papers. News crews had surrounded the house by morning. Autumn had come to her. Kept her together through the funeral. They'd moved into a hotel suite because the house was a crime scene.

But enough of that for tonight. She would not let herself slip into the hole she so often found herself in lately. Yes, it was horrific. But she was still here. She had life left in her. Ways to contribute.

What can I do to make the world a better place?

She set aside her pen and picked up her wineglass and took a sip. There was a little something niggling at her. What was it?

The inheritance. She could do so much good with it. Battered women. Hungry families. School funding for poorer communities. Scholarships for low-income kids. Homes to get people off the streets. A clever money manager could continue to grow the funds. Ripple upon ripple, she could change lives.

For all that, one year of her life in a fake marriage seemed like a small sacrifice.

Next, David's face appeared before her. He was struggling financially. She could solve all that. Give him enough out of the inheritance that he would never worry again.

The idea was crazy. Of course it was. But it was also a good one.

She picked up her glass and went to the window. The three-quarter moon hung over the ocean. All this was hers when so many suffered. She had to do this.

Would David agree? She had to try. Tomorrow could be the beginning of a whole new purpose. If only she could get him to say yes. She went back to her notebook and jotted two more sentences down.

I'll try. That's the least I can do.

THE NEXT DAY, Sara stood at the bottom of the steps of the Victorian and looked up to the second-floor windows. She carried a bag of art supplies containing watercolor tubes, paintbrushes, pencils, good paper, and a small table easel. Trey had assured her it was enough to get him started.

Could she really do this outrageous thing? *It's only a proposition*, she reminded herself. *If he's not interested, then so be it.* She'd tried, at least.

All that money. All the good she could do with it. *Remember that.*

She took a deep breath and let herself into the foyer. A set of stairs led up to the second floor, where she knew David lived. It was the weekend, so she assumed he'd be home, although she hadn't called. One more deep breath before she tapped on the door. The sound of children's footsteps, then a high-pitched voice calling out, "Daddy, someone's here."

A second later, David appeared, dressed in slouchy jeans and a T-shirt that did nothing to hide his muscular chest. His eyes widened when he saw it was her. He had a dishcloth in his hand, which he threw over his shoulder. "Sara, what are you doing here?" His children peeked from behind each leg. A towheaded toddler in a pink dress wearing a tiara looked exactly like her aunt Lisa. The little boy had on a San Francisco football jersey. Big blue eyes just like his father's stared up at her.

"I'd like a moment of your time." She thrust the bag toward him. "And I have this for you."

He took the bag and peered inside. "What's all this?"

"Trey told me what to get."

His mouth formed a circle as he rocked back on his heels. "I don't know what to say. This is really sweet." He looked up at her. "Where are my manners? Come in, please." He moved aside, which caused his daughter to stumble and fall on her diapered bottom.

"I'm sorry, baby." David scooped her up in one arm and held her against his chest. "You all right?"

Laine nodded before pointing a finger at Sara.

"This is Miss Sara. Daddy's friend. This is Laine and Oliver."

"Hi, Laine and Oliver. It's nice to meet you," Sara said as she stepped inside the front room of the apartment, which smelled of bacon and maple syrup. "Did I interrupt breakfast?"

"No. We finished a bit ago. I was cleaning up," David said.

"I'm sorry to come unannounced," Sara said.

"It's no problem. As long as you don't mind the mess." David set the bag of art supplies near the door. "They can mess it up faster than I can keep it picked up."

The front room was decorated tastefully with a slouchy, comfortable-looking sofa and chairs arranged in front of the gas fireplace. High ceilings and the original molding salvaged during the reconstruction gave the place character. An open wooden cart in the corner looked as if it had spewed toys all over the room. Stacks of children's books crowded the coffee table. A pillow on the couch cushions reminded her that David's father lived with them. He must be sleeping on the couch. She remembered there were only two bedrooms. How was he keeping his sanity?

This is a good plan. It would be good for all of them.

Oliver moved behind his father's leg. Sara had been painfully shy at that age. She'd felt invisible if she could hide behind her mother or father.

Sara reached into her purse. "I have something for each of you." She handed Laine a small stuffed white dog.

Laine looked at it for a second, then up at her father. He nodded. "It's all right."

Laine took the dog and hugged it tightly to her chest.

"She doesn't talk," David said. "Much anyway."

She put that away to think about later. "Oliver, do you like Matchbox cars?"

From behind David's legs, a portion of Oliver appeared. "Yes."

She pulled the package of four sports cars from her bag. "Do you have these ones?"

Oliver shook his head.

"Here you go then." Sara knelt to give it to him. The pretty eyes on these two were enough to melt anyone's heart.

Oliver took it from her outstretched hand. "Thank you," he said.

"You're welcome." Sara straightened. "I was wondering if there's someplace we could talk privately?"

"Privacy isn't a commodity around here," he said. "But we can talk in the kitchen. My dad's out with Ria. In fact, he didn't come home last night."

Sara did a double take, unsure if he meant what she thought he meant. "Do you mean they're dating?"

"Yep. Sleepovers and everything." David set Laine down. "You two play out here or in your bedroom. Daddy's going to talk to Sara in the kitchen."

They were busy with their new toys and didn't seem overly concerned with the adults' whereabouts.

"Would you like coffee?" David asked as he led her into the kitchen.

"No, thank you. I've had enough." The kitchen was painted a light yellow with white cabinets and honey-colored wood floors. A hum from the dishwasher accompanied the radio, which played instrumental jazz. Several pots were stacked on a drying rack. She caught the faint scent of lemon dishwasher detergent.

"Please, have a seat," he said. "You sure I can't get you something?"

She sat at the kitchen table. "A glass of water would be terrific."

He grabbed a glass and went to the refrigerator to fill it up. "What's going on?" He set the glass in front of her.

She took a grateful sip. Her mouth had gone completely dry.

"I have a proposition for you. It's going to sound really crazy, but I'd like you to hear me out."

He sat across from her. "Sure."

"Okay, so I'm just going to tell you the whole thing. I got this phone call last week from an attorney." She shared the content of the conversation, including her grandfather's strange request. "So, in a nutshell, I have to be married within the month in order to inherit his fortune."

"Otherwise it goes to the dog and Moxie?" David's eyes twinkled with humor. "Only in California."

"It's not funny," Sara said, laughing. "I mean it is, but I can't let it go to this obviously manipulative grifter. We're talking about a billion dollars."

"Not to be rude, but you don't really need the money, right?"

"Technically, no. My father's wealth wasn't as vast, but I'll never have to worry over money. That's not why I want it. This is enough to start a serious foundation. One that could help a lot of people." She listed off her areas of interest.

"That's what you want to do with it?"

"Yes, I want to model it after Bill and Melinda Gates. You can't imagine the impact they've had on the world."

"That's great, but what're you going to do about the husband part?"

"That's where you come in."

He blinked as his mouth opened, then shut.

"Now, hear me out," she said. "Here's how it would work. We would write up a prenup where you're guaranteed a hundred million dollars if we divorce. That way, we're married for a year, complying with the will, then you walk away with a lot of cash. Which would solve at least some of your problems."

He continued to stare at her, a little the way one would at a hungry bear, equal measures of the desire to flee and complete terror. "Did you say one hundred million dollars?" He drew each word out with a space in between.

"Yes."

He stood and began to pace around the small kitchen. "A fake marriage for a year in exchange for one hundred million dollars?"

"Correct. We'd have to make it seem real, though. Even to our friends and family."

"Wait, why?"

"It's in the will that a private investigator is going to make the call about whether or not the marriage is real."

"How would they do that?" He leaned his backside against the sink and crossed his arms over his chest.

"I'm not sure, exactly. I imagine it's like the FBI or something, where they interview people and spy on us. That kind of thing."

"Like they did to my wife," he said. "They figured out everything when I was clueless." He waved his hand in front of him. "Never mind that." He started to pace again. "So how would this work? We just up and get married and tell everyone we fell in love?"

"I haven't totally thought it all through yet, but something like that."

"My sister will never buy it," he said. "She knows everything about me."

"You'd have to sell her on it," Sara said. "She's a great actress. Maybe you got some of those genes too?"

"I'm pretty sure I didn't." He went back to leaning against the sink. "What about our kids? This will be totally confusing to them."

"I have an idea about that," Sara said. "To make it easy for them to understand, we tell them you guys are moving in with us because you want more space. They don't have to know more than you're simply staying with us until you can find a house of your own. That way their hearts aren't broken when you move out. They'll already know that's happening."

"That's brilliant."

"They're still young," Sara said. "A year in their lives they probably won't even remember anyway. However, they'll be able to enjoy my pool and the big yard. As you know, there are enough bedrooms for everyone to have their own."

"I don't know. Mine have been through so much change already."

She laid her hands on the table. "How much would make it worth it to you?"

"A hundred million is a lot," he said, chuckling. "But how much are we all going to need in therapy after the year's over?"

She smiled back at him. "Would it really be that bad to live with me for a year?"

He drew in a long breath. "If it were just you and me, that would be one thing. But the kids. I'm worried about how this would be for them. Like, what if they fall in love with you? We'll be basically selling them on a blended family. They'll grow attached to you."

"We'll make them understand it's a temporary arrangement. And we'll remain in each other's lives after it's over. Plus, like I said, they're so young. Think of all the good we could do."

He didn't say anything for a long moment. The sound of Oliver's voice floated into the kitchen.

"Think about all the space. Your dad wouldn't have to sleep on a couch." She had to sell him on this idea. He was close to the edge. She could feel it. "Did I mention the pool? And the outdoor kitchen?" She snapped her fingers. "And a nanny that you can use for your kids."

"My dad wouldn't have to look after them anymore," David said. "He won't admit it, but they wear him out."

"You'd never have to worry about that again. College educations are paid for. You can design a house exactly how you want. If Wolf Enterprises goes under for any reason, you'll be fine and still get to live here with your family and friends."

He winced as he brushed a hand through his hair. "I don't know if we can sell this. You haven't made it a secret that you don't like me."

Sara flushed, embarrassed. "That was before. I like you now.

We can tell everyone we started talking after our support group and one thing led to another."

"We'll have to lie to Autumn and Trey," he said. "And all the Wolves."

"That's going to be rough," Sara said. "But we can do it."

He stuffed his hands into the pockets of his jeans. "I've never lied to my sister about anything. We're twins, so this may be tricky. She knows me very well. I think it's best if we wait to tell everyone until after we're married. That way they'll simply have to accept that we've already done it."

"After the year goes by, we can tell everyone why we did it," Sara said.

"I have an ask," he said. "I want part of your foundation to fund combating the opiate crisis."

She placed her hand over her heart, moved by his plea. "Yes. Done."

"And will you keep me informed of the work you're doing? Even after we're divorced?"

"Yes, yes, of course. You can be on the board if you want."

He shook his head. "I'm probably delusional, but yeah, I'm in."

She jumped up from her chair and threw her arms around him. "Thank you."

His arms wrapped around her waist, as if on instinct. For a second they stood together, looking into each other's eyes. Against the sturdiness of his chest, her body felt alive suddenly, betraying her.

She unwrapped her arms from his neck at the same time he let her go.

"Okay, well, we should probably get our plan together," she said. "Should we fly to Vegas to elope?"

He rubbed his hands over his face. "That's probably easiest. My sister's going to kill me when she finds out I got married and didn't tell her."

"Should we have a little ceremony here in town instead?" she asked. "Would that make it easier for you?"

"No, if we do that, the kids have to be there. Vegas is better."

"There's one more detail," Sara said. "We have to sell this to my nanny. They're sure to interview her." The girl practically lived at the house. They would have to keep up the act even at home, at least for the times when Zoey was present. "We have to act like a couple in front of her. She's in and out of the house all day long. There's not much that happens that she doesn't know."

"Acting like a couple? You mean barely speaking to each other and never having sex?"

She threw back her head and laughed. The two of them were actually perfect for each other. Bitter, angry, and with a shattered belief in happy marriages. "No, not the kind of marriage we had, but the kind all our friends have. Happy ones where they can't keep their hands off each other."

"I really wish I'd gone to acting school with Lisa." He tugged on one ear. "Or taken lessons from my wife about how to have a secret life."

A sharp dart of pain shot through her. "We have all the worst stuff in common, but maybe we can help each other because of it."

"Support sounds nice," he said softly. "I'd like to feel less alone."

"We'll just make it a game. Any time anyone's around, we make a point to hold hands and touch each other. You know, like all our happily married friends do."

"Nauseating." He grinned at her.

"Totally." She smiled back at him. "Come over first thing in the morning with the kids. We'll leave them with Zoey while we go to Vegas. I'll get us plane tickets and a car."

Between then and when she arrived home, she needed to come up with a tall tale to convince Zoey that she'd fallen in love overnight with the man she used to despise. Talk about an acting job.

"Good plan." She turned toward the door but looked back at him before walking away. "This will be good for you and your kids. Just keep that in mind."

"I will."

"I'll call my attorney and have the paperwork drawn up," Sara said.

"Great. I'll have my signing hand ready."

She walked out of the kitchen and through the living room to the front door. Oliver and Laine were playing with their new toys. Oliver had made a slope for his cars using a book and the bottom shelf of the coffee table. Laine had put her stuffed animal on a chair and was pretending to feed him with a toy fork.

They were precious. The last thing she wanted was for them to be hurt. Was this the right thing?

Yes, she told herself. The money would be good for them and for all the people she wanted to help. One year out of their lives? How could it possibly go wrong?

D avid
      After she left, David watched Sara walk down the street toward her car. White noise between his ears drowned out Oliver's humming like an engine as he drove one of his new cars over the arm of the couch. What had he just agreed to? A fake marriage for money. A lot of money. An amount that would change his life forever.

This was a good thing. A great thing.

A wonderful turn of events fraught with problems. How would he explain it to his sister and father? What effect would it have on his children?

There was another thing, too. His attraction to Sara was possibly the worst part of all. He didn't want to be attracted to her. During the hours they'd spent together on her house, he'd been too newly widowed to think of her that way. He barely remembered the first months in Cliffside Bay. He'd gone through the motions like a man asleep. How he'd done such a fine job on her house was actually a mystery. The part of his mind that controlled his work had remained intact, while the rest had closed down. If it hadn't been for Lisa, the kids would surely have suffered even more than they already had. She'd replaced a mother figure for them. As much as she could, anyway, given her work schedule. He knew she'd turned down offers for television series because of his children. She wouldn't admit it to him, but he could read between the lines.

He had a feeling that's why she and Rafael had waited before having a baby of their own. She probably figured she needed all her energy for them. A baby would take her attention.

Thus, another reason for him to go through with this. A full-time nanny and a mother figure in Sara would free Lisa up to have her own child.

But what happened after the marriage was dissolved? What did he do with the kids then?

He wanted to be the type of man who felt comfortable alone, raising his kids without relying on a woman, but he wasn't. He felt uncertain and confused and paralyzed with fear that whatever he did for the children would be the wrong thing. They'd end up a mess on his watch. Without Lisa and his dad, the whole thing would be even more of a disaster than it was currently.

With a sigh, he sat on the floor next to the couch and asked the children to come sit with him. "I have something I want to tell you."

Laine crawled onto his lap. Oliver sat with his legs crisscrossed and his hands folded as they'd taught him at preschool.

"The lady who brought you the toys," he said.

"Sara," Oliver said.

"Right, Sara. She has a giant house that Daddy designed. There's a swimming pool and a big yard and lots of bedrooms. She's invited us to come live with her so that Papa can have the apartment to himself. Would you like that?"

"Could Papa come visit us?" Oliver asked.

"Yes, any time he wanted. And after I save enough money or sell the house in Iowa, I'll be able to buy us a house of our own."

"Does she have kids?" Oliver asked.

"A baby. Her name's Harper."

Oliver shrugged. "Too bad it's not a boy my age."

"You can have friends over, I'm sure. She has a nanny who will look after you while I'm at work."

"Is she nice?" Oliver asked.

"I'm sure she is," David said.

"What if she's a wicked witch?" Oliver asked.

"Did Sara seem nice?" David asked.

Oliver nodded. Laine, pressed into his chest, also nodded.

"Then wouldn't it seem like she would have a nice nanny?" David asked. "Nice people usually hang out with other nice people."

"Okay, then it sounds pretty great," Oliver said. "When are we going? I want to swim in the pool."

"We're going tomorrow. You're going to stay with the nanny while Sara and I go on a short trip."

"Why?" Oliver asked.

"Just grown-up stuff we need to take care of."

A knock on the door, followed by Lisa's voice, drew their attention. "Perrys, anyone home?" She opened the door and poked her head through. "Can I come in?"

"Aunt Lisa's here," Oliver said, as he ran to her and threw himself around her legs.

Lisa, dressed in jeans and a cotton peasant blouse, knelt on the floor and pulled Oliver into a hug. "How's my favorite nephew?"

"I got some new cars," Oliver said.

"Great," Lisa said.

Laine scrambled off David's lap and held the stuffed dog out for Lisa to see.

"And you've got a new pet?" Lisa asked.

Laine nodded, smiling as she hugged her dog to her chest. Lisa rose to her feet and grabbed Laine up into her arms to plant a kiss on her cheek. "That doggy's almost as cute as you." She sat in the easy chair with Laine on her lap. His daughter snuggled into her auntie's chest.

The image brought tears to David's eyes. Since Marigold's

death, he found himself on the verge of crying at the smallest things. He rose from the floor and went back to the window, wiping his eyes with the back of his hand. From this vantage point, he could see almost the entirety of Hugh Shaw Avenue. Instead of going to her car, Sara had stopped at the flower stand outside the grocery store. He watched as she gathered a bouquet of bright pink peonies and combined them with another made up of white flowers he didn't recognize.

"Who brought them the toys?" Lisa asked.

Before he could answer, Oliver beat him to it. "A lady named Sara. We're going to stay at her house."

Lisa raised her eyebrows as she turned her focus on David. "You are?"

The front door opened and Dad came inside, carrying a bag of groceries. "Hey, gang."

"Hi, Dad," Lisa said. "David was just about to explain what Sara Ness was doing here. Is she having you design another house? Like a vacation home or something? I'm so jealous if that's the case."

"No, it wasn't business." David knew there was no way out of this. He had to tell them today. Otherwise, how would he explain to his father that the kids were going overnight to Sara's house to be looked after by the nanny?

Lisa wrinkled her nose. "Are you guys friends now? I got the impression you two didn't really like each other."

"Ollie, can you take your little sister and go play in your bedroom? I have to talk to Papa and Aunt Lisa about some grown-up stuff."

"Okay, Daddy."

Lisa set Laine down, and Oliver took his sister's hand.

David waited until they were inside the bedroom before he turned back to face the music.

"What's going on?" Lisa asked. "You look weird."

"Well, the thing is...Sara and me...we've been seeing each

other. Ever since that one night I took her home from the brewery."

Lisa's mouth dropped open. The bag of groceries slipped from his father's arms. Several cans of corn rolled across the floor and stopped at David's feet.

"Are you kidding me?" Lisa asked.

"No, you know, we have a lot in common." David picked up the cans from the floor and put them on the coffee table.

"Is it serious?" Dad asked.

"Yeah, it is." David perched on the arm of the couch. *God forgive me for my lies.* "We're getting married. Tomorrow, in fact. We're flying to Vegas. Neither of us wants to make a big deal out of it."

Dad and Lisa were both staring at him with their mouths open.

"What about the kids?" Lisa asked.

"They're staying at Sara's with the nanny."

"The question isn't about tomorrow," Lisa said. "What about the kids, like in general?"

"Sara's a terrific mother," David said. "We'll be a blended family. There are a lot of those. Together, we're stronger. Our kids will have a mother and father."

"Are you doing this because you think it's best for them?" Dad asked. "Or because you're in love?"

I do think it's best for them, David thought. Focused on the financial angle, he hadn't really thought about how this would benefit the kids in a positive way emotionally. Having a woman like Sara in their lives on a daily basis would be good for them. *For all of us.*

Ah, there it was. There was the danger. What would this do to him and the children when it all ended? Would they have all fallen for Sara Ness with no hope of her returning their affections?

"I'm doing this because it's a second chance for all of us," David said.

"Do you love her?" Lisa asked. "Because if you don't and you're just doing this to have a mother for the kids, then it's wrong. It'll be too hard."

"Don't you want a new marriage to be a love match?" Dad asked. "After what you went through with Marigold, I want you to have it all this time."

"This is, Dad." How did people do this? Lying was hard. "I'm crazy about her. She's completely different from Marigold."

"But it seems so fast," Lisa said. "I thought she didn't even like you?"

"She didn't, but she changed her mind," David said.

"Obviously." Dad scooped the fallen bag back into his arms. "Well, we know she's not after your money."

"Since I have none."

Lisa narrowed her eyes. "Is she doing a prenuptial?"

"Yes. If we divorce, I'll get a tidy sum of a hundred million dollars." David pressed the palms of his hands into his knees. Stay strong. Keep up the pretense.

"Are you marrying her for the money?" Lisa asked.

"The fact that she's rich is convenient," David said. "But that's not why. I'm in love with her. Like head over heels."

"I can honestly say I've never been more shocked in all my life," Lisa said.

"Do I have your blessing?" David asked.

"I'm not sure I totally approve, but if you think you know what you're doing, then who am I to say?" Lisa asked. "Rafael and I knew pretty quickly that we wanted to spend our lives together. It's just that you tell me everything. To keep this from me is not how we do things."

"You've been busy," David said. That was true. She'd spent six weeks over the summer filming a movie. "I didn't want to bother you with this."

"And Vegas? What about a celebration?" Lisa asked.

"We can still do one," Dad said. "A party to celebrate."

"You have to promise me," Lisa said. "That you'll let me throw you a party?"

"I promise."

Lisa got up from the chair to give him a hug. "I'm happy for you. I truly am."

"Thanks. That means a lot," David said.

Dad patted him on the shoulder. "I'm happy for you too, son. A new beginning for you and the kids."

"And you won't have to sleep on the couch any longer," David said.

"I should get this into the kitchen," Dad said. "There's ice cream at the bottom of this bag."

After Dad left for the kitchen, Lisa placed her hands on his upper arms. "Tell me you're not doing this just for Dad and the kids?"

"I'm not. I swear." He was doing it for her, too. For all of them. Money was freedom for them all.

"Get married here," Lisa said. "In the church. I want to be there. Please. Not to mention how this is going to be for the kids if you suddenly come home married."

"I can't," he said. "Please, try to understand." He scrambled to come up with an explanation that made sense. "I want to do it totally differently than I did the first time. Vegas. No church or all the fuss and theatrics that Mom and Marigold made me do."

She nodded, her thin eyebrows coming together in a sympathetic frown. "That makes sense. You're right. You do this however you think best."

"Thank you."

Now he just had to convince his family that it was a real thing between them. He was afraid Lisa would figure it out the moment she saw them together. He had to take that chance. This was too important. Let the acting begin.

11

Sara

Sara walked along the stone path to the pool. The afternoon sun kissed her bare shoulders. When she reached them, Zoey had Harper in a floating contraption. Harper squealed as Zoey steered her around the shallow end of the pool.

Winding rock paths connected the house and pool as well as the cottage where Zoey currently lived. Growing up, Sara had wished for privacy. A place where she could be with just her parents instead of the myriad staff. She'd had that in mind when she chose to add the small dwelling for a nanny or housekeeper.

Her goal in life from now on was simplicity. No more parties or party people. She wanted a calm environment for her daughter. One where they could be connected to place and community in a real way. She wanted her daughter to value the way the sun glinted off the ocean, not how a diamond glinted on a person's hand.

This was silly, of course, but she blamed wealth for her parents' deaths. If they hadn't been coming home at midnight from some event, they might not have been killed. She kicked off her sandals and padded across the warm pool deck. "Hey, girls," she said.

"Mama," Harper shouted and splashed the water. A pink hat protected her head and face from the sun. The blue plastic of the swim diaper peeked out from under her cherry-red bathing suit.

Sara lifted the skirt of her dress out of the way and dangled her feet in the water. Zoey and Harper drew closer, both grinning. Zoey, as she always did when outside, wore a wide-brimmed straw hat to shield her fair skin from the sun. A modest blue suit covered her slim figure. She was such a tiny girl that she seemed closer to Harper's age than her own, which wasn't at all accurate. Zoey was twenty-five and Sara was thirty-one. The numbers didn't matter, because Sara felt at least eighty. The weight of her grief and anger heavier even than the extra pounds she'd carried around.

"How's your day been?" Sara asked.

"About as perfect as can be," Zoey said. "Here in God's country."

Zoey was from North Dakota. She continued to be awed by the sight of the ocean as if every day were the first day she'd seen it. Sara appreciated her enthusiasm and wonder about life. She always saw the bright side of things, unlike Sara.

"How was yours?" Zoey asked.

"Well, I have some news." Sara hesitated. How was she supposed to sell this? "I've fallen in love."

"What?" Zoey lifted her gaze from the baby to look at her. "Fallen in love?"

"I know, it's unexpected, but, well, we started talking after the support group and one thing led to another."

"The support group? Haven't you only gone to two?" Zoey squinted into the light. "And what single men are there besides Bobby and David? Please tell me it's not Bobby. I know it can't be David, because you don't like him."

"It is David. I don't know why I didn't like him before. Maybe I was just in denial and trying to talk myself out of my attraction to him. Anyway, we're flying to Vegas tomorrow to elope."

Zoey stared at her. "I don't understand."

"We're ready to start the next phase of our lives. We both have young children who need two parents. It makes sense."

"You sound like it's a business deal."

This was not going well. She needed to ramp up the romance angle. Pretend that she was madly in love the way Autumn was with Trey. What were some of the things she'd said about him? He made her heart thump when he walked into the room. "I can't explain it, really, but my heart thumps louder when he walks into a room."

Zoey continued to stare at her.

Change the subject. Zoey would want to know how this would affect her, most likely. Or she would once she got over the shock.

"So, I'm thinking we're going to have to hire another nanny. Three children under five is too much."

Zoey shook her head vigorously. "I hadn't even thought about that part. But I don't think that's a good idea. I'd rather have all three so that I can do things my way."

"I'll double your pay."

"Really?" Her face transformed from worried to delighted. "That would mean so much to me. I can pay off all my debt and still have some left to buy a house in a few years."

"Oliver will be starting kindergarten next week. Laine still takes naps, so that'll give you some peace in the afternoons." Zoey already used the minivan for traipsing around with Harper. Two more would fit easily.

"Are they good children?" Zoey asked.

"They're very well behaved. David told me the little girl rarely speaks. Losing their mother no doubt caused them a lot of pain, even if they're not totally aware of what happened. They'll need extra nurturing from both of us."

As if she agreed, Harper splashed the water with her hands.

"And you're sure about all this?" Zoey asked. "Taking on two children who aren't yours? I mean, being a stepmother can't be easy."

"I'm sure. Now stop worrying. You two finish your swim. I'm going to pack a bag."

"Will you be gone long?" Zoey asked.

"Overnight."

"No honeymoon?" Zoey's mouth turned downward into a frown.

"Later, once we have the kids settled in." She lifted her feet from the water. "I have to call Trey and have him order some new beds for the kids' room."

"And what about a prenup?" Zoey asked. "You have to protect yourself."

"Already drawn up," Sara said.

"All right. As long as you're sure."

Sara knew by the tightness in Zoey's voice that she didn't think any of it was a good idea but was wise enough to keep her mouth shut.

"Don't worry," Sara said again. "This is going to be great for all of us."

Remember the mission, she reminded herself. The money could help so many. This was a small sacrifice. One year of her life spent in the company of a nice man and his two sweet children. There were worse scenarios.

12

David
The next morning on the ride from the apartment in town to Sara's property, Oliver chattered away in the back seat. How excited he was to go swimming in the pool, and how big was the yard, and had Daddy really designed the entire house?

David answered the best he could, despite his nervous stomach. He'd slept poorly, tossing and turning until the early morning when he'd finally fallen asleep, only to dream of Marigold.

As he climbed the curvy two-lane road up to her property, his ears popped. He swallowed and told the kids to do the same. Her home was not far from the Brody estate as the crow flies, but they were separated by a dip in the cliff.

When she'd come to them as a client, the two-acre piece of property had an old, run-down beach cottage and a dirt road riddled with potholes. Stone's crew had cleared away the old house. Then, working with Nico on the landscape design, they'd created an oasis that overlooked the Pacific. The house itself was inspired by Sara's love of traditional architecture but with a modern flair. From the beginning of his career, David had focused on this aesthetic. He'd found Sara to be his ideal client in this way. She had an eclectic mix of the past and present. Classic yet fresh. Like her.

When they arrived, he turned the car off and gripped the steering wheel with both hands. He took a deep breath in and out as he said a silent prayer. *Please, God, let this be the right thing for my kids.*

His mind tumbled over the list of positives, just as it had most of the night. Who passed up this kind of money over a year? What a beautiful setting to spend twelve months—stone paths that meandered through the property and the pool and the view of the mighty Pacific. A grassy yard for them to run and play. Lastly, when it was all over, he could build or renovate a place of their own.

"Daddy? Are we getting out?" Oliver asked.

"Yes, sorry. Daddy was thinking for a minute," David said.

He asked Oliver to unbuckle himself from his booster while he helped Laine out of her car seat.

"Wait here for a second," he said to Laine as he set her on the cement driveway. He gathered their backpacks on wheels from the back of the car. Oliver took hold of his and pulled it across the driveway as if he'd been there a hundred times.

Laine, however, was having none of this. She clung to David's leg. He picked her up and balanced her on his hip, then reached down for her bag.

He'd explained again that morning that he and Sara were going on the airplane and that she and Ollie were going to stay with the fun nanny. Laine hadn't fussed or cried, just watched him with big eyes. Not unusual, but it made it damn hard to tell what she was thinking. He hadn't been sure she'd fully under-stood. Now, however, she seemed to be panicking.

"Laine, honey, don't be scared. You're going to have so much fun today."

She clamped her short legs around his waist and buried her face in his neck. With her clinging to him, he trudged across the driveway and up to the front door. Even so, he admired Nico's landscaping. Tidy rows of shaped shrubbery and pots with flowers lined the front. Vintage lanterns hung on each side of the covered entry.

Oliver had already rung the doorbell. Sara opened the door just as he reached the front steps.

The moment she saw Oliver, her face lit up in a bright smile. "Oliver, I'm glad you're here. Zoey's excited to meet you."

David's stomach fluttered at the sight of her. She looked downright gorgeous in a light blue dress and flat sandals that tied around her ankles. He'd noticed before what nice legs she had, muscular and toned. She also had the loveliest complexion. Not the typical fair skin of a redhead but more of a creamy beige. Her hair was the color of a Moscow mule cup, and as shiny as one too.

"Hi, David," Sara said. "And hello to you, little miss." She placed the tips of her fingers on Laine's back, ever so briefly.

Laine lifted her head to inspect Sara. Her round eyes seemed to take Sara in like those of an old soul destined to be a judge or a preacher. Sara kept smiling, however, seemingly undaunted by the appraisal of a toddler.

"Have you eaten breakfast?" Sara asked. "Zoey's making pancakes if you're interested."

"I am," Oliver said. "Can I have syrup?"

"If it's all right with your dad." She met David's eyes. "It's pure maple syrup. No corn syrup."

"Sounds great," David said. What was it about her deep green eyes that stirred him? They had the depth of someone who'd suffered. Was that the source of his response? One broken soul to another?

She gestured for them to come inside. "Zoey's in the kitchen. She has a lot of fun things planned. Including an art project."

Laine twitched slightly in his arms. An art project might tempt her into letting go of her death grip on him. She took after him that way. Always coloring or splashing paint onto a piece of paper.

"Dad says you have a pool," Oliver said.

"We do. And Zoey's going to let you swim after lunch," Sara said.

"I love swimming," Oliver said.

"I do too," Sara said.

"You can swim with me sometime if you want," Oliver said.

"I would love to." Sara smiled at David. "As soon as your Dad and I are done with our trip, we'll have a pool party."

"Is there cake at a pool party?" Oliver asked.

"No, just pool toys," Sara said.

David hadn't been inside the house since he and Trey had wrapped up the project. Cathedral ceilings and windows at every turn gave the house a light and airy feel. He knew each room, having designed them himself, but this house could never be fully appreciated on drafting paper. This house was a living, breathing structure, designed with all five senses in mind. Dark hardwood floors and white trim made the interiors timeless.

"Would you like to see your rooms or have pancakes first?" Sara asked.

"Rooms." Oliver picked up his backpack. "I have my clothes in here. Daddy says Papa will bring over our toys later."

"All right then," Sara said. "Follow me."

Sara and Oliver took the lead. He couldn't help but notice her muscular calves as he followed behind her. The scent of her perfume made him a little dizzy, and not in the bad way.

"The first door is Harper's room." Sara opened it to show the kids. He spotted a white crib and green-and-white-plaid rocking chair, and an unlit gas fireplace with a mirror above the mantel. The windows looked out to the backyard.

"This room will be yours, Oliver," Sara said as she opened the door to a bedroom painted robin's-egg blue. A queen bed was made up with a red comforter and pillows in various patterns.

"Wow, that's a big bed," Oliver said. He slipped his hand into David's, looking unsure for the first time.

"It's very soft, though," Sara said. "Would you like to try it out?"

"I guess so," Oliver said. "But how do I get up there?"

Sara reached under the bed and pulled out a double-tiered stepping stool made for kids. "I picked this up yesterday. One for in here and one for your bathroom." She pointed toward the open door that led to his bathroom.

Oliver, clearly delighted with the stool, kicked off his sandals. He marched up the steps and flopped onto the bed. "It *is* soft, Daddy." He moved his arms and legs as if he were making a snow angel.

Laine, who had been watching with suspicion, patted David's cheek, then pointed to the doorway.

"You want to see your room?" David asked.

She nodded.

"Right this way," Sara said. "I hope you like yellow things."

The room next to Oliver's was painted a butter yellow. A toddler bed with a tulle canopy draped over the four posts was tied with yellow ribbons around each post. Laine wriggled out of David's arms and ran toward it. She touched the material that hung over the closest post.

"It's a princess bed," Sara said. "Do you like it?"

Laine nodded.

"How'd you know what to get?" David asked. "Or did you have this?"

"Trey found the bed at an antiques shop, and it just seemed to scream for a canopy. I'd planned on moving it into Harper's room when she was older. But now it'll be yours, Laine." She turned to David. "Once your dad brings their things over, we can put them on the shelves and in the closet."

"Great." He wanted to ask where his room would be but before he had the chance, Oliver asked about breakfast.

"Yes, let's go eat," Sara said. "I have fresh orange juice, too."

Laine tugged on his pants leg. David lifted her up and balanced her on his hip.

"This place is nice," Oliver said. "Like a palace."

"Did you know your dad designed this entire house?" Sara asked as they filed out of the room.

"Sure. Aunt Lisa says he's the best house maker in the whole world," Oliver said with a note of pride in his voice.

"I'd say so," Sara said.

They went down the stairs to the kitchen. Stacks of pancakes and bacon plus a pitcher of orange juice were waiting for them on the island. A young woman with dark hair fixed in a ponytail scrambled eggs at the cooktop. Harper was in a high chair, babbling between bites of pancake delivered to her mouth with sticky fingers.

"Everyone, this is Zoey," Sara said. "And Harper."

"Well, hello there." Zoey set aside the eggs and came around the island to greet them. "Pleased to meet you."

"Likewise," David said. "This is Oliver and Laine."

Laine had buried her face in his neck again. Oliver, however, was fixated on the pancakes and bacon.

"I'd say you're hungry," Zoey said to Oliver. "Would you like to sit up here to eat?" She gestured toward a row of tall stools on one side of the large island.

"Yes, please," Oliver said.

Zoey lifted Oliver onto the one at the far end, then bustled around putting a plate together for him. David, in the meantime, tried to figure out what to do about Laine, who continued to cling to him as if they were about to be swept out to sea.

The mostly white kitchen was flooded with sunlight. A bank of windows faced west. Sara's property was built on one of the highest peaks of the southern hill. From here, the view was of the Pacific as well as the long, sandy beach that drew so many tourists and day-trippers. Today, on one of the last afternoons before school started, the sand was dotted with umbrellas. From here, they looked no bigger than the ones used in tropical drinks.

"Oliver, can you cut up your food?" Zoey asked. "Or do you need me to?"

"I can do it." Oliver picked up his fork and dug it into the stack of two pancakes.

"You're so grown-up," Zoey said.

Oliver beamed. "I'm going to kindergarten."

"Sara told me," Zoey said. "Are you excited?"

"Yeah. I'm not scared at all," Oliver said.

"You shouldn't be," Zoey said. "You're going to have a lot of fun. In fact, I know your teacher, and she's awesome."

Oliver's eyes widened. "You do?"

"Yes, she's a good friend of mine. We went to teacher school together."

"How come you're not a teacher?" Oliver asked.

"I like being a nanny better," Zoey said.

"Why?" Oliver picked up a piece of bacon and took a bite.

Zoey shot David an amused glance. "For lots of reason. One of which is that I get to hang out with you and your sister in the swimming pool today."

Sara had disappeared through a door that led to the garage. She returned now with a booster seat. "I picked this up for Laine. We can secure it to one of the stools."

"Do you see that, Laine?" David asked. "You'll get to sit up there with your brother."

Sara set the booster seat on the stool next to Oliver, then used the straps to fix it securely.

"Would you like some bacon?" David asked Laine. She liked bacon at home. Would she here?

Laine nodded.

"Okay, then. You'll have to sit in your big-girl seat if you're going to eat."

She nodded again. Her body relaxed its grip. He set her gently into the booster, then buckled the safety belt around her little body. He'd dressed her in a white sundress with a pattern of small yellow flowers. She'd wanted to wear her pink sandals that fastened with Velcro. Those precious feet, tanned from days at the beach, in those sandals made his chest ache. A wave of immense love for his sweet little girl washed over him. He would do anything to keep her safe, to make her joyful the way she'd been as a baby. Everyone said that at a year and a half, she would be too young to remember her mother and would not grieve her absence. That had turned out to be completely false. She might not consciously remember, but she'd changed after Marigold's death. His once babbling brook of a baby girl had grown quiet and shy. It was as if the light had gone out inside her.

"Do you want pancakes, too?" Zoey asked Laine.

Another nod as Laine fixed a wary gaze on Zoey.

"She doesn't talk hardly ever," Oliver said as he stabbed a piece of pancake with his fork.

"I've noticed," Zoey said. "But that's just fine. Some of us like to wait until there's something important to say."

Harper, as if in agreement, let out a shout from her high chair and kicked her chubby legs.

"This one, on the other hand, is hardly ever quiet," Sara said as she scooped a pile of eggs into a plastic bowl. She then set it in front of Harper.

"She's adorable," David said. Strangely, given their fair hair and blue eyes, Harper looked as if she could be his children's sibling.

"David, would you like coffee?" Sara asked.

He glanced at his watch. "No, we better get going if we're going to catch our plane."

"Yes, you're right," Sara said. "The morning's gotten away from me. I already put my bag in my car. We can take my car into the city and leave it overnight at the airport."

His neck flushed with heat. She probably didn't think it was safe to drive there in his outdated Honda Accord. There was nothing wrong with the car, other than a few weary years under her belt. Kind of like him. "Sure, whatever suits you."

Her eyebrows came together briefly, but she didn't say anything further. Sara Ness was an astute woman. He'd have to be extra diligent to keep his thoughts and feelings to himself.

"Laine and Oliver, I'm going now," David said. "You be good for Zoey." He kissed them each on top of the head.

Laine lifted her arms and strained against the booster seat belt.

"Just go," Zoey said. "She'll be okay once you leave."

His stomach turned. Laine's face had changed shape, almost like the twisted form in a Picasso painting. Tears ran down her reddened cheeks.

"Seriously, it's best if you go," Zoey said.

He nodded and turned away. "I'll get my bag and meet you out front," he said to Sara.

She'd already kissed Harper and nodded, then took off for the garage.

His heart might burst with guilt during his journey out of the kitchen and into the foyer. He had to go. That was all there was to it. He yanked open the front door and sprinted down the steps and then across the driveway to his car.

Sara backed out of the garage and waited as he grabbed his overnight bag. He tossed it into the back seat of her Mercedes SUV and hopped into the passenger seat.

Neither of them spoke until they were out of the driveway and on the highway that would lead them to San Francisco.

"Do you really think she'll be all right after I left?" David asked. "Because that was really bad."

"Zoey's always right about these things," Sara said.

"I hope Laine won't be too much for her. My daughter's not good with change."

"She's been at day care, though?"

"Yes, three days a week. My dad takes care of her the other two."

"And she does fine there, right?"

"She cries every single day I drop her off." He sighed and

pinched the bridge of his nose. "The teachers assure me she stops the minute I leave."

"See there, then? Don't worry."

He settled back into the seat and closed his eyes for a second. His fatigue seemed chronic these days. Ironic, since he couldn't sleep when he was supposed to. Most nights he fell asleep quickly, only to wake at two in the morning. Unable to shut off his mind, he lay awake until the birds began to chirp their cheery songs.

"You tired?" Sara asked.

"All the time. I don't sleep well."

"Me too, and I have Zoey and only one child."

A bug splattered against the windshield, smearing yellow guts on the clean glass.

David yawned. "Most days, I'm not sure I'm going to make it through the next few years. I'm completely inadequate." Why was he telling her this? He'd promised himself he'd be stoic in front of her. But again, he was just so tired. Feigning that he was doing fine made him even more tired.

"You're not inadequate," she said. "My observation is that you're doing a fantastic job. They're really sweet kids."

He turned his head to look at her. Her high cheekbones and perfect nose gave her an extremely attractive profile. The sunroof was open a few inches, bringing in the scent of the ocean as they climbed in elevation.

"Thanks," he said. "If it weren't for my dad and Lisa, I would've been completely screwed."

"Not having any family is hard. Autumn helps with that, though." The sun glistened in her hair. He longed to feel the texture. What would it feel like in his hands?

"Trey told us in our meeting the other day that they're expecting," he said. "That'll be nice for you."

"It will, yes."

A sudden curve in the road caused Sara to slam on the brakes. He lurched forward.

"I'm sorry," she said. "Are you all right?"

He made a face, meaning to tease her. "Other than the seat belt bruise, I'm fine."

Her mouth turned downward. "I was going too fast. I'm one of these people who can't drive and talk at the same time."

"I'm just teasing you. That curve in the road came out of nowhere."

"Kind of like life," she said.

"Amen." He yawned again.

His yawn was contagious. She mirrored his, then slapped him on the arm. "Now look what you've done."

His eyelids were like lead. "It's the sun that makes me sleepy."

"Lower the seat back and take a little rest. We're at least an hour from the airport."

He yawned a third time as he lowered the seat. "Maybe just a catnap."

The next thing he knew, they were pulling into the San Francisco airport.

13

S ara
Sara lifted a glass of champagne to toast her new, albeit fake, husband. "Here's to us keeping a fortune away from Moxie and the dog."

He clinked glasses with her. "To you and me and the craziest thing I've ever done in my life."

David really did have the sexiest mouth, she thought, as he lifted the slender flute to his lips. They had just the right amount of pucker.

"What's the name of the dog?" David asked.

They were in a hotel suite in one of the swankiest hotels in Vegas. Outside, the sun was about to set, casting an orange glaze over the city. She lounged on the couch with her legs spread out in front of her. He sat opposite her in an engulfing armchair. They'd both changed from their wedding outfits into jeans and casual shirts. For the wedding, they'd agreed to a suit and tie for him and nice dress for her. They'd figured the photographs from the chapel had to look real for the private investigator. They'd posed in the lobby right after the ceremony to have their photo snapped and sent directly to their phones.

She laughed as she flexed her feet. The high heels she'd worn for the ceremony had caused a cramp in the sole of her foot. "You know, I don't know. He only mentioned Moxie, not the dog."

Her phone buzzed from where she'd left it on the coffee table. A quick glance at the screen told her it was the attorney. "It's Lodge calling me back. He must have gotten my message."

She'd called him on the way back from the chapel. He hadn't answered, so she'd left a message. "I've gotten married. I was hoping you could tell me what to do next and reassure me that I haven't lost my mind."

"Hello, Mr. Lodge," she said into the phone.

"Ms. Ness, I got your message. Well done."

"The certificate is sitting right in front of me," she said. "What should I do now?"

"Quite simply, spend the next six weeks convincing everyone and their mother that you're a real couple. The investigator is unknown. He has his methods, I'm sure. Whenever you're in public, act like a couple. The only time to let your guard down is behind closed doors. And keep your window shades drawn. He might try to photograph you in your own house. Any staff must believe in your relationship as well."

"All right, yes. We're on it."

"How's the lucky young man holding up?" Lodge asked, with a hint of humor in his deep voice.

She lifted her gaze toward David. He held his champagne flute in one hand and appeared to be watching the bubbles rise to the surface. His shoulders curved inward, as if the weight of the world rested there. A pang of sympathy went through her as it always did when witnessing the suffering of others. A tiny part of her wakened. The piece of her that had remained tucked away since her husband's betrayal. Desire for connection? The possibility of friendship? Or was it something else? Something deeper and more primal?

"We're having champagne," Sara said. "And fancy cheese and crackers. Exactly what any other happy couple would do on the night of their elopement." The staff had left the champagne on ice along with a tray of snacks and best wishes for the wedding night.

"Any chance you could fall for him for real?" Lodge asked.

She shot a nervous glance David's way, hoping he hadn't heard. He didn't look up from his champagne glass. "Why would you ask that?"

"I'm a romantic. After what you went through, I'd like to see you with a nice man. I did my research on him, and from all accounts, he seems like one of the good ones. Terrible thing about his wife."

"Yes, it was."

"All right, I'll let you get back to your champagne," Lodge said. "You let me know if you need anything."

"I will, thanks. Also, thank you for encouraging me to take a stand on this. The more I think about it, the more I know that I can do so much good with that money."

"It's my pleasure." He paused. She heard rustling, as if he were moving the phone from one ear to the other. "I was at prep school with your father. We were friends back in the day—before the rift between him and his father. He always struck me as an old soul, so much more mature than the rest of us. His vision for his life was always to give back however he could. You take after him, obviously. He'd be proud."

"How did you become Lincoln's lawyer?" she asked.

He chuckled. "I inherited him from my father."

"Lucky you."

"Yes, well, the hourly rates make most clients more tolerable than they otherwise might be. Anyway, you get back to your night. I'll speak with you soon."

Sara hung up and set the phone back on the glass coffee table. The suite was large, but she would have preferred a two-bedroom. However, when she called to book the room, it occurred to her that the PI would surely have a way to check records. So far, David hadn't mentioned anything. She would take the couch, since she got him into this mess.

"You all right?" She poured herself more champagne.

He lifted his gaze to her. "Yep, fine."

She could see the careful way he rearranged his features to appear bland and benign. That's what it was—what she'd disliked about him. She was suspicious of people who hid their feelings so well. Her husband had done that. She wouldn't make the same mistake again.

Today, however, David had been open, even kind of fun. Actually, quite a bit of fun. They'd giggled all the way back to the hotel about the five-minute ceremony.

"Give me your glass. I'll pour you more bubbly," she said.

He handed it to her. "Fill her up."

"I've been thinking. Since this is probably the first night we've had without our kids since our dearly departed, departed, let's have some fun."

"What do you have in mind?" He sipped from his filled glass. "This is really good, by the way. Better than the cheap stuff I'm used to."

"Only the finest for my groom." The bubbly had given her a wonderful floaty feeling. "We could go downstairs to the best restaurant and have dinner, then gamble or see a show. I don't know. What do you like to do in Vegas?"

"This is my first time."

"Really?"

"Yes, I'm a virgin," he said, smiling.

"Would you like to gamble?"

"This is going to make me sound like a total bore, but not really. I don't have the money to spare. Given my luck, I'm sure to lose. Do you like to gamble?"

"Not at all," Sara said. "I'd rather read a book or watch a movie than waste money on gambling." He didn't have the money to spare? Had it not sunk in that he was now wealthy? Or maybe he didn't count the money as his until their year was up. Given his practical nature, the latter made sense.

"You know what sounds great to me? Ordering room service and some good wine and talking or watching a movie. Or both. Not at the same time. I hate when people talk during movies."

"I do too. It's like make a choice. One or the other."

He rubbed his right cheekbone. "Exactly. Anyway, we should probably know a little more about each other if we're going to pretend to be in love."

"You make a great point." She got up and ambled over to the wet bar to find the room service menu. "They have pretty much anything you could want." She set it on the table in front of him. "I'll probably just have a salad with grilled chicken and dressing on the side." No reason to go off the rails simply because she was on her fake honeymoon.

"You sure?" He had the room service book open. His finger trailed down the page. "They have a rib eye steak that sounds pretty great. It's grilled with an herb butter sauce poured over the top."

Her stomach growled. She hadn't eaten much, what with getting married and everything. "It's tempting."

"But you don't eat stuff like this?"

"Not any longer, no." Sara went back to the couch and took another sip of her champagne. "That's the part no one thinks of when they're in the process of losing weight. Keeping it off is still part of the journey. Daily choices and habits and all that crap."

He closed the book. "You know what? I'll have the salad too. Chowing down on a steak in front of you is not supportive. No way to start a marriage, right?" He flashed her a sheepish smile. "I mean if we're going to do this, I'm going to be the best fake husband ever."

She laughed. David Perry was charming today. Completely different from the way he'd been the entire time they worked together on her house. "Absolutely not. You're getting that rib eye. Remember, we're supposed to be doing whatever we want tonight."

"Fine. But only because I'm a selfish bastard and am dying for that steak. It's the Midwesterner in me, I guess."

"Here, give me that so I can pick out a good wine. Do you like red?" She took the menu from his outstretched hand. "Oh my gosh, we *don't* know anything about each other. I don't even know what kind of wine you like."

"Actually, I know quite a bit about you. Designing a house for someone gives me great insight into my client's tastes and interests."

"No fair, then. I get to ask the questions tonight."

"I like red, especially with a good steak," David said. "But I'm more of a scotch kind of guy."

She scribbled in the air. "Making a mental note."

"Such a good wife." He grinned, then polished off his champagne.

She reached for the hotel telephone and pushed the button for room service, ordering their dinners and a Napa cabernet from one of her favorite wineries. When she hung up, she marched over to the wet bar and searched through the mini bottles of booze. "Ah, yes, here's a scotch for you. How do you like it?"

"Neat, please. Only way to drink it."

She dumped the contents of the small bottle into a glass. David had risen from the couch to meet her.

"Thank you," he said as he took it from her. He wandered over to the window. The last of the sunset was a brilliant pink. She joined him, standing close, suddenly uninhibited. Too much champagne. She would slow down before she got herself in trouble. This was a gorgeous man, and they were together in a hotel room with endless amounts of booze. What could go wrong?

She stifled a giggle and meandered back to the couch. "Tell me, husband, about your favorite things."

"Should we make flash cards?"

"No need. I have a great memory," Sara said. "About people, anyway."

"All right. Favorite things? The smell of Laine's head. I swear to God, it's the sweetest scent. Doesn't matter when or where, I can stick my nose into that kid's head and I'm in heaven."

Sara's stomach fluttered. This sweet man wasn't at all what she'd thought. "Same with Harper's. I love watching her sleep, too. It's kind of the same type of thing, right?"

"Totally."

"What else. Music?"

"If I tell you this, you'll think I'm the biggest nerd."

"Hello? Look at me. You can't get nerdier than yours truly," Sara said.

"Okay, well, I like old country like Waylon and Willie. Folk music like James Taylor and John Prine."

"Johnny Cash?" she asked.

"Of course. George Strait. Reba. Emmylou."

"You're on a first-name basis with them?" Sara asked, laughing.

"Only in my mind." He took a sip from his glass. "I like scotch, obviously, although I never buy it because it costs too much. I like IPA when it comes to beer. The beach is preferable over mountains. Pie instead of cake. My favorite movie of all time is *A River Runs Through It*."

"I love that movie, too," she said. "Classic Brad Pitt."

"For sure. It was on the other night. After our first support group session. I watched part of it and thought about you." He leaned back in the chair with his legs stretched out and his ankles crossed. In loose jeans and a Dog's Brewery shirt, he looked younger than when he'd been in the suit earlier. She liked this look on him.

"Me? Why?" Sara asked.

"I'm not sure. I guess after what you'd shared, I felt a connection with you."

A connection? She'd felt it too. Now even more so. "What's your ideal Saturday?" Sara asked.

He cocked his head to the side. "I'm not sure. I don't really ever think about what I want. Growing up, I focused on pleasing my hard-to-please mother. Or looking after Lisa during her rough patches."

"Rough patches?"

"She had depression. When we were in high school, she had a breakdown. She tried to...end her own life." His voice cracked. He sipped his drink.

"I'm sorry. I'd never have guessed." To Sara, Lisa was the woman with everything: talent, beauty, sweetness.

"Thanks. All I wanted during that time was for her to get better. Then, after that, it was all about what Marigold wanted. She had a strong personality. One of those women people describe as wearing the pants in the family. My mother was the same way, so I guess I just followed in family tradition. Marigold wanted to get married, so we did. She wanted a certain kind of house, so I designed it and had it built for her. She wanted kids, so we did that too. I can't remember ever thinking about whether any of it was what I wanted. It's embarrassing to admit."

"Why?"

"Aren't men supposed to be strong?" David asked.

"Being generous to your partner isn't a bad thing."

"I suppose not. But it was so much like how my dad was with my mother. Giving in to whatever she wanted. A purse holder."

"Tell me what that is."

"It's a phrase I came up with to describe men who do whatever their wives tell them. My dad was always holding her purse while she did whatever. Like a lapdog waiting for a treat from a mistress who'll never give them one."

"To me, it sounds like he was a thoughtful, sweet husband,"

Sara said. "There's nothing wrong with being attentive to a partner's needs."

"That's not what this was, though. This was about control. Having the upper hand in the relationship. My mother was the queen of manipulation. Then I married a woman who did the same to me. I knew it, too, but somehow couldn't stop myself."

"When did you guys get together?"

"We were in high school." He set aside his drink and cracked the ring finger on his left hand. "Sixteen, I think, when we started dating. Lisa describes me as the golden boy growing up because I was an athlete and a good student. To everyone else, it seemed like I was on top of the world. Inside, not so much."

"Don't tell me you were a jerk and break my heart." She said it teasingly, but she'd immediately been flooded with memories of *that* guy in her high school. Clark Meyer had been blond, good-looking, and the star of the football team. He'd nicknamed her Fat Cow Nessie. That had spread like wildfire through the small private high school. "There was a guy in my high school. The 'it' guy. He tortured anyone outside of the 'in' crowd."

He was sitting forward now and waving his hands like a traffic cop. "No, no. I could never be cruel to anyone. We had a guy like that too, but after my buddy James broke his nose, he wasn't so pretty anymore. Things got a lot better after that."

"I wish someone had broken Clark Meyer's nose," Sara said.

"What did he do to you?"

"We're supposed to be talking about you." She gave him a weak smile. Talking about her high school experiences woke the demon in her gut, crying out for nourishment. A cookie or ice cream. Maybe macaroni and cheese.

"I should know who your nemesis was in high school," David said. "That could be on the test."

"Good point." She looked up at the ceiling as the memories came, one after the other. Walking down the hallway at school when she'd heard her name and looked over, hoping for a friend. Instead, it was a huddle of popular kids. A mixture of girls, all thin with perfect hair, and boys, athletic and nice-looking. They'd sneered and fixed narrowed, beady eyes on her. Their ringleader, Clark Meyer, wearing his signature leather jacket, had called out to her again, only this time with the nickname that would stick. "There's Fat Cow Nessie." He'd tossed a candy bar at her. "Hungry, Nessie?"

"He called me Fat Cow Nessie. You know, because Nessie's a cow name. And I was fat." She left spaces between the words of that last sentence. Since she was fourteen years old, that string of words had controlled and consumed her. They'd filled her with shame and self-hatred. Ironically, the only thing that assuaged all those feelings, temporarily anyway, was food. For a few minutes, the bliss of taste and texture had made her feel better. Food was her friend.

And her enemy.

"You're beautiful, Sara," David said softly. "Yours is the timeless kind. When you're eighty, you'll still shine because it's from the inside out. Don't let some spoiled, insecure boy's cruel words haunt you."

Her eyes stung. What a sweet thing to say. A surprising one, too. "My mother used to say that to me. Or something similar, anyway."

"Yet you don't believe it," he said.

She blinked away her tears. "Turns out it's easier to change the outside of me than the inside. I still feel like the fat kid."

"You're not that. You were never that," David said. "There's so much more to a person than their appearance. I know it's impossible to digest that when you're a teenager. But now? The purity of your heart, your generosity, is what makes you as beautiful inside as you are out. Giving up a year of your life because you want to start a foundation is no small gesture." He set aside his drink and tilted his head, watching her with such intensity that she had to look away.

"I'm sorry," he said. "I've said too much."

"No, it's just that I'm not used to so much kindness all at

once." She folded her legs under her and ran a finger over the distressed fabric on a section of her jeans. "When I lost the weight, after I married Brent, I credited his unconditional love. I thought he'd filled this hole inside me. I couldn't believe I'd met a man who would love me. Fat Cow Nessie. When I learned of his betrayal, it reawakened all the feelings of worthlessness. I thought, 'If I were thinner this wouldn't have happened.' I'd just had Harper when I found out he was cheating."

"How did you find out?"

"A friend saw them out at a bar one night. She snapped a photo of them kissing and sent it to me."

"A gut punch," he said.

"Yes. I couldn't actually absorb it at first." She'd been nursing Harper when the text came in from her friend. All she could do was stare at the photo. She had the irrational thought that it was a mistake, just someone who resembled her husband and her good friend. "He was with my friend Joanna. She and her husband were friends of ours through the country club. The four of us golfed together and partied together. What I didn't know is that Brent and Joanna had been sneaking around behind our backs for the entirety of my pregnancy." Her voice caught. "Can you believe that? I mean, that I didn't know. Looking back, I can see all the clues. How they all stacked up together. At the time, I was blissed out to be pregnant. I guess that's how I missed so much." She paused for a moment, swallowing the bile that rose to her throat. "After my friend told me what she'd seen, I asked Autumn to meet me for dinner. I needed to talk through what to do. We had a nanny who lived with us, and she'd offered to stay with Harper so I could have a night out with my friend. Once I'd told Autumn what I'd learned, she told me to go home and kick Brent out of the house. So I drove home, psyching myself up for a confrontation. What I didn't know is that Brent and Joanna were in bed together. Rupert was there as well. He shot them and then himself as I stood in the hallway." Her throat ached, but she continued. "My nanny got to me before I could see the bodies. She spared me that, which I've been grateful for ever since."

"What about Joanna's husband?" David asked. "When did he find out?"

"I'm assuming the same day I did," she said. "Rupert had drug problems. He was volatile on a good day. Honestly, I was a little afraid of him. One time during a round of golf he beat the side of the cart with his club." The three of them had watched in horror. Driving home afterward, she and Brent had talked about how they felt sorry for Joanna. Brent had ranted, actually, about how awful Rupert was and that Joanna should leave him. Later, Sara had understood just how much he wanted her to leave her husband.

The only problem? Rupert was the one with the money and a solid prenuptial. Brent was in the same predicament. Sara had an impenetrable prenuptial as well. If they divorced for any reason, he would be left with nothing. "They didn't want to leave us because Rupert and I were the ones with the money. In the end, it didn't matter. Rupert must have gone crazy when he learned of the affair."

"Poor bastard," David said.

"I learned later that Rupert was a frequent visitor to the gun range. Quite a sharpshooter. Three shots was all it took. One for each of them and then one for himself. It happened so fast I couldn't quite believe what had happened. The police said they most likely never even knew what hit them. For days, I questioned what I'd seen. Like, was it real? Could something like this really happen to me?"

"I know what you mean. When the Feds showed up at my house to tell me about Marigold—both that she was dead and what she'd been doing—it felt mostly like a bad dream."

"One you keep wishing you could wake up from," Sara said. "But we didn't."

"And then it all breaks in the newspaper." David picked up

his drink. "All the dirty details. Everywhere you go, people stare at you."

"Yes. That's one of the reasons I moved to Cliffside Bay. People don't know me there. If they do, they're too polite to ask about my past. Some days it feels like I wouldn't have made it if not for our little town and Autumn."

"Same here. I can remember walking down to the beach that first day after our move. I stood there, watching the waves come and go, and thought I'd take it one day at a time. Your house and the kids were my primary focus. Sadly, there are chunks of time I can't really remember from that first year. I was so out of it."

"You did a beautiful job with my house," Sara said.

"The Wolves and Lisa have caught me every time I thought I would fall and never get back up. And designing your house may have saved my life."

"I guess we've been thrown together more than once to save each other."

His blue eyes softened. "I suppose we have." He lifted his glass. "Here's to year two after our worlds fell apart."

She raised her flute to clink his glass. "To year two. Together."

14

David
David's stomach growled as the server entered with the cart of their food. He'd been too nervous to eat much before the wedding ceremony. Now, however, a warm buzz had overtaken the pricks of anxiety and doubt that had plagued him since the plane landed in Las Vegas. The booze helped. As did the company. He found Sara surprisingly easy to talk to, probably because of their similar experiences. Fate had dealt them harsh blows. Their children were what kept them striving for a better life.

She was also easy on the eyes.

How did he keep himself in check here? What a disaster it would be if they slept together. He had a feeling it would be much too easy for them to start something they shouldn't. They were both lonely. If she were like him, there had been no sex in her life since their spouses' deaths. Who had time?

"Yes, please set it up for us on the table there," Sara said to the server.

David excused himself to use the restroom and wash his hands. When he returned, the table had been set with their meals. Wine had been poured. A candle flickered from the middle of the table. Sara sat with her chin in her hand, gazing out the window. He stood for a moment, watching her. The sun had disappeared by then, leaving only a pink streak behind. Her skin glowed in the shadows thrown from the flickering candle. The blouse she wore clung to her curves. What would she feel like under him?

He ran his hands through this hair. This was not good. His libido was not his friend.

"How are you feeling?" David asked as he sat across from her. "Having any doubts about this absurd plan?"

"No doubts," Sara said. "I was just thinking how nice it is to have someone to talk to."

"I think so too." He closed his eyes to savor the scent of grilled steak mixed with garlic and butter. "This smells incredible."

She laughed as she picked up her fork. "Go ahead. Dig in."

They ate in silence for a few minutes. The steak was as good as it smelled, melting in his mouth. He had to restrain himself from groaning with pleasure.

"How's your salad?" he asked.

"Very fresh." The candlelight reflected in her eyes when she looked over at him.

He had to tear himself away from staring into them for too long.

"I got a text from Zoey," Sara said. "The kids are doing great. All three of them went down like bricks. They swam for hours in the pool. Zoey gave Laine and Oliver swimming lessons. She said to tell you that she got Laine to put her face in the water. Did I mention Zoey was a lifeguard and swim instructor?"

"What doesn't that girl do?"

"I know. She's a marvel." Sara brought a cherry tomato to her mouth. He was mesmerized for a split second, imagining how nice it must be for that lucky tomato. He'd like to know what it felt like to have those sexy lips take a bite out of him. *Okay, dude, you've got to get yourself in check. Think about the kids, not Sara.*

121

"What else did they do today?" This was more of a croak than a spoken sentence.

"After the girls took naps, she blew bubbles for them in the yard. Laine and Oliver chased them all around the grass. She put Harper in her swing to watch them. Zoey said she laughed and laughed and clapped her hands. It's nice for her to have other kids around."

His stomach clenched, suddenly missing his babies. "I'm terrible. I've barely thought of them since we returned...from our wedding." He made a face. "God, that sounds weird."

"It truly does." She flashed a sassy grin his way. "There's something kind of fun about all this at the same time."

Their eyes locked for a second. His pulse quickened. The space between them became suddenly heavy with a current of desire. He sensed she felt it, too, this undeniable attraction that heaved them toward the other. He looked away first. Using his knife, he cut off several small pieces of his steak. This entire evening had unnerved him, thrown him off-balance. *Turn the conversation back to the kids*, he told himself.

"I'm relieved they're doing so well," he said. "I wasn't sure how Laine would do without me to tuck her in."

"Zoey has tricks." Sara's cheeks had flushed, and she seemed unusually intent on examining the piece of lettuce on her fork.

He spread more sour cream over his baked potato, thinking about how much fun the kids must have had that day. Swimming and playing in the yard. What could be better? "You know, I can't tell you how much it means to me that the kids had that experience today. Dad's taken them to the beach this summer, which is great, but they've never really had a chance to swim in a pool since we left Iowa. Oliver has had swimming lessons but Laine hasn't. She hasn't had any of the stuff we did for her brother. Sadly, she's stuck with me. I never have time to do the activities I should be doing with them."

"You'll have more time now that we can help each other," Sara said. "And Zoey, of course."

Embarrassed by the tears that pricked the backs of his eyes, he looked away, focusing on the glass of wine he hadn't yet tasted. He nabbed a sip. "Holy crap, that's good."

Her face lit up with one of her pretty smiles. "I'm glad you like it. This is one of my favorite wineries in Napa. We should go sometime. Zoey could stay with the kids and we could spend a weekend there." She pursed her lips as a flush crept up her neck. "I don't know why I said that."

"There's no reason not to say it," David said. "We're spending a year together. We might as well have some fun while we're at it. Life's kind of sucked for both of us. There's no reason we can't enjoy a weekend away. In fact, we could take Lisa and Rafael with us. More ammunition to prove this is a real marriage."

She set down her fork and picked up the glass of wine. "There's the problem of separate bedrooms. Whenever we're with other people, the facade has to continue."

His stomach fluttered. Just the mere mention of bedrooms and his mind went to all the wrong places. "I'm not afraid of a couch or the floor. No one needs to know what does or doesn't happen behind closed doors."

She placed both arms on the table and gazed into her plate. The muscles in her jaw twitched.

"What is it?" He grazed her forearm with the tips of his fingers.

She sucked in a breath. Had his touch moved her?

"Nothing, really," she said.

She sounded so sad that his heart felt as if it had been wrung out like a sponge. "Hey now, you can tell me anything. We're in this together."

She met his gaze. "Do you think people like us, with all our baggage, could ever love again?"

He wrapped his fingers around the stem of his glass and looked past her to the still life painting of a bowl of peaches.

"Sure. Look at our friends. They've all been through a ton of crap, and they were able to get past all that and fall in love."

"I agree. Sort of."

"What do you mean?"

"I don't like to sound pitiful or angry, even though I am. But no one has been through what we have. My husband was shot to death in my bed with his girlfriend, who was one of my best friends. He left me with an infant who will never know her father. Your wife was distributing drugs across Iowa while your precious babies slept in their car seats. And then she was murdered by really bad people. Now you have to raise them all by yourself. Surely you can agree that we've had particularly bad blows." Her eyes had filled by the time she finished. One teardrop traveled down her cheek.

Without thinking, he reached across the table and wiped it away with a corner of his napkin. "I do agree."

"You know that adage that God never gives you more than you can bear?"

"Sure."

"I don't think that's true," Sara said. "Because I feel all the time like I can't bear what happened." Several more tears escaped. She wiped them away with her own napkin this time. "Sometimes I lie awake at night and think, if only my parents had lived, maybe then I'd have a fighting chance. I wouldn't be totally alone with only me to love this baby. I would have someone else to call family."

He dabbed at his mouth with his napkin, then set it back in his lap. "I have my dad and Lisa, and I feel that same way. What happened to us is not something most people can relate to or understand, so they don't know how to offer support. Even when they want to." His voice grew husky. "But I understand. You can talk to me about anything, no matter the time of day or night. I'm always here to listen."

Her bottom lip trembled. "That's very sweet."

He pushed his chair back a few inches, done with his dinner. "I thought it might be easier for you because you don't have money problems. When everything happened, the Feds froze all of our accounts. I had one bank account I kept separate from my wife, so I could put money away. Anything I made, she spent. Thank God I had that, because the rest was seized by the Feds. I spend all day and night thinking about how to get out of debt. Do you know I'm afraid to pick up my phone because I'm worried it's a debt collector? It's humiliating. I did everything right, like I was supposed to, and at thirty-four, I'm a mess." He picked up his glass and swirled the wine. "I've run up credit card bills. It's the mortgage in Iowa that's killing me. I wish I could sell it. I spent way too much building the house Marigold wanted but that I couldn't afford. Story of our marriage right there."

"Let me pay off all your debts," she said. "We can do it when we get home tomorrow, so that you don't have to worry all year."

"I don't know about that." His reptile brain immediately kicked in at the thought of a woman rescuing him. Then again, what was this whole thing? This was about money. Whether she gave it to him now or then didn't really matter. "It's a lot."

"David."

He laughed. "Right. It won't be a lot to you."

"How much are we talking? Like five hundred thousand?"

He did a double take. "Oh my God, no. It's around twenty thousand, plus the mortgage on my house in Iowa. That's close to eight hundred thousand."

"We'll take care of it when we get home." She watched him from across the table, as if he were about to bolt from the table. "Does my wealth bother you?"

"If this were a real marriage, it would. I'm not sure I'm evolved enough to be this unbalanced financially."

She nodded, obviously thinking about what he said for a moment before answering. "My situation is unfortunate that way. Either men are like my late husband—interested in my money. Or, like you, thrown off by my wealth."

"You need a guy in your tax bracket," David said. Why did imagining her with another man bother him? Again with the reptile brain. This woman wasn't his, and yet he felt possessive.

"That's unlikely," she said. "I'm not sure I'll ever be ready to trust someone again. Plus, he would have to be good enough for Harper. That adds another element to the mix."

"For sure," David said. "And the other way around, too. What woman is going to want to take on two kids that aren't hers? I'm pretty much doomed when it comes to love."

She smacked the table with her hand and smiled. "Well, that settles it then. For the next year, it's you and me. We'll get your finances on track. Have some adventures together. Help each other with our kids."

He smiled back at her. "I can imagine worse people to spend a year with."

"Me too. In fact, I was married to him."

"We really have all the wrong things in common," he said, chuckling.

They locked eyes for a second. A warmth traveled through the length of him. The depth of those eyes was dangerous. This was merely a way to secure a future for him and the kids. Not a relationship.

But damn, she was pretty. What did she look like under those clothes? Was she a lacy panties and bra type of woman? She seemed pragmatic and methodical in the ways she ran her life. Would that translate in the bedroom? Or was she the type who transformed into a wild woman during sex?

"What're you thinking?" Sara asked. "You have a strange look on your face."

Her words jerked him from his daydream. "Oh, nothing. Just thinking about what we should do next on our night of freedom."

"Do you want to rent a movie?" Sara asked.

"Sounds good to me." He paused, hoping to read what she wanted. "But if you'd like to go out, I'm happy to escort you. I don't think I've asked you what you want."

She picked up her wineglass and rose from her chair. "Going out sounds exhausting."

"It does. The curse of single parenthood. A night in and early bedtime trumps a wild turn in the casino." He tossed his napkin onto his mostly empty plate and picked up the bottle of wine and his glass.

Sara had returned to the couch and had the remote in her hand. "What kind of movies do you like?"

"I haven't seen a movie that wasn't animated since Oliver was born." He topped off her glass and did the same to his, then set the bottle on the coffee table.

"We've got five years to choose from then."

The television was directly opposite the couch, which meant he'd have to sit next to her. *Don't be ridiculous,* he told himself. *She's not poisonous.* Anyway, the couch was plenty long. He would sit on one end and she on the other.

He plopped down in the corner as she pulled up the movie listings.

The selection was mostly horror, musclemen in car-chasing movies, or animated.

"Let me guess," he said. "No horror or car chases?"

"Good guess."

"What about this one?" she asked. "I've seen part of it, but I fell asleep somewhere in the middle."

The movie blurb said it was an ensemble piece about five friends in Los Angeles looking for love. "Sounds benign enough," he said.

"It'll probably have a happy ending. I could use that right now."

"I'm warning you now, it might make me cry," he said. "Ever since Oliver came, any hint of sentimentality and I cry."

She turned to him and said softly, "I love that."

An overwhelming desire to grab her in his arms and kiss her powered through him. This was not good. Why was this happening?

If he didn't get himself under control, this was going to be one long year.

THEY SHARED a bowl of microwave reduced-fat popcorn as they watched the movie. He'd placed it on the couch between them and so far he'd managed to keep from reaching into it at the same time as Sara. If his hand touched hers, he might lose all control.

The movie was surprisingly good and reminded him a little of his group of friends in Cliffside Bay. Their paths to love were circuitous and full of mistakes. Mostly by the men.

Sara giggled at a funny line. He turned from the movie to watch her. The television light illuminated her face. She had a handful of popcorn, which she ate from, a kernel at a time. Her self-discipline was impressive. In general, she was impressive.

He'd never seen her this relaxed. Other than the night he had to drive her home. She'd been a little too relaxed that night. He'd felt bad for her. A night of freedom had caused her to overindulge. Being cooped up at home with a baby would do that to a person.

The hour was nearing eleven when the credits began to roll. She yawned and stretched her arms over her head. "I'm pretty tired. Are you ready for bed?"

"Yeah, we probably should. I'll take the couch." He picked a few stray popcorn kernels from his lap and put them in the empty bowl. "I'm sure there's some extra blankets in the closet." He uncurled his legs to rise from sofa.

"Are you sure? Maybe we should flip a coin."

"Absolutely not. Let me at least be a gentleman in this arrangement." He smiled to make sure she knew he was teasing. "It's all I have to offer."

She turned to face him. "That's not true. Spending time with you today has been so much fun. It's easy between us. To be honest, I was worried it would be awkward."

"I was too. I'm glad you feel the same way I do."

"All right then. I'm going to get ready for bed. I'll be quick so you can have the bathroom."

"Great." He watched her cross the room toward the bathroom, admiring the view of her backside before averting his gaze, then busily gathering up the empty glasses and bowl.

They'd already put their dinner trays outside the door, so he put the dishes on the wet bar. He liked this hotel room a little too much. Nothing to clean up. No sticky hands and faces to swipe. A floor empty of stray toys. A whole day with a beautiful, funny, smart woman. He wouldn't think too carefully about what they'd done—the utter craziness of their decision to marry. He'd had a fantastic day. He couldn't remember the last time he'd had such good conversation or laughed as much. Even his weekly outings with the Wolves, whom he loved spending time with, couldn't compare to today.

Sara came out of the bathroom wearing a pair of white cotton pajamas. He willed himself not to look at her chest. If he saw her breasts without a bra under that thin cotton, he might explode.

"Good night, David," she said. "Thanks for a great day."

"Thank you." He drew closer. "This isn't completely nuts, right?"

She lifted her chin slightly and met his gaze. In the dim light, it was harder to see the nuances of her expression, but he detected a resolve in the setting of her jaw. "We're doing this for all the right reasons. You and I are adults who made a decision that will benefit your family and allow me to do really good work for a lot of other families. I'm happy with our decision."

He let out a sigh. "You're right. Thank you. All right. Sleep well." He put his hands in the pockets of his jeans and clenched his stomach muscles as a fortress against his own lascivious thoughts. It had been too long since he touched a woman.

Anyone would be tempted. This meant nothing. *Do not look at her boobs*, he ordered himself.

"You too." She shook her hands as if they had water on them. "I feel like we should hug or something."

He hesitated, scratching the nape of his neck. "I understand the sentiment, but I'm not sure I can be held responsible for what might happen if we do. That's a thin cotton you're wearing. And you're a sexy, gorgeous woman."

"David, really?" She grinned. "I didn't think you thought of me as a woman."

"What else would you be?" His mouth had gone suddenly dry.

"A friend. A partner in crime."

"This is *not* a crime. Is it?"

She laughed. "No, it's not a crime. We've agreed to marry for financial reasons. We're not committing insurance fraud or anything. It was just a turn of phrase." She stepped toward him. Before he knew what was happening, she'd placed her hands flat against his chest and looked up and into his eyes. "For the record, you're pretty damn hot yourself."

He stiffened. God, she smelled good. Floral and fresh.

She took her hands off his chest and stepped back a few inches. "We're going to have to pretend to the outside world that we're husband and wife. Behind closed doors, though, there's no reason we can't be good friends. As a way to...I don't know... feel less alone. This single-parent situation is hard. As you said earlier to me—there's nothing you can't tell me. I'll always be available to listen."

"Thanks." David's throat constricted, moved by this kind gesture from a woman who didn't need to be. "It'll be nice to have a friend."

"You won't hesitate to ask me if you need anything?"

"I promise," he said.

She held up her hand and wriggled her pinkie finger. "Pinkie swear?"

He laughed. "As a man, I normally don't do anything with my pinkie, but I'll make an exception for you." He hooked his finger with hers. Her pinkie squeezed his.

The moment they separated, he wished to have her back.

"I'll see you in the morning," she said. "We can have breakfast and then head to the airport."

He watched her walk to the bedroom and disappear behind the closed door. How exactly was he supposed to keep his hands off her for 364 more days?

15

Sara

When they arrived home from Vegas, the house was empty.

"Maybe they're out in the pool," Sara said to David. They walked out to the patio. Sure enough, delighted screaming was coming from the direction of the pool.

"Should we put on our suits and join them?" David asked. "A swim would be great after the flight."

"Great idea," Sara said. Was it, though? Did she really want to parade around in a bathing suit in front of David? The California sun showed every flaw.

"Why the hesitation?" He peered at her with a concerned glint in his eyes. "What's going on? Does it feel weird to have me here?"

"No, no, nothing like that. I feel fine." She turned to go inside. He grabbed her gently by the wrist. His touch sent sparks up her arm.

"Remember our promise? Tell me."

She evaded his gaze by looking up at the sky. A jet made a white streak in the blue. "I don't like how I look in a swimsuit. Normally, I swim alone."

"What don't you like?" David asked.

She couldn't tell him. The list was too long: her stretch marks left over after her weight loss; the additional ones from her pregnancy; cellulite on her bottom that no amount of exercise fixed; the C-section scar.

"Imperfections," she said.

"Women are so hard on themselves," David said. "I can guarantee you I won't see what you see. I'll see a fit, long-legged redhead with curves in all the right places."

His words made her want to cry.

"And I'm not just saying that to get you into a bikini," he said. "Although that would be a happy outcome."

"Are you flirting with me?" Sara asked, hoping to hide the emotion that threatened to spill out onto the patio and drown them both. *Too much. I'm always too much*, she thought.

He smiled down at her. "If flirting with you helps you to see how freaking ridiculously sexy you are, then yes."

She pushed into his chest. "You're a very good husband so far. Now, let me go and I'll put on the stupid bathing suit if it makes you happy. But first, I'll show you your room."

They passed through the kitchen and upstairs.

"I never thought I'd be out of bedrooms," Sara said. "But with three kids here, that left only one." She opened the door, and he passed through. His aftershave smelled sinfully good.

"Dad brought some of my clothes over earlier," David said. "Zoey told him to put them in the closet in the master."

"She told me," Sara said. "We can sneak them back in here later and hang them up in this closet."

"Good plan."

"I'm glad you won't have to deal with that today. If you're like me, you're anxious to see your kids."

"As nice as it was to get away, yes. You did very well, by the way. I know it's not easy to leave them when they're babies. At least that's how it was for me."

"I've missed Harper," Sara said. She had, but not as much as she'd thought she might. Instead, she'd had a heck of a time. "But getting away was good for me."

"It was nice to have a chance to talk to an adult without someone asking for apple juice."

"True enough. Will the room be all right for you?"

"It's great," he said. "Better than great. At the time, bathrooms off every bedroom seemed like overkill, but I'm glad you asked for it, given our current circumstance."

She'd purposely saved this one for him, as it was larger than the children's rooms and had the best view besides the master, plus a little balcony. "I thought you'd like to have your coffee out there in the mornings. Or do some of your work."

"That was thoughtful of you." He perched on the edge of the bed, wrinkling the dark blue spread with his weight. "What are we going to do about Zoey? Won't she know I'm sleeping in here?"

"I already thought of that. If she asks, which she might not, I'm going to tell her that one of us has restless leg syndrome and we keep the other awake."

"Where did you come up with that one?" David asked.

"Television. I told you I've been watching way too much late-night TV. There's all these medication commercials. It's depressing."

"Maybe we can binge-watch some Netflix tonight instead." He sprang from the bed. "But I like your deviousness. Very impressive."

"Thank you. I try."

"I'm dying to see the kids," he said. "I'll meet you down at the pool?" A question, she noticed. With a hint of yearning. He wanted her to go with him. A pleasant buzz hummed a happy tune in her chest.

"Yes. I'll see you down there in five." She gave him one last smile and went to face the bathing suit.

SARA STARED INTO THE MIRROR. Instead of a bikini, which she did not own, she wore a one-piece that supposedly made you appear ten pounds lighter. Whether that was true or not, the suit made it slightly hard to breathe. It also squeezed the fat around her thighs into hard lumps. She turned around to see her backside. Same issue there.

Her mother had always told her to focus on her good qualities. The problem with that advice was that Sara didn't feel as if she had any. Even after losing fifty pounds and weighing well within the appropriate BMI for her five-foot-nine-inch frame, she couldn't look in the mirror without seeing flaws.

She and Autumn had bonded over this same feeling when they'd met during their freshman year of college. Autumn's legs were scarred and misshapen from a car accident. Sara was overweight. Their friendship had grown as they shared how isolated and embarrassed they felt. Instead of watching movies and eating ice cream alone, Autumn had joined her. However, her friend did not have the same relationship with food. For Sara, it was comfort. In Autumn's case, there had never been enough of it growing up, so she saw food for what it was—nourishment.

Autumn had come out of her shell here in Cliffside Bay. Sara knew it was because of Trey's unconditional love. He didn't care about her physical imperfections. The man loved her just as she was. Because of him, she swam in public now, with no more self-consciousness. Sara wasn't quite there.

She grabbed a cover-up from the closet and slipped her feet into flip-flops and headed downstairs. By the time she reached the pool, David was already in the water with the kids.

Zoey stood between Laine and Harper with a hand on each of their floating devices. Harper splashed and squealed, whereas Laine rested her chin against the front of the floaty and smiled.

"Mama," Harper called out as she splashed her hands in the water.

Sara untied her cover-up and used the stairs to walk into the shallow end of the pool. She forgot her self-consciousness at the sight of Harper. This child was her heart. She knelt in the water and kissed Harper's cheek. "Mama's so happy to see you."

"Mama," Harper shouted, and clapped her hands together.

"We've got the kids for the rest of the day," Sara said to Zoey. "Take some time for yourself."

"Really?" Zoey asked.

"Absolutely. You've done enough over the last few days to deserve a few hours off."

Zoey said goodbye to the kids. "I'll see you guys in the morning."

"Bye, Zoey," Oliver said, waving.

"Thanks for everything, Zoey," David said.

"My pleasure," Zoey said. "They did really well."

"Even Laine?" David asked.

"She woke up this morning a little disoriented," Zoey said. "But we've kept busy all day. She had a good nap in her princess bed."

Zoey got out of the pool and grabbed a towel from a stack on the end of a chaise. "I'm going out tonight. So don't worry if you see activity in and out of the gate."

"Have fun," Sara said.

Sara pushed Harper and Laine around the shallow end of the pool. The sun on her bare shoulders felt good, as did the sound of her daughter's delighted laughter.

David's chest and arm muscles rippled as he tossed Oliver into the water. Sara tried to keep her eyes averted, but no woman would be strong enough to keep from staring at his lean, muscular chest and arms or the tapered waist. Blond hairs on his tanned arms glistened in the sun.

He dove under the water after Oliver. Both came up at the same time with the beads Zoey must have tossed in earlier. David shook his wet head, then slicked back his hair with the palms of his hands. Even his head was symmetrical.

Laine, still in her floaty, shivered. She was on the thin side, which meant she didn't have body fat to keep her warm. "Laine, do you want to get out?"

Laine nodded.

Sara pushed both of the girls to the steps, then unbuckled Laine and lifted her from the floaty and set her on the side of the pool. "David, will you keep an eye on Harper while I get Laine dried off?"

"Sure thing," David said. "Buddy, you swim around without me for a bit, okay?"

"Okay, Dad," he said before diving headfirst into the water, like a happy duck who spotted a fish.

16

D avid

David walked through the water to get to Harper. She grinned at him. "Hey there, sweetness. You want out too?"

Harper babbled a response. He'd go ahead and take that as a yes. He unstrapped her and lifted her into his arms. She was absolutely adorable with her big blue eyes and the tuft of blond hair that reminded him of a baby chick. He kissed her pink cheek. "You are such a pretty little thing."

More babbling. She patted his cheek, which melted him. "This one's a charmer," he said to Sara as he walked up the steps and out of the pool.

Sara sat on one of the chaise longue chairs with Laine on her lap. She'd wrapped a towel around his girl, who continued to shiver.

He sat next to them with Harper on his lap. Her swim diaper was heavy with water. A bag next to the chaise contained a diaper and a change of clothes for Harper and Laine. Zoey thought of everything. How many times had he been out recently without the proper supplies? "Do you want me to put her in a regular diaper?" David asked Sara.

"If you don't mind," she said. "We're kind of snuggly here."

Laine studied Sara with an intensity that reminded him of himself. The way she scrutinized the smallest details was exactly like him. Her serious demeanor and quietness, more comfortable as the observer than the participant, was also like him. Would she ever talk more? A wave of shame clouded the beauty of the day. Life had already damaged her. Would he be able to make it better?

He spread a towel over the chaise and set Harper down lengthwise. She kicked her legs but didn't fight as he pulled her bathing suit top over her head, then slipped the bottoms and the swim diaper off. With the dexterity of a man who'd already diapered two children, he slid a clean diaper under her and fastened it tightly. A cute cotton dress was folded into a neat square in the bag. He sat her up to pull it over her head.

When he was done, he took a toy tambourine from the bag and gave it to Harper to play with. Then he sat back with her on his lap. The sun warmed his bare legs and torso. He'd been so occupied with his task that he'd forgotten to keep an eye on his son. A guilty glance toward the pool told him Oliver was fine. He hadn't yet tired of diving for treasures on the bottom of the pool. "That's going to be one tired boy tonight."

"He loves the water," Sara said. "I'll keep the pool open for as long as we can this fall. I can turn the heat up if we need to."

"When he was six months old, I took him to one of those 'baby and me' swimming classes," David said. "It was our little outing to give Marigold a break. He loved the water from the first. Laine, on the other hand, cried the entire time. She got so cold her mouth turned blue. I never took her back."

"Maybe she'll get acclimated to the water if we spend more time in the pool." Sara had her arms wrapped around Laine and rubbed her back. "Are you warming up, sweet pea?"

Laine answered by burying her face in Sara's chest.

"She likes you," he said quietly. She was that way with Lisa as well. Maybe his little girl craved the touch that only an auntie or a mama could give.

Harper shook the tambourine and bonked him in the nose. "Watch it, rock star," he said, laughing. "This one might be headed for a life as musician." He rubbed his nose.

"Are you all right?" Sara asked, looking as if she wanted to laugh.

"I'm fine. This isn't the first wallop I've had from a baby."

Sara suggested he put dry clothes on Laine. "I've got one of those thick picnic blankets in the pool house. The girls can play on there while Oliver swims a few more minutes."

They exchanged babies. He changed Laine out of her bathing suit and swim diaper into dry clothes. She still wore Pull-Ups at night, but he'd managed to get her potty-trained a few months back with only a few days' effort. Oliver had taken a good six months. Finally, they'd bribed him with Fruity Pebbles cereal for every time he used the toilet. At three and a half, he'd finally been able to switch out of his Pull-Ups. That had been right before Marigold was killed. A lifetime ago.

Sara returned with a weighted blanket she spread out on the pool deck. The sun had lowered by then and filtered through the clump of trees on the west side of the pool. She lifted the lid on a plastic bin filled with toys. "Laine, would you like to pick something to play with? There's a tea set in here."

Laine scurried over to peer inside and pulled out a small case resembling a picnic basket. She sat on the blanket and flipped the latch, then began to set a pretend table with plates and cups.

Sara set Harper on the blanket and gave her several toys, including a set of blocks and a doll with a mermaid's tail. She lowered back into the chaise next to him and stretched her legs out.

Those long, toned legs were enough to break him. He had no idea what she thought was wrong with her body. From his perspective, she was gorgeous. In fact, he was thankful for the kids or he might lose his resolve and touch her smooth, tanned skin.

"Did your kids walk by this age?" Sara asked. "She's thirteen months and no sign of even being interested."

"Oliver walked right around his first birthday. Laine…this is awful…but I'm not sure. All I know is that Marigold never saw her walk, so that means it was some time after her first birthday." He scrunched his eyes closed as the ache came. Guilt and regret and anger mixed up in one pain package. "I've reconciled this thing for myself. Marigold made her choices. She took terrible chances, and they cost her everything. But I can't forgive her for leaving our children without a mother. Wanting designer clothes at the expense of her children is not something I will ever understand."

"You think she did it for the money?" Sara asked.

"What else would it have been?" He turned to look at her, genuinely curious.

"I don't know. Maybe a need to have control or be the boss of something. Or it could've been the danger she was attracted to. The thrill of it all."

"I never thought about it that way. I've blamed myself for not being a good enough provider. Like if I'd just given her more of what she wanted, she wouldn't have had to turn to drug dealing."

"You did nothing wrong. If she hadn't overspent, your income would've been fine."

"I don't know. Looking back, I should've clued in to what was happening and done something."

"God, we're pathetic, the two of us," Sara said. "They're the ones who screwed up, and we're the ones taking the blame."

"It's not a natural human instinct to blame the dead," David said. "Even though I do."

From the blanket, Harper babbled as she smashed two blocks together.

"This kid. I worry she's going to be a wild child," Sara said. "A party girl like her dad was."

"I wouldn't worry. With you as a mom, she's going to grow up to be a wonderful human."

Her expression turned serious. "She's so different from me. Lighthearted and easygoing. Even as an infant, she hardly ever cried. If she were wet or hungry, she'd let out a little squawk. Once those things were taken care of, she'd either go back to sleep or want to eat or play. I don't know what I would've done if she'd been difficult. My mom told me I was a hard baby. I didn't sleep through the night until I was Harper's age. There's a reason they had only me."

"Really?"

"I'm kidding. That may be the reason, but they never said. They died before I could ask them any of that kind of thing. Before I was interested in them as people outside of being my parents."

"As cramped as we were at the apartment, it's been great to know my father in a whole new way. Without my mother controlling him, he's able to be part of my life on his own terms." He told Sara about his parents' divorce and that his mother was now in Paris living with a man half her age and his father's recent confession about Ria. "I never in a million years would have predicted that one. I guess that's what happens when two people unsuited to each other finally break up and go on with their lives."

"Ria seems like she'd be a great partner for your dad."

"She may end up my stepmother." David hadn't really thought that far ahead, but it was certainly possible. "Which is weird to me."

"Are you one of those types who don't want their parents to remarry?"

"No, it's not that," David said. "It's that things were the same in our family for a long time. Then, Lisa finds Rafael right around the time Marigold's murdered. Half a year later, my parents announce they're getting divorced. My mom told us on Lisa's wedding day. That should tell you a lot about my mother."

"Did you pick a woman like your mother?"

"Very astute of you," he said. "I'd laugh, but it's too true."

"Speaking of your wives, have you thought about how you want to announce our marriage?" Sara asked.

"Um, yeah. About that," David said. "I kind of promised Lisa she could throw us a party."

"You did?" She sucked in her bottom lip.

"Are you mad?"

"What, no," Sara said. "I think that's sweet. I see no reason why we shouldn't let her. We're going to have to be great actors, though."

"It'll just be for a few hours," he said.

"We might have to kiss."

"I can think of worse things." He said it casually while brushing an imaginary bug from his bare leg.

"Right. Like those people on television who eat spiders for a million dollars."

He laughed and tapped her knee with the back of his hand. "Kissing a lovely woman is not the same as eating a spider."

She nudged him in the rib cage with her elbow. "You're good for my ego."

"Happy to be of service."

They sat and watched the kids for a few minutes. This wasn't bad at all. He could think of worse ways to spend a year.

"Do you worry about Laine's speech?" Sara asked, startling him.

"Yeah. She's always been quiet, but even more so after Marigold died. Dr. Waller said I shouldn't worry. Apparently some children talk later or when they're ready. He said that since she does speak every so often, it should put my mind at rest. I couldn't tell if he was just being nice or if that's the truth."

"She's the sweetest little thing," Sara said. "Maybe it'll be good for her to be here with Zoey and me."

"There's something about a woman."

"I'm glad for some male energy around here," Sara said. "For Harper's sake, that is."

They shared a smile.

And for a moment, David was filled with a sense of peace. For the first time since his wife died, he felt that maybe everything was going to be all right for him and his children after all.

AT THE OUTSIDE GRILL, David turned the chicken. Smoke wafted upward as the fat caught fire. Temperatures remained warm as the sun set over the ocean. They'd decided it was too nice not to eat outside. He'd offered to grill, and Sara had agreed.

Laine and Oliver were taking turns on the slide on the playground equipment. Sara was inside with Harper, preparing a side dish. He stole glances of her through the window. Barefoot and wearing a cotton dress, she moved about the kitchen with her usual gracefulness. She'd braided her hair, which hung down her back and emphasized her long neck.

He turned back to his chicken. The outside kitchen, which he and Trey had designed, was made of flat rock and granite. No detail had gone unnoticed, including the pizza oven that Sara had asked for. They'd done a great job creating a home that was both traditionally elegant but also one where a family would live. He'd think about that when he built his own home. After the year was up, he'd have the opportunity to do whatever he wished. He would definitely have a pool and an outdoor kitchen. Spending the afternoon here had convinced him of that.

The idea of financial freedom was intoxicating. To be without worries over money was still such a foreign concept. Sara had promised that after dinner they could get online and take care of all his bills. He'd finally be able to answer his phone without fear of it being a creditor.

Sara came out with the baby on her hip and set her inside a bouncy seat next to the table. "I'll be right back with the rest of dinner. How close is the chicken to being done?"

He stuck the thermometer into one of the thighs. "A few more minutes."

"Great. Keep watch on Harper for me?"

"Sure."

There wasn't much to do. Harper was safe in her chair and playing with the built-in toys. He was about to take the chicken off the grill when Sara returned with plates and silverware.

"How many more days will we have like this?" David asked.

"I'd say maybe one or two more weeks." Sara plucked Harper from her bouncy seat and put her in the high chair. "I love fall out here."

"I love the weather in general," he said. "Back home we have such harsh winters."

Sara looked out toward the ocean. The orange-and-pink sunset gave her a rosy glow. "Beautiful, isn't it?"

"I'd say so," he said, huskily. She was, too.

She called out to Laine and Oliver. "Come eat, guys." She tugged a sanitizer wipe from a packet on the counter. "You mind if I wash their hands this way?"

"Not at all. Saves a trip inside."

In minutes, she had them washed and sitting at the table. David cut up some chicken and green beans for Laine and set the plate in front of her. She stared at it for a second before picking up the child's fork and eating a bite of chicken.

She hardly ever ate meat. This was a good sign. Maybe she just needed to be physically worn out to tap into her hunger.

"I'm starved," Oliver said.

"You got a ton of exercise today," Sara said as she placed a piece of chicken on Oliver's plate and cut it into small pieces for him. "You'll need to eat these green beans, too."

"Why?" Oliver asked.

"You want to grow up tall and strong like your dad, right?"

"Yeah."

"Then you have to eat your vegetables. They work with the sunshine to make you grow," Sara said as she chopped up another piece of chicken.

Oliver picked up a green bean with his fingers and snapped off an end with his front teeth. "These are yummy."

"I put a special ingredient on them." Sara put the bits of chicken and some beans on Harper's tray.

"What is it?" Oliver asked.

"I can't tell you. Otherwise, it won't be a secret," Sara said.

"Oh, man. No fair." Oliver grinned. He ate another bean. "I like it here."

"I like having you here," Sara said.

"It's kind of like a family," he said. "Like at Dakota's house."

Dakota was Violet and Kyle Hicks's oldest child. Oliver worshipped him.

David glanced at Sara. Had she felt the same pang that had pierced his chest? *Kind of like a family.* Were they doing the wrong thing? Letting these children become lulled into the idea of a family unit when this was a business transaction?

"They have a pool too," Oliver said. "Have you ever been there?"

"I have. They have a wonderful pool."

"They have a slide on their pool." Oliver said this matter-of-factly. "I think we should get that."

"I'll take that under consideration." Sara smiled slyly at David. "I'll have to talk to my favorite architect about why we didn't think of a slide."

David laughed. "Terrible oversight. Unforgivable."

"Easily rectified." Sara sat between Oliver and Harper's high chair.

"What about you?" David asked Sara. "Would you like one or two pieces of chicken?"

"One breast, please."

David slid his spatula under a breast and laid it on one of the empty plates.

She thanked him as she scooped some beans next to her chicken. David helped himself to two thighs and some beans and sat next to Laine.

No one spoke as they ate. David devoured his chicken and went back for more. He'd just sliced into a third juicy piece when he heard a woman's scream.

"What was that?" he asked.

"It sounded like Zoey," Sara said. "Coming from the guest cottage."

He stood, ready to investigate. However, the sight of Zoey running across the yard stopped him.

Sara, clearly alarmed, stood as well.

Zoey was out of breath by the time she reached them. "My cottage is flooded. I think a pipe burst. I just got home from the beach. There's like two inches of water on the floor."

"I'll go shut off the water to the cottage," David said. He remembered it had a separate valve from the main house. He sprinted down the path and around the shrubbery to the cottage. The valve was around back, he was pretty sure. Yes, there it was. He knelt and turned it all the way off.

He was afraid to look. The cottage had been a fun and challenging project for him. Sara had asked for a cottage for staff that was away from the main house. He was proud of the way he'd utilized the seven-hundred-foot space.

He flung open the back door and gasped. There were at least four inches of water on the floor. The wood might be ruined. Furniture could be salvaged but would require reupholstering.

Sara came up behind him. "Oh no. It's a mess."

"I'll call Stone and have him send some guys out here to clean everything up. He can come out in the morning and tell what needs to be done. In the meantime, there's no way she can stay out here."

TESS THOMPSON

She stared at him with wide eyes. "Crap. That means she'll naturally assume the only available guest room is her temporary place."

His stomach turned as he realized the implication. If she didn't sleep out here, Zoey would be in the house. In his room. There was no way to hide.

"We'll have to pretend you're sleeping in my room," Sara said, slowly. "There's no way we can get away with you sleeping anywhere else if she's in the house."

"I can sleep on the floor." He spoke calmly and reasonably, as if he weren't in a complete panic. If he had to be in the same room with Sara, how would he keep these traitorous thoughts from raging out of control? Seeing her in her bed and not being able to touch her would be torture.

"Yeah, okay. I guess that's the only choice we have." Sara wrung her hands. "This is a disaster."

"I'll tell Stone to be quick about making this livable. Maybe it'll only be a week or two." Two weeks of pure hell.

His children might not be the only ones who left this situation wanting them to be a real family. A real marriage. One where he took this lovely woman into his bed and made her forget everything but the feel of his hands on her skin.

17

Sara

In the shower, Sara let the water wash over her as she processed this latest development. Zoey was in the house. She would expect them to act like newlyweds, which meant they had to be in the same room. This house was supposed to be their sanctuary from the lies, and now Zoey would be here, witnessing their every move. Pretending everywhere other than the house had seemed manageable. They could go to their separate bedrooms and have alone time. Now they'd be in the same room with no escape.

She stepped out of the shower and focused on her breathing. The important thing was not to panic. This was not a big deal. David would sleep on the floor. She would sleep on her king-size bed. Sharing a room like friendly roommates, just as she and Autumn had their freshman year in the dorms. Each in their own beds. Platonic as could be. They'd shared a hotel room last night. And anyway, Stone's crew would get the cottage fixed up in no time. All of this was temporary.

She dressed in a pair of cotton pajamas, then dried her hair. Before exiting the bathroom, she threw on her robe. Walking around braless in front of David would be awkward at best.

She drew in a deep breath and walked out of the bathroom. The dark hardwood floor felt cold on her bare feet. Bedside lamps cast a soft light. David had made a nest on the floor from blankets and a spare pillow. He sat on one of the green-and-yellow striped easy chairs hunched over his knees. His phone was on the floor near his feet as if it had dropped from his hands.

Something was wrong. "David?"

He straightened his posture and looked up at her. "They arrested someone in my wife's murder. I had a voice mail from the Feds."

She sat in the chair next to him. "That's great, right?"

"I guess so. They've known who was responsible all along, but they couldn't prove it. They must have gotten someone to talk in exchange for a lesser sentence or something."

"Will you have to do anything?"

"Probably not. Unless it comes to sentencing, in which case they'll want me to speak about how her death left two small children without a mother."

"I'm sorry." She placed a hand on the arm of his chair.

"It never seems to end." He sighed. "I just want it all to be over."

"I know. It will be, though."

He leaned his head against the back of the chair and looked up at the ceiling. "I never thought this would be my life. A widower at age thirty-four with two little kids."

She didn't say anything. What could she say, other than she knew exactly how he felt. But he already knew that.

"I don't think you should sleep on the floor." The words had tumbled from her mouth before she could think through the offer. "You won't get a good rest, and you seem so tired. The bed is huge. We can share it without touching."

He turned to face her. "Are you sure? I don't want you to feel uncomfortable."

"I'm sure. It'll only be for a few days."

David hung his head. His face was cast in shadow, making it hard to read his expression.

"David?" She touched his shoulder. "What is it?"

He met her gaze. "I'm not sure I can trust myself to be in your bed and not try something I shouldn't."

"But you don't feel that way about me."

"I'm not sure why that's a statement instead of a question," he said.

"Let me ask then. Are you attracted to me?" She held her breath as she studied her hands in her lap. Her stomach fluttered as she realized exactly how much she wanted to hear him say yes.

He gently pulled back her hair that fell over her face. "Look at me."

She lifted her face.

"I spent the afternoon watching you in a bathing suit. No single man alive would be able to think about anything but taking you to bed."

Her mind couldn't keep up with this conversation. He was attracted to her. It wasn't only her who felt the pull.

"I'm sorry," he said. "Have I scared you?"

"No, you didn't. It's just that I don't see myself that way. I stood in here this afternoon, dreading going down to the pool, so certain you'd be disgusted by me."

He startled her by standing. "Give me your hand."

She gave it to him, and he pulled her up. He led her over to the antique swing mirror that occupied a corner of the room. Standing behind her, he put his hands on her upper arms. "Look at yourself."

She lifted her eyes to stare at her own reflection. Her hair shone in the lamplight but without makeup, she looked plain and pale. The thin bathrobe did little to hide her figure.

He ran his hands down the length of her arms, then traveled to the tie wrapped around her waist. "May I?"

She nodded, unable to utter a word from her dry mouth. Her heart thumped in her chest. Could he hear?

Still behind her, he untied her robe. With his dexterous fingers he slipped the robe from her shoulders. It fell around her feet, leaving her practically naked. The bottom portion of her cotton pajamas came to mid-thigh of her long legs, and the tank top clung to her breasts.

"Do you see what I see?" David asked, gruffly.

"I don't know," she whispered. Totally shaken, she was as frozen as a scared animal.

His hands hovered just inches from her hips. She could almost feel them on her skin. "The way you're made is the perfect design. Do you see the way your waist curves in here and then the swell of your hips and those long, long legs? Do you see how beautiful they are? I can only imagine what they would feel like wrapped around me."

He made her buzz. She was under his spell. A desire, deep in her belly, burst into bloom. She wanted him to touch her. Possibly more than she'd ever wanted anything in her life.

"Do you see now?" David said, his mouth close to her ear.

"Not yet. Tell me more." Her voice sounded strange, husky and lustful. The voice of a temptress. A goddess. That's what she felt like standing here with this magnificent man behind her. What did she sound like to him?

"Can I touch you?"

"Yes," she whispered. "I want you to."

He took in a deep breath as he swept aside her hair with one hand and ran one long finger down her neck. "This neck of yours is a work of art." He brushed her earlobe with this thumb. "When God made you, he left no detail unchecked." His knuckles traced her jawline. "Do you see here—the angle of your chin, how it's perfectly rounded?" He moved to stand at her side. "Then there's your eyes. Can't you see how unique they are? How exquisite?"

"Just an ordinary green."

"No, not true. I once hiked ten miles up a mountain to see a lake famous for its green color. Yes, the green was as spectacular as promised. Yet here you are staring back at me and I can tell you with certainty that your eyes are prettier." The corners of his eyes crinkled as he smiled. "I'm fairly certain I'll drown in them if I'm not careful."

She ducked her chin, shy suddenly. A man had never spoken to her this way. She didn't know what to make of it. "You're a little too charming, Mr. Perry."

"You bring it out in me."

"What're we doing here?" She was on a precipice, teetering on the edge. One nudge and she'd fall. "Two lonely people stuck in a bedroom? Are we so weak?"

"Weak or opportunistic?" He raised one eyebrow as he drew closer.

She laughed and reached up to nudge him in the chest, but he caught her hand and brought it close to his heart.

"Your skin is as soft as I imagined."

"You've imagined it?" Sara breathed in his clean, spicy scent.

"More than you would believe."

"You never seemed to notice me. That's one reason I didn't like you, I suppose."

"You're intimidating as hell," he said. "Rich and drop-dead gorgeous. All my insecurities came roaring to the surface. When I'm insecure, I go quiet."

"You're not quiet right now."

"Desperate times call for desperate measures." He grinned, then quickly sobered. "Honest to God, you've gotten under my skin. I can't stop thinking about you."

Stunned, she grasped for the right thing to say. Words were elusive. The space between her ears was a white-noised chant. *Kiss me. Kiss me. Kiss me.*

"Sara, what do you want?"

"I want you to kiss me," she whispered.

She watched him in the mirror as his head dropped to her

shoulder. He planted a soft kiss on her skin. A quiver, as though she'd been shocked, coursed through her. He yanked her to him and kissed her on the mouth. She almost moaned with pleasure.

Somehow, they fell onto the bed. She hadn't realized they'd moved at all. More frenzied kissing. His hands went under her pajama bottoms and gripped her thighs.

"But doesn't this complicate everything?" She panted and arched her neck as he trailed kisses down her chest. Of course sex complicated things. Sex was what got her into the mess with her late husband. If she hadn't been so blissed out from orgasms, she might have seen what a lying cheat he was.

He raised his head to peer down at her. "If we're going to be trapped in this bedroom for tonight or however many nights, I can't keep my hands off you."

"What will this be then?"

"Does it have to have a name?" His thumb found her nipple.

Sara shuddered as desire shot through her like a bullet.

"Can't we just enjoy each other?" David asked. "We're married, after all."

"I don't want to get hurt."

"I'm not going to hurt you."

"You don't know that," she said.

"If we both go in with our eyes wide open, then it's all fine. We keep it casual. Friends with benefits."

"I'm not a casual type of person," she said.

"Listen, we have a unique opportunity to be a team this year. No reason why we can't enjoy each other in all ways. Neither of us wants a relationship ever again. But we can partner up as parents during the day and spend nights doing this. What's the harm? We're adults. If you think about it, we're perfect together. We've both been majorly burned and are raising these kids by ourselves. We're the best team ever."

"We are?"

"Yes, we are. There's no way we can hurt each other, because we're on the same page."

He was right. They were adults stuck in this strange circumstance. Why not enjoy their mutual attraction? A year from now they'd both be on their merry way.

"Do I need a condom?" David asked.

"I have an IUD. And I'm free of diseases. I had every test known to man after Brent died."

"I'm safe too." David pushed back her hair. "Yet another sign that we should do this."

She put her arms around his neck and brought him to her. Strangely, kissing him felt right, as if she'd done it hundreds of times already. "Why do I want it so badly?"

"You mean me?" He traced his thumb down her stomach.

She grabbed his hand. "Not there." She didn't want him to feel her C-section scar.

He shook his head. "No, that's not the way this is going to work." He looked into her eyes as his finger gently caressed her scar. "That right there is your warrior tattoo. You earned it. Be proud. Anyway, I think it makes you even hotter."

"You do not." She had to laugh. Or rather, giggle. Since when did she giggle like a girl?

He smiled as he lifted his head to look down on her. "Sara Ness, there isn't one inch of you that isn't sexy. I'm quite happy to spend the rest of the year exploring." He kissed her. "And not just with my hands."

You wicked man. Bring it on.

SARA COVERED her face with a damp arm and attempted to catch her breath. David Perry might be mild-mannered in life, but in bed he was a wild man.

He'd already left to use the restroom. The toilet flushed, followed by the sound of the tap turned on and off. Seconds later, he returned. They'd left the lamps on during their escapades because of his insistence that he wanted to see every inch of her.

She'd have preferred him to see a little less of her, but who was she to argue when it gave her so much pleasure to look at him? Talk about a well-designed person. David Perry was made just right.

Half the bedding had fallen to the floor. The rest was a twisted knot in the middle of the mattress. He straightened the sheets and pulled the comforter back into position. "Can I get you anything?"

"No, thank you." She turned on her side to gaze at him. He'd put his boxer shorts back on. She, on the other hand, had no idea where her pajamas were. "Do you see my jammies anywhere?"

He dipped under the mattress and came up with them. "Not that you should feel any pressure to put them back on."

She laughed as she sat up, conscious of the way her stomach wasn't flat like women on television. "If one of the kids needs us, it's probably best to be dressed."

"Good point." He turned off the lamp on his side of the bed.

Quickly as possible she pulled on the shorts and top. After turning off her light and sliding in the covers, she turned once more on her side. She could barely make him out in the darkness.

"Are you all right?" David asked.

"I don't know."

"It was undeniably great, right?"

"Yes. Undeniably," she said.

She felt the bed shift as he scooted closer. "Why do you sound so sad?"

"I don't know."

He stroked her hair. A tear slipped out of her left eye. She didn't want to cry. But it had been so long since anyone but the baby and an occasional hug from Autumn had touched her. She had an image of a ball of yarn unraveling. Layers of herself, too, had slipped away until here she was, naked and raw. No clothing could hide her from David. He saw right into her. "I'm discombobulated," she said.

"But it's just me. Your partner in crime."

She smiled as another tear slipped down her face. "Again, this is not a crime."

"I know. My only point is that we're in this together. I'm not going to hurt you." He kissed her forehead before pulling her close. Her hair spilled over his chest as she curled into the crook of his arm.

"You smell so good," he said.

"You smell pretty good yourself."

"Can I tell you a secret?" David asked.

"Sure."

"Other than my wife, you're the only woman I've ever been with."

She was glad for the dark just then, as her mouth dropped open in surprise. "Really?"

"We were together in high school. Even though I was tempted a few times during college, I never cheated on her."

"What did it feel like to be with me, then?" She had to ask. "Was it like visiting a foreign country?"

He didn't answer for a few seconds. She knew him well enough by now to know that he was mulling over the exact words in order to explain his feelings as precisely as possible. "It felt like the time I went to Italy and I thought it looked like California. Familiar but not at the same time. And mind-blowingly exciting."

She'd felt the same. In fact, he'd done things to her that her husband had never done. She was so inexperienced when she married that she didn't know much about how adventurous couples should or could be. They hadn't had sex that often. Of course, he was sleeping with her friend, so that might have satisfied his needs.

"Your body fits with mine," he said. "Not too tall or too short."

"Was she pretty? Your wife? What did she look like?"

"She was petite and cute. The girl-next-door type." His tone had flattened.

She wanted to ask if they'd been intimate up to the end. Or had her lies ruined any hope of sex? But she kept the questions to herself. It didn't take an emotional genius to know he didn't want to talk about her.

"Why do you want to know?" David asked.

She jerked in surprise. Perhaps he did want to talk about her? One could carry both desires at once. The need to be understood and the desire to forget the past. "I'm not sure. Natural curiosity, I guess."

"What did your husband look like?"

"He fancied himself an arty bohemian. Pretentious beret. That kind of thing."

"Nothing like me then, with my boring khakis and collared shirts?" David asked.

She chuckled. "The two of you are about as opposite as it's possible to be. For one thing, you're a real artist, and he just talked about being one."

"For the record, you're nothing like Marigold. Never in a million years would it have occurred to her to do something like this with no reward for herself."

"You mean the foundation?"

"Yes."

"One can only have so much money," Sara said. "I mean, what could I possibly buy with all that?"

"People buy islands and small countries," he said.

"I couldn't. Not when so many suffer."

"I don't get it. You were raised rich. How do you have a heart for the poor?"

"My mom and dad made sure I understood that not everyone was lucky like us. We spent a lot of time at soup kitchens and food banks. I can remember being very small and seeing this homeless lady digging through the trash. I don't know how anyone could see that and not be changed somehow."

"Maybe that was Marigold's problem. She never saw anything but our safe, middle-class world."

"You know what I want for us?" Sara asked.

"What's that?"

"I want to go out to dinner tomorrow and make it a point not to bring up either of our dearly departed."

"I think that's a great idea," he said, sounding sleepy.

She snuggled closer and shut her tired eyes. Tomorrow would come soon enough. For the first time in a long time, she looked forward to the rise of the sun.

David

David never claimed to be a smart man when it came to women. This time he'd really set himself up for a doozy of a mistake. *Sleeping with her? Really, man?*

At the same time, he wanted to tell himself to just shut up. Couldn't he just enjoy this thing with Sara? This thing? This affair. *Call it what it is,* he thought. An intense physical attraction to a woman he was supposed to be involved with only for financial reasons. *Way to muddy up the waters, buddy.*

"Hey, David, are you listening?" Stone asked.

David blinked. "Yes, sort of. I'm sorry, what did you ask me?" The Wolves were having their weekly meeting at the office, and he was supposed to be paying attention. Sunlight streamed through the large windows of their work space. Rafael had his laptop open, updating the project plan for The Oar. Next to David, Trey had a fabric sample book open but was looking at him expectantly. Stone sat on the other side of David, playing with his pencil like a baton in his giant hands. Nico stood at the end of the conference room table, leaning over his sketch for The Oar landscape.

"I asked if you heard back from the city council about the patio at The Oar," Stone said.

"Yes, we're all set," David answered. "They agreed to the extra square feet." Sophie had asked in the new design to have the back patio extend farther into what had once been grass. Other than teenagers making out on the grass, the area had gone unused. Open container laws made it so customers couldn't imbibe past the patio. Sophie wanted as much real estate as she could get.

"Great," Nico said. "Sophie will be pleased. And you know what that means for me."

"No one wants to know that." Trey threw an eraser at him. Nico caught it and tossed it back.

They spoke for an additional fifteen minutes about the project. Stone's crew had laid the foundation the day before and were going to begin building this afternoon.

Rafael shut his laptop. "David, did you have something you wanted to tell us?"

Obviously Lisa had told him about his nuptials.

"I do, yeah," David said.

The guys all looked at him. "What's up?" Stone asked. "Are you sick?"

"What, no. I'm not sick," David said. "Why would you ask that?"

"You look like crap," Stone asked. "Like you haven't slept for a few days."

"You're white as a ghost under that tan," Trey said.

"I'm...well, I'll just come right out with it. I married Sara Ness over the weekend." David placed his palms on the table. "That's all."

The guys stared at him. No one said a word or moved. It was as if they had suddenly frozen in the middle of a meeting.

Trey was the first to speak. "You got married? To Sara?"

"That's correct. We went to Vegas." His stomach churned. He

hated this. These guys were all so good to him, and here he was lying.

"But why? How?" Nico asked. "You two don't even like each other."

"I changed my mind." He spread his fingers wide and pressed into the tabletop. "We fell in love quickly. Which, you know, you've all done at one time or another."

"Holy crap," Stone said, shaking his head. "I did not see this coming."

"Why didn't you tell us?" Trey asked.

"It all happened so fast," David said. "Just a whirlwind type of thing."

Rafael was watching him with narrowed eyes. If anyone would see through him, it was Rafael. As a former cop, his superpower was reading people. He could spot a lie better than anyone. He'd also fallen in love with Lisa in less time it took for paint to dry. That would work to David's advantage.

"You know how it is," David said. "When you know, you know."

"But no wedding?" Trey asked. "Autumn and the other ladies are going to be devastated that you robbed them of a party planning opportunity."

"We didn't want to make a big fuss. This isn't our first rodeo, so to speak." David leaned back in his chair and placed his hands in his lap under the table.

"How are the kids doing?" Stone asked.

"They're good. Sara fixed up bedrooms for them." David scratched behind his neck. The room was too warm.

"Lisa wants to throw you guys a party." Rafael's tone was biting and clipped. "I hope you'll at least give her that."

Rafael was mad. David hadn't thought he'd care one way or the other. However, in hindsight, Rafael was protective of Lisa. She must have been hurt.

"Sure, yeah," David said. "Whatever she wants to do is fine with me. With us, that is."

"Are you sure you're okay?" Stone asked. "You're not all glowy like these two were when they got married." He gestured at Trey and Nico.

"Glowy?" Nico laughed. "I do not glow."

"Me either," Trey said.

"But he has a point," Rafael said. "You look like crap, and that sad quality in your eyes is still there."

"Did you do this for the money?" Stone asked. He flushed. "I'm sorry. I shouldn't have said that."

"You shouldn't have, no," David said, offended even though it was exactly what he was doing.

"But did you?" Rafael asked.

"How could you ask me that?" David asked.

"Because this is totally out of character for you," Stone said. "You take forever to decide what to order for lunch. Leaping into a marriage is just not you."

"How could I resist her?" David asked. Finally, something truthful. "She's gorgeous and smart."

"And rich," Rafael said.

"We have a prenup," David said. "The financial situation is covered."

"What's that mean?" Rafael asked. "Did she agree to an amount should you divorce?"

"No one would fault you for it," Stone said. "We've all been broke."

"I'd fault him for it," Rafael said. "Because of the kids. Is this the right thing for them, David? Have you asked yourself that?"

David flushed with heat. What the hell did Rafael know about his kids? Or any kids, for that matter. Men without children telling him what was right for his family had a lot of nerve. "My kids are my business. Until Sara, they were looking at life without a mother. Can you really sit there and tell me they'd be better off with only me to raise them?"

"You have Lisa and me," Rafael said. "If this was about money, we could've helped you."

David shot up from his chair. "You know that's not an option for me. I'm not taking money from my sister. I'm a man, if you haven't noticed."

Rafael, on the other end of the table, jumped to his feet and spoke through gritted teeth. "Family is different. We would've done anything for you and the kids. Marrying a woman you don't love was better than taking money from your sister?"

"You have no idea what you're talking about," David said.

"You can really look me in the eye and tell me you love her?" Rafael asked.

"I don't answer to you," David said. "Or to my sister. Despite what you two seem to think, I'm an adult perfectly capable of making my own decisions."

"We're family," Rafael said. "We take care of our own."

"This is how you take care of me?" David asked, shouting now. "By belittling me in front of our business partners?"

"Hey now, let's not get carried away," Stone said quietly. "Rafael, this isn't really our business."

"Right. I mean, we don't know what's happened between them." Nico smoothed his hands through his hair. "Stranger things have happened in this town than two people with a lot in common falling in love rather quickly."

"None of you have any right to question or judge me." David's volume was louder than he wanted, but he was pissed. Rafael had completely overstepped. "Rafael, you all fell in love in like two minutes. I didn't say crap to you about my sister when you two showed up in Iowa." They'd come for Marigold's funeral. Lisa had brought Rafael with her even though none of the family knew of his existence. To make matters worse, she'd dropped the ultimate bombshell. She planned to marry him after being together for three days.

"You were hardly in the position to think rationally," Rafael said. "Which is not the case now."

Trey, who had been quiet during the entire exchange, finally spoke. "If you're happy, we're happy. This just took us off guard.

We've always talked through everything together. I mean, we're more than business partners."

"You all talk through everything together," David said. "If you think about it, I keep to myself. No offense, but none of you get it." He cracked one of his knuckles as it occurred to him that there were certainly many things he didn't have to lie about. Sara understood his situation better than any of the men around this table. "You know what? Sara gets it. She gets me. I'm sorry if I didn't think to share my innermost personal thoughts during one of our coffee klatches."

Nico barked out a laugh. "Dude, easy now. They're more like beer klatches."

Stone grinned. "I like the sound of that. Gossip and beer."

David knew what Nico and Stone were trying to do. Make peace. However, right now he wanted to punch Rafael in the face.

"How about we call it quitting time," Trey said, obviously on the side of peace, "and head out to the brewery for some beers?"

"I don't think that's a good idea," David said. "I promised Sara I'd be there when she gets home. She was going to tell Autumn we got married. She's worried it'll go about as well as it did here. I want to be there in case she's upset."

Stone slapped the table. "Well, if that doesn't sound like a man in love, I don't know what does. And if you remember, I'm kind of an expert."

"Landing Pepper doesn't make you an expert," Nico said, "but simply damn lucky."

"Amen," Stone said. "And right back at you."

"No truer statement," Nico said.

Trey started gathering up his sample books. "Speaking of lucky, I should get home too. In case Autumn is upset."

"Do you think she will be?" David asked. He hated to think of sweet Autumn mad at him.

Trey grimaced. "I'm thinking so. She won't like it that she didn't know about you until now."

Rafael had wandered over to the window. David packed up his laptop and walked out without another word. If his brother-in-law wanted to be on good terms again, an apology would have to come out of his judgmental mouth. Screw him. This was his life. No one got to tell him what to do.

DAVID TOOK the stairs up to his former apartment two at a time. An urgency to return to Sara's surprised him. However, he needed to check on his dad first. He hadn't talked to him since his return from Vegas.

He used his key to open the door. The apartment was quiet. And clean. No toys strewn about. No more bedding on the couch.

"Dad, you here?"

"In here," Dad's voice called out from the kitchen.

David crossed the front room to the kitchen. Dad was at the counter with his hands in a bowl of ground beef.

"I'm making meat loaf," Dad said. "I have a date with Ria."

"When did you learn how to make meat loaf?"

"Since now." Using his chin, he gestured to the open cookbook next to the bowl. "Turns out there's these tools for cooking called recipes. All one has to do is read and follow instructions. Your mother always made it seem so complicated."

"Mom likes control and admiration." David left it at that. He didn't want to make a habit of bashing his mother. She wasn't perfect, but she'd done her best to give them all a good life.

"How are things with you?" Dad asked. "Did you do it? I don't see a ring on that finger."

"We did it. Rings will come later."

"I've been alive almost sixty years. Nothing, other than Marigold's alternative career, has surprised me more than your announcement about Sara. I thought you might back out, but it looks like you didn't."

"It's a good thing, Dad. I promise."

"How's the sex?"

"Um, Dad. I can't believe you just asked me that."

"It's important. Everyone's always talking about how important it is to be friends with your spouse because sex fades away. That might be true, but as a man deprived of it most of his marriage, I can tell you a woman's willingness to participate in a few nightly escapades is meaningful."

Again, a moment when he could tell the truth. "The sex is mind-blowing."

"That's my boy." Dad beamed at him before returning to his ground beef.

"How come you never asked me that?" Lisa said from the doorway.

Both David and Dad jumped.

"Jesus, how long have you been standing there?" David asked.

"Not long," Lisa said.

"Why are you here, honey?" Dad asked. "Checking on me again?" He turned to David. "She checked on me twice yesterday."

"I'm just concerned you're lonely," Lisa said. "You've never lived alone."

"He has a date tonight," David said. "I'm not sure he's too lonely."

Dad grinned as he patted the meat into a loaf pan. "I've been decidedly not lonely."

Lisa flushed. "For heaven's sake. Is that all men think about?"

"Sometimes we think about food," David said.

"And beer," Dad said.

"You two are in good moods," Lisa said. "Maybe having women in your lives is just what you needed to stop moping around like a couple of Eeyores."

"Listen, Piglet, you don't have the monopoly on being in love," Dad said.

"You're in love with Ria?" Lisa's eyes widened. "Like for real?"

"I'd say so, yes." Dad went to the sink to wash his hands.

"How serious are you two?" Lisa asked. "Because if you announce a sudden wedding I'm going to lose my mind."

"I'm serious about her," Dad said. "How she feels about me is still uncertain."

"Why?" David asked.

"She's reticent," Dad said. "Maybe a little afraid to trust. She's not had the best experience with men, including the one who left her alone with a little boy to raise."

"We'll talk more about this later." Lisa pantomimed putting a pin in a board, then turned to David. "So you really did go through with it?"

"I did."

Lisa raised an eyebrow. "Okay then, let's plan on a party at our house Saturday night. I'll invite the whole gang."

"I'm not sure it's a good idea," David said.

"You promised me," Lisa said.

"Your husband's not happy with me," David said. "We got into it at the office."

"About what?"

"He basically accused me in front of the other Wolves of marrying for the money and said if I needed money so badly, why didn't I just take you up on your offer to bail me out of debt. Oh, and that I'm a terrible father for putting my children through this."

Lisa had paled. She sank into one of the kitchen chairs. "I can't believe that."

"He was a total jerk, if you want to know the truth," David said. "The other guys handled it well, but he made me feel like crap. And I lost my temper."

"I'm sure you did," Lisa said.

"The whole thing was completely embarrassing," David said.

"He feels protective of you," Dad said. "He's worried you've made a mistake. Sometimes with men, it comes out as accusatory when he's simply concerned."

"Regardless, that was completely out of line. I'll talk to him. He owes you an apology." Lisa tented her hands and pressed them between her knees. "I've never seen him be anything but kind. I wonder what got into him?"

David shrugged as he leaned against the counter. "It's okay, really. I'm sure it's like Dad said. He's just concerned about the kids."

"I think he's hurt you didn't tell him yourself," Lisa said. "He's come to think of all you guys as family."

"I could tell Trey was bummed too," David said. He'd hidden it better, but he'd been hurt. His silence spoke louder than words.

"How'd the other guys respond?" Lisa asked.

"You know how Nico and Stone are. So easygoing and empathetic," David said. "They allow more room for error than Rafael and Trey."

Lisa stood as she tucked her blond waves behind her ears. "I'm going home to talk to him. He will make this right before Saturday night."

She kissed each of them on the cheek and strode out of the kitchen. When the front door closed, David turned to Dad. "Now I've created problems between them. I should've kept my mouth shut."

"Nah. She'll straighten him out, and you'll get your apology."

The oven beeped, indicating it had risen to the right temperature. Dad opened the door and plopped the meat loaf on the second rack. "You know, son, I've been thinking. One of the challenges you're going to face is exactly what happened today. People, not just family, are always going to wonder if you married her for the money. You have to learn to let it go.

Water off a duck's back. Not everyone is as purehearted as you."

"I don't know how anyone could look at her and not know exactly why I fell in love with her," David said. "She's stunning, smart, articulate, and a great mother. She's generous and down-to-earth, despite how wealthy she is."

His dad's eyes twinkled at him. "Well, you don't have to convince me. I can see plain as day you're in love with her. I couldn't be more delighted for you. She's going to be the best thing that ever happened to you and my grandchildren." Dad patted him on the shoulder. "If you don't mind a little advice from your old man, make sure she knows how you feel every single day. Little things like coffee in bed, a bouquet of flowers for no reason, loading the dishwasher. She's been through hell and back. She deserves you showing up for her. Being present. Do you understand what I mean?"

"Are you saying I wasn't for Marigold?"

"I was speaking about myself and your mother. You're the only one who knows what kind of husband you were."

David gazed up at the ceiling. "I worked hard to provide for her."

"That's not the same as being present."

Had he been checked out with Marigold? All he could remember was feeling a deep fatigue. The days were an endless exercise in survival. "After the kids came, I was tired, Dad. And the way she spent money. I couldn't work hard enough to keep up. I failed her, probably. The last thing I could be was present, vacillating between stress and fear. All in all, I was pretty much failing everything."

"You're being too hard on yourself," Dad said. "Life has a way of beating a man down."

"Is that how you felt?"

"Sure. And when I wasn't beating myself up, your mother was sure to remind me what a failure I was. Do you know the worst part of all? I taught you how to do the exact same thing in your marriage. This is your chance for a fresh start with a wonderful woman. Maybe this time around, we'll have a fighting chance."

"I hope so." In that moment, David forgot that his marriage was fake. He thought about how much Sara had endured and that he would help make up for all she had lost by being good to her. Cherishing her. Loving her.

Then the truth came flooding back. That was the job for a man she loved. Not a business transaction.

Where did that leave him? Falling for a woman who couldn't possibly love him?

God, I'm in trouble, he thought. *I'm falling for her.*

Sara

At a table by the window at Dog's Brewery, Sara watched Autumn butter a piece of bread. For the last five minutes, she'd tried to come up with the words to tell her best friend that she'd married David. The confession had to be today, or Autumn would hear it from someone else. David was telling the Wolves probably at this very minute. They'd all go home and tell their wives. The news would be around town in the time it took to order a coffee.

Sara poured a packet of sugar-free sweetener into her glass of iced tea and stirred slowly, searching for the right phrase and tone.

"What's going on with you?" Autumn asked. "You've barely said two words since we got here."

"I have news."

"News?" Autumn's perfectly plucked eyebrows raised. "What kind of news?"

"It's big news, so prepare yourself for a shock."

Autumn set aside her buttered bread. "Are you all right? Please don't tell me you're sick."

"No, no. Nothing like that. I got married over the weekend."

"Very funny." Autumn rolled her eyes. "What is it really?"

"That's the truth. I'm in love with David Perry, and we got married. In Vegas." Not that Vegas was an important detail.

"What's gotten into you?" Autumn frowned. "This isn't funny. Now I'm getting irritated. Just tell me what's going on."

"I'm telling you. David and I are married. He and the kids have moved in."

Other than a tiny quiver in her eyes, Autumn didn't move for at least five seconds. "Oh my God, you're serious."

"Yes, I'm serious."

"Why would you do this and not tell me?" Her voice shook. She sat back in her chair and stared at her with wide eyes.

"It was spontaneous." Under the table, Sara clasped her hands together.

"You flew to Vegas and married a person you barely know? Are you out of your mind?" Autumn's voice had raised in volume. Several people from other tables glanced over at them.

"Can you lower your voice, please?" Sara asked. "I do know him. We've gotten close. Over the last few…" What could she say? Not weeks. Not even days. She'd just had lunch with Autumn where she'd declared herself single for life.

"No, you haven't. I know that's a lie." Autumn crossed her arms over her chest. "What the hell is going on here?"

"The marriage happened. Legally and everything," Sara said.

"You haven't gotten close to him. Last time I checked, you didn't like him."

"I changed my mind," Sara said. "This is a great thing for me. For all of us. The kids need a mother and father." She inwardly cringed. This was true. They did need a family unit. What happened to them when they ended it? Next, a twinge of pain. She didn't know if she wanted it to end. After last night, she couldn't be certain their plan had been a good one. All day she'd replayed their night in her head. The way he'd touched her had brought her back to life. How could she ever let him go now that she knew what it felt like to fall asleep next to him? What had he said? *We fit together.*

"I can't believe this." Autumn's gaze darted to Sara's hand. "Where's the ring?"

"We haven't gotten it yet."

"So walk me through this." She spoke quietly, leaning over her bread plate as if she wanted to reach across the table and give Sara's hair a good yank. "You're just talking after your support meeting one night and you're like, 'Hey, it would be good for our kids if we got married.' And he agreed and off you go to Vegas." Her tone had gotten progressively sharper and louder until she was practically shouting.

"Not so loud." Sara glanced at the tables near them, occupied by a couple with a baby and another with a group of women. They quickly looked away when they saw her glancing in their direction. She'd had enough scandal back in her old life. Enough for a lifetime. Cliffside Bay was supposed to be her fresh start. A place where no one knew she was the heiress of a beer company.

"Sorry," Autumn said. "But I can't figure out what's going on here. You tell me things. I was the first person you called when everything happened. How could you not tell me this?"

Tell the story. Convince your best friend that you fell madly and deeply in love.

"We wanted to keep it for ourselves for a few days, that's all," Sara said. "We didn't want anyone telling us not to do it."

"I suppose I would have," Autumn said. "Because it's insane."

"In a town full of romantics, it's hardly the craziest thing that's ever happened between two people. Anyway, it's done. Can't you just be happy for me?"

"Did you get a prenup?"

"He's not after the money," Sara said. "That was my first husband, remember?"

"Do I need to repeat the question?"

"Yes, we got a prenup. My fortune is safe from any nefarious plans." She said the last part in a dramatic voice, then smiled to lighten the mood. It had little effect. Gentle, sweet Autumn looked as if she were about to burst into tears.

"I can't believe this," Autumn said in a dazed voice. "I don't even know what to say."

"You really like him, though. You've told me that how many times. Can't you admit that he'll be good for me and Harper?"

"How did it happen?"

She drew on the truth for the answer. "That first night at the support meeting, he gave me a look after my embarrassing tirade and everything changed."

"What kind of look?"

"It was just a nod, but his eyes told me everything. He understood. That's the thing, Autumn, we have so much in common. The trauma of our spouses being murdered. Raising these babies by ourselves while trying to work through what the hell happened to our lives. No one can understand that like him."

"You're basing a marriage on the fact that your spouses were murdered? That's not enough."

"There are other things, too," Sara said. "Like hot sex, for example."

Autumn let out a long, shaky sigh. "Is that supposed to make me feel better? You barely know him, but the sex is hot so what could possibly go wrong?"

"I'm sorry this has come as a shock to you," Sara said, doing her best to keep her temper in check. "I can understand how that might feel like a betrayal, and I know that's a trigger for you. However, this is my life. I've done what I think is best for Harper and me."

"You said you'd never bring a man into her life. No one was good enough. Do you remember that?"

Sara flushed. "I know I said that, but that was before David swept me off my feet."

They were interrupted by Sophie, who had their salads in hand. Tall and blonde, she reminded Sara of a human Barbie. If she weren't so relentlessly cheerful and kind, Sara might have hated her. No one could hate Sophie. Not even bitter, jealous women like Sara.

"Hi, ladies," Sophie said. "It's great to see you. I have your two salads."

"What are you doing here?" Autumn asked. "I thought you'd be down at the work site."

Sophie set both salads down in front of them with one fluid motion, as if she were in a choreographed dance. "Zane and Honor took the kids up to Stoweaway to shop for some school clothes for Jubie. I was only too happy to fill in for him. Waiting for The Oar to open back up is killing me. I just get in the way when I'm down there."

"Trey said they're done pouring the foundation, right?" Autumn asked.

"Yes. And Stone assured me his crew will get it built before the first rains," Sophie said. "But that's not the only big news of the day. Nico just texted me about you and David." She smiled, flashing those perfect teeth. "I'm so, so happy for you guys."

Finally. Someone was happy for them. Leave it to Sophie to be the one.

"How did he find out?" Autumn asked, with a little squeak in her voice. The jealous voice.

"David told them at their partner meeting just now." Sophie bounced on the balls of her feet. "I love David so much, and this makes my heart ache with happiness." Her high ponytail swung back and forth. She looked about sixteen. "And the kids. You'll be such a help to each other and make such a wonderful family. Even though we're not married yet, I know how you're feeling right now. Isn't it just the best thing in the whole world?"

Sara smiled, unable to resist Sophie's enthusiasm. "It's pretty great, yes."

"Especially after what you two went through. Now this? Isn't it amazing all the twists and turns in this life?"

"It is," Sara said.

"We need to celebrate," Sophie said. "A party or something."

"Lisa is throwing something at their house on Saturday," Sara said. "All the Wolves are invited, obviously."

"Lisa knew about your marriage?" Autumn's eyes flashed with temper. "As in before today?"

"They're twins. They tell each other everything," Sara said.

"You know what, I'm not hungry any longer." Autumn rose abruptly from the table.

"Please, don't go," Sara said.

But it was too late. Autumn had already stalked away, fast despite her slight limp.

"Sorry about that," Sara said. "I just told her about David. She didn't take the news well."

"She's hurt because she didn't know about it first," Sophie said. "As close as you two are, I guess I can understand that."

"It was such a whirlwind. We got caught up in the moment."

"I get that. Nico and I were the same way in Paris. If we'd been able to, I'm sure we would've gotten married right then."

"But you didn't, which means no one's mad at you."

"My parents would've been really sad, not to mention Zane. He can be a little overprotective."

Sara's invitation to Sophie and Nico's wedding had come last week. She'd sent a reply right away. No plus-one. How much difference a week made.

"Don't worry," Sophie said. "She'll come around. You've been best friends for too long to make this a permanent riff. Once she gets over her own feelings, she'll realize what a miracle it is you two found each other."

"Thanks, Sophie." Sara sucked in her cheeks and willed herself not to cry.

"I guess this means we'll have to change the seating chart up a bit," Sophie said. "You and David will be seated together."

"I'm sorry to cause you more work."

"It's no problem. My mom's doing it all, and she loves every minute." Sophie brushed Sara's shoulder. "I'm truly so delighted for you. David's always had a special place in my heart. And those little ones of his are sweet as can be. I'm glad you're a team now."

After Sophie left to take care of another customer, Sara picked at her salad and thought about her next move. She hadn't thought Autumn would take it this badly. In hindsight, given Autumn's abandonment issues, she should've seen it coming. Somehow, she'd have to make it up to her.

Sara caught a glimpse of herself in the mirror that hung on the wall across from her table. The face of a liar. Never in her life had she lied to anyone, let alone her best friend.

Remember why you're doing this, she reminded herself. *So much good will come from this lie.* That made it all right, surely?

"AND THEN SHE stormed out of Dog's." Sara tossed slices of cucumber into the salad bowl before turning back to David.

He stirred a pot of sauce on the stove and nodded sympathetically. "I didn't fare much better with the Wolves."

"What happened?" She reached into the wine refrigerator and pulled out a chardonnay. "First, wine?"

"Great, thanks."

The sounds of the kids playing chase on the lawn came through the open window. Zoey had offered to watch them while they made dinner.

As she opened the bottle and poured glasses, David recounted his experience. "Everyone was shocked, of course. But Rafael already knew because of Lisa."

"Right. We figured."

"Yeah, so he'd already had a few days to get really pissed. He basically called me out for jeopardizing the kids' mental health and accused me of marrying you for the money."

"Well, technically that's true, but still, how rude." Sara smiled at him. "Yeah, we don't really have a moral ground to stand on here." He laughed as he lifted the glass of wine to his mouth and took a sip.

Her stomach did a happy dance when he laughed. "I felt really bad about Autumn."

"Yeah, at first I was angry at Rafael made me angry. After I calmed down, I felt bad."

"He pushed just the right button bringing up the kids," Sara said. "The one aspect of this that's been dicey for you, which is why it bothered you."

"That's right." He dropped his gaze from her and turned the knob on the cooktop down to simmer. "We're doing the right thing. For all of us. It's really no one else's business." He crossed his arms and leaned against the sink. This was the way he stood when he was worried about something. She'd noticed it several times over the last few days. It was as if crossing his arms over his heart protected him.

"This is going to give you financial freedom, which means you can do so much for your kids," Sara said. "It's a year in their lives they won't even remember."

David uncurled his arms and gripped the edge of the island. His head bent downward, which shifted his wavy hair over his forehead.

"What is it?" Sara went around the island and placed her hand on his shoulder.

He flinched at her touch, then straightened, before pulling her hard against him. "I'm not sure I'm going to be okay."

"How do you mean?" She drew in a deep breath in response to his strong frame.

"I mean, I'm not sure how I'm going to feel after spending a year with you." He stroked the side of her face with his knuckles. "Last night kind of rocked me. I'm not sure what to do about it."

"I thought we had a plan," she said, hoarsely. "Partners during the day; fun at night."

He traced her bottom lip with his thumb. "I thought about

you all day. All damn day. Imagining what I want to do to you tonight."

"There's more than what you did last night?" She tucked a hand into the back pocket of his jeans and looked up at him. *I'm flirting*, she thought. Screw it. Why not? This man wanted her, and she wanted him. If the children hadn't been outside, she would have let him take her right there on the kitchen island.

"Every inch of you, inside and out, intrigues me. I want to know everything you think and your memories and dreams and worries. I want to explore every inch of your body at night and talk to you all day. Any man who gets to spend time in your life, in your home, and your bed should know what a privilege it is. You better believe I do. You're not a woman I'm going to be able to let go of easily. That scares the hell out of me."

She sobered as the weight of what he said sank into her consciousness. Her chest ached. "David, I've never had anyone talk to me the way you do." She placed her hand on his chest. "My first instinct is that I'm not worthy."

He kissed her softly on the mouth. "Trust me, you are. I have exquisite taste in all things."

"I'm scared too. I'm scared to get used to this, to you, and then have to watch you walk out of my life."

"What do we do?" He looked into her eyes, without any camouflage, as if it was his very soul staring into hers.

"We take it one day at a time," she said slowly. "Like we have for the past year. All the time fighting through the pain and regret and anger just to stay alive for our kids. Only now, maybe finally, it's our turn to laugh and do normal, wonderful things like cooking dinner together. Do you think it's possible that there's something real here?"

"I think it's possible," he whispered. "But I keep wondering when I'm going to wake up from this dream."

"I'm real. This is real." She took her hand from his back pocket and wrapped both arms around his waist. With her cheek resting against his chest, she listened to his heart beating and knew that he, too, was real. "We're alive. They didn't kill us, after all."

He lifted her up to the island. She gripped him with both legs and let him kiss her.

Yes, I'm alive.

David
David drove straight from work for the third support group meeting. He'd spent the day at the office working on the plans for Crystal Whalen's new home. The rest of the Wolves had not appeared. He wasn't sure if they were avoiding him or if they were simply busy elsewhere. Other than business correspondence, Rafael had been silent. Lisa must not have convinced him to apologize after all. David was past anger and now just really missed his brother-in-law.

Sara had already arrived by the time he got there, chatting with Zane by the coffeemaker. As it had that morning when she'd come down for breakfast in her swimsuit, his stomach fluttered. He had it bad. The more time he spent with her, the worse it got. All day, he'd thought about her. Their second night in her bed had been as satisfying as the first. Maybe even more so, because they were growing closer emotionally.

He hadn't meant to admit that he was falling for her. The words had jumped out of his mouth. Her response had eased his mind somewhat. At least he wasn't the only one feeling things.

She waved to him as he crossed the room. They'd agreed that

most everyone in town knew about their marriage and that it wouldn't have to be revealed to the group.

"Hi there," David said as he leaned in to kiss her cheek. "Zane, how are you?"

"I'm good. Thanks. Congratulations, man." Zane held out his hand, and the men shook. "Good job. You've got a keeper with this one."

"Thanks. You don't have to tell me," David said. "I know."

"Zane was just saying it's all over town that we eloped," Sara said.

"This is Cliffside Bay," Zane said. "Not much stays a secret for long."

"True enough," Sara said.

"Lisa sent a note to Honor and me this morning about Saturday's party," Zane said. "We're both excited to help you celebrate."

"My sister and Pepper know how to throw a party," David said. "It will most likely be epic."

"It's not a party unless someone falls in the pool, right?" Zane asked.

Ria called out that it was time to start. Judi and Bobby were already seated, talking quietly with their heads together. Bobby's chair was kind of close to hers. Interesting. Were they a love match like him and Sara?

Love match? Was that what this was between them? Or were they simply hot for each other? There was a difference, wasn't there? Just because people lit each other up didn't meant they were a match.

He and Sara took seats next to each other. Zane sat on the other side of the circle by Judi.

"Who would like to start this week?" Ria said. "I'm interested to hear how your assignments went." She patted her notebook. "I have them written down in here, so don't think you can wriggle out of telling us if you did them or not."

David raised his hand.

"Yes, please, go," Ria said.

"This isn't about my art, but I have something else I want to share. In case anyone here hasn't heard, Sara and I married," David said.

"This wouldn't be Cliffside Bay if we hadn't already heard," Judi said. "I didn't know you two were dating."

"It was whirlwind," Sara said.

"This group helped us realize our feelings for each other," David said. He hadn't thought of this persuasive argument until just now, but it sounded legitimate.

Ria's brows had knit together. She was worried, David thought. There was probably some rule about how long you were supposed to wait to get remarried after your spouse's death.

"I think it's groovy," Bobby said. "Young love. Nothing better."

"I agree." Judi beamed at them. "And how wonderful for your children."

A twinge of guilt accosted him. *So good for them. Until they split up.*

"I don't like to be that guy, but I did tell you there was life after loss," Zane said.

Sara smiled, remembering how skeptical she'd been. "You did say that, didn't you? I'd forgotten."

"My sister's throwing us a party on Saturday night," David said. "And you're all invited."

"How wonderful," Judi said. "I'll be there."

"I'll escort you," Bobby said. "If you'd like."

"What a grand idea," Judi said.

Ria gave a small nod. "Your father and I will be there, of course."

"Now, wait just a minute," Judi said. "Are you and David's dad an item?"

Ria, despite her dark complexion, flushed pink. "Yes, that's correct. It's not a secret anymore. Now that the kids know."

"Well, butter my butt and call me a biscuit," Judi said.

"We should probably get back to the reason we're here," Ria said. "Who else would like to share?"

Judi raised her hand. "I'll go next. Bobby and I had a fantastic night. I hired a car and we went to a fancy steak place. We had martinis and oysters on the half shell and steaks smothered in garlic butter. I had a splendid time. There were whole segments of time where I forgot I'm old as the hills."

Bobby hadn't stopped smiling as she'd described their evening. "We had a good time."

"Having a new friend to share a meal with was just what this old goat needed," Judi said.

"And you, Bobby?" Ria asked. "Have you surfed since we saw you last?"

"Four mornings last week," Bobby said. "Thanks to Zane."

"I love seeing you out there," Zane said.

"Young Dr. Waller joined us, too," Bobby said. "I felt like one of the gang."

"Good to hear," Ria said before turning to Zane. "Did you take a drive over the weekend?"

"I did, but not like you suggested," Zane said. "I didn't take my family. I decided for this first time that I should go alone. During the drive, I played all my dad's favorite songs." He folded his hands in his lap. "I let myself think about him and miss him. I stopped at his favorite lookout along the way. Then I drove to the pier where we used to fish and watched a man with his son. I cried but also smiled, remembering how much he enjoyed the smallest, simplest things in life. I realized something that I wanted to tell you guys. Part of my grief has to do with how the last few years of his life he was here but not really. The dementia took him from me years before he physically left. I never got to tell him all the stuff I should have. How much I loved him and admired him."

"He knew," Ria said. "Parents always know even if you don't say the words."

"Did you feel better after the drive?" Judi asked.

"Not really, no," Zane said. "But I realized the only way through this is to face my grief. Feel the pain. Mourn the loss. I've made myself busy so that I didn't have to think about him. As usual, my wife was right. Keeping all that inside me was a time bomb. I don't want to be the kind of man who buries everything inside. Not for my kids. Not for Honor. But I can't lie. Facing this crap is hard work."

"I'm proud of you," Judi said. "I understand how tempting it is to just keep moving, doing, building. But you're right. The grief is there no matter how fast you run on this treadmill of a life."

"Yes ma'am," Zane said.

"How does it feel to see your father's bar in the beginning stages of resurrection?" Sara asked.

Zane ran a hand through his hair. "That's a great question. Emotional, for sure. But also nervous that seeing Sophie's vision of The Oar is going to hurt. She has her own ideas of what she wanted, and I as much as I support her, not ever seeing it again as it was…well, it's just a symbol of my dad. I'll leave it at that."

"Fair enough," Ria said.

"Have you seen the plans?" Sara asked.

Zane shook his head. "I didn't trust myself not to say something and hurt Sophie's feelings or poke holes into her dream. I gave her the bar to do with what she wanted. It's not fair for me to try to influence her."

"The design I came up with pays homage to the original," David said. Sophie had made sure every detail honored the past. "Maybe it'll seem like the perfect merging of old and new. Sophie and your dad."

"I like that idea," Zane said. "Thanks for saying that, man."

"What about you, Sara?" Ria asked. "Did you have a chance to write this week?"

"Things have been a little busy at the house, you know, with everything," Sara said. "There hasn't been a lot of time.

However, I have written a few journal entries about things from the past."

"Has that helped?" Ria asked.

"It has, actually," Sara said. "I'd forgotten that writing used to help me work through things. Make decisions."

David watched her, proud. What a courageous person she was.

"Good for you," Bobby said.

"Thanks. It's a small step, at least," Sara said.

"And you, David?" Ria asked.

David smiled, thinking of the thoughtful gift Sara had brought him less than a week ago. It seemed like a lifetime. "I haven't done a thing. Like Sara said, it's been a lot moving in with Sara and getting adjusted."

"Can you find time in your schedule this week?" Ria asked. "Just to dabble. There's no pressure to paint the next *Mona Lisa*."

"Yeah, I can." He glanced at Sara as his chest surged with gratitude and affection. "Thanks to Sara, I have a few moments to myself these days. Having support has been life-altering. In a good way."

"I'm sensing less anger from both of you," Ria said. "Is that true?"

They exchanged a look. David stifled a laugh. Nothing like hot sex every night to take the edge off.

Sara leaned over her knees. "I haven't thought about my late husband once today." She shook her head, as if in disbelief. "Isn't that strange?"

"You've been joyful," Judi said. "Spending time with your new love. No time to think about that bastard."

"Why does it concern you?" Ria asked.

"I don't know, really," Sara said. "It's not like he deserves my attention. I understand that part. But my anger fueled me. Kept me from crumbling. I've been angry for so long that I'm not even sure who I am without it."

"You're you," Zane said. "You weren't made to be angry.

We're made to love, not hate. Take it from me, holding on to the past means you can't live in the present. I'm the most stubborn idiot in the world. I was determined to hold on to my anger after my fiancée called off the wedding. Once I forgave her and myself, I was able to see that Honor was right there, waiting for me to notice her."

David swallowed a lump in his throat. Was it possible that he and Sara had a chance? After all the crap they went through, could they have a happy ending? Together?

"Am I supposed to forgive him?" Sara asked. "Is that the only way to move forward? Because I don't want to."

"Forgiving him means you're free," Judi said. "There's a difference between forgiveness and forgetting."

"You won't forget," Zane said. "Forgiving him is for you. The only one the anger is hurting right now is you. He's gone."

"I'm here," Sara said softly. "I get another chance to have the life I want."

"That's right, sugar," Judi said. "And living well is the best revenge."

"You're both young," Bobby said, gesturing toward Sara and David. "You have your whole lives ahead of you. When I think of how many memories you still have to make, I'm envious. Don't waste one more minute in the past."

"Bobby, you're not as young as these two," Ria said. "But is it possible that you too might have more memories to make in this new chapter of your life?"

Bobby blinked a few times. "I guess I do."

"We're old goats," Judi said. "But we're not dead yet."

"That's right," Ria said. "As we know with each passing day, life is short. Our only goal should be to live each day as fully as we can. Tell people how we feel before it's too late. Take a chance on love by trusting."

David had the feeling that Ria might be speaking to herself as well as the others around the circle. Would she decide to trust his dad? He hoped so, for both their sakes.

What about him? Could he make the choice to trust Sara, to love her? Was this his second chance?

He glanced over at Sara. She met his gaze. He took her hand and brought it to rest in his lap. She shifted in her chair to sit closer to him, until their shoulders melted together. This woman might be the passageway to the rest of his life. Only time would tell if they were brave enough to try again.

BY THE TIME David pulled into the driveway, the hour approached the kids' bedtime. He'd stopped at the store to buy a bouquet of flowers for Sara. They weren't as fresh as they'd probably been that morning when the flower guy arranged them in buckets on the sidewalk, but they were beautiful just the same. When he entered through the front door, Laine and Oliver rushed toward him.

"Daddy's home," Oliver shouted.

He set the bouquet on the side table in the foyer. He knelt on his knees and opened his arms.

Laine and Oliver hurled themselves into his embrace. They were already in their pajamas and smelled of shampoo and baby powder. "Did you already have your baths?"

"Yep," Oliver said. "Zoey said we should be clean for when Daddy came home."

"I'm glad, because now we'll have time for a book before bed." David hauled Laine up with him as he rose from the floor. Oliver took his free hand.

Sara appeared with Harper perched on her hip. "There you are. I was starting to worry."

"I stopped by the market to get you these." He picked up the bouquet from the table. "Every woman should have a bouquet of flowers once in a while."

Her face went blank for a split second, as if he'd said something in a foreign language. Soon, however, she rewarded him

189

with a dazzling smile. "How sweet. Thank you. I'll put them in a vase after I get Harper down."

"I'm going upstairs to read to these two rascals," David said.

They all headed into the great room.

"I had Zoey thaw some steaks," Sara said. "For our dinner."

His stomach growled as he followed her up the stairs. "I'm starving."

"Won't be long," Sara said before disappearing into Harper's room.

Laine rested her head against his neck and sighed. Her eyelashes fluttered and tickled his skin.

"Are you tired, baby girl?" he asked.

A small nod was her answer. He kissed her sweet-smelling head. "Shall we read in your room tonight?"

Another nod.

Oliver broke free from David's hand and ran ahead. "I'll pick out a book," he called back to them.

He lifted Laine in her bed and kicked off his shoes. She snuggled against the pillows and watched him with serious eyes as he settled next to her. Oliver came into the room with a book he'd never seen before.

"What's this?" David asked.

"A book from the library." Oliver got into the bed and lay by his sister. "Zoey took us. There was a lady who reads a book to us and a bunch of other kids there."

"That sounds fun," David said.

From across the hall came the sound of Sara singing a lullaby to Harper. Goose bumps prickled his arms.

He opened the book about a little girl who wanted a dog. In order to convince her parents, she made up an imaginary one. Eventually, the dog of her imagination showed up at her house, and the parents couldn't refuse.

By the time he finished, Laine was fast asleep. He kissed her forehead, then swung his legs to the floor.

"Piggyback?" Oliver whispered.

"You bet." David went around the other side of the bed and let Oliver climb onto him. They lumbered like a two-headed monster down to Oliver's room. Once there, David pulled back the covers and dropped Oliver onto the bed.

David sat on the side of the bed and peered down at his little boy. "Did you have a good day?" He pushed Oliver's bangs off his forehead.

"Yeah. The library was fun. We played in the pool after lunch. I love it here, Daddy. Do we get to stay?"

"Yes, we get to stay."

"Is Sara going to be our mom?" Oliver asked.

His stomach dropped. "What makes you ask that?"

"I saw you kissing her."

"Oh, well, yes, we did kiss." Flustered, he wasn't sure what else to say.

"And Zoey said you got married to her."

What had he expected, though? Zoey would assume it was perfectly natural to talk about their marriage. She believed it was real. Rightly so, since they'd told her. "Yes, we did. How do you feel about that?"

"Pretty good."

"Do you remember much before we moved to Cliffside Bay? Like our old house?"

He shook his head. "Not really. Just Mommy. Sort of."

"If you ever want to talk about her, it's fine. Like if you have questions or anything."

"Okay, Daddy." Oliver yawned and turned over on his side. He tucked his hands under his cheek. "I don't have any right now."

He kissed Oliver before standing.

"Daddy?"

"Yes?"

"How come you didn't have a wedding? Aren't people supposed to have those before they get married?"

"We didn't want to make a fuss."

"But it still means we're a family now, even though you didn't have a wedding?"

Guilt twisted his stomach into a knot. "Is that what you want? For us to be a family?"

"I want a mom, especially for Laine. Maybe she'll start talking now that Sara's her mom."

"Why do you think that?"

"Well, Harper never stops talking, so I figure that's because she has a mom."

That was as good a theory as any. He smiled down at his pink-cheeked son. "I hope you're right."

"Night, Daddy."

"Good night, Oliver." He switched off the bedside lamp. Sensing the dark, the night-light plugged into the wall turned on and cast a dim glow about the room.

He slipped into the hallway. Sara stood against the wall just outside Oliver's room. Tears swam in her eyes.

He shut the door softly. "Did you hear all that?" he asked, whispering.

"Yes," she whispered back.

He took her hand. "Come on, let's talk downstairs."

As they passed Harper's nursery, he looked through the open door to the baby asleep in her crib. His heart softened at the sight of her. Dressed in a onesie with feet, she lay on her tummy with her thumb in her mouth. She was a beautiful baby. Like her mother.

What was happening to them? Was Oliver right, they were becoming a family? Were they all getting too deep, too fast? If they were, he didn't really feel like stopping.

21

S ara

Darkness had come by the time David returned to the kitchen with their grilled steaks. He'd insisted on grilling them outside, citing a Midwestern manly desire to be in charge of the beef. In the meantime, Sara had made a salad and opened a bottle of red wine. She'd set two places for dinner. The bouquet of Japanese anemone she'd placed in the middle of the island. The delicate white flowers with their yellow centers were her favorite. Had David known? At the last minute, she'd dimmed the pendant lights that hung overhead and lit a candle. He was going to so much trouble with the steaks, after all. The least she could do was make the atmosphere suit the meal.

Zoey was out with friends, so she knew they wouldn't be interrupted. Not that Zoey would intrude. Sara sensed that her nanny much preferred the cottage. She couldn't blame her for that. A young single woman needed her privacy. Being stuck in the same house with the children and what she thought were blissed-out newlyweds was probably the last thing she wanted.

David came in through the doors from the patio with the steaks. The smell of the grilled meat made her mouth water. She would only have half, she promised herself.

"Do you mind just salad and no starch?" she asked.

"Not at all," David said. "These filets must have cost a fortune."

She didn't comment. Many times over the last few days she'd been aware of how much she took for granted. Seeing the extravagances through his eyes, she suspected he thought her frivolous and spoiled. He was right, of course. She thought nothing of grilling twenty-dollar steaks on an ordinary weeknight. The bottle of wine was from a boutique winery in Washington State that cost as much as a week's worth of groceries for him and the kids.

"I like the candle," he said. "Nice touch."

"Kind of fancy, but why not?"

He transferred the steaks onto their plates while she poured them each a glass of wine.

Once they were seated, she cut into her steak and took a bite. Medium rare, just as she'd asked for. "Cooked perfectly."

"I know my way around a steak."

That wasn't all he knew how to do. Given the last few nights, she could safely say with confidence that he was skilled in the bedroom.

"Did you know Japanese anemone is my favorite flower?" Sara pointed at the bouquet with her fork.

"I didn't even know what they're called, but I saw you choose them from the flower stand the other day," he said. "After you proposed to me."

She narrowed her eyes and playfully poked his shoulder. "Mr. Perry, were you watching me from your window?"

"Is that creepy?"

"Kind of sweet," Sara said. "You notice every detail, don't you?"

"Only about subjects that fascinate me."

She flushed, pleased. "You're a quick study."

They ate in silence for a few minutes. Sara's body hummed

from his compliment. She felt different about herself when she was with him. As if she were as lovely as he seemed to think.

"I almost forgot to tell you," David said. "Stone came out earlier and assessed the damage to the cottage. He said it's not as bad as it looks. The floors are easily replaced, and a new coat of paint will take care of the rest."

"Will it be done quickly then?" Her heart sank. If Zoey went back to the cottage, would he return to his own room? Well, not return. He'd never actually slept there. She didn't want him to.

"He said about a week. His floor guy is finishing up a project but will do the cottage next. He's the same guy who did these floors."

She loved her floors. Dark cherry in wide planks had been one of the elements of the house that had been an immediate decision. She'd probably driven Trey crazy working through some of the other options.

"So, listen, we should probably talk about what you over-heard," he said slowly, as if he'd really rather not.

"The whole thing was totally sweet and kind of broke my heart." There was no "kind of" about it. Listening to that inno-cent child talk about his desire to be part of a family was enough to thaw the most frozen of hearts.

"Does it worry you? That we're all getting so attached?"

She leaned closer and wrapped her fingers around his knee. "Yes, I'm worried, but that doesn't mean anything. Since I became a mother, I worry about everything every minute of the day. I'm sure I'm going to mess Harper up in ways I can't even imagine right now."

He covered her hand with his. "It's only a period in time. One they won't remember."

She dropped her gaze to her plate. Perhaps he was right. The kids would be fine. But what about her? A breeze traveled through the patio doors and brought the scent of the late-blooming roses. "I'm not sure that's correct. What if we've stum-bled into the perfect situation? For the kids, I mean?"

"Maybe your grandfather was onto something," he said lightly. "It's obviously good for Oliver to have you in his life."

She lifted her eyes to look into his. "I want to be." The candle wick quivered as the breeze threatened to extinguish the flame. She shivered. The air had cooled quickly tonight. Fall would be here soon.

"Are you cold?" David asked.

"A little."

He jumped from his stool and closed the French doors. "Would you like me to get you a sweater?"

She laughed silently. How had this man just fallen into her lap? Men their age weren't chivalrous like David. He was of another era.

"What's so funny?" He sat back in the stool. "Are you laughing at me?"

"I'm laughing because I'm not used to a man surprising me. Thank you, but no, I'm fine now that the doors are closed."

He kissed her lightly on the mouth. "I'd go around the world to fetch anything you needed."

"Everything I need is right here in this house."

He picked up his wine. "Well, I did try to think of everything when I designed this for you."

"You did. But I'm not talking about the structure or even the objects. It's the people who live inside a house that take it from a beautiful showpiece to a home."

His expression grew serious as he turned his gaze toward her. He lifted his glass. "I could spend a lifetime trying to design a house worthy of your beauty and grace and never come close. You're the essence of this place. I'm happy to be along for the ride for as long as you'll have me."

"Do you mean that?" She might be dreaming. This could not be happening. Not to her.

"Despite the strange circumstances that require us to lie to the rest of the people in our lives, I'll never lie to you. You have my word."

She sighed as she picked up her fork. A part of her wanted to lean in and allow herself to fall for this man. Another part of her was screaming loudly to be careful. Was it right, though, to deny this obvious chemistry and affection simply because an unworthy man had hurt her?

His forehead wrinkled. "What is it?"

"I don't want the cottage to be fixed." She blurted this out without any warning that it was coming.

"But why?" The space between his eyebrows deepened.

"Because I don't want you to go back to your bedroom."

A short bark of a laugh escaped from his chest. "I don't want to go back."

"What if at some point you do? What if this is all just a result of two lonely people in the same house?"

"We've both been hurt and have felt very alone," he said. "No one would blame us if that's all it was."

She nodded. How stupid she must seem. How desperate. And insecure. Was this the beginning of driving him away with her self-doubt and need for affirmation?

"Hey now, don't look like that," David said as he lifted her chin with the tips of his fingers. "We don't have to decide anything other than day by day. For now, I'm content to be here by your side. Let's not overthink anything, okay?"

It wasn't her brain that was ruining this. Her needy heart had wakened. She was falling, and falling hard. God help her if David wasn't there to catch her.

A FEW DAYS LATER, Sara knocked on Autumn's door. She was fairly certain it was her best friend's day off, and she hadn't wanted to text or call for fear Autumn wouldn't answer. Dropping by would force her to have to talk to her.

Sure enough, Autumn opened the door. She immediately burst into tears. "I'm so sorry. I don't know what got into me."

Autumn grabbed her into a hug. "I think it's the pregnancy hormones."

Sara breathed in the scent of Autumn's perfume. "I'm sorry I didn't tell you before we got married."

"Come inside. I made some herbal iced tea. Would you like a glass?"

"That sounds great."

She followed her inside and watched as Autumn poured them both a glass and then added a mint leaf.

"Let's sit on the back deck," Autumn said. "There aren't many sunny days left."

Autumn's deck faced the boardwalk and a long strand of beach. There weren't as many people out today as there had been during the summer. School would start soon. That morning at breakfast Oliver had chattered on about how excited he was to go to school and that his dad had promised him a new set of tennis shoes because his old ones had holes. She'd caught David's gaze across the breakfast nook, and the shame in his eyes had made her chest ache.

She and Autumn took seats at an outside table shaded with an umbrella. The temperatures were in the midseventies with a pleasant breeze.

"How are you feeling?" Sara asked.

"Nauseous and cranky," Autumn said. "Which Dr. Waller says is all good news."

"Having gone through it myself, I'd have to agree."

"I got an invite from Lisa for the party," Autumn said.

"And you'll come?"

"Yes, of course. I was acting like a child."

"I can understand," Sara said. "You were right to be angry. We've never kept anything from each other."

"It's water under the bridge now. Tell me the story. I want to hear every detail of how you fell in love."

Strangely, given the situation, she hadn't thought of what to say if asked this question. They really should get their stories straight before the party. For now, she would have to draw on the events of the last few days.

"I don't know. During the support group sessions, it became obvious that he and I have a lot in common. I think we might have realized it before if we hadn't been shell-shocked after our spouses' deaths. If you think about it, we were both in zombie mode just then. He says he barely remembers anything from his first few months here."

"So you weren't getting the real picture of what and who he is." Autumn said this with a slight note of inevitability. As in, of course that's what it was. Sara supposed she deserved that. Especially after the last few days.

"I think I disliked him because of the attraction I felt. I translated that into angst. Falling for anyone after what happened with my husband seemed impossible. Looking back, I can see that quite clearly." To her surprise, this was all true. Over the last few days, all the feelings she'd pushed down had come bubbling to the surface.

"What was the wedding like?" Autumn asked.

Sara thought for a moment. Her nerves had been such that she could barely remember the blessed occasion. "The whole thing took like five minutes. We did it and then went back to the hotel and enjoyed a nice meal." The hours after the ceremony were the beginning of affection and intimacy they shared. "We talk really easily. It's like I've known him forever."

"That was true for Trey and me too," Autumn said. "Only I thought it was just a friendship, not a love match."

"You were a little slow on the uptake," Sara said. "I'm pretty sure you were the only one who didn't know what was going on between you."

"A foundation of friendship goes a long way in a successful relationship," Autumn said.

Sara inwardly cringed. She and David had jumped into bed without a foundation of friendship. Would that come back to hurt them in the end? Would there be an end?

"What's the worry frown about?" Autumn asked.

Her best friend knew her too well. "If I'm being honest, I'm worried all this went too fast. I fell for him just out of the blue."

"The paths to love vary in every relationship," Autumn said. "Don't overthink it. I'm pleased for you. You deserve to be happy. And this will be so good for the kids. All of them." She paused as she looked out toward the beach. "Are you worried about being a stepmom? It's no small thing you've taken on."

Sara wiped condensation from her glass. She hadn't thought about that element, because they'd gone into this thing knowing it would be only for a year. Yet another aspect that required a lie. "His children are young enough they'll think of me as their mother. Same for Harper and David. If they were teenagers, it might be different."

"Do you think you'll have one together?"

A further concept she hadn't pondered. Leave it to Autumn to ask all the questions. During the history of their friendship, the two of them had always analyzed and dissected whatever was on their minds.

"I'm not sure," Sara said. "Four would be a lot."

"Tell that to Violet and Kyle." Autumn laughed. "I still can't believe he talked her into a fifth one."

"God forbid it's another set of twins."

"Can you imagine?" Autumn patted her still-flat stomach. "I was a little relieved when we found just one heartbeat. Twins run in families, you know."

The sound of keys dropping onto a table and footsteps interrupted their talk. "That's Trey, home for lunch," Autumn said. "He's started coming by to check on me, both here and at work. I'm not sure what he's worried about exactly. I'm not the first pregnant woman in the world."

"I think it's sweet," Sara said. For a second, envy swirled around in her gut. But then she remembered David and how thoughtful he was to her. If she were to have his baby, he would be like Trey. She'd never known what it felt like to be cherished.

Did her future hold what Autumn had with Trey? Dare she dream?

Trey came out to the patio carrying a bag from the market. "Hello, ladies." He leaned down to kiss Autumn on the cheek. "I've brought sandwiches and salads from the deli."

"How'd you know I was here?" Sara asked.

"David mentioned it at the office this morning," Trey said. "I thought it would be nice for you to have lunch."

"Can you stay, honey?" Autumn asked.

He shook his head. "No, I have a meeting with Sophie. We're picking out tables for The Oar."

Driving through town, Sara had been surprised that the foundation was poured. A construction crew had been there, putting together the first boards.

"If all goes well, Stone says we'll have it completed by Christmas, interiors and all," Trey said. "Sophie's counting on a Christmas reopening."

"That'll be so exciting for the town," Autumn said.

"She and Zane want to do a huge party for the opening. Maggie's agreed to give a concert with Christmas music." Trey took several takeout cartons from the bag and set them on the table.

"How will they have room for such a party?" Sara asked. "The whole town will want to be there."

Trey separated a foot-long sub wrapped in paper and set the halves next to the salad cartons. "They're installing outdoor heaters on the patio and in front. Sophie had David use the space that had once been an apartment for more seating, which doubles the capacity."

"I can't wait to see it finished," Autumn said.

"A mix of breezy California bar and grill and a French bistro was challenging and fun for David and me." Trey grinned down at them. "Aren't you two lucky to be married to two such clever beasts?"

Autumn laughed. "Yes, we are."

"I'll be off now to let you ladies enjoy your lunch and the sunshine," Trey said. "The weather report calls for rain tomorrow."

After he left, Autumn unwrapped a sandwich. She covered her nose with one hand. "Does it smell bad to you?"

Sara opened the other half and sniffed. "No, it smells fine to me."

Autumn pushed her sandwich aside. "I think it's the cheese. My sense of smell is completely off. I can't even brush my teeth with mint toothpaste without feeling sick."

"Love of cheese will return," Sara said. "And it's all worth it the moment you hold the baby in your arms."

"I'm sure it's true, but right now I feel nauseous and hungry all at the same time."

Sara reached across the table to squeeze her friend's hand. "I'm excited to be Auntie Sara."

"This baby will have the best auntie in the world."

"I'm sorry we fought," Sara said.

"Never again, okay?"

"Agreed." She slid a carton of the salad over to Autumn. "Now eat up. Baby needs some calories."

David

Standing at Rafael and Lisa's front door, David squeezed Sara's hand as he rang the doorbell. Lisa had called that morning to ask them to come to dinner. His sister was too polite to admit to the reason for the spontaneous invitation, but it didn't take a clairvoyant to know this was a peacemaking evening between him and Rafael.

Sara wore a white halter dress that showed off her sculpted arms and tanned skin. In the light of the evening sun, a sprinkling of freckles on her shoulders beckoned to him. He'd plant a kiss on each one if he could. She had her hair up tonight, and his fingers itched to undo the knot just to watch how it cascaded down her back. A masterpiece in motion. The perfect design in a living woman. No matter how hard he tried, God's creations would always beat the ones of his own imagination.

"You look beautiful," he said.

She lifted her gaze upward to meet his. His stomach fluttered at the sight of her green eyes. They sparkled in the light as her mouth curved into a smile. "You look nice, too."

He'd dressed in a pair of khakis and a muslin shirt Lisa had given him for his birthday. He could only imagine what it cost, which was why he'd never worn it before tonight. Around the kids, he was sure to have it spotted with ketchup or peanut butter in a matter of minutes. "It's nice to be out, isn't it?" David asked. "Or does that make me a bad parent?"

"It's very nice to be out," Sara said. "Especially with you."

He kissed her quickly on the mouth a split second before the door swung open, revealing Lisa.

They jerked apart like guilty teenagers.

"Hello, there, newlyweds," Lisa said, looking like the movie star she was in a light blue skirt and white tank top. She had fairer skin than he, and was always careful to wear sunscreen, so that even after a long, warm summer, she had the complexion of a crab apple blossom—white with smudges of light pink.

"Hey, sis."

"Hi. Thanks for having us," Sara said. A tightness in her voice hinted at her nerves. This endeared her to him even more.

Lisa grabbed Sara into a hug. "I'm happy you're here. Welcome to our family. Now come inside. I have champagne on ice."

They walked inside, and Lisa closed and locked the door behind them. She remained cautious after the shooting she'd witnessed at a concert. For the most part, her anxiety had eased, thanks to therapy. Yet he often caught subtle hints that she would never be the same. Locking the door was one of them.

"Lisa, your house is stunning," Sara said.

"You can thank your husband and the other Wolves for that," Lisa said. "We gutted this place when we bought it."

Their home was located at the top of the northern slope of town. From this stunning view, the ocean was an azure blue with silver sparkles that seemed to dance for the sun. The house had been lived in by the same couple for sixty years and hadn't been updated since the late seventies. He and Trey had worked together to design a modern, open concept. Trey had cast a palette of grays and whites on the walls and furniture.

Lisa led them out to the patio. The stunner of a yard was

another of Nico's successes. They'd cleared the overrun area of dry grass and overly mature plants to put in a stone patio and an infinity pool that made it seem as if they were on the edge of the world. Pots of various sizes and shapes were planted with lush flowers and decorative bushes to create a Mediterranean feel.

Tonight, the outside table had been set for dinner. A bottle of champagne on ice waited on a low table surrounded by four lounge chairs. "Have a seat," Lisa said. "I'll pour the champagne."

"I'll do that," Rafael said as he came out on the patio from the open doors off the kitchen. Given his damp hair and a clean-shaven face, he must have just come from the shower. Rafael ambled over to them and held out his hand for David to shake. "Sorry to be late. I had a last-minute call with Garth Welte about his project." He turned to Sara and took one of her hands in both of his. "Welcome to our home. And our family."

"Thank you, Rafael," Sara said

Rafael poured glasses of champagne while he and Sara sat. The chairs were comfortable, as was the temperature. An over-hang protected them from the rays of the sun, which hung low on the horizon. Tropical flowers that climbed a trellis sweetened the air.

Lisa handed them each a glass of champagne, then sat next to Sara. "Cheers. I hope you'll be as happy as Rafael and I are."

"Thank you," Sara said, catching David's eye. "So far so good."

"Have you told Mom yet?" Lisa asked.

"Not yet," David said. "I've been putting it off. I'm afraid of what she'll say."

Lisa closed her eyes as if she had a sudden headache. "Yes, well, given that she's living with a man our age, I don't think she has much moral ground to stand on."

"She's different now," David said. "That's for certain."

"Happy, maybe?" Rafael asked. "It's amazing what love will do for your personality."

"Sara, you have no idea how nauseating it was," Lisa said. "When we were in France for Stone and Pepper's wedding, she surprised us with him. Boom, here's my French artist lover." She shuddered. "Totally gross."

"He's like something out of a movie about a middle-aged woman getting her groove back," David said. "Not what a son wants to think about."

"And now with Dad dating Ria, I don't know what to think," Lisa said.

"I'm happy for them," Rafael said. "Ria's been alone for as long as I've known her, which is all my life. Finding your father is a huge blessing to us."

Lisa laughed. "Fine. Way to be the better person than me or my twin."

"I'm not." Rafael patted his wife's hand. "Everyone knows you're the better person in this relationship."

"Have you heard from Uncle Dominic or your mom?" David asked Rafael.

"Nothing but a postcard or two from Italy," Rafael said. "Which tells me they're having too much fun to think about us."

"What is it with this town?" Sara asked. "People are always falling in love."

"Sea breeze is my guess," Rafael said. "Makes men amorous."

"How are the kids adapting?" Lisa asked.

"The girls are too young to really know what's going on," David said. "Oliver told me he's happy we can be a family like other people have."

Lisa's eyes filled. "That's the sweetest thing I've ever heard."

"Hey now, no tears," David said.

"You know how much I love my niece and nephew." She turned to Sara. "Thank you for being there for them. They've been through a lot."

"I know," Sara said. "And it's not hard to love them, as I'm sure you know."

"What about Harper?" Rafael asked. "Can you tell if she knows what's going on?"

"So far, she seems thrilled to have the other kids around," Sara said.

They all went quiet. A moment of awkwardness passed before Rafael turned to David. "You want to take a walk with me down to the wine cellar? You can help me pick something out to go with the fish Lisa's making."

"Sure thing." David would rather not have gone. Sitting outside with his two favorite women was better than an awkward exchange with his business partner. He took the opportunity to kiss Sara on the cheek before he followed Rafael into the house.

THE WINE CELLAR had been the sewing room of the previous owner. When David had first drawn the plans, he'd quickly decided the cool, dry spot would be perfect for wine. Now, as Rafael ran a finger along the racks, David smiled to himself. Seeing his work in this house pleased him. With everything that had gone wrong in his life, joining Wolf Enterprises had breathed life into his creative process.

"I'll just come right out and say it. I'm sorry about the other day," Rafael said. "I don't know what got into me. Lisa gave me an earful when she got home. If that makes you feel any better."

David plunged his hands into the pockets of his pants. "Think nothing of it. I shocked you. I know you were just concerned for the kids."

"Not my place, man. I'm sorry." Rafael crossed his arms over his chest. "You guys seem like you're in love. I can see I was wrong. I'm not childish enough to not admit when I screwed up."

He hadn't been wrong. A surge of self-condemnation rushed

over him like the high tide. "Yeah, well, it was weird to spring it on you guys like that."

"I shouldn't have questioned you. Like you pointed out, Lisa and I moved quickly once we figured out how we felt. Fate has a way of doing that."

"Sure does." Was this fate?

"Listen, man, I wanted to say one more thing. As far as the money is concerned, I've been where you are."

"Meaning?" He bristled. Was he going to accuse him of being in it for the money after he just apologized?

"Meaning I had very little and my wife was rich."

His shoulders eased. "Oh, yeah. Right. Got you."

"I had issues with it. I'm not proud to say so, but the Neanderthal in me didn't like that she had so much more money than me. I remember the first night we were ever together in that fancy hotel, I didn't know how I was going to manage my way through it."

"Did you?"

"Sure. You know how your sister is. It's impossible to remain petty in her presence."

David smiled. "She's always been that way."

"She's my angel. Has been from the minute we drove to LA that first day."

"I'm glad it's you she loves," David said. "Couldn't ask for a better brother."

Rafael ran a hand through his thick brown hair. "There's something else."

"Okay?" Now what?

"There's a reason I got so boiled over the money thing. It set me off, because I'm feeling conflicted about my role in my own marriage. Your sister wants me to bow out of Wolf Enterprises."

David jerked backward and knocked into a shelf of wine. Fortunately, nothing fell. "Why?"

"She wants to have a baby, and she wants me to be able to go with her on her jobs so that I can look after her or him while she's on set or wherever."

"Is that what you want?" David asked.

"I want a baby. I know that for sure. Being separated because of my work, when we don't need the money, makes no sense to her. She wants us to be together more than apart. With the roles she's being offered lately, she could work as much as she wants to. I feel like I'm holding her back because she doesn't want to be apart from me."

"That's no good," David said. "She'll start to resent you."

"Right."

"On the other hand, what about your work? It's not always about the money."

"Agree. But the truth is, this was never the passion project for me as it was with the rest of you. I got involved because I needed the money."

"We're just starting to really make it," David said.

"You guys can hire another business manager. There are a lot of talented people out there who would love the opportunity."

"I'm sure that's true. But the five of us have been through a lot together."

"That's the part that gives me pause," Rafael said. "Our friendships have been the best part of the gig."

"Have you talked to anyone else about this?"

A flash of guilt glinted in Rafael's eyes. "Yeah, man. I'm not the only one getting pressure to bow out."

"Stone?" *Please don't say it. Not Stone too.*

"Yes. Now that the theater's up and running, Pepper wants to have a baby too. Her career's exploding, and she wants Stone with her."

"I can't say I blame either of you, but Nico and Trey need this job. Walking away isn't really a choice for them."

"What about you?" Rafael asked. "Does marrying a woman with money change things for you?"

"It takes the pressure off," David said. "But it's the opposite for me. Now that I don't have to stress about money, I have more desire to be creative."

"Stone and I are prepared to sell our part of the business to you guys. That way you're a partnership of three. You can hire a contractor and a business manager. If they work out, you can offer them part ownership."

"You guys have really thought this through." An ache had started in his chest. He didn't want everything to change. Not with so many changes in his personal life. Or, rather, his *fake* personal life.

"Wives come first," Rafael said.

"As your brother-in-law, I appreciate that. As your buddy, not so much."

Rafael turned to the wine rack and pulled out a white, and then a red. "We better get upstairs before the ladies run out of champagne."

He followed Rafael out of the wine pantry. The rest of the basement had been turned into a recreation room, with pool and Ping-Pong tables as well as a bar.

"Have you figured out when you're going to tell the others?" David asked as they walked up the stairs.

"Stone's having them over tonight. Since you and I had other things to talk about, I told him I'd talk to you."

"I can't imagine Stone without physical work," David said. "What will he do with all that energy?"

"Man, Pepper's a full-time job."

David laughed. "True enough." As they walked into the kitchen, he sobered. Trey and Nico were going to take this hard. Like him, their work was an extension of themselves. Not doing what they loved would not be an option, even if they could. "Replacing you guys is going to be impossible."

"We'll still go out for beers once a week," Rafael said. "We never end up talking about business anyway."

"Good point." Usually they talked about the women in their lives. One by one, they'd won the hearts of the women they loved. Everyone but him. Now, another change, just when he'd started to count on these guys always being his business partners.

"Hang on," Rafael said. "I need to open these first."

David stood by the windows and looked out to sea. The sun had lowered to just above the horizon. Soon it would disappear, as if the sea had gobbled it up for dinner. That was the crux of it anyway. Change always came. He'd never been good at letting go or moving forward, even when life forced him to do so.

He turned back to Rafael, who was opening the bottle of red. "I hate this, but I understand."

"Your sister's my world. I have to do what's best for her."

"I know."

"Even if it means being a house husband." Rafael shot him a rueful grin. "I promised her from the beginning that I'd be Mr. Perry if that's what she needed. I never break my promises."

"I know, man, but this is a tough one," David said.

"Sometimes I think God had a plan to humble all of us Wolves by making our soul mates badass women. Took us all down a notch."

David nodded. "Probably true. That said, do you think we could have a beer instead of wine? I mean, we've got to hold on to something."

Rafael laughed as he opened the refrigerator. "Beer it is."

S ara
The weather on the night of their party snapped with a crispness that hinted fall would soon arrive. Standing near the pool, Sara clung to David's arm, almost dizzy. Music played through the outdoor speakers, competing for attention with the laughter and chatter of the guests. Several servers scurried about with trays of appetizers. A bartender served drinks from a temporary bar on the other end of the pool.

Outdoor heaters placed strategically around the patio warmed her bare shoulders. She'd chosen a pale halter dress that she'd bought online during one of her sleepless nights. Earlier, she'd caught a glimpse of herself in the wall mirror in Lisa's living room. The sight hadn't made her cringe as it sometimes did. This dress, with its full skirt and plunging neckline, suited her tall frame. David had said she looked stunning. His compliment had warmed her all the way to the party.

Overwhelmed by the attention and crowd, she longed to escape. Why was it that everyone else seemed to enjoy parties and for her they were a chore? She'd rather be home reading a good book or watching a show. Or curled up with David in bed.

She wished Autumn were here. She'd texted Sara earlier that

she might not make it. The nausea was particularly bad, and she'd spent most of the day in bed. Sara had texted back that she should rest. They could celebrate some other time. But it had increased her nervousness. Autumn was the only one she really knew well.

Stone and Pepper, holding hands, came over to congratulate them. What an odd pair they made. He was big and rugged—the type of man who could chop wood for hours and never break a sweat. Pepper was petite and thin as a whippet with eyes almost too big for her delicate face. She belonged on the red carpet in that white dress no bigger than a handkerchief. Black curls tumbled around her face in perfect symmetry. Next to her, Sara felt like a lumberjack.

"What a fabulous party," Pepper said. "Thank you for inviting us."

"A party without a Pepper is an impossibility," David said.

"I *am* a delightful guest," Pepper said. "Seriously, I couldn't be happier to celebrate with you two." She turned to Sara. "I've known this man for a long time, and it's great to see him like this."

"Like what?" David asked.

"For lack of a better word, radiant," Pepper said. "The look of a man in love."

Stone patted him on the shoulder. "She's right, man. You deserve all the happiness in the world." He tipped his head toward Sara. "Welcome to the Wolves family."

"And the Bobcats," Pepper said, tossing her curls. "That's what we call the wives of this mangy crew. Married to these jokers, we have to stick together. You're one of us now."

Sara smiled, surprisingly touched. She'd never really been part of a group. These were nice women. The opposite of mean girls, in fact. "Thank you, Pepper."

"We try to have a girls' night out at least once a month," Pepper said. "Will you join us?"

"Yes, I'd like that very much," Sara said.

"Great. We're off to get a drink," Pepper said.

Lance and Mary Mullen came over next. Sara knew them from the bookstore, where she was a regular customer. Mary always suggested the perfect book.

"We just wanted to say congratulations." Lance flashed them his gentle smile, soft-spoken and well-mannered as always. "Rafael and Lisa are like family to us. We look forward to getting to know you better."

"Thanks," David said. "Same."

"Yes, thank you." Sara's voice shook slightly. Damn these nerves. "We appreciate you being here."

Mary placed her fingers lightly on Sara's arm. "It's a bit overwhelming, isn't it? All the people swarming you."

Sara nodded, feeling a kindred spirit in the tall, slender Mary Mullen. "A little, yes."

"And everyone so pretty and sparkly," Mary said.

"Exactly," Sara said.

"You're both pretty and sparkly," Lance said.

"My husband always says just the right thing," Mary said.

Sara's heart twisted as they exchanged a look of deep and profound love.

"I agree," David said, gruffly.

Sara looked up at him and gave him a smile. He pressed her more firmly against his side.

"This crowd grows on you after a while," Mary said. "They mean well, even if they are a tad intrusive."

Lance laughed. "That's the truth. You're part of us now, which means you'll be getting unsolicited advice on a regular basis."

"But also a group of people who will always have your back," Mary said. "It took me a while to acclimate. I'm more of a loner. But somehow this group of people wriggled their way into my heart. Before I knew it, I started thinking of myself as one of them. My life is so much richer than I ever thought possible."

Sara wanted to believe it to be true, but she had her doubts.

"We eloped to Vegas, too," Lance said. "What an adventure that was, right, honey?"

"Something like that," Mary said. "We still laugh about the chapel where we got married."

"Our experience was definitely on the surreal side," David said.

"How come you two don't have adult beverages in your hands?" Lance asked.

"We haven't made our way over to the bar yet," Sara said. "So many people."

"Let's get these ladies some drinks," Lance said to David.

"Sure thing," David said. "Will you be all right for a minute?"

"Yes, I'm fine." Sara calmed under the compassion of his gaze. He knew she was nervous without her having to explain it to him. "I'll have a white wine."

"Me too," Mary said.

After the men walked away, Kara Mullen came over to them. She and Mary embraced. Kara was married to Lance's brother Brody, which made them sisters-in-law. Sara had met the Mullens a few times before but didn't know them well. Kara had deep brown eyes and a full mouth. Long dark hair cascaded over her muscular shoulders. She wore a blue dress that hung a few inches above her knees, showing off her toned legs.

Kara congratulated her and thanked her for inviting them.

"You're very welcome," Sara said. "But truthfully, Lisa did everything. We just had to show up."

"In my opinion, that's the best kind of party," Mary said. "But my sister-in-law here will disagree."

"I love throwing parties," Kara said. "In fact, we need to have one soon. I've been so busy with the kids that I haven't had time. Brody's been traveling for work, which I'm not in love with, but what's a football widow to do?"

Brody, retired professional quarterback, was now a color

commentator on one of the sports networks. Sara enjoyed his on-air presence.

"He's so good at his job," Sara said. "He's my favorite."

"He would love to hear you say that," Kara said. "Despite his self-confident demeanor, he's often racked with self-doubt."

"Aren't we all?" Sara asked.

"God yes," Mary said.

"Nothing brings it out worse than motherhood," Kara said. "Just ask Mary how many parenting books I buy."

Charmed by her honesty, Sara laughed. "I think every mother wonders how high the therapy bills will be when her children are adults." How much damage were she and David causing their children? She put the worry aside and focused on her new friends.

They were joined by Violet, looking like a blooming rose in a dark green dress that clung to her baby bump. "Oh, Sara, I'm so happy for you guys." She gave Sara a warm hug, then pulled back to fix her almond-shaped brown eyes on her. "You're absolutely gorgeous tonight."

"You too," Sara said.

"Oh, God, I'm big as a cow. If Kyle doesn't stop getting me pregnant, I'll never be able to fit into regular clothes again."

"You look exactly the same," Kara said. "Other than your tummy."

"You're a liar, but I love you anyway," Violet said.

Kara was right. Violet's toned arms were proof of her daily yoga practice, which she taught at the newly opened dance and theater space.

Kara gestured toward Kyle, who stood with Brody and Zane over by the bar. "You should've heard Kyle bragging to the guys at poker last week."

Violet rolled her eyes. "Was he talking about his super sperm again?"

"Yes." Kara dissolved into a fit of laughter. "I was dying."

"The sad thing is—he might be correct," Violet said. "He only has to look at me to make another baby. I told him after this one, he's getting snipped. Five children is enough for a basketball team, for heaven's sake. It's embarrassing when people stop me in the store to ask how many children do we have now. I can see the look of judgment in their eyes." She directed her gaze at Sara. "Honestly, I figured it would take at least a few months of trying. But no, first try did the trick."

"You have a beautiful family," Sara said. She'd seen Violet at the park in town a few weeks ago, pushing her twins in the baby swings while her oldest, Dakota, supervised his other sister on the slide.

"Thank you," Violet said. "They're especially pretty when they're asleep."

"I'd have to agree with that," Kara said. "I don't know how you do it with four."

"Don't remind me. I'll start crying, and I want to have a good time," Violet said.

"How's it going with the kids?" Violet asked Sara. "Are they adjusting?"

"Remarkably well," Sara said. "Oliver seems especially happy to be with us."

"That sweet boy," Kara said. "He's lucky to have you."

"He has a giant heart. Like his dad," Sara said.

David and Lance returned with drinks, then begged off to join the other guys, who had gathered around the firepit.

Lisa floated up, looking angelic in a white dress and platform sandals. "Kara and Violet, why don't you have drinks? I had the bartender make a fresh batch of lemonade for those who can't imbibe."

Kara and Violet excused themselves and headed toward the bar. Out of the corner of her eye, she saw Zane and Honor arrive with Sophie and Nico right behind them.

"Do you know Honor?" Mary asked.

"Not well, no," Sara said.

"Come with me," Mary said. "She's fun, and you won't have to worry about thinking of anything to say."

Honor said something to Zane, who nodded and ambled toward the bar.

"Honor, nice to see you," Mary said. "You know Sara, of course."

Tiny and curvy, Honor had long blond hair and an infectious smile. She wore a shorts jumpsuit and high pumps that displayed her trim thighs and shapely calves. "Yes, yes. How are you, Sara? This is a kick-ass party."

"All Lisa," Sara said.

"She's full-on class all the time," Honor said.

"Yes, she is," Sara said.

"What's it like being married to a twin?" Honor asked.

"I'm...it's too early to tell." She hadn't really thought about Lisa as a twin.

"It's obvious how close they are," Honor said. "I'm jealous. I'd love to have a sister or brother."

"I've always wanted one too," Sara said.

"That's what you have us for," Mary said. "Family we chose, not just born into."

"Way better," Honor said.

Zane showed up with a martini in his hand and gave it to his wife.

"Hallelujah, a drink." Honor took a modest sip.

"Nice to see you, Sara. Congratulations again," Zane said. "I'm going to check in with the guys."

"Yes, go," Honor said. "We want girl talk."

He kissed her on the cheek and headed toward the guys.

"I couldn't wait to get out of the house," Honor said. "I swear to God, we're raising the devil child. That boy of ours is out of control. Today Sebastian tried to dress one of the cats in a doll dress and got himself scratched."

"Oh no. Was he hurt?" Mary asked.

"Um, no. He didn't even cry over the scratches," Honor said.

"It was only when I gave him time-out on the naughty step that he cried. He hates getting in trouble, but it doesn't seem to deter him from his evil ways. He kept saying how it was the cat who should have the naughty step. I had to go in the other room to keep from laughing." She took another sip of her martini before continuing. "I don't know how, since my DNA is not in that child, but he's just like me." She looked at Sara. "I couldn't have a baby so Zane's sister, Sophie, carried a donated egg."

Sara nodded, unsure what to say. Autumn had told her about how Sebastian had come into the world. Fortunately, as Mary said, Honor didn't seem to need a response. She kept right on talking.

"And then there's Jubie. She's so well-behaved and stoic. I'm afraid she's going to reach age twenty-five and decide her childhood was ruined by her naughty baby brother."

"I doubt that," Sara said.

"Are the guys pouring shots?" Mary asked, sounding worried.

Sara looked over at the huddle of men. They indeed had a row of shot glasses lined up on the edge of the firepit. "Is that Dr. Waller pouring them? And is that tequila?"

"Yes, that's Jackson," Honor said. "That's so out of character. Usually he's the one holding them all back."

"Where's Maggie?" Mary asked.

"She's doing a show up in Portland," Honor said. "Last one until after the baby comes."

They'd heard one of Maggie's songs on the radio on the way here.

"She's going to take at least six months before she works again," Honor said. "Performing, anyway. She said she's going to record a third album at Sophie's dad's studio." She directed her comments to Sara. "He's a big music producer. That's how she got her big break."

A cheer rose from the clump of men, followed by clinking of glasses.

"They're obviously happy to be out of the house and without their children," Mary said. "Lance doesn't normally do shots. Although tequila is what got the two of us into the mess we're in."

"The old 'three margaritas and let's make a baby' situation?" Honor asked.

Mary blushed and ducked her head. "Embarrassingly enough."

"It looks like the ladies will be driving home tonight," Honor said as the guys let out a collective rebel yell. "I have a feeling church will be empty of Dogs and Wolves tomorrow morning."

"I better check in with the sitter," Mary said. "And make sure she can stay late. This is going to be an epic night if they're starting out with shots."

Honor turned to Sara. "Let's sit. My feet hurt already."

They sat around one of the tables Lisa had had brought in for the party.

"Those idiots are going to pay tomorrow," Honor said. "Especially when kids wake them up at six o'clock."

Sophie had gotten a glass of wine at the bar and was headed their way. She plopped down at the table. "What's up, ladies?"

"We're just talking about how much pain the boys are going to be in tomorrow," Honor said, sounding delighted.

"Not Nico," Sophie said. "He never drinks anything but red wine and never too much. He's annoyingly perfect. But God, I love him to death. Isn't love grand?"

"It's better than a kick in the eye," Honor said, smiling.

Sara had heard Nico describe his fiancée as sunshine personified, and it was true. She was tanned and blond and had a smile that could light up the darkest room.

"How are the wedding plans going?" Sara asked Sophie.

"I'm jealous you eloped, to be honest," Sophie said. "My mom's driving me a little batty with the wedding plans."

"It saves a lot of hassle," Sara said. "My first wedding was ridiculous. But that was all my husband. He wanted the most extravagant wedding of the year."

The other ladies seemed suddenly interested in the contents of their glasses.

"It's okay," Sara said. "You can talk about it or ask me questions. It's not like the scandal didn't make the tabloid headlines."

"I'm sorry," Honor said. "It's just hard to know what to say."

"Other than it must have been awful for you," Sophie said. "I'm sorry you had to go through such a horrendous thing."

"Thanks. I appreciate you saying that," Sara said. "I'm through it now. And I have David." It was no longer hard to lie, now that the fibs had become truth.

"I went through some rough stuff myself," Honor said. "So I one hundred percent get how you feel. The past is just that, though, right? The present looks pretty damn good."

Sara looked over at the men, who were now sprawled in chairs around the firepit. They'd retired the tequila and replaced it with beer. David glanced her way, and their eyes met. He winked. She gave him a swift wave. A moment of contentment swept through her. How good it felt to have a special person to go home with at the end of the night.

"When you're going through all the bad stuff," Sara said, "it feels like this kind of day will never come again."

"So true," Honor said. "And when it does, you almost don't trust it. Like, if you give in and enjoy, you might jinx yourself or something."

Sara studied the small, feisty woman across from her. In her designer clothes and perfect hair, you'd never know that Honor had ever faced anything harder than deciding what to order for dinner. But like most, she'd faced the darkness. She'd come out on the other side.

As if she read her thoughts, Sophie said, "There's not a person here tonight who hasn't had hardship and pain, but we all made it to this moment."

The golden sun had lowered over the sea. Tonight would be a

sunset without color. In her time here, Sara had watched the sun crawl into the ocean many nights. Not once had it been the same. Sometimes orange, others pink or a combination thereof. But no matter how it went down, it always came back the following morning.

"When it happened," Sara said. "All I could think about was my infant daughter. What would I tell her about her father when the time came?"

"Understandable," Sophie said.

"What did you come up with?" Honor asked. Her voice shook slightly, giving Sara insight into the source of her pain.

"I haven't yet." Sara sipped from her wine, continuing to watch the sun.

"I was that kid," Honor said. "The one left behind after their parent disappeared in the worst of ways. Tell her the truth, but make sure to tell her the happy ending. David came to be her father. That's what matters. How the story ends. Not how it began."

"And the middle too," Sophie said. "Like right now."

Sara's arms covered with goose bumps. How would this story end? Were she and David headed for a happy ending or more pain?

God, how she wanted it to end happily. She wanted David. She wanted him to be her real husband. Harper's real father. And sweet Oliver and silent Laine. She wanted to love them and be the mother they'd lost.

She decided right then. She would do her very best to win his heart. Hers was already his.

David

He agreed to let Sara drive them home, even though he hadn't had anything to drink after the second tequila shot hours before. As they drove down the skinny street toward town, Sara was quiet.

"Everything okay?" he asked.

"Yes, I'm fine. Do you mind if we stop for a minute down at the beach?"

"Not at all. I'm kind of wired from the party anyway," he said.

She turned right instead of left, heading toward the strand of beach. They parked in front of the bench. She shut off the car and turned to look at him. "Do you want to get out?"

"Sure." He grabbed his jacket from the back seat where he'd tossed it earlier. "But you need to wear this. It's chilly."

She took it from him and got out of the car. He joined her, helping her into his jacket. The still night air smelled of seaweed. He took her hand and led her over to the bench that resided on a grassy knoll. "Let's sit for a moment."

They sat together. She faced outward, seeming small in his jacket. He rested one arm on the back of the bench and turned toward her. Her beauty took his breath away, made his stomach flutter. Waves crashed against the shore, interrupting the quiet night. Sea-foam glittered under the moonlight as the tide ebbed and flowed.

"I've never seen a more beautiful thing than you here in the moonlight," he said finally.

Her eyes shone as she turned her gaze to him. "Where did you come from?"

"Iowa." He smiled as his fingers found a groove in the wood. Someone, who knew when, had carved a pair of initials. What was it like to love someone with such surety to mark it here forever?

She pressed her fingers into his chest. "That wasn't what I meant."

"I know." He longed to kiss her, but he wouldn't. There was something bothering her. He sensed the heaviness in her body.

"Spill it," he said softly. "What's on your mind?"

She looked out to the ocean. "Stone told me at the party that the cottage is ready. Zoey can move back in tomorrow."

His stomach clenched. Was she telling him this would be the last night he spent in her bed? Had she decided it was only loneliness that had prompted her to share her bed with him?

"Which means we no longer have the excuse to share a bedroom." Sara pulled the jacket tighter around her middle.

"Are you glad? Relieved?" He held his breath, waiting for the hammer. A seagull screeched from somewhere in the darkness.

"No, I'm not glad." Her voice sharpened. "I'm not relieved. That's the opposite of what I am."

He breathed in, filling his lungs with air as his chest expanded. Was it possible she felt what he did? "Tell me, then. What are you feeling?"

"I feel so many things I don't understand. The line between fake and real is blurring. This isn't what I thought it would be."

A tendril of hair had fallen from her bun. He reached over

and twirled it around his finger. "We don't have to change anything. We're making the rules."

"There don't seem to be any rules."

"Do you want there to be?" David brushed the back of his index finger across her exquisite cheekbone.

"I want things to be clearer."

"I don't know what that means." His chest tightened. This was it. The moment she would tell him they should take it back to a business partnership. She must have realized how silly it was for them to have become involved. What would a woman like her want with him anyway?

"I need to understand how you feel about me." She tucked her chin and looked into her lap and spoke just above a whisper. "For me, this thing between us is more than sex. Is that all it is to you?"

He smiled to himself. "No, not at all." Did he have the courage to tell her how he felt and risk humiliation?

"Tell me, David, what am I to you?"

Tell her the truth, he thought. *Tell her how you feel. Risk it all.* "It was never about sex. I'm falling in love with you."

Her head jerked upward. "You are?"

"If I'm being honest, I think I've felt this way for longer than I wanted to admit. All those months we worked together on the house, I kept you at arm's distance for a reason. Maybe that's why I was so distant, which made you think I was arrogant and aloof. I was trying not to embarrass us both by making a move. All subconscious, mind you."

"I felt the rejection, maybe. Because of my issues and what happened to me, I reacted in anger. All my insecurities were triggered. I've been drawn to you from the beginning."

"Is there any part of you that thinks you could love me?" He swallowed his fear and waited for her answer.

"Every part of me could love you."

His heart pounded hard inside his chest. "What do we do now?"

"We go home," she said. "And go to bed in *our* bed."

DAVID SWALLOWED the lump in his throat as Oliver bounded down the stairs dressed in his new jeans and polo shirt. The first day of kindergarten had come too quickly. People had warned him when his son was born not to blink. Nothing had proven more true.

"I'm ready, Daddy." Oliver grinned.

"Teeth brushed and hair combed," Sara said from behind Oliver. She had the baby on her hip and had somehow managed to get Oliver ready for school while David made lunches. Oliver's hair had been dampened to take care of the cowlick that had stood straight up that morning during a quick breakfast.

Laine wandered into the hallway from the kitchen, carrying her dog. At the slight of her brother, she started to cry.

"What's the matter, honey?" David asked as he scooped her into his arms.

Laine pointed at her brother.

"Don't be sad, Lainey." Oliver marched over to them and patted Laine's bare calf, which had wrapped around David's stomach. "I'll always come back."

Sara set the baby on the floor and pointed at the small chalkboard she'd bought for the "first day of school" photograph. "We have to take your picture before you go." She looked over at David. "Should we do it on the front porch?" David had done the lettering in his precise architectural handwriting. In blue chalk, the sign read:

Oliver, age 5

Kindergarten

David nodded, too emotional to trust his voice. With a girl on each hip, he followed Sara and Oliver outside to the covered porch. The sun hung low in the eastern sky, filtering through the trees that lined the driveway. A crispness in the morning air hinted that autumn would soon turn the leaves red and gold. Seasons continued on, despite all human foibles.

Sara asked Oliver to stand on the bottom step and handed him the chalkboard. "Hold this in front of you but don't cover your face."

"Like this?" Oliver asked.

"That's just right," Sara said as she took Harper from David.

David set Laine down and pulled his phone out of his back pocket. "All right, Ollie, give me your best smile."

Oliver grinned. The bright light brought out the blue of his eyes and made his dark blond hair shine. Freckles from days at the beach and pool decorated his nose. His beautiful, beautiful little boy. They'd been through so much together. Too much for a child of five years old. In the months after Marigold's death, he hadn't been sure they would get through the quicksand that engulfed them. But Oliver had risen to the occasion. He'd been brave and caring toward David and his little sister. An old soul peeked out from those sky-blue eyes.

David's stomach hurt as he clicked several photos. The time had gone too fast. His baby was no longer a baby. Yet he still seemed so young with his flushed cheeks and bright eyes. His instinct was to protect him, keep him at home and in a bubble. Questions fluttered through his mind as he put his phone in his pocket. Would there be mean kids? Would he be picked on or bullied? What if no one sat with him at lunch?

"All right, that's good enough," David said. "Everyone into the van."

Sara squeezed his hand as they watched Oliver and Laine gallop toward the minivan. "He's going to be fine. This kid's made for the world."

"How did you know I was worried?"

She kissed his cheek. "Just a guess."

"I feel a little sick," he said. "This is harder than I thought it would be."

"He looks so grown-up in his first-day-of-school outfit. That's the part that got me," she said.

He glanced over at her. There was an attachment and affection in her voice. Was she falling for his children the way he'd already fallen for Harper? Was there a chance they could be a real family?

Hope was a dangerous word, but there it was. He hoped they would be a real family. A forever family.

BUILT IN THE LATE SIXTIES, the Cliffside Bay elementary school was made of brick and to David looked just as it should. Mature bushes decorated the entryway, trimmed low so that the windows of the classrooms could let in light. A massive fenced playground was to the left of the structure. Double doors to the front entrance were open wide. Women he figured were PTA moms held signs that said "Welcome kindergarten students."

Marigold would have been one of those mothers. Or, at least, that was the idea he'd had about his wife. As it turned out, she wasn't the PTA type after all. He felt certain that the women smiling wide and calling out to children as they walked toward the entrance were not dealing drugs out of their minivan. Then again, who knew? People were never only what they appeared on the outside. So many had secrets.

The email from the principal had asked the kindergarten parents to park in the lot for the first day. Seeing the line of cars that spilled onto the street, he now understood the wisdom of that instruction. Students seemed to fall out of cars and SUVs with backpacks on their small shoulders. His heart beat faster. There were so many of them. How would Oliver even maneuver down the hallways with all of these bigger children?

He parked and opened both side doors of the van so they could get the younger ones. Oliver jumped out, bouncing on his toes with excitement. Once they had the girls on their hips, the five of them crossed the parking lot onto the sidewalk. Laine clung to him with all four limbs as if she thought he might drop her into the masses of children.

When they reached the entryway, one of the mothers by the doorway called out to them. He blinked, realizing the woman was Violet Hicks. The familiar face almost did him in. She gave him a reassuring smile. "Hi, do we have a new kindergartner here?" She wore a knit dress that showed off her small baby bump. Her long hair was pulled back into a ponytail.

"It's me," Oliver said.

"I'm glad to see you." Violet's brown eyes twinkled at Oliver. "Are you excited?"

Oliver nodded. "I think so." David glanced down at his son. He suspected the excitement Oliver felt earlier had morphed into apprehension. The number of children, all talking at once and moving in a hive toward the entrance, was enough to intimidate anyone.

"You will love Ms. Trotter," Violet said. "She's wonderful."

"That's good to hear," Sara said. "We're a little nervous. This is all new to us."

"You'll get the hang of it," Violet said. "I was the same way."

"Is it always this loud?" Sara asked.

"Only before school, after school, lunch, and recess," Violet said, laughing. "Do you know where the classroom is?"

"Yes, I was here for orientation a few weeks back," David said. How much things had changed since then. It was nice to have Sara with him today. He'd felt so alone that evening. Most of the other parents had come in pairs.

"Okay, well, go on in," Violet said. "There's a 'boo-hoo' muffin meeting in the all-purpose room after you drop him if you're interested."

"Thanks, Violet," David said. "I appreciate it."

"You'll be fine. I promise." Violet smiled at them and then turned to wave to another parent and child.

Oliver slipped his hand into David's and they headed inside.

Laine continued her intense grip on him as they walked down the hallway toward the classroom.

For a moment, he thought he might burst into tears for real. It struck him how much the three of them had endured together, clinging to one another through everything, just as they were today. These two babies were his whole life, and he was about to let go of one of them. The first step toward the inevitable charge toward adulthood.

"Don't worry, Daddy," Oliver said. "I'll always come back."

"Oh, buddy, I hope so," David said.

Ms. Trotter greeted them the moment they arrived. "Who have we here?" she asked.

"This is Oliver Perry," David said.

Oliver's teacher looked as if she couldn't be much over twenty-five. She had a brown bob and pretty hazel eyes. She wore a conservative yellow dress and tall boots.

"You're Sara Ness, isn't that right?" Ms. Trotter asked. "I'm Laila. Zoey's one of my best friends. We went to college together. She moved to Cliffside Bay after I got the job here. She fell in love with the town."

"Yes, of course," Sara said. "She talks about Laila all the time but I didn't connect the dots. I'm not sure she's ever said your last name."

"Congratulations, by the way," Ms. Trotter said. "It's heartwarming to see your merged family."

"Thanks," David said.

Ms. Trotter turned her attention to Oliver. "We're going to have such fun this year, but first I need to show you where we put our lunch boxes and your spot at the table."

Crap. They'd forgotten his lunch. "I left his lunch at home," David said. "I made it and everything."

"We were a little nervous this morning," Sara said.

"No worries," Ms. Trotter said. "The cafeteria has great food. Just put some money in his account when you get home."

"Yeah, okay. I'll do that." David said, embarrassed. The first day and he'd already flubbed up.

"Now, say goodbye to your parents," Ms. Trotter said. "And go join the others on the carpet. That's where we start each day."

Oliver beamed up at him. "Bye, Dad."

Dad? What happened to Daddy?

"Bye, Laine. Bye, Harper. Bye, Sara," Oliver said. Then, without further discussion or a backward glance, he headed toward the carpet.

"Good job, guys," Ms. Trotter said. "He's obviously well-adjusted. We've had some tears today, and not just from the parents."

David chuckled, but his heart wasn't in it. He wanted to stay and keep an eye on things. That boy near the water cooler looked way too big to be a kindergartner. Maybe he'd had to repeat a grade? Perhaps for bullying? And the little blonde girl with the pink bows looked like she might have serial killer instincts. She looked a tad too perfect.

"Come on," Sara said quietly. "Other parents are waiting."

He looked at the doorway. She was right. There were two other couples waiting. He flushed.

"Let's get a coffee and head home," Sara said. "The day will fly by, and he'll be home to tell us all about it."

David took one last look at Oliver. Great, he'd sat right next to the serial killer and was currently giving her his best Perry grin. Three o'clock couldn't come fast enough.

25

S ara

    The school pickup line extended out to the street. However, Sara had been so nervous to be late, she'd been the first car. David had wanted to join her to pick Oliver up on his first day, but he'd had an important meeting with one of the Emerson Pass clients that he couldn't miss.

She'd left the girls at home with Zoey. They'd both been down for naps, and she hadn't wanted to wake them. This was the first time she'd be alone with Oliver, she realized. Maybe that was good. They could bond.

The bell sounded, and kids began to file out of the main entrance. How would Oliver not be trampled? But then she saw Ms. Trotter with a line of children coming out from a side entrance. An assistant took a set of kids to the buses while Ms. Trotter led the others over to a marked-off zone that said "Kindergarten pickup." Why hadn't she noticed that before? She felt sure the other mothers knew exactly what to do. She should have been there with David at orientation. But they hadn't been married then. How strange. This thing they were doing had started to feel way too real in a short amount of time.

Oliver was the second child in line. The first was the adorable girl with the pink bows. She smiled, remembering David's rant on the way home that morning. He'd tried to convince her the girl looked like a serial killer. They'd had a good laugh over it, and she had plans to tease him unmercifully about his overprotective attitude toward the kids. He'd said he'd much rather keep them in a Bubble Wrapped room than let them out into the world. She understood the sentiment, but she knew, too, that this was the first of many times he would have to let go. That's what no one tells you before you have a child. You have to start letting go the minute they're born. If not, you've failed them. No one wants a thirty-year-old living in his parents' basement.

She rolled down the passenger-side window and opened the sliding door of the van so that Oliver would see her. He grinned and waved wildly. Ms. Trotter nodded that he could go and gave Sara a thumbs-up.

"Hi, Sara," Oliver said as he climbed into the van. "Where's Dad?"

Dad instead of Daddy. Another milestone to break David's heart.

"He had a meeting at work, so I'm here instead." Would that bother him?

"Cool." Oliver pushed the button to close the door and climbed into his booster seat and fastened the belt.

"Did you have a good day?" Sara asked as she pulled forward.

"It was awesome."

"Would you like to stop for ice cream on the way home? To celebrate your first day?"

An enthusiastic "yes" came from the back.

She headed down the street toward the main part of town. Since tourist season had ended, things had settled back into the sleepy town she loved. They passed by the library and then turned right toward the bookstore and café. Lance and Mary Mullen had reimagined the town bookstore when they bought the building a few years back. Now the bookstore took up one side of the building and a coffee and ice cream shop took up the other. During the summer season, it was packed with visitors wanting a cold treat on a hot day. The rest of the year, locals took it back. Teenagers hung out in the café, eating ice cream or having a coffee drink. Women met for book clubs. Families with young children came for the books and the ice cream. Basically, the Cliffside Bay Bookstore was a local hub, as was The Oar. Or it would be once it was done.

She glanced over to see that the walls of the new bar and grill were almost done. Now that permits and insurance had been worked through, Stone's crew was making incredible progress.

Sara found a parking place in the small lot behind the bookstore. Oliver opened the door himself and jumped to the ground faster than she could get out herself. He waited for her, then took her hand.

Touched and pleased, she led him around the side of the building to the front entrance. The one in the back was for emergency exit only.

Mary was at the front counter helping a customer. She gave Sara a friendly wave as they passed through the displays of books to the café. She hadn't been the only parent to think of the idea of first-day ice cream. The place was packed. They got in line just as Violet and her oldest son, Dakota, walked in.

"Well, hello for the second time today," Violet said.

"Seems we had the same idea," Sara said.

Dakota had already greeted Oliver, and they were chatting away about school.

"We're going to take our ice cream and head down to the beach," Violet said. "I'd love some company."

"That sounds perfect," Sara said. "I left the little ones with our nanny, so we're free for a while."

"I did the same," Violet said.

The boys had broken free and were now perusing the different ice cream offerings.

"Sometimes it's nice to focus on only one kid at a time,"

Violet said. "The little ones are still so clingy that I worry Dakota feels abandoned."

"He looks fine to me," Sara said.

"They have him doing all these extracurricular things in the gifted program." Violet's brow wrinkled. "I'm worried it's all too much. He's just a little boy."

"Does he seem all right with it?" Sara asked.

"So far, so good. The teacher says he's thriving. His mind seems to spin faster than the rest of us, and he needed the challenge. I didn't want him to do the program, but Kyle thought it was a great opportunity. I want the kids to get to be kids for as long as they can."

By this point they'd moved to the head of the line. As good as ice cream sounded, Sara ordered an iced tea without sweetener. The boys each got one scoop of mint chocolate chip. Violet let out a long sigh and said how much she'd love a coffee or an ice cream but would settle for the turkey wrap instead, muttering under her breath about being pregnant for the rest of her life.

Treats in hand, they headed down the sidewalk toward the beach. The weather hovered in the midseventies with blue skies. The closer they got to the stretch of sand, the stronger the scent of ocean. When they reached the bench, the women sat while the boys sat crisscross on the grass to eat their ice cream. Seagulls hovered a few feet from the kids, eyeing them with their one-sided glance in case any food was dropped.

"We have a lot in common as far as families go," Violet said. "Only I started out as his nanny. He very unexpectedly became the sole parent of a little baby he didn't know he had." She proceeded to tell the story of how she and Kyle had fallen in love after she went to work for him. "Never in a million years would I have thought Kyle would be the one. I hated him for building the resort."

"I remember hearing something about you protesting," Sara said with a laugh. "I thought I didn't care for David either. Turns out, I was wrong."

"It must be a shock for you to go from one baby to three," Violet said.

"A little. But David's so hands-on it doesn't feel like too much." Sara looked out to the sea. A boat with bright red and blue sails was anchored just out from the shore. Several men were on board drinking beer. "Plus, we have a full-time nanny."

"Thank God for nannies," Violet said. "That's the only way Kyle talked me into another one." She nibbled on her sandwich, then put it back in the bag.

"Five is a lot," Sara said.

"I know. It's downright embarrassing," Violet said.

THE HOUR WAS NEARING four by the time she and Oliver arrived back at the van. She'd just closed the door to go around to the driver's seat when she noticed a man in a leather jacket. He leaned against the side of the bookstore with his arms folded over his chest. Wide-shouldered, tall, with a full beard, he looked like he might ride a Harley.

His eyes were brown and intelligent, and they were fixed right on her.

"May I help you?" she asked as she reached inside her purse for her Mace.

He unfolded from where he'd slouched against the wall and stepped toward her. "No reason to be scared. I'm not here to hurt you." As he drew nearer, she could see he was younger than she'd first thought. Under all that facial hair his skin was unwrinkled. "I'm the private investigator your grandfather hired."

"Oh, well, nice to meet you." Her shoulders relaxed. "I'm Sara Ness, but I guess you already know that."

"I do." His eyes crinkled as he smiled. "I'm Pink Floyd."

Her brows shot up in surprise.

He laughed. "Yes, I know. My parents thought they were

clever. Musical types. Floyd is our real last name, and God forbid they would miss out on the opportunity to call me Pink."

"It's nice to meet you, Pink. Have you been following me?"

"Not all the time, but a little. I've asked around town about you and your husband mostly. I figure a town this size, people don't keep secrets for long."

"And what have you learned?" She drew in a deep breath to settle her nerves.

"That your marriage was unexpected and that some even thought you disliked him immensely."

"We're private people. Not from Cliffside Bay, I might add. People don't know us."

"Sure, sure. That's a valid theory." He stroked his beard. "Still, it's my experience people in a town like this make it a point to know as much as they can about their neighbors."

"Like I said, I keep to myself. So does David."

"The other night you two seemed real close, making out in the car. Then again, you could be doing that for my benefit. I mean, rich people like you don't need to sneak around in the car. That's what your mansion's for."

"We were admiring the moonlight."

"Yep, I could see that. You're what I call a true paradox. This thing could go either way. For example, you looked like the real deal this morning at school. From what I can see, there's an obvious attraction and closeness."

"Yes, of course there is. We're married."

"No reason to get defensive. I'm simply trying to find the truth. For the record, I'm rooting for you guys. That Moxie is a real piece of work."

"You know her?"

He raised one eyebrow. "She's been by my office more than once. And I don't think it's my charming personality she's drawn to. She pretty much said she'd cut me in on some of the money if I did what she wanted."

"And why wouldn't you?"

"That's not how I roll," Pink said. "I don't take dirty money, and I like the good guy to win."

"Then why not rule in our favor?" She smiled at him in a way she hoped was charming.

"I'm not a judge, Ms. Ness. Regardless, I work from a place of integrity. There's no way I'm going to say something I'm not sure is true. No matter how much that woman scares me. And the little dog, too."

"You should come for dinner," Sara said. "See where we live. I'll give you a tour. You can see our bedroom. Our much-used bedroom."

"You're making me blush." Pink reached into the inside of his jacket and handed her a card. *Pink Floyd, Private Investigator.* "Let me know if you have any questions."

"Will do."

Could her life get any weirder?

"YES, he just walked right up to me like he knew me," Sara said. "He scared me to death."

They were in the kitchen. Sara was chopping vegetables for a stir-fry while David kept an eye on the girls. Harper was on the floor with her blocks, babbling to herself. Laine had her stuffed dog in the toy high chair pretending to feed him.

"It's kind of creepy," David said. "Knowing that he's been watching us."

"I thought so too, but once I met him, it didn't seem that way. I hate to admit it, but I liked him. He's on our side."

"What if we aren't convincing enough?" David asked. "If he's as dedicated to honestly as he says, he's not going to do us a favor."

"We did it in front of people the other night at the party," Sara said. "I think people believed us."

"Yes, we've got them all fooled." His features twisted as if he'd eaten something sour.

"What is it?" Sara asked.

"I thought we agreed this wasn't all an act?" His voice sounded gruff and hurt.

She set down the knife and crossed around the island to where he was sitting on a stool. "We did agree." She pushed his legs aside to stand between them. "But it's early, and he may see that. We have to make it seem like we've been together for longer than a few weeks."

"Yeah, okay."

She kissed him. "Although, what a few weeks it's been."

He grabbed her tightly against him. "Is it bedtime yet?"

She shivered. "Counting the minutes."

Oliver came bouncing in, carrying a library book from school. She reluctantly separated from David and turned toward Oliver. Harper squealed when she saw Oliver and rose clumsily to her feet.

Sara dropped to her knees. "Harper, come to me. You can do it."

The baby took one step, then another, then one more before falling into a clump on the floor. Sara, David, and Oliver all cheered, so loudly they startled Laine. She ran to her dad, who picked her up.

"Good job, Harper," Oliver said as he knelt next to Harper.

"Olwie," Harper yelled, and rose once more to her feet.

"Back up a little," David said. "Maybe she'll take a few more steps."

Oliver obeyed and sure enough, Harper walked toward him. She made it at least six steps before falling. They all cheered again.

Harper sat on the floor, grinning and looking quite proud of herself. Sara had to wipe tears from the corners of her eyes. "What a big day it's been." Sara sat on the floor with her back against one of the stools.

David put Laine down and sat next to Sara. "This has been a big one for sure."

Laine wandered over to Harper and put her arms around the baby. "Harper."

They all turned to stare at Laine. Had she spoken?

"What did you say, honey?" David asked, his voice strangled.

But the child didn't say anything else. She picked up her dog and went back to playing.

Sara turned her head toward David. "It happened. You didn't imagine it."

"My heart is beating really fast," David said.

They stared into each other's eyes for a second, all the unspoken words clear between them.

"I'm starved," Oliver said. "What's for dinner?"

And just like that they were back to reality. Dinner always came around again, no matter what miracles had occurred on an ordinary night.

26

David

On the Saturday after Oliver's first week of school, David woke to the sound of rain on the roof. He rolled over to see Sara still asleep. She slept with one pillow nestled between her arms and another where she rested her cheek. He'd noticed she was often in this position, clutching the pillow as if it were a person, even though she had him now.

He glanced at the clock. Not yet 7:00 a.m. The kids would be up soon, as would the baby. The murmurs of Harper waking came through the monitor. Sara stirred, then moaned softly. She'd looked so tired by the time they got the kids to bed last night. He would let her sleep.

She made a move to get up, but he put a hand on her shoulder. "Go back to sleep. I'll get her."

She opened one eye. "Are you sure?"

"Positive."

"Just a few more minutes, I promise," she said.

He swung his legs to the floor and grabbed a sweatshirt from the chair for another layer over his T-shirt and pajama bottoms. The room felt chilly this morning.

He took another second to look back at her. She'd already

fallen back to sleep. Last night, for the first time since they'd started sleeping together, they hadn't had sex. He smiled. They'd snuggled until they fell asleep—a new first in their relationship.

He padded across the hardwood in his bare feet. Harper was standing in her crib, holding on to the bars. She grinned when she saw him and jumped up and down on the mattress.

"Hey there, baby girl," he said as he lifted her out and kissed her cheek.

She patted her hand on his shoulder. "Dada."

He stiffened as a jolt like an electric shock went through him. What had she said? No, she hadn't said his favorite word. He was hearing things.

He placed her on the changing table and undid her sleeper. With one hand he reached for a diaper in the shelf below. After a few sure, deft movements from a man who'd changed many diapers in his lifetime, Harper was in a dry diaper and zipped back into her footy pajamas.

"Are you ready for breakfast?"

"Dada." She lifted her arms and kicked her legs.

She'd said it again. This time he was sure. *Don't overthink this,* he told himself. Over the past few weeks, she'd heard Oliver call him Daddy all day. It was perfectly natural that she would think that was his name. And anyway, it was close to David. She might be saying that instead.

Still, it moved him. Tears pricked his eyes as he picked her up and held her against his chest. She was such a beautiful child with those soft blond curls and big blue eyes. Her mother's eyes. Even at such a young age, he could see her sweet disposition. She would be a darling child who grew up to be a remarkable woman like her mother. He would be her daddy if she wanted him. If her mother wanted him, that is. He stalled in the doorway. A staggering weight fell on his shoulders. He leaned against the doorway as his stomach churned. He wanted her to want him to stay. Forever. Would she want him to stay?

"Dada, milk." She wrapped her fingers in his hair.

"Yes, milk," he whispered. "Let's get you some milk."

He stepped outside the nursery just as Laine came out of her room. She carried her blanket and the stuffed dog. "Hi, Daddy."

She'd spoken again. For the second time that morning, his eyes stung with unshed tears. His baby girl had used her voice to say hello. She'd called him Daddy.

"Hey, baby," he said. "You hungry for breakfast?"

She nodded. Okay, well, that was fine. She'd said a few words, and maybe she wouldn't have any more to say for the rest of the day. It didn't matter. Progress.

Laine lumbered down the hallway toward them, trailing her blanket behind her. She placed her hand in his, and the three of them made their way down the stairs to the kitchen.

He put Harper in her high chair and Laine in her booster, then poured them each some milk in sippy cups with lids. Harper sucked on hers while watching David move around the kitchen. Laine didn't touch hers, though. She didn't love milk the way Oliver did.

"Do you two want some scrambled eggs?"

Laine nodded. The baby continued to suck from her cup.

He took a carton of eggs from the refrigerator and cracked eight eggs into a bowl. It took some opening and closing of drawers until he located a whisk. He'd just finished when Oliver appeared.

"Daddy, I woke up and thought it was school and then remembered it was Saturday," Oliver said. This boy of his was wide-awake from the moment he first opened his eyes.

David smiled back at him. "Yes, we have all day to do whatever we want."

Oliver went into the pantry and returned with Sara's apron. "You have to wear this when you're cooking. Sara said it keeps your clothes from getting messy."

David eyed the apron. The ruffles and sunflowers were not exactly his style, but if Oliver wanted him to wear it, he would.

He lifted it over his head and tied the strings around his waist. "Ollie, can you get the bread out for toast?"

"Sure, Daddy. I'll toast it for you. Sara taught me how."

"When did she do that?"

"When you left for work early the other morning," Oliver said. "She said it's important for kids to learn how to cook."

"Really?" Apparently, they'd had a lot of conversations without him.

Oliver didn't answer. He was too busy carrying a footstool over to the counter where the bread box and toaster were tucked under the cabinet. David watched him, amused by the scrunch in his little boy's brow as he opened the loaf of bread and put four pieces into the toaster.

So far, this day was going pretty darn great. His daughter had spoken again. Harper called him Dada. Oliver was making toast. All small things that represented so much more. A family was forming right under his nose.

Now he simply needed Sara to want him to stay with her forever. For that to happen, he needed a miracle. They existed. One only had to look at the faces of the three precious children in this kitchen to know it was true.

HE'D FED the kids and cleaned the kitchen by eight. With the rain falling quite seriously outside, he scrambled to think of something for them to do. Currently, Harper was yelling to be released from the high chair and had that crazed glint in her eyes that meant she was ready to wreak havoc. Oliver had worked his way through two pieces of toast and a heap of eggs and was now pretending to be driving a car, with his hands balled into fists and making a buzzing sound with his mouth as he moved around the kitchen. Laine had curled under the kids' play table to look through a picture book.

He rubbed his face and yawned. This was going to be a long

day. He unbuckled Harper and picked her up and out of the high chair. The moment he set her on her feet, she crawled over to the toy box and pulled out a play accordion and began to play it, unleashing the most horrifying noise ever.

Oliver stopped his car driving and stuck his hands over his ears.

Maybe they needed a ride in a real car. He could take them to the bookstore and let them all pick out a new book. However, that would require getting them all dressed and out the door without waking Sara. Given the current noise level, this seemed highly unlikely.

He tucked Harper onto his hip and pried the accordion from her pudgy hands. Fully expecting her to start howling, he was pleasantly surprised that she seemed content to put both hands in his hair.

"Dada."

David sneaked a glance at Oliver to see if he noticed Harper's new word. He'd given up on his car game and now stood at the French doors with a mournful expression.

"Does this mean no swimming?" Oliver asked.

"Not today, I'm afraid," David said.

"What do we do all day?" Oliver asked.

"We could go into town and visit the bookstore." The idea of getting them all into the car seemed like an impossible task just then, but he would have to face it.

Laine must have heard this because she clapped her hands, then crawled out from under the table.

"All right," David said. "We can go, but you guys have to get yourselves dressed while I help Harper. And you have to be very quiet, because Sara's sleeping upstairs. Let's pretend like we're invisible. No one can see us but you have to be very, very quiet."

Oliver nodded solemnly.

Laine, who was silent by nature, smiled.

"You're going to be the problem, aren't you, Harper?"

She tugged on his hair. "Dada."

This child really had a way of getting to a man's heart.

THEY STOPPED FIRST at the bookstore's cafe. David, who'd forgotten all about coffee that morning, grabbed a double latte from the teenage barista. The kids weren't hungry, thank goodness, because he didn't want to give any of them sugar right at the moment. He had the girls in the double stroller and had asked Oliver to hold on to the handle while they walked over to the book section.

Mary was at the counter, working on a computer. She smiled when she saw them. "Look who's up bright and early."

"These guys kind of forced the issue," David said.

"They have a way of doing that," Mary said. "My employee who usually works the weekend called in sick. So here I am."

"With the rain, business could be good," David said. As he often wondered, why would she bother with the bookstore? Lance was rich. They didn't need the money. One day he might ask her. But not today.

"Where's your bride this morning?" Mary asked as she came around the counter to stand before them.

"I let her sleep. She was exhausted from the week."

"What can I do for you guys this morning?" Mary asked. "Are we looking for books for everyone?"

"Sure," David said.

"I like books about trains," Oliver said.

"I know just the one," Mary said. "And what about you, Miss Laine?"

Laine held up her stuffed dog.

"Dogs, then?" Mary asked. "Follow me."

He lifted Laine out of the stroller so that she could go with Oliver. "Hold your sister's hand."

"Okay, Daddy." Oliver took his little sister by the hand, and they traipsed after Mary to the children's section.

"You're next, missy," David said to Harper. "Shall we find a book for you too?"

She grinned, showing her row of baby teeth. He'd forgotten how cute they were at this age. With her on his hip, he went to the baby book display of indestructible picture books. Some were made of plastic, others of hard cardboard. He picked up Eric Carle's *The Very Hungry Caterpillar*. "How about this one?"

She babbled something indecipherable and pointed at the cover.

"Okay, this is the one, I take it." He ambled over to the other row. Mary was on the floor with the kids. Several books about trains were stacked next to Oliver. Laine had her hands on one of the tiny Beatrix Potter books, looking at the pictures and smiling.

"I think we've found a few to take home," Mary said. "Now, what about for Daddy, guys? What kinds of books does he like?"

"I like books about trains too," David said.

"How about a good murder mystery on a train?" Mary asked as she got to her feet.

"Sounds great to me," he said.

They came from the stacks just as a figure in black entered the coffee shop. A long black coat and a cap that covered most of his or her face made it impossible to discern gender. The cops had reported a witness seeing a person in black clothing running down the alley after The Oar went up in flames. They'd asked residents to keep their eyes open for such a person.

The person lifted their arm, then shouted something. A loud boom shook the building. Harper howled. Laine's face crumpled as she threw herself against David's leg. Shortly thereafter, the figure ran out the door of the café.

Fear sliced through him.

Mary nodded as the color drained from her face. "The description matches. Black coat and cap."

"We have to get out," he said.

"Willow's in the coffee shop," she said.

The barista. His thoughts raced, then slowed as a calm overtook him. He had to get them all out safely. "I'll get you guys out first and I'll go back and make sure she escaped," he said.

He thrust the baby into Mary's arms, then scooped Laine up in one arm and Oliver in the other.

Mary led them through the shelves of books to an emergency exit that he knew faced the alleyway. She opened the door slowly, quietly, and they slipped out to the rain-drenched alley. "That's my car there," Mary said. "I have the key in my pocket."

In tandem, they ran toward it. Mary used the remote key to unlock the doors. David put Oliver on the ground. "Climb in. Get in the third row." Oliver did as he was asked without questions. He knew David's tone meant this was a serious situation.

David placed a crying Laine into the toddler seat. Mary put the baby in one of the car seats. Thank God she had kids the same age as his.

"Do you have your phone?" David asked.

"No, it's inside," Mary said.

"Take mine. Call 911 and tell them we need police and possibly fire trucks and get the hell out of here. I'm going back to make sure Willow got out."

"Please, be careful," Mary said.

"I will."

Mary nodded and started the engine. He slammed the passenger door shut.

Then he ran toward the shop. Just as he reached the door, he saw Willow coming around the side of the building, dazed and stumbling. He ran toward her and she collapsed in his arms.

"Are you all right?" he asked.

"Yes, I'm fine. The woman tossed something and then ran out the door. A second later, the bomb went off near the ice cream freezer. It was just a small fire. I tossed a bucket of water on it, and I think it fizzled out but I'm not sure."

The sound of sirens told him Mary had successfully reached the fire department.

"Did you get a good look at her?"

"Yes, I think I know who she is."

"You do?" David asked.

"She works at the post office. Her name's Darla," Willow said.

"And you're sure?"

"Positive. She's worked there my whole life. Darla Keene."

Darla Keene. Maggie's stepmother. She'd been married to Maggie's dad when he died a few years back. Lisa had told him the whole story. Roger Keene had left his wife and ten-year-old Maggie. He'd gone to Texas, where he met Darla. After he was gone, Maggie's mother had fallen in love with Hugh Shaw. She'd gotten pregnant and had asked Roger for a divorce. Roger had come back and murdered his estranged wife by pushing her down the stairs right after she gave birth to Hugh's baby.

Hugh had taken the baby to a safe house in San Francisco, knowing she was in danger if he kept her in Cliffside Bay. That baby had been Sophie. Darla had known everything. All those years she'd kept her husband's secret. He'd murdered his wife and yet she stayed with him until the end.

But why the arsons? Was her hatred of the Shaw family what led her to burn down The Oar?

If so, why would she want to burn down the bookstore?

S ara

Sara woke with a start. She'd been dreaming of her parents and could still feel their presence as she rolled over to look at the clock. Nine o'clock? How was that possible? Why hadn't the baby woken her? She sat up, alarmed until she saw a square of paper on the nightstand.

Sara,

Took the kids into town so you could rest. We're hitting the book-store, grocery, and then back home before lunch.

David

He'd taken all three of them into town? So she could sleep? On one of his days off, no less. How thoughtful of him. Her heart twisted. No faster way to a woman's heart than to take care of her child while she slept.

She rose out of bed and went to the window. Rain had fallen overnight. The yard below was damp and the sky gray. She heard the sound of a car coming down the driveway. They must be home already. She threw on her bathrobe and went down to greet them.

She'd just descended the stairs when the doorbell rang. Had David forgotten the code? She hustled over to answer, excited to see him and the kids. But it wasn't her husband. Mary Mullen stood there, holding Harper with the other two hanging on to the side of her pants. Both little faces were streaked with tears.

"Has something happened?" Sara asked as she reached for her baby.

"Mama." Harper snuggled into her neck with her cold nose.

"We're all fine." Mary picked Laine up and settled her on her hip.

Her chest tightened. "Where's David?" Why wasn't he with them?

"He's completely safe," Mary said. "But we have a story for you."

Sara gestured for them to come inside. They all went into the kitchen. She invited Mary to sit, which she did, with Laine on her lap. Sara sat across from her, continuing to hold Harper. Oliver scooted right next to Sara, something he'd never done before, usually too busy playing to sit.

"What's happened?" Sara asked.

"We were at the bookstore, picking out books for the kids," Mary said. "And a woman in black came in and headed toward the coffee area. Seconds later, we heard this loud boom."

"Oh my God. The arsonist?" Sara asked.

"Yes. David and I got the kids out of there and into my car. He went back to see about my barista, Willow. Clever girl had dumped water on the flames and was fine. And she got a good view of the arsonist and was able to identify her. David's down at the police station with her. They wanted them to come in and answer questions. But the cops found her. Darla Keene. She was trying to flee town, but they cut her off at the highway. I'd called it in the minute we were safe in the car, so they knew to block the exits out of town."

"I can't believe it," Sara said as a shiver of fear climbed up her spine. "You could have all been hurt."

"No, we were fine," Mary said in a soothing voice. "Don't even go there."

"Were you terribly scared?" Sara asked Oliver.

He nodded, then rested his cheek against her shoulder.

"The children were very brave." Mary kissed the top of Laine's head. "And they were great listeners when David and I told them to get into my car."

"And he went back?" Sara clutched the collar of her robe. "He could have been hurt."

"There was no way he wasn't going back for Willow," Mary said. "He's a hero."

"Thank God they caught her," Sara said. "Do you know who she is?"

"Yes. I'm afraid she has quite the history with the Dogs and Wags. Her name's Darla Keene. She was married to Maggie Waller's dad."

"Oh, yes, Autumn told me all about that. Was she trying to get revenge on the Shaw family?"

"I suppose. Although it doesn't explain why she'd target the bookstore," Mary said. "But as you said, they caught her now. She won't be able to hurt anyone else."

"Thank you for bringing the children back to me," Sara said.

Mary pulled a cell phone out of her pocket. "This is David's phone. We left in such a hurry that I left my phone in the store." She shook her head. "What's so weird is that I had the car key in my pocket, which I never do. But I was driving Lance's car today because he wanted to take mine in for an oil change. I just stuck the key in my pocket as I left the house and forgot all about it. If I hadn't, we wouldn't have been able to get out of there. In hindsight, it would have been fine, but I wasn't sure the whole building wasn't going up. I didn't want to risk it."

Mary's voice had started to shake.

"You poor thing," Sara said. "That must have been terrifying. Let me put on some water for tea. Or would you prefer coffee?"

"No, thank you. I'm fine. Just a little shaken." Mary glanced down at the toddler in her lap, who had fallen asleep. "This little one cried the whole way here. Silently though. I've never seen anything like it. Broke my heart."

"She doesn't talk," Oliver said. "Hardly ever."

Mary and Sara exchanged a look but didn't comment further.

"I should probably get home. Lance went completely nuts when I called him. I assured him we were all fine, but the whole thing scared him."

She put a hand on Oliver's silky head. "Shall we say goodbye to Mary and get your sister up to her bed for a nap?"

"Sure." Oliver jumped off his chair as Sara and Mary stood. Sara set Harper on her feet and took the sleeping Laine from Sara.

"Again, I can't thank you enough," Sara said.

"That's what friends do," Mary said. "Especially for ones who rushed back to a potentially burning building to rescue my employee."

The moment Mary left, Sara slumped against the doorway. A fury like no other rammed through her. How could he have gone back there with the potential of an exploding bomb? It was incredibly irresponsible. What if he'd died? She would've been left with his children.

She would have been left without him.

What had she been thinking? Allowing herself to entertain thoughts of them as a love match? She could not fall for him. Not when he could leave her. She couldn't go through it again.

It was nearing noon and still no sign of David. Sara paced around the living room while the kids watched a movie. The longer he was gone, the more furious she became. Finally, he arrived home.

Seeing him, rage surged through her. How dare he risk his life like he had.

"I'm back." He glanced at Laine and Oliver, who continued

to stare at the television screen without seeming to notice their father had returned, then grinned at her. "You're letting them watch a movie? I feel better about myself suddenly."

Harper clapped her hands and lumbered on her unsteady legs towards David. "Dada."

Sara's mouth dropped open as she stared at her child. What had she just said?

David swooped Harper up in his arms and kissed her cheek. "Hello, baby girl."

Baby girl? Dada? Holy crap. She'd let this get completely out of control. This man was not Harper's father. He had left her with Mary and run back in to be a big hero. Not to mention his own children.

"Can I see you in the kitchen?" she asked.

His brow furrowed as an expression of puzzlement crossed over his face. "Not exactly the welcome I was expecting, but sure."

"Put Harper down," Sara said. Her voice shook with anger.

He did so, setting her gently onto the floor. Sara scooped her up and charged toward the kitchen.

She put Harper in the bouncy seat and whipped around to David. He stood against the counter with his arms folded over his chest.

"What the hell is the matter with you?" David asked.

"What the hell's the matter with you? What were you thinking? Going into a building where a bomb could have exploded? Do you not remember how fast The Oar went up?"

He stared at her for a second before answering. "There was a teenage girl inside. How could I not?"

"Have you heard of waiting for the police or fire department? It was totally irresponsible of you."

"I'm sorry you feel that way." He spoke slowly, watching her like one would a wild, dangerous animal.

"Leaving the kids with a virtual stranger? And running back

inside? You could've been killed. And where would that leave me?"

"But I wasn't killed. I'm right here. They've caught the arsonist." He continued to speak slowly. Mansplaining, she thought. So typical.

"You would have left me with your children, David. We're married. Do you know the mess you would've left me with?"

"I'm sorry you think my children are a mess," he said, his voice brittle.

"That's not the point. They're not mine." She gestured toward Harper. "And this is not your daughter."

He flinched as if she'd thrown cold water on him. "Wow, okay. I'm not sure what's going on here, other than I scared you. I'm sorry for that, but this is way over the top."

"When did she start calling you that?"

"This morning," he said.

She covered her face with her hands. "This was a mistake. No amount of money is worth screwing with our kids' heads. You running around this morning playing Dada almost got you all killed. I can't do it, David. I can't allow myself to trust a man who would do this."

"Do what?"

"Abandon me to save a stranger," she said.

"You'd rather me be a coward and let someone's daughter die in a fire?" David's jaw clenched. "What's wrong with you?"

"It's what's wrong with you." She was shouting, high-pitched and out of control. "You had no thought of me or the kids. Did you? Tell me the truth. You didn't pause for a second to think what it might do to us if we lost you."

He stared at her blankly. "I guess I didn't. I was thinking only about an innocent girl who would lose her life to a lunatic. If that means I'm a bad man—a man not worthy of your love—then so be it. I'm not changing my principles simply because of your fear of abandonment."

"This is off. You and me. This whole deal. I'll pay you whatever it takes to get you out of my life."

She could feel how bewildered and hurt he was, but the anger was too much.

"I don't want your money," David said. "This stopped being about money the minute you let me into your bed. You know that as well as I."

"We got carried away playing house," she said. "That's all this was."

"It wasn't for me. I fell for you." He unfolded from where he was resting against the counter. "I need a few days to figure out what to do. But we'll be out of your hair."

"Dada?" Harper said from her bouncy seat. Tears rolled down her fat cheeks. "Dada?"

Tears smarted in her eyes. Damn him. Why had she allowed this? Not only was she going to hurt like crazy when he left, so was her daughter.

David knelt on the floor by Harper. "It's okay, baby girl. You have the best mama in the world. You're better off without me anyway." He kissed the top of her head and then rose and left the room without another word.

Sara sank to the floor and wrapped her arms around her knees. He was wrong. They weren't better off without him. Everything was better with him. Why had she freaked out like that?

He was right. She feared abandonment. The risk of loving someone again was too big for a person like her. It was better to do the pushing away now before she grew any more attached.

She couldn't risk this. Not again.

28

David
That night, in the guest room, he stared at the ceiling. He wished for sleep that would not come. His mind was too busy. He had nowhere to go. Once more, he was lost. Moving back in with his dad seemed impossible. Not after giving the kids a taste of this life. Rafael and Lisa would take them, but that would be a disaster. His fragile ego wouldn't survive.

His debts were paid off, so there was a glimmer of good that had come out of this ridiculous arrangement. He had the house in Iowa, which Sara had paid off in full. Maybe the right thing to do was take the children back to Iowa. He could get a job at a firm or maybe go out on his own. Without a mortgage, he could live cheaply.

The thought of that empty house made him want to cry. His kids, who had had a taste of what it was like to have a great mother and a stable household, would now be yanked away from it all and forced to live with him. No Lisa or their papa. Just him. Inadequate, depleted of joy, and brokenhearted over a woman he'd fallen for hard and fast.

He rolled onto his side. The ache in his stomach was such

that he thought he might be sick. Her reaction had been thoroughly unexpected. He'd not seen it coming, but he supposed it made sense. She was afraid to have someone die on her again. Her parents and then that worthless husband. Thinking of him close to death had triggered an irrational response.

She was right, too. He hadn't thought about her or the kids when he did what he did. But what kind of man left a young woman in that kind of danger?

He rolled to his other side, but the pain still engulfed him. A sob came from deep inside his chest. He loved her. Even after the hurtful things she'd said, he loved her. Walking away from her would be the hardest thing he'd ever had to do. And that was saying something. He'd been through a storm once already. But this one hurt more than anything else. No more Sara. No more Harper.

Grief over what might have been consumed him. He sobbed silently into the pillow.

Tomorrow, he would make a plan. Tonight he had to just give in to the loss. One more in a lifetime of them.

29

S ara

At 2:00 a.m. she finally gave up trying to sleep and went downstairs to the kitchen. She wanted ice cream. From now on, that's all she would have to look forward to. No more sex. No more warm David holding her as she drifted off to sleep.

And the kids. She would miss them more than she thought was possible. They'd been such a great unit. A family.

Guilt racked her. What had they done to these kids? What had she done to the kids? This was her idea. She was the one who wanted the money to start her foundation. And why? To feed her ego? To give her life purpose? The poor little rich girl and all that. What kind of woman did this?

She'd accused David of selfish disregard for her and the children when really it was her. She'd caused a major disruption in their lives, probably given them hope that she would be their mother.

And then there was Harper. Calling David "Dada" had broken Sara's heart. How had she gotten so attached so quickly?

The same way she had. Because David was a great man. Kind and thoughtful and so loving.

What had she done? Why had she pushed him away just when things were starting to work so well in both their lives and the lives of their children?

She knew the answer. Because she'd lost her parents. And because her husband had betrayed her in the deepest of ways. All that damage was collateral. Stored up inside her and triggered by something like today. This was the problem, though. Nothing was controllable. Not one thing. People she loved could die. Her precious child could be hurt by a man she wanted to be her father. He could walk away and she couldn't stop him.

Well, she'd certainly made sure he wanted to walk away today. She'd pretty much guaranteed the outcome she'd feared.

She poured herself a glass of wine and wandered into the family room. She curled on one end of the couch and let herself give in to the tears that had been scratching the back of her throat since the anger had dissipated. The moment he walked out of the kitchen, she'd regretted everything. Rage had made her unreasonable. When it left, she was simply sad.

She'd acted horribly and said things to him that he would probably never be able to forgive her for. She hadn't meant them. It was the spewing of a woman in pain. The scared little girl inside who didn't want to be left. The fat girl whom she'd thought no one would or could ever love. But David had loved her. She felt certain he had. Given the way his face had crumpled when she told him to leave, she knew what this whole thing had cost him. They'd been so frightened to feel again, and yet they had. Together, they'd forged an alliance and friendship that could have blossomed into a beautiful marriage. A real marriage.

She downed the rest of her wine and set the glass aside, then curled into a ball and let the tears flow.

"Sara?"

She uncurled to see David standing there in his pajamas and T-shirt and holding a glass of scotch. Swiping at her face with the backs of her hands, she tried to look stoic, but it was impossible. The sight of him made her cry harder.

He rushed to her side, putting his drink on the coffee table. "Why are you crying?"

"Why do you think? Because I'm an idiot." She wiped under her eyes and peered at him. His face was blotchy and his eyes red. Had he been crying, too?

"You're not an idiot," he said softly. "You're just scared to be left again. I am too."

"It was stupid to react that way. I just went crazy for a moment."

"I know. I get it. If I'd thought it through, I would have predicted it."

"I'm sorry," she said. "I'm so sorry for the things I said."

He let out a deep breath. "Sara, I'm in love with you and Harper. The thought of losing you is killing me. Not the threat of an arsonist, but facing walking out of here and leaving you both behind. I can't even fathom how I could do it."

"I don't want you to," she said. "I'm sorry for what I said about you and Harper. She's fallen for you, just as I have."

He took her hands in his. "I know you're scared, but can we give this a chance? I'll promise to be more careful."

"You can't promise me that you'll never die though," she said.

"I cannot, no. But I can promise you that I'd never leave you on purpose. I'll fight like hell to stay here on this earth for as long as I possibly can."

"These last few weeks with you have been some of the happiest of my life," she said. "But that's just the thing. The more I fall for you, the riskier it all becomes."

"As long as you want me, I'm not going anywhere. If I have to tell you that every day, I will."

He drew her into his arms. She placed her damp face on his chest.

"I want us to be married for real," he said.

"You mean a ceremony?"

"God no. I mean for us to come to an agreement that this is

the real thing. We're good for each other. We'll raise these kids together as partners and best friends. Do you want that?"

She raised her head to look into his eyes. "I do."

He kissed her. "I don't want to do the rest of my life without you."

"You won't have to."

He stood and offered his hand, then lifted her to her feet. "Can we go to bed now? In our bed? I was miserable without you tonight."

"Lead the way."

And so he did.

30

David
Four weeks later, David and Sara sat together on the couch with their hands clasped tightly together. Pink Floyd sat across from them with a notepad on his lap.

"How does this work?" David asked.

"I'm going to ask each of you the same questions you answered separately," Pink said. "And then I'll give my recommendation to the attorney."

They'd spent the last half hour filling out a questionnaire. Neither of them had predicted this as part of the process, or they could have practiced.

"Think of it as a newlywed game," Pink said. "Let's see how well you know each other."

"Fine, let's get going," David said. This whole thing bothered him. They shouldn't have to prove themselves to this guy. Sara's grandfather was a first-class jerk.

"We'll start with you, David," Pink said. "What is Sara's favorite meal?"

He thought for a moment. She'd never mentioned one to him. Food was her enemy. Anything she liked, she automatically put on the bad list because she was afraid to eat too much. "I don't know what she put down because this is a loaded question for her. To her, food is complicated. She grew up chubby, which haunts her. Over the last five years, she's transformed how she eats. So, yeah, I have no idea."

Pink frowned. "She put down enchiladas."

He glanced at her. "I've never seen you eat one."

"I don't now," she said. "He's exactly right about everything he said. My relationship with food is complicated."

"Fine, moving on," Pink said. "What's her favorite song of all time?"

Sweat dampened his forehead. He had no idea. How was that possible? He knew she liked classic rock. That's what she listened to sometimes when she cooked dinner. Did other couples know this kind of stuff about each other?

"Take a guess," Sara said quietly.

"I don't think she has one. She wouldn't be able to pick just one," David said. "There's too many to choose from. When we picked features for this house, it took her hours to comb through websites and magazines to decide every detail. She never wants to make a mistake or choose something she regrets."

Sara squeezed his hand so tightly he was afraid his circulation might be cut off.

"She wrote down the Beatles song, 'The Long and Winding Road,'" Pink said.

"Okay, well, I didn't know that," David said. This was stupid. They were going to fail. After falling in love for real, all would be lost. He couldn't bear to think of her losing her dream.

"What about her favorite flower?"

Finally, one he knew. "Japanese anemone."

"Correct. Excellent." Pink marked his paper with a great flourish. "What about something she's shared with you that only you would know about?"

He closed his eyes. These questions were unexpected. Could it be the tattoo on her hip? He'd go with that. "She has a tattoo of a dragonfly on her left hip. No one but me has ever seen it."

"You got another one," Pink said, smiling widely. "Let's switch gears. Sara, what about David's favorite meal?"

"His sister's fettuccini Alfredo." Sara gave Pink a self-satisfied smile.

"Good. How about something from his bucket list?"

She would never get this one. They'd never discussed their bucket lists.

"Visiting Rome to see the architecture," Sara said.

David stared at her. How had she known that one?

"And taking the kids to Disney World when they get a little bigger," Sara said.

Amazed, he continued to stare at her. She met his gaze and winked before turning to Pink. "We've never actually discussed our lists, but I can guess pretty well, given what I know about him."

"Excellent." Pink glanced down at his tablet. "Here's another one. Does David want another child?"

She stiffened. "I'm not sure, but I hope the answer's yes because I'm pregnant."

"What?" David jerked away to get a better look at her. "You are?"

"I took a test this morning." Her eyes watched him, fearful. "I'm only about seven weeks along."

Which meant she'd gotten pregnant on one of their first nights together.

"I have an IUD," she said to Pink. "But somehow it didn't work."

Pink, smiling, set aside his tablet. "I guess that's good enough proof that the marriage is real. We'll do a paternity test and give that to the lawyers."

David had turned to face his wife. "I can't believe it."

"I know. Me either," Sara said. "Are you mad?"

"Mad? Never." He placed his hand over her thigh. "I'm surprised but happy."

"Congratulations," Pink said. "A baby is fantastic news.

However, had you started out with this, I wouldn't have had to ask all those pesky questions."

"I thought the shock factor might work to our advantage," Sara said. "Plus, I wanted to see the look on both your faces when I told you."

"This calls for a celebration," David said. "Pink, can you stay for dinner?"

"Sure. I'd love to," Pink said. "As a matter of fact, I'd love to pick your brains about Cliffside Bay. I'm thinking about relocating here."

"Really?" David asked. "That's fantastic."

The sounds of Zoey coming in the front door with the kids drew their attention. "That's our nanny back with the children." Sara rose from the couch. "She's bringing dinner from the deli. I hope you don't mind sandwiches and potato salad?"

"That sounds delicious," Pink said as he stood.

"Daddy," Oliver shouted as he ran into the room. Seeing a stranger, he stopped and stared.

"I'm Pink." The tall man held out his hand to the little one. "A friend of your mom and dad's."

"He's staying for dinner," Sara said.

"She's not my real mom," Oliver said matter-of-factly. "My mom's in heaven."

Pink dropped down on his knees to kneel before Oliver. "So is my mom. Like you, I have a stepmother who I love a whole lot. Sometimes very special people are sent to love us when our mothers go to heaven."

Oliver blinked, then stepped toward Sara. He placed his hand in hers. "What do you call her?" Oliver asked Pink.

"I call her Mimi." Pink rose to his feet. "I'm not sure why, but that's just the name that stuck for both my sister and me. I was about your age when she married my dad."

"Mimi." Oliver shifted his gaze toward David.

"Has it been worrying you?" David asked.

Oliver nodded. "I don't want to call her Sara. I want a mom like my friends at school."

"You can call me whatever you wish." Sara sat back on the couch and took his other hand. "Whatever you call me, I'm your mom. You have a family now, just like your friends."

A slow smile came to Oliver's young face. "I'd like to call you Mom like my friend Will calls his mom."

"Mom works just fine." Sara let go of one hand to smooth Oliver's bangs from his forehead.

Laine entered the room, followed closely by Zoey holding Harper.

"Zoey, I'm going to call Sara Mom from now on," Oliver said.

"Very cool," Zoey said before turning her attention to Pink. "Hi, I'm Zoey. The nanny."

"Pink Floyd," Pink said. "Nice to meet you."

One of Zoey's brows lifted. "Pink Floyd?"

"My parents were groupies," Pink said.

Zoey nodded slowly. "They took fandom to a new level."

Pink chuckled. "That's one way to put it."

"Pink's a friend of a friend," David said, suddenly unsure how to explain his presence to Zoey.

"May I take that for you?" Pink asked, gesturing toward the deli bag in her hand.

"Yes, please." A slight flush came to her cheeks.

Laine had managed to push her brother aside and had climbed into Sara's lap. She put her hands on Sara's cheeks. "Mama. Not Mom."

They all went silent. Since the first day she'd spoken, she still only gave them a word or two here and there.

"Mama," Laine repeated.

Oliver touched his sister's shoulder. "Is that what you want to call her?"

"Yes. Mama." Laine dropped her head onto Sara's chest.

"I guess Mama's all right," Oliver said. "Here at home but not at school. Big kids don't say Mama."

"Mama," Laine said, even more firmly this time.

Sara kissed Laine. "Mama sounds just fine, little one." She looked over at David and smiled. For a moment, it was just the two of them in the room. No money in the world could replace this, he thought. Two people who fell in love and made a family. Who would have thought a fake marriage for money would lead to this?

"Mrs. Perry, shall I escort you to dinner?" David asked.

"You may, Mr. Perry."

TWO MORNINGS after the visit from Pink Floyd, Stephen Lodge called.

"It's Lodge," Sara said. "I'll put him on speaker."

"Sara, it's Stephen Lodge. I just received the official pregnancy and paternity results. You're definitely pregnant, and David is the father. Floyd's signed off officially. According to the will, we can't transfer money to you until the year is over."

"Thank you," Sara said into the phone. David echoed the same.

"Congratulations," Lodge said. "A child's a blessing, no matter how he or she comes into the world."

"Yes, we're very excited," Sara said. "And for the record, we're madly in love. This baby was not made simply to get the money."

"Oh, I see. Well, that's wonderful news."

Sara almost laughed at the fluster in his voice. "We didn't plan it that way. It just happened."

"As they say, there's no stopping love," Lodge said. "I guess we have your eccentric grandfather to thank."

"Yes, I suppose we do," Sara said. "Mr. Lodge, there's one thing I wanted to ask you. Regarding Moxie, is it possible to give her a bit to help her get started? I mean, she does have the dog."

"That's very kind of you," Lodge said. "However, she's

already moved in with another rich man of a certain age. She's quite fine as far as I can tell."

"What about the dog?" David asked. What if she'd abandoned it once she found out she wasn't getting the money?

"The dog's been handed off to Mr. Floyd. When he went to tell Moxie the news, he found Princess alone in the apartment. No food or water. As you might have picked up, Mr. Floyd's a passionate man. He went ballistic, I think is how you young people would describe it, and took Princess from the apartment. She's now with him."

"Did he tell you of his plans to move to Cliffside Bay?" David asked. "He fell in love with it while he was here following us around."

"Yes, he did," Lodge said. "I might need to take a trip up there myself sometime. After most of my life in LA, a small town sounds delightful."

"Come visit anytime," Sara said.

"There's one thing I wanted to ask you, Miss Ness," Lodge said. "What convinced you to do this? As you said, you don't need the money."

"I've wanted to start a foundation to help impoverished families all over the world since I was a little girl. This will let me do it."

"I thought it was something like that," Lodge said. "Let me know if you need any legal advice."

"I will," Sara said.

They chatted for a few more minutes about the details of the legal matters, then hung up. David pulled her into his arms and kissed her. "We did it. Think of all the people we can help now."

"I like the sound of that 'we,'" she said. "And it means I can offer a job to Autumn if she wants one. Higher pay and working from home. That way she can stay with the baby."

"I love you, you know that?" David asked.

She smiled up at him. "I do."

• • •

David

The Wolves sat around their conference table, all five with their eyes cast downward. Since Rafael and Stone had announced their departures, the five of them had avoided talking about the future, focusing instead on the Emerson Pass projects. Stone and Rafael had bought their way out of the partnerships, so going forward, Wolf Enterprises would only be Trey, Nico, and David. The head contractor and project manager position would be employees, not partners.

Now the two final candidates for the project manager and contractor were waiting in the lobby.

"Okay, guys. This is it," Rafael said. "Are you all absolutely sure these are the people we want?"

"We want you guys," David said. He'd hoped they'd miraculously change their minds. That was not to be.

"But yeah, we're sure," Trey said. "These two just stood out."

"And Zoey vouched for both of their characters," David said. "They all went to college together in Oregon."

Stone spread his big hands out on the table. "It's weird to hire a tiny woman to take my place. However, I have a feeling she's going to get a lot more out of our subcontractors than I did."

"If they can focus," Trey said. "She's very attractive."

"Let's have MariLou in first," Rafael said. "I'll go get her."

"This kind of sucks," Nico said after Rafael left. "I'm going to miss the five of us being a team."

"Me too," Stone said. "But we're still best friends. Nothing changes that."

Rafael held the door open for the woman who would be their new contractor, MariLou Scarpari. "Hey, guys," she said.

"Have a seat," Rafael said.

MariLou was petite and fair-skinned with hair somewhere between red and blond. Today she was dressed in jeans and work boots, having come from a work site. "Excuse my appearance," she said as she lowered herself into a chair. "I didn't have time to go home and change."

"Not a problem," Stone said. "We understand. Your references from your clients and former boss were very complimentary."

"We'd like to offer you the position." David slid the offer letter across the table.

She read it quickly. "That's very generous. I accept."

David had expected her to ask for more money. Perhaps she was young and hungry enough to be grateful for a job. Zoey had told him MariLou had grown up poor and was determined to make it on her own. A woman in a man's world couldn't be easy. They'd been unanimous in agreement that hiring a woman would add a perspective they lacked. Plus, she'd been the best candidate.

A few minutes later, the woman they were offering the project management position looked over her offer letter. Kris Hughes had dark blue eyes and a cap of almost black hair that framed her round face. She accepted the offer without questions, just as MariLou had. From Kris's references, she was adept at handling a myriad of details and would be a great replacement for Rafael.

After the young women left, the five of them remained at the conference table. No one said anything for a moment. Stone was the first to speak. "It's not like we're never going to hang out again. This is just the next chapter of the Wolves."

"David, are you sure you're still on board?" Trey asked. "It's not like you need to work, right?"

"I've wanted to be an architect all my life," David said. "This is not a job to me but a vocation. Sara wouldn't want me moping around the house bored. I'm here as long as you two are."

"I'm not going anywhere," Nico said. "We need the money, even if I wanted to quit. Sophie wants to have a baby sooner rather than later."

"The work in Emerson Pass will keep us busy for the next few months," Trey said. "After that, I hope more will come our way. I'm nervous."

"You're always nervous," Nico said. "And things always work out."

"The three of you will make a bigger part of the profit with Stone and me gone," Rafael said.

Stone got up from the table and grabbed a six-pack of beer from the refrigerator. "Let's have a drink to celebrate everything we've accomplished in the last few years."

They each took a beer and popped the tops. Rafael raised his. "We've built homes, a theater, a new medical clinic. I think we can agree how successful this partnership has been. I'm going to miss working together, but our friendships are strong."

"The mangy wolves of Cliffside Bay have come a long way," Trey said. "We were all broke and bitter. Now look at us. Happily married. Babies on the way."

"That time seems like a lifetime ago already," Stone said.

"I didn't think there was much hope for us," Trey said.

"To the women who saved us," Rafael said.

They clinked bottles.

"To the mangy wolves of Cliffside Bay," Stone said. "Long may we live."

They raised their bottles once more.

David looked around the table at the men he thought of as family. He'd joined the firm on faith and his sister's assurances that he would thrive as the fifth member of Wolf Enterprises. How silly he'd been to ever question the move to Cliffside Bay or joining these guys in business. His life finally made sense. Sara had been waiting for him, neither of them knowing during the heinous moments of their tragedies that a gift would eventually come. The gift of each other and their friends was worth the wait.

"Guys," David said. "I know I've not always been the easiest person to read and have probably been a pain in the rear most days. But I want you to know that this partnership saved me. I don't know what would've happened to me or my kids if we hadn't come here. If you guys hadn't given me a chance without even knowing my work."

"We've never once questioned your commitment to excellence or integrity," Rafael asked. "That we love you like a brother is icing on the cake."

"I can't imagine having done this without you," Stone said. "The three of you are artists, whereas Rafael and I were simply the brains and the brawn. I don't have to tell you which is which."

They all laughed. When the room quieted, Trey addressed Stone. "Are you going to be able to stand not working with your hands?"

"I've got Pepper." Stone grinned as he raised his hands off the table and wriggled his fingers. "She's a handful in every way. I doubt I'll get bored. But if I do, I'll find another way to keep out of trouble. I'm not supposed to tell anyone yet, but she's pregnant. In less than eight months, I'll be a dad."

"No way, man," Nico said. "That's awesome."

"With her work schedule, I'm going to be Mr. Mom for the foreseeable future," Stone said. "That was our agreement. If she had a baby, I said I'd be a full-time dad so she could keep working. I never thought I'd say it, but I'm excited for this next season."

They all congratulated Stone and promised to keep the secret, other than to tell their wives. "Who I suspect already know," Stone said. "They were all having lunch today."

"We won't be far behind," Rafael said. "If the good Lord and my bride have anything to say about it. And I'll be taking care of the babies while Lisa works too, so it'll all fall into place as it should."

David decided then and there to tell them his news as well. "You won't believe this, but Sara's pregnant too."

"Man, the town council will have a fit," Rafael said. "They're going to have to change the sign to add more residents."

"There's another thing," David said. "I don't want there to be any secrets between us. Not if we're going to be a brotherhood for the rest of our lives." He spilled the truth about the fake marriage, ending with the visit from the detective yesterday. "Since we're pregnant, he knows the relationship's real. Before that, I was sweating it. I couldn't stand the thought of her losing the money she wants to do so much good with."

Rafael was shaking his head. "I knew there was something weird going on. Lisa did too. She kept saying that you would have told her before you up and got married."

"We had to keep it a secret in case the detective interviewed you guys," David said. "It was horrible to keep it from our friends, but we couldn't risk it. Other than Lisa and Pepper, no one in this group can act. And except for this one, we've never been able to keep a secret among us."

Nico's eyes softened. "It doesn't matter now. All that matters is that you two found your way to each other. If not for her grandfather and his crazy will, you might not have realized your true feelings."

"You're such a romantic." Trey punched Nico on the shoulder.

"Takes one to know one," Nico said. "All our stories are a little crazy if you think about it. All of us with women way out of our leagues. None of us stood a chance, and yet here we are."

"That's the damn truth," Stone said. "If there ever was one."

"Again, boys, to us," Rafael said. "Lucky bastards that we are."

Sara

For the last night of the six-week support group, Sara and David had them all out to the house for dinner. They'd agreed to a ritual of some kind and to include family members. For days, Sara contemplated just what would be the best way to honor and say goodbye to their loved ones. In a group text, she'd proposed they each light a floating candle for their loved one and set it in her pool.

The weather cooperated with a clear, chilly night. On her patio, guests mingled, enjoying appetizers and drinks. Zane had brought Honor and his children. His little boy, Sebastian, was about Laine's age and the two towheads were currently staring each other down in a battle over a toy car. Zane's daughter, Jubie, was with Oliver and Zoey at the craft table. They'd asked if she might sing "Amazing Grace" for them after they lit the candles, and according to Zane, she'd happily agreed.

Nico and Sophie were there for Zane. Ria had brought David's father. They'd come out to the patio holding hands and hadn't let go all evening. Bobby and Judi had also arrived together. Lisa and Rafael had come for David. Autumn and Trey had come for her.

Sara noticed Bobby heading toward the pool house, probably to use the restroom. She hurried over to Judi, who sat in one of the lounge chairs around the firepit. "What's going on with you and Bobby?" Sara whispered.

Judi grinned and patted her hand. "We're enjoying each other's company, in and out of the bedroom."

"Judi, you sly dog."

"He's a wonderful man," Judi said. "We decided it was time to start enjoying life before it was our turn to go."

"I'm glad for you," Sara said.

Ria clapped her hands and asked everyone to circle around the end of the pool. Sara had asked Zoey to take the children inside during the ritual and she did so now, carrying both toddlers on a hip with Oliver taking the lead. Harper had already been tucked into her crib for the night. A quick glance at the baby monitor assured her that all was well.

On one of the tables, Sara had placed six floating candles.

"Thank you to our family and friends for joining us tonight," Ria said. "The members of our group have been courageous in journeying through the grieving process. They asked if we could have some kind of ritual as our final session, and we agreed to inviting our loved ones to join us. Each of them will take a turn speaking and then light a candle for their loved one. Zane, would you start us out, please?"

He nodded and stepped forward out of the half circle. Ria handed him a candle and a lighter.

"I'm lighting this for my dad." The lighter made a clicking noise as he lit the flame. Shadows played on his face as he spoke. "I miss him every day and will for the rest of my life. However, I know someday I'll see him again in heaven. All I've ever wanted was to be the kind of man he was. For as long as I can remember, he was a living example of what it means to be compassionate and charitable and, above all else, a great father. Now that he's no longer with us, I've felt lost, rudderless. I didn't realize until he was gone how much I relied on his example. He had these eyes—these kind eyes that I could always count on to give me direction. Without him, I'm so often unsure. I want to ask him parenting advice or to weigh in on my business. Regardless of all that, I light this in honor of him and for all the ways he taught me to conduct myself."

Next to him, tears ran down Honor's face. Sara knew from Zane that she had been particularly close to Hugh Shaw. He'd been like a father to her. What was it like to share a loss with someone? She'd never had that. But now she had David. They would share so much in the years to come. The good and the bad. Whatever came their way, it would be together.

Zane knelt to place the candle in the water. "Rest in peace, Dad," he whispered as the candle floated toward the middle of the pool.

Bobby went next. A gentle smile came to him as he lit the candle. "This is for my wife, Lucy. She was splendid. In every way. Too good for me. Everyone knew it, too." He smiled. "Except for her. She made me feel like a prince among men. To have been loved by her was a privilege. In the end, she suffered more than any human should. I prayed that God would give it all to me instead. I let her go, though. Told her it was all right. But I don't want to remember the sick days. I choose to recall instead how splendid she was the day I married her or all the times we spent on the beach. All the memories that make me smile. Because that's what she would've wanted for me. Not the ending but the beginning and all the days in the middle. Until we meet again, my dearest." He placed the candle in the water. Sara watched the ripples cascade outward until they reached the edge of the pool and faded away.

"My turn, I guess," Judi said. She took a candle and the lighter from Bobby. The lighter clicked once, then again, but no flames.

"Allow me," Bobby said softly.

Judi handed it to him and he adjusted the flame size and leaned close to light the wick. "Thank you," she whispered.

"You're welcome." He touched her arm. "Go ahead now."

Something in that small, gentle exchange moved Sara to tears. How careful they were of the other.

"I light this for my husband. He was larger than life. So large, in fact, that I couldn't imagine him ever dying. But he did, of course. I was irritated with him. How dare he die before me. That wasn't our agreement. The man had never once let me down in the entirety of our marriage. Tonight, I honor his steadfastness, his patience, and the way he took care of me and allowed me to care for him. I've learned from this group how very lucky I was to have had that kind of love." She steadied herself against Bobby's arm as she knelt to put the candle in the water. "Rest easy, my love."

Sara exchanged a look with David. "I'll go now," David said.

Bobby handed him the lighter, and the wick flamed to life. "This is for my late wife. When I first started with this group, I was consumed by rage. I could only remember the ending of the story. The ways she betrayed me and the children. The fact that she left her babies behind. I'll always be angry, but I choose to forgive her. I choose to remember the days our children were born and the look on her face when she held them for the first time. Because no matter what she did or how she hurt me, she gave me two very precious gifts. Also, my grief led me to the support group where I got to know my Sara. Together, we're forging ahead into a new kind of family. And for that I'm grateful." His knees creaked as he knelt by the edge and set the candle free.

Sara's heart beat fast as she took the lighter from David and copied the same movements as the others. Once the flame flickered, she drew in a deep breath to steady her nerves. "Like David, I'm grateful for this second chance. Finding each other and making a family together has healed a lot of my rage and grief over my husband's betrayal. I don't think I'll ever understand why he did what he did. But I can choose to forgive. Not for him, but for me. So I light this candle in his memory. I won't be thinking of you any longer. When I do, it steals me from the present. You don't deserve my attention. You never did." She set the candle in the water and then straightened to take David's hand.

"Thank you all for sharing this with us," Ria said. "I hope for all of you, this exercise provides you a little peace. Thanks to all the friends and family who came tonight. Your support means a lot to us."

"There are more refreshments and a cake on the table there," Sara said. "Please enjoy the rest of the evening."

While the others drifted away, Sara and David remained by the pool, holding hands. The candles bobbed in the slight current, their flames reflected in the water.

"Hard to believe where we are, isn't it?" Sara asked.

"I'd never have predicted it, but I'm not going to question our luck. Finally, it's our turn."

AFTER EVERYONE LEFT, Lisa and Rafael lingered. Sara sensed they wanted to talk about what had happened.

David got them all another drink and the four of them went out to the patio. Sara turned on the outside heaters, and they all sat in lounge chairs around the gas firepit.

"Did Dad tell you his news?" Lisa asked.

"What news?" David crossed his ankles and reached over to put a hand on Sara's thigh.

"He's moving in with Ria," Lisa said.

"That seems fast," David said.

Rafael laughed. "As far as that goes, no one here has any right to judge how quickly they're moving."

"Only if we're being reasonable," Lisa said, eyes sparkling with humor. "Which we're not."

"At least she's his age," Rafael said.

Lisa groaned. "Another excellent point." She turned toward David and Sara. "Okay, spill it. I want to know every detail of how this thing happened between you. I knew I was right to be suspicious. This one has never done one thing unexpected in his life. Until now, that is."

"What about at Marigold's funeral?" David asked.

"Oh yes, that time too." Lisa giggled as she brushed a hand through her hair. "That was the most horrifying and humorous moment of our family history."

David cringed, remembering. "And to think Rafael didn't even know me." He turned to Lisa. "That was the first time he'd ever met me."

"I loved you immediately," Rafael said. "Even though it was a total car wreck."

"Anyway, back to your story," Lisa said.

They told them exactly how it had happened, including the initial call from Lodge. "It felt like a weird dream," Sara said. "Or like a prank. I mean, what kind of person demands that their granddaughter get married or all the money goes to a dog?"

"A man with a few missing screws," Lisa said. "And the fact that he hired this detective to follow you around and decide if it was legit is extremely strange. Even for California."

"Named Pink Floyd," Sara said. "That's the best part."

They all laughed.

"Luckily, he's a great guy," David said. "If I'm guessing right, kind of a romantic."

"He said he was rooting for us," Sara said. "Which was really sweet." As long as she lived, she would never forget his kindness during such an awkward time. "He could've been awful to us. Demanded a bribe. Anything like that would've been really tempting. But he has this intense integrity."

"He stayed for dinner that night," David said. "And couldn't take his eyes off a certain nanny."

"He wasn't exactly subtle," Sara said. She couldn't tell what Zoey had thought of him and hadn't brought it up for fear of embarrassing her.

"What happened next?" Lisa asked.

"The pipes burst," Sara said. "And David had to move into my room or otherwise Zoey would've figured us out."

"Anyway, one thing led to another." David spoke hastily, as if he wanted the conversation to end. "And one day I woke up in love with this incredible woman. The end."

Lisa's brow furrowed and her nose wrinkled. "Let me see here—if you're like six weeks along, that means you started sleeping together right away."

"Lisa, that's none of your business," David said. "Boundaries, please."

"I'm your twin. There's no such thing." Lisa flashed him an evil smile. "You totally got her into bed right away."

"Lisa," Rafael said. "Really, it's none of our business."

"I don't mind," Sara said. "The truth is, your brother seduced me. After that, I didn't have a fighting chance. I fell hard and fast."

"This is the greatest love story of all time," Lisa said.

"Not really," David said drily. "It was fate, that's all."

"Do you really think so?" Sara asked. He'd never said that before.

"Sure. We're soul mates, just like these two." David gestured toward Lisa and Rafael. "Once we were forced together, it was obvious what was between us."

"What you're telling us is that you beat our record?" Rafael asked. "It took me three nights before I got her into bed."

Lisa smacked his shoulder. "Talk about boundaries."

"Yeah, that means I win," David said. "One night and boom."

"Oh my God," Sara said, laughing. "The flooding of the cottage helped you out." And the fact that he was the sexiest man in the world.

Lisa's eyes had turned wistful. "I'm so jealous about the baby. We've been trying for months now and nothing."

"It'll happen," Sara said. "Apparently, even with an IUD. Kara said it's something in the sea air. Babies are created out of nowhere."

"I hope she's right," Lisa said.

"She is, baby," Rafael said as he took her hand and brought it to his mouth. "Don't worry. It'll happen soon enough. Especially now that we'll be together all the time."

"Totally," David said. "There hasn't been a month since you got married that you haven't been apart. Now that he's free to travel with you, I bet it happens right away."

"I'm sorry I ruined the firm," Lisa said.

"Pepper's to blame too," David said, teasing.

"Baby, I'd rather be with you than anywhere in the world," Rafael said.

"Me too," Lisa said. The look of pure love on his sister's face made his chest ache.

"Think of all we have to look forward to," Sara said. "A year ago I wouldn't have believed I'd have a family other than Harper."

"You're stuck with us now," Lisa said.

"She's right," Rafael said. "When you marry a Perry, you get the whole package. A twin. Mama Soto and Uncle Perry. Now Mr. Perry and Ria."

"Don't forget our mother and her nubile French man." Lisa rolled her eyes. "We've got the whole dysfunctional family for you to put up with at every holiday for the rest of your life. You're welcome."

"It sounds lovely to me," Sara said. "Growing up, all I ever had were my parents. I used to dream of a big family at Christmas." Sara placed her hand on her stomach. Inside grew a baby that would be part Perry and part Ness. Her parents would live on as they did with Harper. "I always wanted a sister especially."

Lisa smiled her movie star smile. "Me too. And as your new sister, I have to ask. Do you want a real wedding?"

"Definitely not," Sara said.

At the same time David said, "God no."

They looked at each other and laughed. "I guess that's a no,"

Sara said. "Plus, we already had a party at your house. We don't need another."

"And seriously, you should've seen the Vegas wedding," David said. "After that five-minute special, who could want anything more?"

32

David

On the day before Thanksgiving, David, along with the rest of the town, cheered as Sophie cut the ribbon in front of the new bar and grill. For the occasion, city officials had closed Hugh Shaw Avenue in front of the building. They were blessed with sunny skies and a cool, crisp day, as if Hugh himself had asked the man in charge for good weather for his beautiful daughter's grand opening.

David had Harper in a carrier on his back. Occasionally she tugged at the back of his hair and wriggled her legs, but for the most part seemed mesmerized by the activity around her. Sara stood next to him with Laine on her hip so the child could see. Sara had braided Laine's hair into two pigtails with pink bows that matched her dress. Oliver had run up ahead to sit with some of the other children near the entrance.

Sophie hugged Nico, then Zane, before turning to face the crowd.

"Thanks so much for being here," Sophie said into the portable microphone. Later, Maggie would give a short concert on the back patio.

"This place was my dad's first love," Sophie said. "Because

everything was lost in the fire, we weren't able to salvage any keepsakes to put on the walls or incorporate into the design. However, I feel him in every inch of the place. I know he'd be super happy to see what Wolf Enterprises did with his beloved bar."

Next to her, Zane wiped his eyes. Honor linked her arm through his. Jubie, who was holding on to her little brother's hand, smiled up at her daddy. What a beautiful family, David thought. One made from the love of two people.

David glanced down and into the eyes of his wife. Sara smiled and whispered, "The place is amazing, honey. You guys killed it."

He kept himself from touching her slightly rounded belly. She'd teased him last night that he was obsessed with her baby bump, and she was right. In his defense, Sara had never looked lovelier. He couldn't keep his hands off her in general. And the new baby represented the future. Their future together that would merge their family in a whole new way. Already, the three children acted as if they'd always been together. The biggest change, however, was in Laine. She'd attached to Sara as if they'd always been mother and daughter. Laine had started to talk more and more as the days passed. Today, she'd chattered away to her brother all the way to town.

On the short walk from the van to the ribbon-cutting ceremony, Oliver had whispered in his ear that he kind of missed the quiet Laine. David had laughed harder than he should have.

Sophie was continuing her speech. "What I asked the guys to do seemed like an impossible task. After spending time in Paris, I fell in love with the cafés there. I wanted this place to have a little Parisian flair, and I think they accomplished exactly that. Thank you so much, Trey and David, for the design work. MariLou was the best contractor a girl could ask for. Finally, thanks goes to my fiancé, Nico. Not only did he put up with me during this process, he's responsible for the beautiful landscaping." She gestured toward the hanging baskets that were currently planted with mums. David had hung them from hooks all along the front of the building. Movable planter boxes were now lined up along the side of the building, but in warm months they'd be placed along the fenced outdoor eating area.

Nico winked at Sophie and then dipped his chin modestly. He didn't care for attention like this, David thought. He'd rather be playing with his plants.

The project had been MariLou's first job as the contractor of Wolf Enterprises. She'd supervised the latter part of the project and had exceeded expectations by completing the build a month early. All three of them were pleased with their new hires.

Standing here in front of the new bar and grill, a sense of deep pride came over him. During the warm months, tables would return to the outside area, but for now the windows sparkled in the sunshine. The outside walls were partially made of brick to match the bookstore and grocery, but mixed with wood painted white.

For him the challenge had been to best utilize the small lot to the best advantage. Sophie had wanted to expand capacity and to add a kitchen with a wood-fired pizza oven that was partially visible to the customers. The new space included a second-floor seating area, and through careful design, he'd been able to give her everything she asked for. She'd felt strongly that the scent of the pizza oven would enhance the ambiance of the restaurant, and he agreed. What better smell was there on a warm summer day?

What had been grass and the decrepit back patio was now enclosed in glass that could be open or closed, depending on the season. David thought of it as a greenhouse meets a sunporch.

However, as much as he loved the architecture, Trey's eclectic interiors were really the star. Sophie was right. Somehow, Trey had given her exactly what she'd asked for—a restaurant that merged an American bar and grill with a bistro in Paris.

The floors were done in rustic wide planks. In contrast, the lighting fixtures included a wide selection of industrial-like aluminum pendants, delicate glass, and even a row of crystal chandeliers, all of which added to the whimsy of the place. Tables and chairs were not uniform, but made in all shapes and types of wood.

In an homage to the past, a surfboard hung on one wall.

"Without further ado," Sophie said. "I'd like to announce the new name of our bar and grill." Nico moved the tarp that hung over the new sign. In black lettering, the sign read "Hugh's."

"We thought it was only right that the business have his name," Sophie said.

The crowd cheered again.

"My deepest wish is that Hugh's becomes what our father loved the most—a place where people spend happy times with their loved ones over a good meal and a cold beer. He was all about this community. I hope this new chapter will have that in common with the last." Her face lit up in one of her sunny smiles. "Now let's have some food and beer. We don't have room for everyone to come inside, so we'll have staff bringing out complimentary pizza for the next several hours. For those of you who made reservations, please form a line by the door, and we'll escort you to your tables."

Sophie opened the double doors to Hugh's, and people lined up as they'd been asked. David and Sara hung back. The private room upstairs had been reserved for the Dogs and Wolves and their wives to dine together. He could hardly wait.

THE CHILDREN WERE all sent home with nannies or babysitters, leaving their parents to enjoy an adult evening. Trey had cleverly thought to use only square tables for the upstairs portion of Hugh's. This way a long surface could be constructed from the smaller parts. Tonight, they'd been pushed together to accommodate ten couples. Sophie had placed name and menu cards at each setting. A row of mason jars stuffed with strands of white lights decorated the table.

Grand Opening Dinner
Brody Salad
Sophie's Barbeque Pizza
Zane's Sliders
Jubie's Ice Cream Sundaes

Staff had served drinks, and everyone except Honor had sat in their assigned places. Honor clinked her glass, and the room quieted. "Hey, everyone. Sophie asked if I might say a few words tonight to celebrate this grand reopening. I happily accepted, as toasting, talking, and drinking happen to be my specialties."

Zane chuckled as he gazed up at his wife with adoring eyes. "We all know that, honey."

David's gaze darted around the room. Brody Mullen had his arm wrapped around the back of Kara's chair. Next to Brody, Mary and Lance exchanged an amused glance. Kyle and Violet, who were sitting next to David, had their hands on each other's thighs. Across from David, Nico played with a strand of Sophie's hair while directing his gaze at Honor. Autumn, looking very pregnant, rested her head against Trey's shoulder. Rafael sat so close to Lisa that it appeared they were sharing an oversize chair. Jackson held his newborn son in one arm and had the other wrapped around Maggie's shoulders. Pepper was tucked into Stone's thick chest.

Six months ago, the sight of all these happy couples might have hurt. Not now. He had his own love right by his side.

"However, as much as I love attention," Honor said. "I don't want to hog the spotlight. I thought it might be fun if all of the ladies expressed their good wishes to Sophie. As a woman, I'm so proud of how Sophie's risen to the challenge of the last six months. She's a true leader, and I know this reimagined bar and grill will be a great success."

"Thank you," Sophie said, eyes shining. "I couldn't have done it without Nico and Zane."

"Not true," Zane said.

"Ditto," Nico said. "You did this, baby. Not us."

Honor continued. "Hugh was a very special person in my life. He was the first adult who loved me unconditionally and became like a father to me. I miss him every day. But I know in my heart that seeing us all gathered here would make him super happy. I feel sure he's looking down on us at this moment and grinning his enormous Hugh Shaw grin. I know, too, Sophie, that you make him enormously proud. Your kind and generous heart gave us the gift we can never repay, our son, Sebastian Hugh. Congratulations to you and to the Wolves, who did an absolutely amazing job on this place. Cheers to the next chapter of the bar and grill."

A roar of toasts and cheers filled the room.

"One more thing," Honor said. "Since we're all here, I might as well spill the beans. Zane and I learned this morning that our wish for another child through adoption is happening. Our daughter will be coming to us in the next few weeks."

Exclamations of surprise reverberated around the table.

"We didn't want to say anything about our hope to adopt," Zane said, "until we were sure. The young woman who is the birth mother chose us, which we're grateful for."

"That's incredible news," Jackson said as he placed his hand over his heart. "One more baby for us all to love and cherish."

"Seriously, man, that's awesome," Brody said.

"We just felt like our family wasn't quite complete," Honor said. "Even though Sebastian is like two people."

"Like his mama," Zane said, teasing.

Honor laughed as she sat back in her chair.

Kara stood up next. "I came here without knowing a soul or one thing about Cliffside Bay. I'd never felt more lost or lonely in my life. The first thing I did after unpacking my few belongings and promising my cat that everything would be all right was walk into The Oar for a meal and an IPA. Zane Shaw was the first person I met in this town. His warmth and immediate offer of friendship marked the beginning of my new life. It was not just the brick-and-mortar that made The Oar special. The people between the walls are what made it a gathering spot. I look forward to many more years of celebrations of babies and weddings and girls' nights out." Her voice cracked. She took a second to recover. "I never dreamed I would have a life so full of friendship, family, and love. Thank you, Zane, for that first night and for the Brody salad that was the first hint of how much I would love the man it was named after. Congratulations, Sophie."

As she returned to her seat, Brody leaned close and whispered something in her ear. The look of pure love exchanged between them made David's chest ache.

Mary had gotten to her feet. Everyone turned to look at her. "I'm not great at talking in front of people but I just wanted to say how much I love every single one of you. Like Kara, I was alone and sad when I came here. If I'd only known what and who were waiting for me here. You've all proven to me that there are always second chances in life. You've all been mine. Most especially my husband, who never gave up on me even when most men would have. Sophie, I know the business is important to you, like the bookstore is to me, but nothing compares to being cherished by a fine man. Congratulations to you and Nico. I'm looking forward to your wedding and to spending many happy evenings here at Hugh's."

Lance kissed Mary's hand as she slid back into her chair.

Pepper sprang to her feet despite her pregnant belly. "All right, fine. If we're going to be sappy, I might as well jump on board too. I was a hot mess when I came here for the first time. Until I saw this quaint little town, I'd thought Maggie had lost her mind and moved to Podunk. I mean, where the heck was Cliffside Bay anyway? Once I visited, I saw what all the fuss was about, and wanted nothing more than to live here. Then, as if life wasn't great enough, I found my soul mate, who makes my heart sing the sappiest of all songs. So, yeah, Sophie, Hugh's is awesome, and I know we're going to make more incredible memories here. I'm just glad to be part of the gang and that you all accept me as I am, even though a little of me goes a long way." She grinned as she directed her gaze to Rafael. He'd once said something similar about Pepper. Being Cliffside Bay, it had gotten back to her. Obviously, she was never going to let him forget it.

Rafael tipped his head and grinned back at her.

When she lowered herself into her seat, Stone wrapped his arm around her shoulders and kissed the top of her head. "You're just right the way you are," Stone said.

"We wouldn't want you any other way," Rafael said.

Pepper blew Rafael a kiss.

Violet ambled to her feet and wrapped her arms around her pregnant belly. "You guys know how I feel about this place. This town is in my blood. When The Oar went down in flames, it hurt. There are so many memories for me here. I can't tell you how many afternoons I came in for a soda or an ice cream. Hugh Shaw always had a smile or encouraging word, knowing what my home life was like. Many years later, I danced with Kyle for the very first time in The Oar. To see the bar renewed for its second chance warms my heart." Her gaze traveled around the table. "You're all my family now. I'm blessed to be here by the side of this man, who makes my heart flutter every time he walks into the room."

Kyle winked at her. "Thanks, baby."

"I know that someday our children will come here after school for a soda and carry on the tradition of community that Hugh demonstrated so well." Violet waved her other hand in front of her eyes. "Okay, that's enough from the hormonal pregnant lady. Best of luck, Sophie."

Sara surprised David when she stood up and began to speak. "I don't have the memories some of you do, obviously, but I felt like Cliffside Bay was home the very first time I drove into town. There's something in the air here that makes second chances possible. God knows, no one needed a fresh start more than David and me. We found each other here and were able to move forward. For that, I'll be eternally grateful. Before I came here, I could count the people I trusted on one finger." She gestured toward Autumn. "But now I have a roomful. Thanks for that."

She settled back into her chair. David whispered, "I love you," into her ear.

Sara squeezed his knee in response.

David looked over at his sister, wondering if she would be next. Instead, Maggie stood up, wiping her eyes. "I can't talk about Hugh without crying, Sophie. He was one of the great humans. You and Zane are just like him. And I know all about second chances. The life and man I was meant for was here all along, waiting for me to return. Yes, there's something magical in the air, and nothing represents the possibilities of redemption better than Hugh's. Your smile, Sophie, lights up any room, but it shines particularly bright here. Well done, baby sister."

"Thanks, Maggie," Sophie said. "I'll make you proud."

"You do every day," Maggie said.

That left Lisa and Autumn. Lisa stood first. "I can't say anything more than what my friends have already said, other than to reiterate how much this group of people means to Rafael and me. This town and all of you are my safe haven." Lisa's cheeks bloomed pink. "Also, I'm pregnant. It's been long enough now that it's safe to tell you all. I'm due next summer."

The table broke out in more congratulations and best wishes.

When it died down, Autumn stood. She placed one arm over her baby bump and the other on Trey's shoulder. Her voice trembled as she spoke. "One day last year, I stood in front of the women around this table and showed them my scars. In return, they showed me theirs. That experience changed my life. Their kindness gave me the courage to let go of shame and embrace my life fully. Being vulnerable to others is probably the deepest form of love. Like all of us seated around this table, I've been through hard times. But the one thing I've always known is that family matters more than anything else. We're family here, some by blood and others by heart. Sophie, with this group of people cheering you on, I have absolutely no doubt that Hugh's will be a great success."

David swiped at his eyes, self-conscious of his tears. But as he looked around at the other men, he realized he was not alone.

Sophie stood next, beaming at each of them in turn. "What can I say? This life of mine couldn't be sweeter. Finding Zane and Maggie was a dream come true. And now, to have all of you in my life, well, God has blessed me." She touched her fingers to the base of Nico's neck. "Thank you all for being here to celebrate with us." She lifted her wineglass. "Here's to the next chapter in the book of life."

They all toasted one more time as staff brought in the first course. As they dug into their Brody salads, David took one more look at the people gathered for this meal. His people. His community. These were the people who would watch his children grow up right along with their own. There would be school dances, birthday parties, sleepovers, baseball games, weddings and all the other simple and momentous life events and shared experiences among friends. He and Sara would grow old right along with the others. Someday, they would be announcing the births of grandchildren instead of children.

Each season of life was so much sweeter shared with friends and family. That he'd lucked into this one was more than any man could ask for. He glanced at his bride. His blooming, beautiful bride. After all the trials, she was the prize. She was his heart.

The sounds of friends chatting, punctuated by laughter, filled the room. David soaked it all in, promising himself to remember this moment.

Love, not money or fame, made life rich. He'd never known that more than right then.

Jackson had risen from the table. He clapped his hands to get everyone's attention. The room grew silent as he drew his phone from his pocket. "Hugh always told us to make sure to take pictures. I almost forgot that today." He handed the phone to one of the staff. "Will you take one of the whole table?"

The server nodded and walked to the end of the long table. Everyone turned to face him.

"Don't forget to smile," Jackson said as he sat back down.

A flash went off, then another.

Just a moment in time. Gone as quickly as it had come. But even time could not rob memories. One could always return to the places and people they loved by conjuring the image or looking through photographs. Someday this moment would be a long time ago. For now, however, they were here in this bubble of love, breaking bread with no fear of tomorrow.

What a long way they'd all come. From broken to put back together. In the ups and downs of life, there was one constant. Love in all its forms. No matter how hard they were hit, men and women rose again and again to fight one more day. To love, despite fear and hatred that worked so hard to darken the world.

Not here. Not today.

Today love had won.

THE END

MORE TESS THOMPSON BOOKS

I hope you enjoyed the last of the Wolves stories. If you haven't read my other series, I'd love to introduce you to Blue Mountain. The first of the series, Blue Midnight, is available on your favorite retailers here: Blue Midnight.

If you'd like to read the first chapter, simply turn the page.

Much love,

Tess

BLUE MIDNIGHT

I found it at the very back of my bedside table drawer, next to an old bottle of nail polish. I'd forgotten to empty the drawers in preparation for the movers that morning and was doing so now, shoving most of the neglected or forsaken contents into trash bags. But this scrap of paper, it stopped me. Shaped like a duck's beak and wedged between the bottom of the drawer and the back panel, with just its tip exposed, it wasn't enough, really, to indicate something of any significance. But I knew. I knew in an instant. I stood motionless, taking in every jagged detail. Then, I tugged; it came loose easily. This small slip of paper with a man's name and number scrawled in blue ink seemed benign enough. *Finn Lanigan 208-555-2004.* And yet, the pulse at my neck quickened. Heat traveled from my center to every limb. I sank on molten legs to the stripped mattress. I held this scrap of paper, torn from a bar receipt, between damp fingers and stared at it like the ghost it was.

I'd tossed it years before, hadn't I? Surely I had, in one of my moments that first year of marriage when my loyalty was resolute. Hadn't I disposed of it when I embraced my choice? Apparently not. Here it lived. My temptation. My road not taken.

My daughters' voices floated up the winding staircase from

where they chased one another like wanton puppies in the now nearly empty 4,500 square feet of custom floors, intricate finish work, and marble countertops. I went to the window that faced the street and looked out onto our neighborhood park, empty this morning of children. Today was the first day of summer vacation and children and their mothers were sleeping late. How many hours of my life had I spent in that park, pushing my babies in swings, chasing after them as toddlers, and, when they were old enough to climb the play structures by themselves, chatting with other mothers about this milestone or that? The hours could not be calculated, of course, nor the wages lost by choosing to stay at home with my children instead of continuing my career.

The windows were open to let the fresh June air cleanse away all remnants of the scents of my family before the new owners claimed it with their own smells. Outside, the movers shouted to one another as they loaded the family room couch into the moving truck. My neighbor from two doors down walked by the truck, her eyes averted. Her manicured hands grasped the leash of her Labradoodle. She couldn't look. It was easier to pretend the collective nightmare for almost every woman in our affluent Seattle neighborhood had not happened to someone in their circle, someone with whom they exercised, had dinner parties, and volunteered at private school. Someone they liked. A stay-at-home mom, almost forty-five, left by her husband for another woman and forced to leave her beautiful home and sought-after neighborhood. I was everyone's worst-case scenario.

My eyes went back to the slip of paper in my hand.

If you change your mind, here's this. Then he'd kissed me one last time under an Idaho star-scattered sky larger than any other. After the kiss I wished would last forever ended, as all good things must, I turned away, back to the life I'd agreed to, the wedding I'd committed to. It was the last kiss that ever weakened my knees, the last sky I noticed for thirteen years.

Now, Clementine, my seven-year-old, pounded up the stairs,

followed by the tip-tap of her older sister Lola in her flip-flops. I shoved the slip of paper in the pocket of my shorts. I couldn't know then why I didn't just toss it in the garbage like I had so many memories and possessions in the weeks preceding. I know now. It was my destiny, and destinies cannot be denied.

ACKNOWLEDGMENTS

Thank you to MaryAnn Schaefer, my wonderful assistant who takes care of many tasks so that I have time to write. She's the most selfless, caring friend and always has my back.

To my author sisters in My Book Tribe, thanks for all of your support and advice as we maneuver the waters of writing and publishing. I'm so happy to be invited to the party.

A special thanks to my family, especially my husband, Cliff, who believes in my talent and encourages me to chase my dream. His devotion to our family inspires me every moment of every day.

Thanks to my mom for reading every single book. I write them all for her.

ALSO BY TESS THOMPSON

CLIFFSIDE BAY

Traded: Brody and Kara

Deleted: Jackson and Maggie

Jaded: Zane and Honor

Marred: Kyle and Violet

Tainted: Lance and Mary

Cliffside Bay Christmas, The Season of Cats and Babies (Cliffside Bay
Novella to be read after Tainted)

Missed: Rafael and Lisa

Cliffside Bay Christmas Wedding (Cliffside Bay Novella to be read after
Missed)

Healed: Stone and Pepper

Chateau Wedding (Cliffside Bay Novella to be read after Healed)

Scarred: Trey and Autumn

Jilted: Nico and Sophie

Kissed (Cliffside Bay Novella to be read after Jilted)

Departed: David and Sara

Cliffside Bay Bundle, Books 1,2,3

BLUE MOUNTAIN SERIES

Blue Mountain Bundle, Books 1,2,3

Blue Midnight

Blue Moon

Blue Ink

Blue String

EMERSON PASS

The School Mistress of Emerson Pass

The Sugar Queen of Emerson Pass

RIVER VALLEY

Riversong

Riverbend

Riverstar

Riversnow

Riverstorm

Tommy's Wish

River Valley Bundle, Books 1-4

LEGLEY BAY

Caramel and Magnolias

Tea and Primroses

STANDALONES

The Santa Trial

Duet for Three Hands

Miller's Secret

ABOUT THE AUTHOR

Tess Thompson

HOMETOWNS
and HEARTSTRINGS

USA Today Bestselling author Tess Thompson writes small-town romances and historical romance. She started her writing career in fourth grade when she wrote a story about an orphan who opened a pizza restaurant. Oddly enough, her first novel, "Riversong" is about an adult orphan who opens a restaurant. Clearly, she's been obsessed with food and words for a long time now.

With a degree from the University of Southern California in theatre, she's spent her adult life studying story, word craft, and character. Since 2011, she's published 25 novels and 6 novellas. Most days she spends at her desk chasing her daily word count or rewriting a terrible first draft.

She currently lives in a suburb of Seattle, Washington with her husband, the hero of her own love story, and their Brady Bunch clan of two sons, two daughters and five cats. Yes, that's four kids and five cats.

Tess loves to hear from you. Drop her a line at tess@tthompsonwrites.com or visit her website at https://tesswrites.com/

Made in the USA
Middletown, DE
20 May 2022

66017799R00179